Dark Karma

Dark Karma

A novel by
JOYCE VERANDA GRAY

Q-Boro Books
WWW.QBOROBOOKS.COM

An Urban Entertainment Company

Published by Q-Boro Books

Copyright © 2007 by Joyce Veranda Gray

ISBN-13: 978-1-933967-12-7
ISBN-10: 1-933967-12-9
LCCN: 2006936054

First Printing June 2007
Printed in the United States of America

10 9 8 7 6 5 4 3 2 1

Cover Copyright © 2006 by Q-BORO BOOKS all rights reserved
Cover layout/design by www.mariondesigns.com
Editors: Melissa Forbes, Tee C. Royal, Candace K. Cottrell

Q-BORO BOOKS
Jamaica, Queens NY 11434
WWW.QBOROBOOKS.COM

Acknowledgments

The Creator,
The Ancestors,
and
Isaac and Mary,
Andrew, Iris, Debra, Pamela, Kenneth, Shay, and Arnie

A Note From the Author

The Law of Karma teaches that responsibility for unpleasant actions is born by the person who commits them. We move through life carrying all the love, hate, joy, and sorrow that we weave through countless lives. How many lives can a person live? Are we living this life, only to return again and again to complete a full circle, thereby achieving illumination? Are we striving to reach the seventh plain at which our spirit becomes one with the Creator?

With every life we accumulate experiences that must be learned in order to move forward into the next life. The deeds we thrust upon others that cause grief, pain, injustice, and horror, as well as great joy, love, and happiness are sewn into the fabric of our lives. We weave a pattern that moves with us through the annals of time. This web of deeds creates the person we are and determines our fate. If you cause pain in this life, you receive pain in the next life. If you bring joy, you are rewarded with great happiness and love. With every life you learn a great lesson that propels you forward to the next existence until you reach illumination. Those who appear to have no purpose in life, such as drug addicts, drug dealers, thieves, or murderers, may be learning valuable lessons that will relinquish them from a previous debt.

Or, is a single lifetime an anthology of many lives? Study the number of people a person becomes in one lifetime. The person we are at sixteen is completely different from the person we were at six or twelve. Some say we change every seven years. We become someone different. We feel the same, but life is seen through different eyes; therefore, experiences are handled differently. The mind of an infant, a child, or a man has different viewpoints, ambitions, and desires.

Each person goes through life carrying the baggage gained from their life experiences. Who we are today is because of who we were yesterday. Every action taken leaves an imprint on the fabric of a lifetime. If we commit an awful act at seventeen, we are still paying for it at thirty. If we make sound decisions at seventeen, we are reaping the benefits at thirty. Either way, what we do in one phase of life directly affects the next.

For many, the lives lived defy the laws of God and man. It is uncertain if the basic nature of man dictates the insidious nature of a society, or if society breeds unscrupulous characteristics in man. Even the people who are considered goodhearted are not without sin. After all, they are only human.

There is always a reason to kill each other. Society ensures that the things we want the most are always worth fighting and dying for. We kill, maim, enslave, and brutalize each other for little more than a patch of ground or an ideology. We have no idea what the impact is to the families of those who are killed, because we can't stop hating long enough to think about. It is more important that we are right and they are wrong. It is more important that we win and they lose.

When a man is shot, and the bullet tears through the tissues and muscles of his body, pain besieges him and he falls to his knees. Terror takes over as he realizes his fate and wonders about the many lives he has yet to live, but will not. He remembers the moment in his past when the decision was made that put him at this place at this time to be torn apart by hate, ignorance, or fanaticism.

When a woman takes the drug that burns the inside of her noise and takes her to a blissful state of being, she becomes one with her true self. Or does she create another self that fits the image of her dreams, someone completely different than who she really is, another person, another life? She forgets where she is, or even who she is. She has no worries, no cares, and no pain. She knows only that she is alive and complete with all that is good. She loses control and fear overtakes her when she realizes she cannot defend herself from the onslaught of rapists or thieves. She wants to be different, but she has no idea how to change. She wants to be in love and have children, get married, and have a successful career, be proud of herself and for others to be proud of her, but she cannot do these things. She has been lost for so long, she has no idea how to return to the life she had before the drugs crippled her. She remembers the day she met the man who told her she could feel greater than she ever has; that his love for her would never let it go too far. He tells her she can be anything she wants to be as long as she always loves him. She remembers the day she made the choice that has her living on the streets today, sleeping in abandoned homes and prostituting for money. She wonders about the life she could have had if she had made a different choice during another life.

When your livelihood is stolen from you and you cannot sustain yourself, what do you do? You cannot live like you once did in a former life because the actions of one evil person resulted in the desolation of another. Homelessness, hunger, and fear besiege you as you wander from abandoned cars to condemned buildings only to find another sleepless night. You had the money and now it's gone. You remember the fateful day when you realized it was missing and panicked from the hopelessness of not being able to find it. You wonder who took it and what they are doing with it. The money that was so precious to you is gone, and you blame yourself for not being more careful, for not staying awake. The life you live now is completely different from the life you lived a month ago. What choice did you make to end up without everything that matters?

There's always hope for yet another life that will end one devastation and lead to a new and different beginning. One choice can change the direction of the life you live today, and even more choices will change the lives you will live tomorrow.

If you are the criminal who perpetrates the crime against man and God, then your fate could be more ominous and foreboding. Criminals are interesting beings. Their minds take them to a place where most people never dwell. They have the ability to completely detach themselves from the criminal act as if they were not part of it, yet they bear full responsibility for it. They can stand in the crowd and watch the investigation and think *what a terrible thing to happen*. The criminal rarely sees the impact to families and friends that they cause when they perform their awful acts. Some acts are heinous and force one to delve into social and psychological barriers that could cause a person to step over the edge. Some crimes are simply malicious and vengeful. Sometimes it's hard to tell the difference.

It has been said that every year that you live are the number of emotional children that you have. If you are forty, you have thirty-nine children. Each child carries with it the joys and pain of the year they lived. They carry the emotions of that year with them throughout their lifetime. Each child affects the decisions you make at crucial times in your life. When you are scared, the nine-year-old appears and remembers the moment when you were most frightened. He/she perpetuates the fear and feeds you what you want most. If you are lonely, the twenty-year-old reminds you of your most depressing time when you were all alone and abandoned. It's a comfortable place to be, with all your children. They continue to weave the fabric of choices we make that ultimately affect our lifetime. With every life, we take them with us. They guide us to do things which cause us to ask later, *why did I do that?* When we face them and deal with their personal issues, we can begin to erase the baggage that plagues most of us from one life to the other. It is only when we redefine ourselves, and remove the demons that haunt us, that we can reach Redemption. For it is there, and only there, that karmic energy can be expunged.

The lives of three people hang in the balance between good and evil. They are young and they made a choice that horribly affects the direction of their next life. They take on a struggle to save their souls and to give back what they took. In the karmic world you must pay for the things you do to others. As Sir Isaac Newton found, for every action there is an equal and opposite reaction. If you steal something at the age of twelve and cause someone great pain, you will know that pain when you are twenty. The act is long forgotten, but the rule of reaping what you sow will prevail when you least expect it. The life at twenty will pay for the deeds of the life of twelve, and the life of forty will pay for the life of twenty, whether it is good or bad.

Darrell Hunter is a young black man who wants to be part of one of the elite street gangs in Los Angeles. He has his chance—but he has to execute one small task to gain acceptance by his brothers. He has to take a life. Any life will do and he has to do it tonight. His choice changes the direction of his life and threatens his very existence.

Josh Brimeyer deals drugs. He would never touch the stuff, but he ensures he always has a healthy clientele of mostly young, beautiful women. Josh is gorgeous. His tall, beautiful body, blond hair, and crystal blue eyes can trap a woman into doing and believing anything. He attracts a young beauty with a promising future and gives her all she could ever need, and a bad habit she didn't need. Josh shares no blame and has no remorse about her unfortunate condition. "It was her choice," he said. But, he has no choice when he finds himself locked into a world that isn't his, and into a life that threatens his survival.

Carlita Espinoza embraces all of the beautiful things that women should have. She is young and beautiful with long, dark hair and piercing black eyes. Her mother struggles to make a home for her children and gives Carlita everything she needs, but Carlita wants everything she wants. She seizes an opportunity that forces her to take on the most horrific role of her young life. She is transformed and she can't figure out how to escape. She has made a choice that threatens her salvation.

One common thread pulls them together, and together they fight for their souls.

PART ONE

THE CRIME

THE LAW OF KARMA

For every event that occurs, there will follow another event whose existence was caused by the first, and this second event will be pleasant or unpleasant accordingly, depending on whether its cause was skillful or unskillful A skillful event is one that is not accompanied by craving, resistance, or delusions. An unskillful event is one that is accompanied by any one of those things.

Therefore, the law of Karma teaches that responsibility for unskillful actions is born by the person who commits them.

CHAPTER 1

Dray

When the gunshot rang out, the young man standing less than twenty feet away had no chance of escaping its impact. He dropped his bag of groceries and clutched his chest. He looked down to see the blood rushing from his chest and turned toward the sound.

Where did it come from?

"Why?" he whispered as he fell helplessly to the ground. Macy rushed out to see the young man lying in a pool of blood—dead. He looked around, trying to see someone, anyone, but it was dark and the street was deserted. There was no one to be found—just a row of stores and shops along Venice Boulevard with dimly lit lights and bars on the windows and doors. Macy's Convenience Store was one of the few stores that remained open past nine o'clock. He'd never seen anything like this happen before. He rushed back inside and called the police.

This isn't a bad area. Why would something like this happen here, and in front of my store?

Macy Bastowe had owned the store for over twelve years

and offered the neighborhood a quick and convenient place to buy a few items late at night without dealing with the larger grocery chains.

"In and out," he would say, "in and out."

But now, this could change everything. The police arrived within ten minutes, and one of them started to rope off the area along the front of the store.

Macy found another policeman and asked, "How long will this have to stay here?" as he pointed to the yellow tape that blocked the entrance to the store.

"Maybe a few days," the policeman said.

The policeman took out his notepad and his phone and called for the coroner. The paramedics arrived within minutes. Macy could hear sirens blaring down the street.

"What is your name?" the policeman asked.

"My name?" Macy pointed to himself.

The policeman looked at him and waited. He realized the situation was alarming, but he couldn't assume that the man standing before him did not commit the crime. He allowed Macy a moment to calm himself. Macy was a tall man with pale blue eyes and short hair that was mostly gray. His age was showing a bit around his waist, and his chin was not where it used to be, but he was an attractive man in his mid-forties and lived a quiet, peaceful life until that day. Macy had lived with his family in Palms, California for twenty years and finally got enough money to open his small store twelve years ago. He found the perfect spot away from any major chains, and he provided a good service to a small neighborhood.

"Yes, I need to know your name," the policeman said again. "You did phone in the call, didn't you?"

"Yes, I did. My name is Macy Bastowe."

Macy started to quiver a bit. He started to wonder if they would try to pin this on him. His nervousness was concerning to the policeman as he began walking around the area. Several people were on the scene now. The paramedics made a minor attempt to revive the young man, but they knew that there was no hope of reviving him. They waited until the investigators arrived to search the area for clues before removing the body. Several policemen started walking up and down the street, looking down alleyways and inside windows of the adjacent stores.

A man in a gray suit drove up in an old car. He walked over to Macy.

"What happened here?" he asked.

Macy tried to turn away from the horrible cigar smoke that filled the small area of breathable air. "I was inside the store behind the register. I had just waited on this young man. I saw him leave the store, and then I heard one shot. I thought it was a car backfiring, but then I heard bottles breaking, so I came out to see what was going on and I saw him lying there just like that." Macy looked down at the body.

"Did you see anyone in the area?" the man in the gray suit asked. "Oh, by the way, my name is Detective Patrick Hauser." He put his cigar back in his mouth and reached out to shake Macy's hand.

Macy extended his hand and thought the man was a peculiar to policeman. He was tall, but kind of bent over. His hair was gray, but his mustache was black. He had bushy gray eyebrows, and the front of his white hair was yellowed from the cigar smoke. He seemed very unkempt and gruff.

"I looked around when I came out, but the streets were deserted. I didn't see anyone," Macy said, trying to calm himself. "I don't know what happened." He looked as sincere as he could as he stared into Detective Hauser's eyes.

"Yes, well, I hope somebody saw something. We'll need

to get a statement from you. Can you come down to the precinct?" Detective Hauser asked.

"Yes, of course, of course. I'll get my jacket and keys."

A policeman walked Macy back inside the store to get his things. Macy also called his wife to let her know he would be a little late coming home that night.

Detective Hauser began looking around the area. He'd been on the force for thirty years and was set to retire in a few months. He had hoped to do it without interruption, but alas, this young man had been shot and there was no suspect in sight. He was given this case as his final duty on the force. Now that he was on the scene, he knew that this would not get solved in a few months, and his retirement would be put on hold. Detective Hauser was one of the best. He was methodical and meticulous about his work. Every detail was important, no matter how small. Every question had to have an answer until the case is solved. But this one was a mystery that will haunt him. No suspect, no motive. He already knew his search was going to be endless, but he would get there. It was just a matter of time, patience, and perseverance.

The detective walked over to the body, reached into the young man's jacket pocket, and pulled out the wallet. He opened it to reveal the California driver's license inside.

"Mr. Daniel Tanner," he said. "Mr. Tanner, I have to inform your mother that you will not be coming home. You just had to go to the store tonight, couldn't wait, I guess . . . sad." Detective Hauser stared down at the body, wondering what life he might have had.

"Johnny," he called out to one of the policemen standing nearby.

Officer Johnny Mancuso walked over to him.

"Yeah, what do you need?" he asked with a thick Italian accent.

"Take this license and find out who this man belongs to," Detective Hauser said.

"Sure, I'll take care of it," Officer Mancuso responded.

Macy walked toward Detective Hauser, indicating that he was ready to go.

"I'll follow you," Macy said. Detective Hauser turned and walked toward Officer Mancuso.

"Johnny, take Mr. Bastowe downtown and get his statement on record. Now, Mr. Bastowe, you must remain in the area until this investigation is over, or until we are assured that you were not involved in any manner. Do you understand that?" Detective Hauser looked into Macy's eyes to see any sudden reaction to his statement.

"Am I a suspect?" Macy asked.

"Everyone is," Detective Hauser said.

A voice came from across the street. "I found something over here."

Detective Hauser looked at Johnny and told him to stay and guard the crime scene. Then he looked in Macy's direction.

"You stay with Officer Mancuso and don't touch anything."

Detective Hauser, along with four other policemen, walked across the street and into the alley. Officer Stillman was bending over a shell casing he found that could have come from the weapon used to kill Daniel Tanner. Detective Hauser started walking around the area and up and down the alley, looking for anything that could tell him who the perpetrator could be. Officer Stillman carefully lifted the shell casing with a stick and put it inside a plastic bag. It was the only piece of evidence they had so far. Detective Hauser examined the wall near the casing. He used a flashlight to get as close a look at the surface of the wall as he could.

"We may be able to get hair or clothing fibers. Maybe he was sweating before he took the shot. There's got to be something here. We need to get forensics down here."

Detective Hauser noticed Officer Mancuso and Macy still standing across the street, and he directed one of the officers to go and relieve Mancuso so he could take Macy downtown.

"I'm going to hang around over here for a minute and look around. Oh, and tell the coroner that he can have the body," Detective Hauser directed.

Darrell Hunter, better known as Dray, found his way back to Crenshaw without anyone knowing of his encounter with Daniel Tanner. He had waited until the streets were deserted, and, unfortunately, one man, *any* man, standing alone in the open air, became the target.

"POW!" he laughed. "It was like picking apples from a tree. Too easy, too easy." He headed down Crenshaw Boulevard and turned into an abandoned house where his boys were waiting to hear the news.

"Did you do it?" the large, dark man asked. The six other men sat around the room, waiting to hear the answer; They were suspicious that whatever Dray said would not be the truth.

"Hell yes, I took the boy out. You'll hear all about it on the eleven o'clock news." Dray started dancing through the room, feeling very proud of himself as he accepted acknowledgements from his boys.

Darrell Hunter was a fair-skinned young man who just turned sixteen. He was over six feet tall and a bit overweight. His size could be very intimidating, and he used it when necessary. A gang had recruited him and he wanted to show off his manhood. Dray never knew his father. His mother was a hard-working woman, but with her limited education and skills, she could only provide a mediocre life for Dray. She tried very hard to teach him good moral values, but he lived on the street, and it was the streets that raised him.

"Where?" the large man asked. He was the leader, named Kuame. He was twenty-one, and it was doubtful that he would ever see twenty-two. He walked over to Dray and grabbed his shoulder to stop him from moving around. "Where?"

Dray pulled back. "On Venice Boulevard, right in front of Macy's store."

"I know where dat is," Roach said. "I know dis girl that live over dat way."

"Damn, man, you went way out dere," Cash commented.

"Yeah, I figure out there they would never look for me. They would never connect me with a shooting up there. I'm clean, man. It was as easy as pie." Dray laughed as he popped open a can of beer.

"OK den, man, all we got to do is wait for da news, see what's up, and you're in," Kuame said. Kuame grabbed Dray's arm and pulled him toward him. He hugged him in the most masculine way possible and congratulated him on his induction into the gang, knowing that if Dray's story weren't true, he would not live to see another day.

CHAPTER 2
Josh

As Iria knocked on the door, she tried to fix herself up as much as she could. She put on a little lipstick and combed her hair into a ponytail that hung down her back. She had worn her best dress and found a place to shower so she would make a good impression. She had not seen Josh in months. Their breakup was not pleasant, but she had a need that was greater than her hate for him. She had managed to pull together enough money to make the phone call that could get her what she needed, and Josh didn't care where the money came from, as long as it came. She was so nervous about seeing him that her heart sank when he opened the door. She looked into his beautiful face, and all of the hate faded away.

"Hey, come in," Josh said. Iria stepped inside the beautifully decorated apartment on the tenth floor of a high rise in Santa Monica. She walked in, looking all around and feeling a little out of place. It had been a long time since she was in his apartment, but the memories were still strong. She tried to calm herself by taking deep breaths.

"Have a seat. Would you like something to drink?" he asked.

"No, no, I'm fine." She smiled slightly and walked toward the big window looking out over the city. "This is beautiful," she said. He walked over to her and they both stared out of the window for a moment, mesmerized by the view.

"Yes, I like it," he said.

"It must be nice to be able to afford all of this," she said sarcastically as she watched him walk toward the sofa and take a seat.

"Well, you know how it is. We all do what we have to. You know what I mean."

"Yeah, but some of us do it better than others."

"It's all in the choices we make," he said solemnly. "All in the choices."

Josh was a handsome man. His tall, slender physique and his beautiful, blond hair always gave him an advantage with the ladies. He knew he could get them to do almost anything, and he always used this to get what he wanted—money. He knew that Iria cared for him deeply, but he didn't care. He fed her the same amount of drugs as he would anybody else to ensure he would always have a customer.

"What's your fancy today?" He opened a box that sat on the coffee tableand took out various types of amphetamines, a bag of weed, a bag of crack cocaine, and heroin—the sweet drug she couldn't seem to live without. He laid all of it out on the table and started to group the different kinds of pills together.

"You know what I need, Josh. Don't play with me." She smiled at him.

She had been strung out on heroin for a few years. She was once a beautiful girl at a petite five feet, three inches tall with lively, hazel eyes. Her long, golden hair fell over her shoulders, and her perfect smile could light up a room. She was well educated and could have had a glorious life, if she had not loved him so much. Her love for him blinded all things that mattered. He became her reason for breathing. He took away all of her strength and led her to believe that he could love her, care for her, and be the man she had always dreamed of. He also introduced her to drugs, and her life was never the same. Heroin became her drug of choice, and from that moment forward she had no strength, no courage, and no will to try anything. Now she was pale and thin. Her once golden hair was unwashed and dingy. She gave the appearance that all was well and that she had everything under control, but she didn't, and she feared that she never would.

She came from an upper class neighborhood in Canoga Park, California that should have given her every advantage in life, but her life took a drastic turn when she met Josh at a club one night. She fell in love on sight, he fell in lust, and they embarked on a beautiful relationship with a devastating future. When he told her that he sold drugs and that was how he managed to live so well, she didn't understand. But it wasn't long before he gave her just enough of the blissful joy so she *did* understand.

It wasn't long before she started to care more about the drug than anything else in her life. She let herself go, and the beautiful girl started to look unkempt and tattered.

When she arrived at a New Year's Eve party high and half-dressed, Josh was finished. She attempted to apply her makeup, but couldn't keep a steady hand. Her lipstick was crooked and her eyeshadow was smeared across her face. She looked terrible. Josh knew he could not keep her in his life, especially as his woman. She had become an embarrassment to him, and he could not take her around his friends anymore. Josh told her that he never wanted to see her again. He packed her clothes in a small suitcase and put it in the hallway. She was devastated and begged Josh to give her another chance.

"I can quit, Josh. I promise I will quit, but I can't do it on my own. I need your help. I need for you to let me stay and I will stop completely, cold turkey. I promise, I promise. Please, please don't treat me like trash. I will change," she begged.

"Change somewhere else. I've had my fill of you, and I don't want to ever see you again," Josh said as he dragged her to the door, kicking and screaming. She pushed him away.

"You bastard," she said as tears rolled down her face. "You got me in this mess, and now you want to toss me to the side like a worn-out old shoe. I guess this is the way you get customers. String people out and then make them beg. You dog! The scum of the earth is better than you."

"Didn't you know I *am* the scum of the earth?" he asked with a sly grin on his face. "Now get the hell out." He forced her into the hallway and closed the door.

Iria had nowhere to go. She couldn't go home in that condition. Her father would never accept her. She was alone and frightened more than she had ever been. She picked up her suitcase and walked out of the building. She held her head up in defiance of Josh and his horrible drug.

Now she sat on his sofa, waiting for him to give her what she so desperately needed. She thought for sure she could beat it. She thought she could gain control by her will and strong desire to be free, but she couldn't. It was stronger than she was, and regardless of how hard she fought, she always lost. She stared at it as if it were her life force. She craved it and felt her body aching for it. She began to tremble just knowing that she would have it soon. She stared out the window while Josh portioned off the amount and put it in a small plastic bag. She reached in her tattered bag and pulled out twenty dollars.

"Here . . . here's the money," she said. He took the twenty and handed her the bag. She stared at it and wondered where she could go to get the fix. She was hoping the would ask her to stay, so she waited.

"I would ask you to stay here, but I'm on my way out," he said. "I've got some business to take care of. You know how it is."

"Yeah, sure, I know. Always working . . . sure," she said as she stood and walked toward the door. He followed her.

"Are you going to be all right, Iria?" he asked.

"Yeah, sure, you know me I'm a survivor. I'll be fine," she said as she opened the door and stepped into the hallway. She felt alone and hopeless, and she started to realize how dependent she was on this drug and how losing Josh had devastated her life. She loved him, but she knew she would never have him in her current condition. And she couldn't beat it. She wanted to so badly, but it was stronger than she was. Over and over she tried to feed herself positive thoughts about her ability to win.

"I will beat this. Somehow, I will beat this." She walked down the street, not knowing where she was going or what she was going to do. At nightfall she arrived at an alley and decided to spend the night there, eliminating the chance that anyone would see her shame and agony. She found a spot near a large trash can and wedged herself in between the trash can and the wall. She pulled the rubber tubing from her bag along with the needle. She tied the tubing around her arm and filled the needle with the drug, pumped her arm, and found the vein. She forced the needle into the vein and injected the drug into her body. She removed the rubber tubing and the needle and placed them back into the bag and waited for the drug to take hold of her. Within minutes, she could feel herself lift from this cruel place and rise above it all. Now she was living the life she wanted to live. Now she was in heaven. She rolled up her body into a tight ball and tried to sleep.

"Oh God, what have I done? What will I do now? Please help me, please help me," she whispered.

CHAPTER 3

Carlita

David Watkins slept soundly as Carlita boarded the bus headed for Inglewood. He was trying to stay awake to greet his mother when she arrived home from a long day's work. He had an exhausting day in his third grade class, and now he was ready to settle down. He turned on the T.V. and lay down on the couch to watch, but before he knew it, he was sound asleep. He started to feel a presence in the room, but assumed it was his mother coming home. He was so tired; he couldn't open his eyes to see.

"David" a soft, melodic voice whispered. "David." He heard it again. It was not his mother. He did not recognize the voice, but he was not afraid. The smell of lilacs and roses filled the room, and he could feel the comforting warmth of the light shining through the window. He slowly opened his eyes and saw a beautiful angel. He wasn't afraid. Somehow he knew she would not hurt him. He had never seen anything so beautiful. Her soft brown hair seemed to glow as it fluttered about. Her body seemed transparent of white and blue light as she hovered over him.

"David, you are young and innocent. You can see me because your heart is still pure. You are still linked to the heavenly world, and your young spirit will help me in the days ahead."

"What can I do?" he asked.

"Help me guide him. He cannot see me; there is too much anger, too much hate. But your spirit can be understood by his consciousness. I need your spirit to help me."

"Can I come with you?"

"Yes, in time," she said. "Stay connected." She lifted away into the light and out of sight. David fell back to sleep and had a wonderful dream about a beautiful angel.

David's mother, Silvia boarded the bus for the long ride home from work. The bus was full so she didn't notice Carlita sitting in the rear. She was tired, hungry, and ready to go to sleep. There was a seat halfway down, so she took it and settled in. She relaxed and didn't bother to look around to see who else was on the bus. It didn't matter, as long as she got home.

Carlita lived with her mother in east LA, but they had such a turbulent relationship that she spent as little time there as possible. Carlita was a beautiful, young Mexican woman with long, curly, black hair and dark eyes. But her fiery personality and uncontrollable temper always got her into trouble. She had her girls, who would put her up when things were too hot at home. She decided that for today she had heard enough of her mother's disappointed tone, so she was on her way to stay with Maria in Inglewood.

Carlita noticed the pretty, black woman when she boarded the bus. The woman took a seat in the middle of the bus and settled in for a long ride home. The lady was so tired that she could barely keep her eyes open. Carlita watched as she fell asleep. As the bus got closer to the end of the line, fewer and fewer people were on board. She noticed the purse lying unattended beside the sleeping woman. Carlita moved closer.

Today is Friday, Carlita thought. *She probably got paid, and I could use the money.*

The bus was almost empty. Carlita waited for the next stop, grabbed the purse, darted out the door, and ran about two blocks in the opposite direction. She stepped into a corner store and pretended that she was looking in her purse for money. When Carlita opened the purse and found over eight hundred dollars, she was elated. She started laughing out loud, drawing attention to herself. People started to stare at her, so she decided to step out of the store and catch the next bus to Maria's house. She sat on the bus, going through the wallet to see if the woman left anything else in there that she could use. She pulled the driver's license out to read it.

"Silvia Watkins," she whispered. "Well, Silvia, you know how it is. Life's a bitch and then you die." She put the license back in and pulled out a few more cards. "Oh well, no credit cards. Who has no credit cards nowadays?" She shook her head in disbelief. She pulled the money out, stuffed it into her bag, and decided to leave Silvia's purse on the bus.

Just as Carlita reached Maria's house, Silvia woke up to find her purse gone. She screamed in desperation.

"Oh my God, please, please, not my money. Please God, don't let them take my money. Where is it?" She started to look around. A few people tried to help her, but they found nothing.

Silvia sat down in despair and began to cry. She didn't have enough money to take the bus back to look for it. It was hopeless. She stumbled off the bus and helplessly walked the two blocks to her apartment building. David awoke when he heard his mother enter the apartment. He could tell something was wrong when she entered the room in tears. He stood up and watched her every move. She seemed lost and confused as she wandered around aimlessly.

"What's wrong, Mama?" he asked with great concern.

She forced herself to the kitchen table, sat down, and continued to cry.

"What's wrong, Mama? What's wrong?" David walked over to her and took her hand.

"It's all gone, baby. Mama lost the money to pay the rent. I don't know where we will go," she said solemnly. She held her head in her hands.

"What happened?" he asked.

"It doesn't matter. It's gone." She laid her head on the table and cried. She got up and walked into the bedroom and pulled the old black suitcase from the closet. She started putting things inside that she would need to get by. *I still have to go to work*, she thought, so she grabbed a few dresses from the closet. She folded a warm blanket for the cold nights on the street and grabbed two pairs of shoes.

"I'll go talk to Mr. Bellatori in the morning and see if he will let us stay," she whispered as she continued to fill the suitcase. "Go and find the things you'll need, sweetheart. You can't take any toys and games—just the bare essentials. We may be living on the street for a while until I can figure out what to do."

"Maybe the angel can help us," he said.

"What angel? What are you talking about?"

"The angel that came to me and asked me to help her, maybe she'll help us in return."

"You had a dream baby, that's all, just a dream. I wish it were true. I could use an angel right now," Silvia said solemnly. "Go get your things together; we may have to leave by morning."

David entered his room and began to pull things from his closet. He was so angry he started to throw his toys and games around the room. He threw an electronic game on the floor and stomped on it over and over again. He fell across the bed and cried. He couldn't understand what was happening. He only knew that life would be different and harder than it had ever been before. He hated what was happening to them, and he hated being helpless.

"It wasn't a dream," he whispered. "I saw her . . . I think."

He sat on the bed and prayed that she was real and that she would return and help them.

Over at the mall, Carlita and her girls spent a family's rent money.

PART TWO

SWITCH

Be not deceived; God is not mocked: for whatsoever a man soweth, that shall he also reap

Galatians 6:7

CHAPTER 4
Dray

After confirmation from the eleven o'clock news of the murder of Daniel Tanner near Macy's convenience store, and the celebration of Dray's courage and loyalty, Dray managed to make it home in his intoxicated state. He opened the door to the small cinderblock house and tried to control the loud, squeaking noise from the rusty hinges and the cracking wood. He walked into the kitchen as quietly as he could. He didn't want to wake his mother and get the third degree about his miserable, worthless life. After he ate the last of three cookies and finished a glass of milk, he tip-toed down the hall and entered his bedroom. He stretched out across the bed and inhaled deeply.

The little house in Crenshaw was a step up for the family. His mother was finally able to move out of Watts. She thought she was separating Dray from his boys, but it didn't work. He simply found a new set of derelicts to hang out with. He knew that he was a disappointment to his mother, but he didn't know what to do to change it. He didn't apply himself in school, so it made no sense to stay. He knew he could make the kind of money he wanted and have all the things he desired on the street. He sat up, took his clothes off, and tossed them in the chair at the foot of the bed. He pulled the covers up, slid in underneath, and thought about Daniel Tanner.

Dray couldn't forget the look on Daniel's face when he realized he had been shot. He pretended to be brave amongst Kuame and Cash, but deep down inside, his emotions were in chaos. He couldn't believe he took someone's life today, and now he had to move about like nothing happened. He tossed around in the bed, but he couldn't get comfortable. He began to realize that what he did was going to haunt him for a very long time, and he wondered if he would ever have to do it again to prove himself to the gang. Without him realizing it, a tear rolled down his cheek. He started to feel great despair and sorrow. The doors of the window flung open, a warm breeze entered, and the room filled with the scent of lilac and roses. Dray fell into a twilight sleep, so he was aware of everything around him. He wanted to move, but he couldn't. Something held him. He stared at the ceiling and felt his soul lift away. He wasn't afraid. He was at peace and wondered if this was what death was like.

If it is, I'm ready to go.

He closed his eyes and waited for the final outcome.

Where will my next existence be?

He calmly drifted into nothingness.

The night seemed to pass in a moment. Dray heard sobbing and crying, but couldn't seem to open his eyes to see who was crying. His body was heavy, and his mind flowed into a semi-conscious state. He heard a sorrowful sound.

Who is it? Why is she crying? I've got to find out. Wake up, he told himself.

He repeated the words until his eyes opened. Everything

was a blur, and he couldn't figure out where he was. He knew he was dead, but where was he—heaven or hell? He thought he would go to hell, but he couldn't understand why he would be in a soft bed in a beautifully decorated room if he were in hell. He forced himself to turn over, and he noticed the woman standing at the window. The soft green curtains flowed about her as she embraced the cool breeze. Her sadness was so painful to watch. Dray stared at her and wondered who she was and why she was part of his death journey.

"Why are you crying?" he asked softly.

"I'm sorry. I just can't seem to stop. I don't know if I will ever get over this, not ever."

She took the tissue and wiped the tears from her soft, white cheeks. Her face was red and raw from crying and wiping. She was an attractive woman of forty with short, dark hair and brown eyes. She was slightly overweight, but it was her New Year's resolution to lose twenty pounds. Her wish looked as if it may come true. She hadn't eaten much since the funeral five days ago.

Dray lay in bed, wondering who she was and why he was there. He couldn't understand how she fit into his eternity.

"Don't cry. It will be all right. I'm sure it isn't that bad," he said.

"Not that bad! Your son was shot down by a vicious animal on the street, and you say it is not that bad? What would it take to get worse? Are you really that cold, Madison? Did you love the boy at all?" she lashed out at his insensitivity and uncaring attitude.

"No, no, that's not what I meant," Dray said as he tried to recover from a colossal mistake. Dray's eyes were adjusting to the minimal light in the room. He began to notice some of the small details in the room—the satin chaise lounge by the wood burning fireplace, the large Persian rug and the huge armoire against the wall,the stately dresser on the far wall with all of her personal things canvassing the top, and the beautiful handcarved wooden jewelry box that sat on the edge of the dresser.

Where am I? I'm living pretty well for this to be hell. I just don't understand how this woman knows me and why she called me Madison. Who is Madison?

Dray scanned back across the room and noticed the photographs that lined the fireplace mantel. He stopped to focus on one picture in particular.

I've seen that face before. He looked harder, trying to bring it into focus when . . .

"Danny is gone, gone forever. Why, God, why did you take him from me? I can't . . . I can't go on. I can't bear this."

The woman started to cry uncontrollably as she moved slowly to the lounge chair and stretched out over it. She covered her face with the throw blanket that lay across the back of the chair.

"Danny," whispered Dray as he sat on the side of the bed and stared at the picture. *Daniel Tanner—that's the face of the man I shot. What the hell is going on?* He jumped to his feet and started to frantically move around the room. He walked over to the fireplace and picked up the picture of Danny. He stared at it and tried to understand what was happening to him. He heard the woman sobbing, and he realized she was Daniel's mother.

But why am I here? Is this my hell, to spend eternity with the mother of the man I killed? This makes no sense.

He put the picture back on the mantel and tried to focus on his situation and what, if anything, could be done about it. He walked into the bathroom to throw some water on his face. As he passed the mirror, he screamed and jumped back and stared at the image in the mirror.

"Who the hell am I?" he asked in a state of terror.

"Are you all right, Madison?" Barbara shouted. "Is everything all right?"

"Yes, I'm fine, I think." His voice softened as he repeated over and over again that he was fine, just fine.

He felt his face, hoping that the illusion was only in the mirror.

"I don't use drugs, so I can't be hallucinating, unless Kuame or Roach put something in my beer. Yep, that's what happened. Those bastards spiked the beer and this is all a hallucination. Yeah, guilt, maybe a little guilt. That's why all of this is going on. They will pay for this."

He looked in the mirror, scared to death and hoping that it was just a really bad dream.

"I'll get back in bed and go back to sleep, and when I really wake up, I'll be back home in my own bed," he whispered. Dray went back into the room. He looked over at Barbara and became saddened by her grief. He got back in the bed, pulled the covers over him, and tried to go back to sleep.

As the sun shone through the window, it woke Barbara. She forced herself off the lounge chair where she slept and walked to the bathroom. She took off her clothes and stepped into the shower, hoping that it would make her feel better. She let the water run down her face and over her shoulders, feeling the warmth caressing her body.

"It'll be all right" she whispered.

Dray heard the water running and turned over in bed. He remembered the strange dream he had last night and figured that when he opened his eyes everything would be back to normal.

With his eyes closed he yelled out, "Mama, don't use up all the hot water." He turned over and pulled the covers back over his head to catch a few more minutes of sleep.

"Since when do you call me Mama?" Barbara asked as

she opened the bathroom door and walked over to her dresser in her slip and bra.

Dray knew that this was not his mama's voice. He recognized it from the dream. He peered from beneath the covers to see Barbara searching through her jewelry box for her gold hoop earrings. Dray was afraid of what was going to happen when she saw that he was not Madison, and not her husband. He jumped out of bed and threw up both hands.

"Look, I don't know how I got here. I'm not even sure who I am, but if you just let me get my things and leave, I promise nothing will happen." Dray stood next to the bed in his dark blue silk pajamas, frantically begging for mercy.

She looked over at him, shook her head, and went back to the earring search. Dray noticed the pajamas. He ran his hand down his arm to feel the silky fabric.

"These aren't mine," he said. He was extremely nervous. His hands started to shake as he looked around the room and realized that it was the room from his dream. "Oh, God, this isn't a dream." He was still standing by the bed trying to figure out what to do next.

"Found them," she said as she put her earrings on and walked to her closet for her brown cotton dress. She stepped into the dress and into her brown slip-on sandals. She walked over to Dray, turned around, and waited for him to button her up. He wasn't sure what to do. He hesitated and decided that he better play along until he could figure things out. He began to close the buttons. After he finished the last button, she turned around, kissed him on the lips, and walked downstairs.

"Get dressed. I'll start breakfast."

She thinks I am him. I must still look like him, but I'm not him, I'm not. I'm me. I'll play it cool until I can figure this out.

Dray went into the bathroom and took a shower. He found a huge closet and picked out a pair of pants, a white shirt, and a pair of shoes. He located socks and underwear, combs and cologne. As he got dressed, he wondered what his mother was doing.

Does she know I'm missing? Are Kuame and the gang looking for me? Somehow I've got to contact them and let them know I'm all right.

He walked downstairs to find Barbara in the kitchen sitting at the table crying. The eggs were in a bowl ready to be scrambled, and the bacon strips lay on the counter. Dray stood at the kitchen door and watched her. He felt alone and empty inside, like someone took his heart out and left a hollow space. He didn't know why he was having these feelings. Dray watched her and wished he could do something about her grief, but what does he care?

Hell, I caused the grief and I don't care. I'm a member of the gang, and if Danny had to give up his life for it, then so be it. I've got my boys backing me, so once all this shit is over, I'll be right back where I want to be.

He pulled himself together and walked into the kitchen. She noticed him and tried to stop crying.

"I'm sorry," she said.

"There's nothing to be sorry about." He looked around at the unfinished breakfast. "Don't worry about breakfast. I'll go out and get us something. You just rest and try to get your mind off of it," he said. Off of his son, the man he killed.

Did I kill my own son? He's not my son. I owe nothing to him or her. Nothing. There was a stab to his heart. The face of Danny entered his mind, and he couldn't shake it off. He walked over to her and put his hand on her shoulder to try to comfort her.

"I'll be right back." He walked to the coat closet, got his full-length wool coat, and headed for the door. He looked back and wondered how he knew where the coat was.

A black Mercedes was in the driveway. He pulled the keys from the coat pocket and hit the unlock button.

"This is it."

He smiled at the luxury and style as he walked over to the car, opened the door, and got inside.

"Well, I live really nice, really nice," he said. "Wait till the boys see this."

He started the car and backed out of the driveway. He headed toward home, hoping that his mother would know who he really was.

CHAPTER 5
Josh

She had beautiful, black hair with deep, dark eyes. It was a stark contrast to her pale, white skin. He held her in his arms as he thrust himself into her. Her moans and groans were pleasurable to him, and he wanted to hear her over and over again. Sweat soaked the sheets as he passionately kissed her over and over. She wrapped her legs around him as he forced himself harder and harder into her.

"Oh God!" he yelled as he reached the point of ecstasy.

She screamed his name as she released in joyful bliss. She kissed him passionately and relaxed her arms as they fell to her side. He calmed himself and she tried to catch her breath. He rolled over to the other side of the bed and stared at the ceiling. He had no idea who she was.

They met at a club and he forgot her name before she finished saying it. He didn't care. All he wanted were those beautiful breasts and long legs. They shared a few dances, and he convinced her that he had much more to offer. He knew he would never see her again, but he wanted that night to be memorable.

He sat up and reached for the pack of cigarettes on the night table beside the bed, and suddenly he became very dizzy and light-headed. He laid back down to gather himself. He lay there for a few minutes and then tried to rise again, and again the room started to spin around and his stomach became very nauseous.

"That damn reefer I got hold of must be some bad shit," he whispered.

He looked behind him at the girl lying in the bed. He couldn't focus. Her image kept fading in and out. His heart started to beat faster and faster. He looked around the room to try and focus, but he couldn't. The entire room was moving in and out of view. Other images appeared and disappeared.

"What's going on?" He tried to stand up. He held onto the table, but he couldn't get his balance and he stumbled to the floor.

"Hey you," he yelled. "Hey you up there. Do you hear me?" He tried to get her attention, but she didn't answer. She couldn't answer.

The room changed to a dark alley strewn with trash and debris, and then it changed back to his room where he found himself sitting on the floor by the bed, frantic.

"That reefer was laced with something lethal," he said. "Damn, wait till I get my hands on that bastard. I'll kill him. I'll kill his ass for selling this shit."

He tried to stand up when the room shifted back to the alley. He grabbed a trash can to pull himself up from the ground. The trash can was where his bed was. He looked all around and couldn't understand how he got there.

"I'm hallucinating. That's what this is—a hallucination. That shit needs to be taken off the street. Damn, I'll stay right here and when I come down, I'll still be in my bed in my room."

Josh sat back down on the ground and nestled himself in between the wall and the trash can. Time passed as he slept. Deep inside he knew something was wrong, but he was sure that as long as he slept it wouldn't hurt him, so he slept for as long as he could. The chill in the night forced him awake. When he opened his eyes and realized where he was, he jumped to his feet. He frantically ran to the street as fast as he could to see where he was. He looked out onto the street and watched the cars go by and people leaving the clubs and bars along the street.

"What time is it?" he asked as he looked at his arm for his watch. It was not there. He noticed his arm and hand. They were small and feminine. He looked down at his body and . . .

"Oh my God. Oh God, what the hell happened? Am I still hallucinating? What's happening to me?"

He frantically ran down the street until the light from the street reflected his image in a storefront window. He stopped suddenly. He couldn't believe it. He stared at himself and knew who he was, but the image that looked back at him was Iria.

"How could this happen? I'm Iria. If I'm her, is she me? This makes no sense. Why? What is this about? I've got to find her."

He started walking around in the chill of the night hoping to find someone who knows Iria. "Where does she live?" he asked out loud. "Probably nowhere. Iria hasn't had a job in two years. That shit got her all strung out. She's probably living on the street." Josh approached a prostitute who was standing near the street light.

"Excuse me, excuse me, but I'm looking for a woman, her name is Iria. Do you . . ."

"Bitch, you need to get away from me," she said. "Shit,

just being near you could get me killed." The prostitute stepped back from Josh in a defensive posture.

"I'm looking for Iria," Josh said, looking very anxious and nervous.

"Iria, stop fucking with me, girl, and get the hell away," she said.

"I'm not Iria," Josh said as he pointed to himself, and hoped that this woman who obviously knew Iria would believe him.

"Oh no? Then who the fuck are you?" she asked sarcastically. She began to walk away from him. Josh followed her. He had to, for now. She was the only link he had to Iria.

"My name is Josh Brimeyer," he said. He positioned himself in front of her so she could see the sincerity in his face. *She has to know I'm not lying.* He tried to make her believe him, but she kept walking.

"It's OK," she said. "If I were you, I'd want to be somebody else too."

The tall, dark-haired woman with long braids and a shiny gold tooth was dressed in a short red skirt and a tank top that was two sizes too small. As she stepped around Josh to move on her way she noticed the long, black car turning the corner and coming toward them. Josh noticed the fear on her face and looked behind him. The car stopped and a tall, black man stepped out and raced toward them. The prostitute turned in the opposite direction and ran as fast as she could.

Josh looked back at her and assumed that the man must be her pimp and she owed him money, but before he could turn completely around, the thrust of the man's hand crossed Josh's face with fierce malice. The strike left a burning, agonizing sensation and Josh fell to the ground. A huge hand lifted him up and another struck him across the face again, forcing him against the wall. When his shoulder hit the wall, the pain was unbearable. He screamed and grabbed his shoulder. He fell to one knee and hung onto the wall. He wanted to fight back, but he didn't have the strength. He felt as light as a feather as the man grabbed him again and forced him to stand.

"Where's my money, bitch?" he bellowed. Josh was so afraid and in so much pain he could barely breathe. He looked up into the face of his accuser and wondered how he would survive another blow.

"Where's my money?" he asked again as he grabbed Josh by the collar.

"What money?" Josh asked.

"Oh, so you got amnesia now. I bet you remember snorting that shit up your nose and now you gonna forget the part where you supposed to pay for it? Well, maybe I'll have to remind your ass."

He raised his hand to strike Josh again, but using all his strength, Josh reached up and stopped his arm. He pushed him back just far enough to give himself a narrow lead in the chase. Josh ran for his life. Right now he knew that was all he had, and he had to stay alive long enough to find out what was happening to him. He darted into an alley and over a fence. Elroy, AKA Diamond, decided not to mess up his new suit by climbing that dirty, rusty fence.

"You got till five o'clock tomorrow to get me my money. Five o'clock," Diamond yelled as he smiled at the sight of Iria dashing around the corner.

Josh never looked back. He heard him and felt the fear of eminent death all around him. He couldn't stop hearing the words *five o'clock tomorrow*. Josh started walking. He walked toward Santa Monica, toward home. He hoped the apartment was still there. So many things were upside down that he couldn't be sure who or where he was. All he knew was he wanted to go home. He walked during the night and stayed off the main streets as much as he could.

Josh walked past a window and caught his reflection in the glass. He couldn't believe what happened to him. He stared at Iria's blue cotton dress that was soiled with dirt and blood. His arms were bruised, his face was battered and beaten, and Iria's long, golden hair was matted with oil and dirt. He held his bruised shoulder and wished that this nightmare could end now.

CHAPTER 6

Carlita

Flaunting some of her new clothes, Carlita walked onto the bus as if on display. She was pleased with her new look and was ready to show the world how beautiful she was. She was on her way to meet her boyfriend at the beach, where they planned to spend the day. She took a seat at the back of the bus and checked her hair to make sure every curl was in place. *Everything is fine*, she thought. She sat back and relaxed.

Carlita looked around at the other people on the bus and wondered if they saw just how hot she was. *They're all nerds*, she thought. She watched a young woman try to deal with two small children. She had all of her baby gear with her and worked frantically to hold onto it while holding a baby and controlling a toddler. She noticed an old man whose hard life showed in his rough exterior. He worked hard for every penny, trying to survive, and now all he had to show for it was being poor. *I'll never do that*, she thought. She glanced over at the middle-aged woman sitting across from her who was trying desperately to hold onto her youth. She had on far too much makeup and a skirt that was a little too short and a little too tight. She wondered if the woman envied her youth and if she would be like that when she was older.

I'm never getting old, she thought and smiled. *I will always be just like this.* She looked at the young man behind her with his CD player plugged into his ears. She wondered if she was any different than any of them. She watched people get on and off at every stop until her eyes started to tire. She took her small purse and tucked it under her arm. She had the last of the stolen money in there and she wanted to keep it safe. She had a little ways to go before she reached her destination, so she laid her head back and closed her eyes for a moment.

A bump in the road jolted her and she opened her eyes. The bus was empty except for a small black boy standing at the front of the bus staring at her. He never said a word. He never took his eyes off of her. His eyes were daunting and sad. The whole scene was ominous and chilling.

"What's going on?" she asked.

The boy said nothing. He was motionless. He stared at her with his dark, piercing eyes.

"Who are you?" she asked with concern. She stood up and started to walk toward him. She was starting to feel a little scared. She didn't know why, but his staring at her made her very nervous. *Why is he staring at me? I don't know him. I wonder who he is,* she thought. The bus stopped and the boy turned around and walked off. The door closed behind him and the bus started to move again. She peered through a window and watched the boy as he stood on the corner staring up at her. She watched him as he disappeared into a thick, white fog.

"This is eerie," she whispered to herself. "I'm the only one left on the bus. Where is everybody?" She looked out the back window, but the fog was so thick she couldn't see anything. She moved from one side to the other hoping to get a glimpse of something through the awful fog. Suddenly she felt the bus moving faster and faster.

"Driver, aren't you going a little too fast?" she asked. There was no response. "Can you hear me? You are driving too fast," she said frantically. Her heart was racing as the bus moved faster and faster. She held onto the seat backs as she moved to the front of the bus, and she was horrified to find that there was no driver.

"OK, OK, what's going on? Where's everybody? Who's driving the bus?" she asked all of the logical questions that didn't seem to fit into this illogical situation.

Carlita turned around and walked down the steps to the door as the bus moved even faster. She began to bang on the door and yell and scream for help, but she was crying to a dense fog. There was no one to hear her, no one was there. She was shaking with fear. She looked back to see the steering wheel moving as if there was a driver. She stepped back onto the landing and slowly moved backward, watching the steering wheel move as if the bus was being driven. She slowly moved to the back of the bus. She was frightened beyond words and hoped she was dreaming, but somehow she knew this was real. There was a break in the fog, just slightly. She could see light and, little by little, a few buildings and trees. The fog was dissipating. The bus was still speeding, but now there was hope. She was out of the fog. Just as she began to calm down, she saw the direction the bus was traveling. A three-story building loomed directly ahead. The bus did not appear to be turning or stopping.

"Oh no!" she screamed frantically. "God please, please don't let me die!" She fell to the floor, covered her head, and waited for the disaster. The bus hit the building, but there was no impact. She opened her eyes to see the bus moving through the building like a ghost through a wall. Nothing fell. There was no destruction.

"Oh shit," she screamed as she watched the wall coming toward her through the bus without any stones crumbling or ceilings falling.

"What's happening? Oh God, oh God, what's happening?" she cried. She had never been so scared. She stepped back as far as she could, but the wall kept coming. The bus passed through the building with no disruption and deposited Carlita on the first floor of the building. She was standing in the hallway watching the bus vanish into the wall before her. She was severely shaken and tried to calm herself. She was so thankful she wasn't dead that nothing else matter. She took a few deep breaths and tried to relax. She looked around to figure out where she was. Confused and baffled, she raised her hand to knock on the door in front of her without knowing why. She stopped when she noticed that her hand was dark brown. She looked at her other hand and it was the same color. She noticed that the cute outfit she left home wearing was gone and had been replaced with a dark gray dress and a pair of flat black shoes and black stockings.

"Where are my clothes? Why am I a black woman? Am I on a spaceship or something?" she whispered. "This is too weird."

"Mama, is everything all right?" a small voice came from the top of the stairs. Carlita turned and looked upstairs to see the face of the boy who was on the bus. The same child stared at her and called her mama.

"I don't . . ." Just as she began to answer, the door in front of her flung open.

"What do you want?" a gruff Italian man asked.

"I don't know," Carlita said, looking very confused and disoriented. "I don't know."

"Your rent is due tomorrow. If you don't have it, don't be here." He slammed the door. She stood in the hallway with a thousand questions and no answers.

Carlita walked upstairs and looked all around, not knowing whom she was, what to do or where to go if she had to leave the apartment. She looked into David's eyes and wondered who this child was and why he was calling her mama.

"Why are you calling me that. Where am I?" she asked as she continued to study the apartment and her hands and clothing. "What the hell is happening to me. Who are you?"

David was worried that his mother was sick. He had never seen her like this before, and he wanted it to stop.

"Mama, are you all right? Did you ask if we could stay? What did he say mama? Can we stay?" He studied her and was starting to get a little scared. He turned and walked into their apartment where she was packing to leave.

"Where are you going?" she asked.

"Mama, didn't you say we had to leave because you lost the rent money? Didn't you say to pack because we were going to leave?" He looked at her puzzled and concerned.

"I don't know what you're talking about. I don't know you or this place, I . . ." She stopped talking as she suddenly passed by a mirror. She glanced at the image, but was afraid to take a second look. She stood still for a moment and tried to rationalize that what she thought she saw was a mistake. She only thought she saw it because of some guilt she may have had for stealing the purse. She took a deep breath and stepped back and looked directly into the mirror. She couldn't move. She couldn't scream. She was frozen. She reached up and felt the mirror hoping that the image was wrong and that it was another person staring back at her, but only the mirror was there, along with her fear.

"This can't be real. I can't be her. How did this happen?"

"What happen, mama, what?" David asked

"I can't be her, I am me. I have to go back. I have to go back like I came and then it will reverse itself back to me."

"Go back where, Mama?" David was scared.

"David, your name is David?"She had no idea how she came up with that name.

He hesitated. "Yes."

"David, please go into your room and finish packing and I'll come in a few minutes. Can you do that for me?"

David stared at her. He walked into his room and closed the door.

She stared at the mirror and started to cry. "What have I done? I can't go back, the bus I was on disappeared. What am I going to do? I can't go back."

She cried and prayed for guidance. She didn't understand what happened, but she did recognize the face in the mirror, the face that looked back at her, Silvia.

"I'm Silvia Watkins. I stole this woman's money. That must be her son and this is her apartment. Oh my God, she's getting thrown out of this apartment because I stole the money. She can't pay her rent. Oh no, God, please don't let this happen. I didn't mean it. I didn't know she had a son. Damn, I wish I hadn't taken the money. What am I going to do? I can't stay here and I can't leave the boy by himself; he thinks I'm Silvia and I guess I am, in a way. How could something like this happen? This isn't the thirteen hundreds with witches and warlocks. This is impossible. Maybe, I'm having a hallucination from that bus ride that I just had. It's all a hallucination. Maybe it will be over soon. I'll sit here on the sofa and close my eyes and wait for it to pass."

Carlita sat on the sofa, closed her eyes and tried to clear her mind. She focused on pleasant things and happier times. She tried to forget the events that led her here and she asked God for forgiveness for taking the money. She fell into a semiconscious state. She was aware of what was going on around her, but she was meditating on God's ability to change her back. She sat for about twenty minutes when the sound of David's voice startled her.

"Mama, what are you doing? I'm scared, Mama. Are you all right?" He began to cry.

"I'm all right, baby. Just know that I'm going to take care of you no matter what, OK?" she said as she tried desperately to comfort him. She could see that her hands and arms were still that of a black woman, and so, she knew she had not changed back. This was real, and somehow she was going to have to deal with it.

"Are you going to pack, Mama?" he asked

"Yes . . . yes, I guess I am," she said as she stood up and walked down the hall and found what must be Silvia's room.

She walked inside and looked all around. "What would she want me to take?" she whispered.

She noticed the suitcase on the bed with some personal things thrown inside. "She already started. What ever happened, happened in the middle of her packing. I guess I have to take up where she left off."

She started folding clothes from the dresser and pulling clothes from the closet and putting them inside the suitcase. She found a few photographs on the dresser and put them inside along with her Bible and a few pieces of gold jewelry. She stopped for a moment and picked up the Bible. She held it close and closed her eyes.

"I know what I did was wrong, and I'm so sorry. Please help me to get back to being myself. Please, I promise I won't ever do anything like this again." Tears rolled down her face as she fell across the bed and cried.

PART THREE

KNOW THYSELF

A double minded man is unstable in all ways

James 1:8

CHAPTER 7
Dray

Dray knocked on the door to his house, the house where he lived with his mother. He waited, but no one answered. He knocked again, harder and harder.

"Mama," he yelled. "It's me, Dray."

The door opened very slowly and a small, meek woman with dark brown skin looked at Dray. Her sadness and despair overshadowed her beautiful, long locks of curly hair. She looked up at Dray with some hesitation. It was not very often that a well-to-do white man entered her neighborhood, no less one claiming to be her son.

"What do you want?" she asked.

"Mama, it's me, Dray. Please recognize me?" Dray asked in a manner so helpless and needy that she almost listened.

"Who are you? What do you want?" she asked again.

"Mama, please know me. I know I look different, but it's me, Mama, it's really me," he pleaded.

"This is cruel. Why are you doing this?" She started to cry as she stepped back from the door.

"No, no, you must know me. I have to make you know

me somehow. It's me, your son, Dray." Dray pleaded with her to listen, to give him a chance to explain. He didn't know what he could say to explain himself, but he had to try.

"We lived in Watts before we moved to this house. I broke my brand new red bike the same day that I got it for my ninth birthday. I remember when you had to sell Grandma's diamond pin to get food, and how you saved to buy it back. I remember . . ."

"STOP IT, STOP IT!" she screamed. "How dare you? I don't know who you are, but this is sick, sick. You can't be Dray. I lost my son last week. Some hoodlum shot him down in the street. He's dead. Do you hear me? Dead! I cremated the body yesterday. I don't know who you are, but you're not Dray." She slammed the door.

Dray didn't know what to say or where to go. For the first time in his life, he felt totally lost.

"Cremated . . . shot . . . who, by who, how? What is she talking about? I'm not dead. There's been a big mistake, a terrible mistake," Dray mumbled to himself. He walked back to the car, stopped and looked back at the house, and wondered what he should do.

Maybe I should go back and make her understand, or maybe I should leave and try to figure out what's happened to me and then I'll come back, like I used to be, like me, he pondered as he walked to the car.

As he stood by the car, he looked out over the street where he lived. He remembered the Johnsons, who lived next door; the Rymes, who lived two doors down; and Tina and her two boys on the corner. Part of him wanted to stay right there in familiar surroundings where things were comfortable and certain, in a place with which he could identify; his home, his friends, and his neighbors. He leaned against the car with his head in his hands, trying to hold back the tears. He realized how he took his life for granted and used it to do awful things.

"Who the hell are you?" a voice asked from behind him. He turned around to find Kuame, Roach, and Cash.

"Hey, Mister white man, who are you and what the fuck you doing at my boy's house?" Kuame asked again as he moved closer to Dray. Dray realized quickly that Kuame did not recognize him, and knew it'd be best not to try and persuade him.

"I'm a friend of Mrs. Hunter. I came to express my condolences," Dray said. He wanted to tell him, but knew that it would be just as hard to explain as it was with his mother. *How can I explain this? I don't understand it myself.*

Kuame backed off and smiled at Dray. "You know Mrs. Hunter?" he asked.

"Yes, yes I do. We worked together once," he said.

"Well, OK, man, if you know her, it's all right," Kuame said as he backed away.

Kuame, Roach, and Cash walked to the door and knocked. Mrs. Hunter opened the door and became very disturbed to see them.

"What do you want?" she asked.

"We thought you may need some help, so we came by to give you a little something that may help you get through these hard times," Kuame said as he pulled a roll of money from his inside pocket and handed it to her.

"No, no. I don't want your dirty money. Dray's dead because of people like you. That's why he's dead now, people like you. Get out, get out of my yard and never step foot back here again." She slammed the door.

Kuame stepped back in amazement and stared at the door for a moment in disbelief.

"She's just upset," Roach said.

"Yeah, upset, you're right," Kuame said in agreement.

They walked back to the street and passed by Dray, who watched the exchange between his mother and his friends. Dray stared at Kuame intently, hoping he would see some piece of him somehow, but he didn't. Kuame, Roach, and Cash walked by without a word.

Dray wasn't sure what to do now that his mother hadn't recognized him. He got back in the car and drove around for a while. He had no idea where he was going. He was just driving and hoping that an answer would come to him.

"I can't figure out how I got here, so how the hell can I figure out how to get out of it?" He passed through Venice and onto Highway One.

The ocean is so large it makes my problem small. The coolness of the ocean feels great. I'll just follow it until I wake up.

He noticed a small café and decided to stop in. He stepped inside the smoke-filled room and took a seat at the bar. He looked around the room at the unsavory class of people and began to feel a little out of place. The unruly crowd around the pool table would most likely take exception to a man in a five hundred-dollar coat pretending to be one of the boys.

"What'll you have, mister?" the bartender asked.

"Scotch and soda," Dray answered.

Scotch and soda, what the hell did I order that for? I don't drink that, or at least I didn't used to. I don't know who I am anymore. Maybe I'm just crazy for real. This place, I should be as comfortable here as anyplace, but I'm not. I don't fit in. I mean me, or the other me, doesn't fit in. I guess I'm too upper class now. Damn, what am I going to do? I hate this sadness. I can't seem to escape it. The loss is overwhelming, but I didn't lose anyone, or the real me didn't. I don't know . . . I just don't know.

The bartender returned with his drink and Dray pulled ten dollars from his wallet.

Somehow I seem to know things about this guy. His clothes, his drink, and I feel his hurt and his confusion, or maybe that's my confusion.

Dray thought about his situation and tried to come up with the answer to it all, but he couldn't. He couldn't even figure out the questions, no less the answers. He finished his drink and asked for another. He sat for a while in deep thought over this nightmare he was in. The noise from the poolroom quieted down. Dray knew that the next focus for their amusement would be him—the prissy white boy all polished and clean. He decided to leave before they realized that he was in the room. He walked to the car without knowing where he was going. His body belonged in the upper class neighborhood with his upper class life, but his heart was in Crenshaw. He found himself in Los Feliz walking around Griffith Park. He couldn't go home. He couldn't even decide where that was.

"I've got to figure this out. I'm not dreaming, that's for sure. Something really happened. I may be the only one, or there could be others. Yes, but how do I find out? I've got to find out."

He leaned against a tree and tried to figure out how to start. "Everything has always been so easy for me. I take what I want. It's as simple as that, but now, now!" He hit the tree with his fist to release his anger and the pain that gripped him forced him to his knees.

"God, please help me. I don't understand these feelings. It hurts, God, it hurts. I killed my son. I killed Danny. Help me, help me." He leaned against the tree and cried.

It was five o'clock when Dray pulled into the Tanner driveway. He realized that he had nowhere else to go, and part of him seemed to belong there. "I'll stay here until I can figure this out," he said as he turned the key and walked in to find Barbara in the kitchen. Her mood was better. She was moving around with grace and ease, humming a beautiful soft melody. Potatoes were cooking on the stove and a roast was in the oven.

"Where have you been all day?" she asked lovingly. She looked at him and smiled as he walked into the kitchen.

"I had something to do. I'm sorry about breakfast," he said.

"That's OK. I made out all right. Dinner will be ready in a few minutes. Go get washed up and relax a bit. I'll call you," she said. Dray walked into the study and noticed the liquor cabinet. He walked over and fixed himself a drink and relaxed on the soft, leather sofa. He laid back and closed his eyes.

This guy lives pretty well. I should just stay in his body and say the hell with it. If it's what God wants, then so be it. It's the best deal I ever got. Suddenly he got a wave of nausea that brought him to his knees.

OK, OK, it was just a thought, just a thought. Besides, my mama thinks I'm dead and I can't let her live with that. I can't. His stomach calmed and he sat back on the sofa. "Wow, what caused that?" He took a drink and relaxed. He heard the doorbell, but he was so relaxed he really didn't want to move. It had been a trying day. Barbara opened the door and walked Roman into the study.

"Madison, Madison, it's Roman," Barbara said. Dray tried to tap Madison's memory, but he couldn't seem to remember this man. He had to play along and hoped it would work out.

"Roman, nice to see you." He extended his hand and smiled. "Please, have a seat."

"Thanks," Roman said.

Roman Cantell was one of Madison's closest friends and coworkers. He was a heavyset man with very dark features. His dark hair was cut short, and his dark eyebrows and mustache complemented his tanned complexion. He was a pleasant man with a substantial portfolio that would keep him and his family living well for the next three generations. He was polished and groomed, and presented himself in a manner befitting the upper class.

"How are you holding up?" he asked.

"I'm fine," Dray said cheerfully. He noticed the confused look on Roman's face and remembered that he was in mourning. "I mean, I have my good days and my bad days," he corrected himself with sorrow in his voice as he turned away from Roman. "Would you like something to drink?" Dray asked as he walked to the liquor cabinet and poured himself another drink.

"Yes, bourbon will be fine," Roman answered. "So, Madison, when do you plan to come back to work? Everyone misses you and wishes you well. We all understand what you are going through and want you to know that we are here for you."

"Thank you," Dray said. *Oh my God! I have a job.* Dray started to panic. *What do I do? How am I supposed to do it? This is crazy.* "Roman, do you have one of my business cards on you?" Dray asked.

"Yeah, sure. I believe I have one somewhere." Roman searched his wallet until he found the card. "Here it is." He handed it to Dray. *Attorney at Law for Simons, Biddle and Laten Law Firm. Oh no, I'm a lawyer. The only thing I know about the law is how to break it.* Dray stared at the card in disbelief.

"Are you all right, Madison?" Roman asked.

"Yeah, of course, of course, I'm fine." Dray took another drink knowing he would not be able to keep up the charade for long.

"We need you in the office. It'll be good for you to get back to work. The antitrust case is waiting for you, and I could use your help on a copyright infringement case I'm working on."

Antitrust, what the hell does that mean? Lord, I'm in trouble.

"Sure, anything I can do," Dray said. "Roman, I'm a little tired. I need to think. I mean, I need to be alone for a while. Would you mind?"

"No, no of course not. Hey look, you just take all the time you need and we'll talk in a few days. I know everything will be all right." Roman grabbed Dray at the neck and gave him a hug. Dray tried to reciprocate, but failed miserably. "You take care," Roman said. He walked out of the room and said goodbye to Barbara as he left.

Dray was disturbed. *What am I going to do?* He looked over at his desk and noticed the picture of Danny. He felt an overwhelming urge to cry. *I can't understand this. I know I'm not Madison, but I can't help but feel this great weight when it comes to Danny. Why? It shouldn't matter to me.*

He wiped the tears from his eyes and noticed the smell of something burning. When he entered the kitchen he found the potatoes burning and the roast still in the oven. He turned the fire off, took the roast out of the oven, and looked around for Barbara. The towel was on the floor by the kitchen door that led to the backyard. He walked out onto the porch and found Barbara sitting in the flowerbed playing with the soil. He walked over to her and sat down with her. Dray felt a great sympathy for her, a closeness that he couldn't explain. Her pain was so deep, he knew he caused it and he wanted to cleanse himself of it, but he couldn't. He kneeled down, wiped the tears from her face, took her in his arms, and held her.

"How can I help you, Barb? What can I do?" he asked as the tears began to roll down his face. *Why am I crying? What am I crying for? He wasn't my son. I have no reason to care,* he thought as he held her and wondered why he stood in that alley on that night.

"How can I make this right?" he whispered. He guided her back inside, walked her to the study, laid her on the sofa, and covered her with a blanket. He walked to the liquor cabinet and poured her a drink. Her sobbing was heartbreaking and Dray could feel anger building inside. He walked over to her.

"Here, drink this. It will make you feel better," he said as he helped her sit up. She drank the liquor and lay back down. He covered her and stroked her forehead gently.

"I need for you to be strong, Barb. I need for you to get ahold of yourself and be strong. You must move forward. You must let go. Danny is dead and there's nothing we can do about it." He heard himself say the words, but he felt a rush of guilt that he'd never felt before. *I could have done something about it, I could have done something.*

He walked to the liquor cabinet, poured himself a drink, and began to take a swallow when he started thinking about the killing and the reason for it. He wanted to scream. Barbara's sobbing was driving him crazy, and he wanted her to stop. He couldn't stand it anymore.

"STOP IT! STOP IT NOW!" He hit the glass in the cabinet and broke it. His hand was bleeding, but his anger kept him from feeling any pain. He grabbed a napkin, wrapped his hand, and stormed out the door.

"I can't take this. I am sick of her crying. The man's dead, and that's that. Why can't she get over it?" He headed upstairs and collapsed on the steps in tears. "Why can't I get over it?"

Barbara heard him fall and ran to him. She got a clean cloth from the kitchen and cleaned his wound. They walked upstairs and he fell across the bed. She bandaged his hand, removed his shoes, pulled the covers over him, and kissed him goodnight. When he lost control, it forced her to be strong. She had someone to care for, someone needed her again. She gained strength from his weakness. For a brief moment, she felt strong and in control. She embraced it, knowing that it would only last a short while. She lay across the lounge chair and fell asleep.

Dray felt the warmth of the sun coming through the window. Barbara had opened the curtains and began picking up around the room.

"Are you going to work today?" she asked.

"Work? I don't know. I . . . I'm not sure if I'm ready,"

"Sure you are. You need to go to work. Occupy yourself."

Dray had no idea where he worked, or what he did there. He knew he had to face it somehow, but how?

"Roman called and he wants you to contact him," she said.

"All right, I'll call him."

He stepped out of bed and went into the bathroom. He sat on the toilet and tried to figure out how to get in touch with Roman. He stepped into the shower and remembered the card—the card that Roman gave him with the name of the company on it. *I'll use that.* He got dressed and went downstairs into the study to look for the card.

"There it is," he said as he spotted it on the table next to the liquor cabinet. *Simons, Biddle and Laten Law Firm, that's the name.* He picked up the phone and dialed the number on the card. His secretary answered.

"Mr. Tanner's office. May I help you?"

"Yes, yes, I . . . I am Mr. Tanner," Dray said hesitantly.

"Mr. Tanner, it's great to hear from you. We're all very sorry for your loss. You and Barbara are in our prayers."

"Thank you, thank you very much."

"How is Barbara?"

"She's doing better. I think she will be all right. It's an

awful blow to our family and she is taking it pretty hard, but I'm sure she'll be fine."

"I'm glad to hear that. If there is anything I can do, please let me know."

"Somehow I've forgotten Roman's number. Can you get it for me?"

"Sure, Mr. Tanner. Please hold." A moment passed. "Are you ready?" she asked.

"Yes."

"The number is 213-559-1238."

"Thank you."

"Is there anything else I can do for you, Mr. Tanner?"

"No, thank you for your help. Goodbye." He hung up the phone and dialed Roman's number.

"Hello," Roman answered.

"It's me, Madison."

"Hey, how are you?"

"I am planning to come in. I'm having a late start. Barbara had a rough night, so we didn't get much sleep. You understand."

"Yes, of course. Take all the time you need. I'll see you when you get in."

"Great, see you then."

Dray had gotten over that hurdle. He had the card, so he could find the place. He walked back upstairs to say goodbye to Barbara.

"Barb, I want you to stay busy today. Try to keep it together. If you find yourself losing it, call me. OK?"

"I'll be fine." She walked over and kissed him. "Now go and enjoy your day."

Dray pulled the car out of the driveway and headed toward Imperial Highway. He found the building, drove into the parking lot, and parked the car. The seven-story glass building was impressive and intimidating. Dray walked inside the lobby and looked around, hoping that someone would tell him where his office was. People were moving all about who didn't seem to notice his confusion. He noticed the directory on the wall and walked over to find his name.

"There it is, on the sixth floor," he whispered

"Madison." Dray heard Mr. Tanner's name being called. "Madison."

Oh, that's me, he remembered. He turned around to see two well-dressed men waving at him. *Oh God, who are they?* He tried to smile and walked toward them.

"Hello, how are you?" Dray extended his hand and acted like he was genuinely glad to see them.

"How are you is a better question," the taller man said.

"I'm doing fine. It was a little rough at first, but I'm going to be fine," he said.

"Good, good. We're all glad to have you back," the shorter man said. "Jack, here, is handling the Carter case and he will need all the help you can give him. You know he's a little slow," he laughed.

OK, I got one name. Jack. The taller man is Jack.

They walked to the elevator, stepped off onto the sixth floor, and walked down the hall laughing about Jack's sharp wit and attention to detail or lack thereof. The shorter man stopped at an office door and stepped inside.

"I'll get with you later, Madison. Maybe we can have dinner one day this week?"

Dray quickly looked at the name on the wall beside the door. *William Laten. His name was on the card. He is one of the partners. If I'm talking to one of the partners, then Madison's pretty high up in the organization. Can it get worse?* "That'll be great, Mr. Laten."

"What's with this Mr. Laten stuff? It's Bill, remember?" He pointed his finger at Dray and smiled.

"Yeah, Bill. No, I haven't forgotten. Just a little disoriented, that's all. You know, my first day back."

"OK, I'll get with you later," William Laten said as he closed the door behind him.

Dray walked with Jack down the hall until he stopped again. He looked at Dray as if waiting for him to do something, but Dray didn't know what. He waited and was saved when he heard his name from the woman at the desk inside an office.

"Mr. Tanner, it's wonderful to see you." The gray-haired woman came out into the hallway. "Welcome back. I have everything you need on your desk to get you started. I know it will take a little time, but if you need anything, just yell," she said as she walked him into what must be his office. He looked at the nameplate on her desk, Janice Collier.

"Thank you, Janice. You are very kind." He looked back at Jack standing in the hallway and waved goodbye. Janice had control, so Jack smiled and walked away knowing that Madison was in good hands..

"No trouble at all, Mr. Tanner."

Dray walked into Madison's office and closed the door. For a moment he felt a little calmer. His nerves had been on edge all morning and now, behind closed doors, he felt like he could hide from the reality of this strange life. He sat at the desk and looked all around. He picked up a file and began to read it, and realized that he had no idea what it was all about. All of the herewiths and therefores meant nothing to Dray.

Allowable this and permissible that, what does judiciary mean? This is crazy. How am I going to talk to these people? There's a dictionary in the bookcase that may be useful.. He pulled it off the shelf and thought he would have to get real smart, real fast. He hoped he wouldn't have to do this for very long, because he was going to figure out what had happened to him, and try to change it back to the way it was.

"Do you need anything, Mr. Tanner?" Janice asked as she opened the door and peeked inside.

"No, Janice, I'm fine. Could you see that I am not disturbed?"

"Yes sir." She closed the door and walked back to her desk. She felt the sadness of his loss and wished she could do something. But she couldn't and she knew it was going to take time for him to be strong again.

Janice Collier was sixty-years-old and had worked for the company for twenty-seven years. She was the obvious choice as Madison's secretary when he made junior partner five years ago. Janice's take-charge personality helped balance Madison's kind nature. She never allowed anyone to walk all over him. She was there like an impenetrable wall.

Madison was one of the best attorneys they had, and he was well respected in his field. He was a corporate attorney and had accounts with several multi-billion dollar corporations. Simons, Biddle and Laten relied on his expertise and sixth sense about the law and the client. Madison won his cases through the expert use of diplomacy and wit, rather than aggression and force. He could make you believe the sky was green and you wouldn't understand why others couldn't see it. He knew the law, and he could manipulate it to his advantage. He was a prime candidate for the next senior partner position.

Dray, however, knew nothing about the law. He read the file with little comprehension. He realized that he was in over his head, with no idea what to do about it. He labored over the file, using the dictionary to try and understand the meaning of the words, but how they were used in context was beyond him. He was in trouble. He knew he couldn't use Danny's death as an excuse forever. He sat at the desk and stared out the window, trying to figure out what to do.

"Mr. Cantell, you can't go in. Mr. Tanner does not want to be disturbed," Janice said as Roman barged his way into Madison's office.

"Hey, Mad man, it's lunch time. Come on."

"Lunch, I don't really want to go to lunch today. I'm not very hungry," Dray said.

"Come on, man. It'll just be us. I didn't invite the crowd. You gotta try and get back into the swing of things." Roman walked over to his desk and physically lifted him from the chair. "Come on. We'll go to Little Italy's. You always liked that place."

"OK." Dray grabbed his blazer and walked out behind Roman. "I'll be back in an hour," he told Janice.

"Better make that two," Roman said. Janice closed the door to Madison's office and went back to work.

Roman parked the car in front of the restaurant and hesitated before getting out. He looked at Dray. He wanted to say how sorry he was about Danny, but he couldn't quite get the words out. Dray noticed his expression.

"You don't have to say it. I know what you're thinking," Dray said.

"I wish I could have been there more for you and Barb. I let my work come first, and I'm sorry about that," Roman said.

"You were always there for me. I always knew that. I knew if I called you for anything, you would be there. I didn't expect you to interrupt your life to care for me. One of us had to go to work."

"You shouldn't have had to call. I should have been there for you."

Dray smiled and patted Roman on the shoulder.

"I had to work through it alone, and there was a lot to

work through. You have no idea, and I will need you, and when I do, you will be there. I know it. Now, come on. Let's eat." He looked Roman squarely in the eyes and spoke with great sincerity and friendship. Dray could see that Roman and Madison had a special bond that was more than just coworkers.

I'll have to be careful how I handle this relationship. I may have to tell Roman the truth someday if I stay in this body, and I'll need him to understand, maybe even help me. I must maintain this illusion until I have to explain myself, but if the time comes, I will need a friend.

They walked into the restaurant, both secure that they were brothers and would always be there for each other, or at least for as long as the lie lasted.

Dray pulled into the driveway, relieved that he had gotten through the day without making a complete fool of himself. When he opened the garage door, he noticed that Barbara's car was gone. He parked the car and went inside to looked around.

"Barbara, you in here?" he yelled, but there was no answer. He walked into the kitchen and noticed where she started to prepare dinner, but left the food and utensils on the counter. He turned and walked upstairs to the bedroom and searched the bathroom and closet. He looked out the window at the backyard to see if she could be in the garden, but she was not there. He began to worry. Barbara was so fragile. He hated the idea of her being alone.

Maybe she's with one of the neighbors, but who? I really don't know these people. But I've got to ask.

Dray started panicking a little. He was starting to feel a lot of guilt about what she was going through, but he didn't realize how entangled he was until the thought of something happening to her became possible. He raced down the stairs and outside. Jean, their neighbor from across the street, was standing in front of Tracy's house next door. Dray approached them.

"Have either of you seen Barbara?" he asked hesitantly.

"Hi, Madison," Jean said. "Yes, I saw her just a little while ago. She said she needed to talk to Danny. I asked her where she was going, but all she kept saying was that she needed to talk to Danny. I don't know what that meant, but we are really concerned. She didn't seem rational. I'm really worried, Madison."

Dray tried to figure out what that could mean. *Where would you go to speak to someone who is dead? The cemetery, yes, the cemetery, but what cemetery? I have no idea where Danny was buried. How can I find out? I can't ask them. They'll think I'm crazy not knowing where my own son is buried. There's got to be something inside that will tell me.* The unsettled look on Dray's face concerned Jean and Tracy.

"Are you all right, Madison?" Tracy asked.

Dray looked over at her. "Yes, yes, I'm fine." He turned, walked back into the house, and went upstairs. He began to look around the bedroom hoping to find something with the name of the cemetery on it. He searched through Barbara's dresser and through some boxes in her closet. *Where would she put something that personal?*

He walked around the room for a minute trying to find the spot. He noticed the jewelry box on the dresser, walked over, lifted the top tray, and there it was. The brochure from the funeral home was in the bottom of the jewelry box. He looked at the picture and saw Danny's eyes staring back at him. The eulogy made him cringe at the thought of the life he took.

Daniel Tanner, graduate from Michigan State University, served two years in the United States Army, had just started graduate school when his life was tragically cut short.

He played soccer and the piano. He was an honorable man with a great life ahead of him.

"Damn, what have I done?" Dray felt a tear roll down his cheek. He tried to control the sadness. He tried to remember who he was and that this man was not his son, but it didn't help. He felt the anguish and emptiness that came from the loss of a loved one. "This isn't happening to me."

Dray wiped his face, looked for the name of the cemetery, and found it on the back page. He put the brochure back in the jewelry box, rushed downstairs, grabbed his keys, and headed to the cemetery. As he turned into the gate he got an eerie feeling. He saw all the headstones and realized that he lost much of his youth by taking on Madison's body. He began to realize the depth of his own mortality. He couldn't believe he was coming to the grave of the man he killed. It was a little overwhelming. He could hardly contain himself. His heart was beating faster and faster, and his shallow breathing was frightening. He gasped when he noticed Barbara sitting on the grass under the huge maple tree. He stopped the car nearby and walked toward her. She was sobbing and talking to Danny as if he was standing next to her. He stopped and waited, uncertain about approaching her.

What am I going to say? What do I do? Do I walk up to her and say, "I'm sorry, but I'm not your husband and I am the man who murdered your son and I guess I will be committing you to an asylum momentarily."? This is insane.

She turned and noticed Dray standing near her. She turned back to the grave and continued to weep. Dray walked over to her and helped her to her feet.

"It will be OK, Barb. I promise you, it will," he said.

"It will never be OK. There's nothing anybody can do to make it OK. I can't take this. I want to know why this happened. I want to know who is responsible for this. Why did God let this happen to me?" She was so angry she started to rant and rave. She lost control, ripped the flowers to shreds, and fell to her knees. "Who took my baby away from me? Who?"

"We must have strength. We will get through this," Dray said as he caressed her neck and shoulders, hoping to help her get control.

"Strength, strength, I am so sick of people saying that to me. You must have strength in God. There is no God. What God would let this happen for no reason at all? Where was his strength to stop this madness? Don't talk to me about strength. Danny was strong and look at what it got him— dead, that's right, dead." She pointed to the grave as she tried to calm herself. "I wish I could meet him."

"Who?" Dray asked.

"The person who did this. I wish I could meet him face to face."

"What would you do?"

"Kill him!" she said. She said it with such fierce hatred that Dray took a step back. He could not believe that a woman of such wealth and refinement could come to a place of such hate and despair. If she only knew that it was he who took her soul away. He replaced her joy with despair. *How can I ever fix this*? He watched as she lay upon the grave crying in pain and anger.

"I can't help you, Barb. I don't know what to do." He walked away and left her with her grief.

Maybe, if I can stay in this body, I can make life better for her, he thought. But just as he thought this, a wave of nausea came over him and he could barely stand. He grabbed his stomach and stumbled to the car.

"OK, OK, I can't stay in this body. I won't even think it anymore, but if I can't stay and I can't seem to leave it, what should I do? The last time I thought about staying in this body, I got sick. I can't go and I can't stay, why? Someone or something is manipulating this situation and I am going to find out who." Dray started to feel better. He looked back at Barbara as he got inside the car and drove off.

The drive home was long and sorrowful. Dray's self worth had dwindled to nothing. He felt so much guilt and shame.

"Who the hell am I to decide another man's fate? Who am I, God? That must be who I think I am. But obviously I'm not God, I'm just a damn fool, that's what I am, a fool, I'm not God, that's for sure. I'm just stupid . . . just stupid."

Dray pulled into the driveway, walked inside, went straight to the liquor cabinet, and poured a drink. It went down nice and soft. One more, then another and another. He took the bottle to the sofa and decided to knock himself out. He wanted to ease the pain and for a moment forget about all of it. He stretched out across the sofa and drank himself to sleep.

The desert sun was hot on his face. Dray looked at his hands and noticed that he was back to being his old self again. He rejoiced and literally hugged himself. He laughed out loud and thanked God for his life back. He looked around at the desolate desert around him and wondered where he was. He saw the swinging doors to the saloon. He walked over and peered inside to a dark room. As he stepped inside, he could feel himself being pulled into the room. It was very dark, and he could feel a presence all around him. Suddenly, hundreds of eyes come from the darkness and stared at him. Sharp lashes struck him from everywhere. He couldn't see where the deadly strikes were coming from.

"Who is doing this, where are you?" Dray yelled.

He fell to the floor and crawled out the door. He crawled

into the dirt road and forced himself to stand. He could feel the sun and the wind on his face, but he still could not see anything. He struggled to walk, but he couldn't see. He felt his face and cried horribly when he touched the sockets where his eyes used to be. He fell to the ground and cried. He screamed so loud he woke himself. He heard a voice from the corner of the room. He turned and looked upon the face of evil. It was a ghastly demonic creature in the form of a man that reeked of foul odor. He brought a chill to the room that caused Dray to shiver.

He looked at Dray and smiled. "How do you plan to spend eternity? I will have your soul." He laughed. "Your eternity will be mine."

The pounding on the door startled him as he jumped to his feet. He looked back at the entity, but it was gone. "It was a dream, I was still dreaming." He said as he stumbled to the door and opened it.

"Does this woman live here?" the policeman asked.

"Yes, she's my wife. What happened?" Dray stared at Barbara as she stepped inside, covered with dirt and grass, and walked upstairs.

"The groundskeeper at the cemetery called and said she was just lying on the ground and refused to leave, so he called us. Is everything all right?" the policeman asked.

"We lost our son. It's been extremely hard on her. I will take care of it," Dray said as he looked back at her stumbling upstairs with her coat hanging off one shoulder.

"I'm sorry to hear that," the policeman said. "We'll let you deal with it. I hope she'll be all right."

"She'll be OK. It'll just take some time. Thank you, officer," Dray said as he closed the door and went upstairs to try and comfort her.

"Barbara, are you all right?"

"No."

"Maybe we should get you some help."

"You know what's amazing to me is that you don't need any help." She turned and looked him squarely in the eyes. "Danny was your whole life. You were so proud of him. Why aren't you crazy, too?"

Dray didn't know what to say. He hesitated and watched her stretch out over the lounge chair. "I can't afford to have a breakdown, Barbara. You seem to be having one for both of us. One of us has to be strong or we will lose everything."

"I already lost everything." She turned over, closed her eyes, and tried to forget that awful day ever happened.

Dray picked her coat up from the floor and lay it across a chair. He walked into the bathroom and threw some water on his face. *I can't leave her alone,* he thought. He walked into the room and lay across the bed. *How am I going to go to work and leave her alone? This could be a way out of going to work,* he thought. *I'll think about it.*

Dray drifted off to sleep and was left undisturbed until he smelled the bacon and coffee coming from downstairs. He opened his eyes and noticed the sun shining through the window. He tried to move, but his headache was more powerful than he was. He grabbed his head and fell back down on the bed in agony.

What did I drink last night—a brewery? He tried again and made it to the bathroom to shower. The warm running water eased the pain a little. As he pulled himself together, he realized that he should be at work.

"I can't go in. I can't leave her alone." He picked up the phone and called Roman.

"Hello," Roman said.

"Roman, this is Dray. I mean, Madison. This is Madison." Dray stuttered for a minute and tried to remember who he was now.

"Madison, how are you? What's going on?" Roman asked.

"Roman, I won't be in today. Barbara had a bad night last night and I don't want to leave her alone."

"Oh my God, what happened? Nothing serious I hope."

"She went to the gravesite and stayed there almost all night lying on Danny's grave. The police brought her home. She was really depressed and withdrawn. I am afraid of what will happen if I leave her."

"Yes, Madison, I understand. I'll tell the boss, and you just take it easy. Maybe you should stay out until Monday. Yes, take the next two days and do something together. Get out of the house or something."

"Yes, that's a good idea, Roman. We'll take a short trip somewhere. Thanks. I'll call you and let you know where we'll be just in case you need to contact me."

"No problem. Take care, Madison," Roman said.

Dray hung up the phone and went downstairs. Barbara was in the kitchen cooking breakfast. He watched her move around with ease and grace as if last night had never happened.

"Good morning," Dray said.

"Hi, sweetheart. I'll have breakfast ready in a jiffy," she said in a cheerful, pleasant tone. Dray was concerned. She seemed to be a different person today. Her mood swings were driving him crazy. One day she was singing, and the next she was laying on graves.

Maybe she has one of those multiple personalities.

"Take a seat," she said. Dray walked over to the table and she placed his food in front of him.

"Would you like some coffee?" she asked.

"Yes, please," Dray said. She brought the pot to the table and poured him a cup of coffee. He looked at her as if she was somebody he had never seen before.

"Stop looking at me like that. I'm all right today. I just needed to say goodbye that's all. I needed to let go, and so I stayed with him until I was finished, and now I can close the book on it and move on with my life. I'm fine," she said.

"That's wonderful, Barb. I'm so happy we can finally get past this. I have decided to take off today and tomorrow so we can get away for a few days. How do you feel about that?"

A strange, sad look came upon her face as if she couldn't leave because she couldn't separate herself from the house, the house that Danny lived in. Then she remembered she was supposed to be all right now. She quickly changed her mood and seemed elated about the idea.

"I'd love it. Where are we going? I'll start to pack right after breakfast."

"Great," Dray said. He took a swallow of the coffee and finished eating. He could tell that the little speech Barbara gave was a poor effort to hide the madness that was really going on inside.

I can tell she has a long way to go before this is over, but I'm going to get her through this if it kills me.

By early afternoon they were standing in the airport waiting to catch a flight to Las Vegas. They arrived in less than an hour. Dray checked into a hotel, dropped off the luggage, and headed straight for the gambling tables. He dragged Barbara along, kicking and screaming.

"Madison, please let me change shoes first."

"No time. The winnings are waiting." Dray smiled at Barbara's giddy expression and hoped she could hold onto it for awhile.

"Papa needs a new pair of shoes," Dray said as he rolled the dice across the table. "Come on number eight."

"Seven and the shooter craps out," the attendant said.

Dray walked away with a joyous smile on his face. He

had always wanted to go to Vegas, but never had the money. Now he was here on Madison's nickel, and he intended to enjoy every minute. Vegas was the right place to go when you want to have too much to do and not enough time to do it in. There was no place outdoors where Barbara would find spiritual healing and be one with God. Nope, that's too close to heaven and too close to Danny. He didn't want her wondering about anything, so it was either Vegas or white water rafting through the Grand Canyon, and there were any number of reasons why that wasn't going to work. So, Vegas it was.

He mingled around the room at Caesar's Palace, watching the people move about. The fabulously decorated rooms and the luxury restaurants gave him a feeling of importance. *I am somebody*, he thought and smiled. He moved around from blackjack tables to roulette, making one hundred-dollar bets. He was playing with the high rollers and he loved it. He found Barbara glued to a slot machine dumping in one quarter after another. She was intent on winning and refused to leave until she did.

"Hey, Barb, how are you making out?" he asked.

"Win a little, lose a lot." She smiled.

Dray was pleased to see her smile. For the first time since the incident, she seemed happy. Maybe this was a good idea to get her away from that house and all those memories. She pulled the handle and three sevens appeared in the window. The light started flashing and the high dollar receipt rolled out of the machine. She was elated. She started to jump up and down and screamed with joy. She threw her arms around Dray and kissed him passionately.

"Thank you," she said.

He knew what she meant. She kissed her receipt and headed for the cashier. "Wow, this is so great." She couldn't stop smiling. "What'll we do now?"

"Let's get a bite to eat and then catch a show," Dray said.

"Great, I'm hungry. Where to?"

They walked along the strip and found a small, quaint restaurant with a patio. They sat outside and enjoyed a wonderful meal and the pleasure of each other's company. Dray never thought he would be able to talk to a lady of class and stature. He always felt out of his element around these people, but she was different.

She's like me, whoever that is nowadays.

He listened to her intently as she talked about one of her trips to Africa when she was in the Peace Corps. She spoke of the hunger and desolation of the people.

"But even in their worst condition they were sweet and humble, kind and innocent. Even in their despair they would give what they had to help another person. They are different than us. They see life differently than we do. They can find great joy in things that we would never even notice. I don't know if that's good or bad," she said. "You can't stand still as time goes by, but the price you pay for progress can be so unforgiving."

Somehow Dray understood her. He could relate her African experience to living in the hood. The average person is kind and generous and their only crime is being poor and uneducated. Just like the African, most people carry their own weight and would help anyone if they could. The conversation went on for hours. They finished the bottle of wine and decided to go back to the room. The television was left on, and Dray heard the name Kuame Kafurue on the news. He turned the volume up and listened.

"Tony Underwood, AKA Kuame Kafurue, was gunned down by a rival gang in Watts, California last night. Kuame Kafurue has been linked with running numbers, drug use, and possession with the intent to sell."

"No! No, we weren't never into anything like that. We didn't mess with drugs," Dray said without thinking about his current situation. He realized his mistake and stopped himself from saying another word. Barbara stared at him while he tried to recover.

"Do you know this man, Madison?"

"No, no, I don't know him . . . no."

"You used the word 'we' as if you were associated somehow. Are you?"

"Barb, how could I know him?"

"Well, what did you mean?" she asked suspiciously. Dray stumbled over his words for a minute.

"I . . . uh . . . I mean that they always try to say it is drugs, but it isn't always, not always. I believe that many of these gangs are together simply to help each other through difficult times."

"Bullshit."

Dray looked at her in amazement. "What did you say?"

"Bullshit. People like that come together under the disguise of helping you, but the moment you don't do something or they see you as a liability, your life is over. They are ruthless. I'm surprised at you, Madison. These are the kind of people who probably killed Danny. You should know better. You're a lawyer." She turned and walked into the bathroom. Dray knew he messed up and took her right back to square one. *That was stupid. I'll have to be more careful and watch what I say from now on.*

"Is there anything you want to do now?" he yelled. Barbara walked back into the room.

"I have always wanted to see the Grand Canyon. Can we do that?" she asked.

He wanted to say no, but he couldn't. He knew he couldn't. The explanation would be more painful than going.

"We can do anything you want. We'll leave in the morning." Dray contacted Madison's travel agent to make the arrangements.

This is the life. I can do anything I want to on the spur of the moment. I knew white people had it good, but I never thought it was this good. I can't imagine what it must be like for those people who are super rich. Man, I'm liking this. He poured a drink and stretched out across the sofa with the remote control.

"I could do this forever, but I can't, I know I can't." Dray sat up and made it clear to whatever it was that made him sick every time he thought of staying as Madison. "This is crazy. I can't go and I can't stay. Crazy." He took a drink and lay back on the sofa for the evening.

Flagstaff, Arizona is a beautiful city—not too small and not too big. It's quite unique with beautiful green trees that seem out of place in the middle of the Arizona desert. The drive up the mountain was long. It was amazing how high up you had to go to see something that ran so deep into the ground. The ride to the top of the mountain was scenic, with tall trees, but nothing prepared them for the wonder that awaited you they you reached the top. The canyon went on forever, as far as they could see in all directions. There were cliffs and hills and plateaus everywhere. It was unbelievable.

While standing at one of the many scenic lookouts, Dray and Barbara tried to get the whole canyon in one picture frame, but couldn't. It was too vast. The setting sun's colors of red, orange, yellow, and purple cast a surreal shadow over the canyon. They looked down as far as they could at the seemingly small stream that is the Colorado River. From where Dray stood, it looked like a stream struggling to survive.

"It is hard to believe that a river created this vast canyon," said Barbara.

"Is this God?" Dray asked.

"Yes," she said. She reached over, took his hand, and closed her eyes for a moment.

"It makes me feel so small and insignificant," he said.

"We are. That's why it always amazes me how we seem to make ourselves so great. We come and go, but this . . . this is forever. We cannot own it, we cannot overpower it, and we cannot control it. We can change it, but we cannot destroy it. It is greater than we are, and that's what I have to hold on to. It is greater than me and Danny."

Dray understood, and silently they drifted into their own private prayers while they held hands and stood before the wonders of God.

Dray left the Grand Canyon with a renewed sense of value. He realized now how small and insignificant his puny life was and how he tried to make himself grand without really deserving it. The emptiness he felt for Danny was real, and he hated the realization that people cause this kind of pain to other people all the time, without caring or honoring the life of the victim or their loved ones.

Dray rode to the airport in deep regret and sat in the car quiet and solemn. He couldn't get Danny off his mind and began to feel the life force moving out of Danny. He sensed it as if it was happening to him now. The fear was so great, it seemed to cause his heart to stop. The anger was so deep, he didn't have time to seek forgiveness. Questions were left without answers for an eternity, and he felt Danny's momentary hope that God was real and that He accepted him into his arms just before total darkness enveloped him and his last breath was taken. He understood the agony of senseless death. In a moment he lived Danny's death, and he was devastated. He broke into tears and scared Barbara to death. He was so concerned about the effect of seeing the Grand Canyon would have on Barbara, he was shocked at the affect it had on him. He couldn't control the tears. He was so angry that Danny was gone and even angrier that he caused it and had to live with it for the rest of his life.

"What's wrong, Madison? What is it?"

"He's gone, Barb, gone," Dray cried helplessly. As much as he wanted to stop, he couldn't. He saw the darkness and he didn't like it. The darkness was him.

Barbara started to cry with him, but deep down she was glad to see him showing emotion about Danny's death. She held him and let him cry.

"It was great being away," she said as she fell across the bed in a sigh of relief. "But it's good to be home. The trip was wonderful. Thank you for taking me to the Grand Canyon. Danny always wanted to see it. I wish he had. I guess there are a lot of things that he'll never do," she said with a look of sadness in her eyes.

Dray walked over to Barbara. He realized that the reason he was in Madison's body was to help pull Barbara through this terrible time. He caused her pain, and it was his purpose to make it right. He knew he couldn't right the wrong he caused, but maybe he could get back to being himself by helping her survive this awful moment in her life. *She needs to be whole again, and I am going to help her get there.*

"Barbara, Danny's loss is a big thing, but it is not bigger than we are together. We will survive it and we will move on. We just have to get through this tough time. I remember when my grandmother passed away. My mother was beside herself and it took a few years before she was all the way right again." He sat beside her and held her hand gently.

"Madison, I thought your grandmother died before you were born," she said suspiciously. She looked at him with a keen eye, and waited for his answer.

"Yes, well yes. I mean, that's what I heard people say. I heard people say that she had a tough time of it after she died. I guess anyone would."

Dray nervously got up and walked toward the bathroom. He looked back at Barbara and noticed her staring at him with some concern and doubt. He turned and walked into the bathroom and closed the door. He realized his mistake and wondered how he was going to backstep out of it, but even worse, it made him think of his mother and the pain she was enduring for the loss of her son. He sat on the toilet in somber despair about this situation.

I wonder if I'll be stuck here forever. I will never really fit. Sooner or later she will figure out that I don't have Madison's past, then what? What am I going to do?

Dray didn't want to leave the bathroom, but he knew he had to. He threw some water on his face and tried to calm down. He opened the door to see Barbara undressing. He hesitated and tried to avoid that part of their marriage, but he knew that eventually he would have to be with her intimately. She had been so distressed over Danny's death that she hadn't been strong enough to even desire him, but as she got stronger, he knew he would have to try and be Madison.

"I'm kinda hungry. I'm going to make a sandwich. You want one?" he asked.

"Madison, you can't be hungry. If you keep eating like this I won't be able to get my arms around you," she said

"It won't get that bad, you think?" he said as he grabbed his love handles and wiggled them. "I guess I am starting to grow outward a bit."

"A bit? In a minute I'll be throwing you peanuts," she laughed.

He looked at her, smiled, and walked downstairs.

* * *

The night passed without incident, and Dray was ready to face the next day. He was planning to retrace the path he took on the day he shot Danny and try to figure out what happened to him along the way that caused this switch. He drove to Venice where the shooting took place and walked back into the alley facing Macy's store. He looked all around hoping to see something. He had no idea what he was looking for, but he felt that when he saw it he would know it, whatever it is. He walked up and down looking for a clue.

"It's an alley, just an alley like any other. What caused this? I've got to figure this out. I've got to."

Dray stood at the place where the gun was fired, looked out across the street, and remembered Danny walking to his car. He remembered the look on his face when he realized he had been shot. Dray stared at the spot where he fell and remembered the body laying there. He couldn't stop thinking about it. The cruelty of it made him sick to his stomach.

What kind of animal am I? I'm not a bad person. Why did I do this? Damn, I must have lost my mind and thought I was important. I thought I could do anything, with no limitations. That's the problem. I feared nothing, so I had no limitations. If there had been somebody who was strong enough to kick my ass a few times and shake some sense into me, maybe I wouldn't be here right now. I guess my mother tried, but I didn't listen.

He found himself sitting on the ground, contemplating his life and how he managed to give it away. After a few hours, he pulled himself together and went to Watts, to the place where he met up with Kuame and the boys after the shooting. He knew he couldn't go inside, but he walked around hoping for an answer. He couldn't find it. He drove toward his house in Crenshaw and stopped at the corner store. Dray noticed a young man standing near the register when he walked inside. He walked to the back of the store and waited. The young man looked scared and anxious. Dray stayed in the back unnoticed and watched as the young man pulled out a gun and demanded the cash from the register. The cashier was scared to death. He slowly stepped to the register.

"Don't touch anything," the young man yelled.

The three other people in the store were cowering behind shelves and racks.

"All of you, over here where I can see you."

The young man waved the gun toward them and forced them to move to the front of the store near the counter. The young lady was crying, which distracted the young man.

"Stop all that noise. Stop it, or I'll stop you," he yelled.

Dray realized that he had not been seen, so he remained in place. He watched as the cashier moved toward the register and started to remove the money from the drawer. Dray moved forward slowly and got right behind the young man. No one let on that Dray was there. The cashier slowly brought the money to the counter and handed it to the young man. Just as he let his guard down and reached for it, Dray grabbed his arm and forced the gun toward the ceiling. A shot was fired, but Dray was able to hold him.

"Get out," Dray yelled to the people cowering at the door. They turned and ran for the door. One of them called 911 and alerted the police of the robbery. The cashier also ran outside and stopped at the door and peered inside to see what was happening. Dray placed his arm behind the man's head and banged it against the counter.

"You stupid, stupid idiot. How dare you use other people to support your stupid, useless life?" Dray yelled as he continued to pound the man's head against the counter.

Dray was so much stronger; the young man had no hope of freeing himself. Dray turned the man around, looked at him, and yelled in his face over and over.

"You can't do any better than this? Is this the best you can do with your life; kill and rob other people to give purpose to your stupid useless, lazy, selfish life? What kind of man are you? What purpose do you have for existing? You don't treat people this way. Doing anything you want to anybody. You earn your own way, you don't just take and take and take!"

Dray held the man with one arm and slapped him with the other. He slapped the young man over and over again. The man stepped back and tried to free himself. Dray tightened the grip on his arm and banged it on the counter until he dropped the gun on the counter. Dray grabbed the gun and threw it to the other side of the store.

"Are you crazy? You white motherfucker; I'll kill your ass. I will kick your ass if you don't let me go," the young man yelled.

"Let you go? Let you go? The only place you're going is to jail, and I hope you have a record so they keep your sorry ass for a long time. Maybe it will give you some time to think about how useless and pitiful you are. Maybe jail will force you to be something other than a back street thug who wants everything given to him just because he was born. I'm going to lie and say that you said you were going to kill all of us one by one. Who do you think they're going to believe—me, the fine upstanding white man, or you and your scummy ass?"

"Hold it right there." A policeman stood in the door pointing a gun directly at Dray. Dray held up his hands and backed away from the young man. "Back away, back away," the policeman yelled. He walked inside the store and forced the young man to the floor. Two other policemen entered and assisted in getting the handcuffs on him. Dray watched as they took him to jail, and he realized how easily that could have been him. He walked out behind the police and stepped in front of the young man.

Dray looked into the young man's eyes and with great sincerity he said what he wished someone had said to him. In a way, he was talking to himself and hoping that he was smart enough to listen.

"Try to do something with your life. Don't throw it away."

"What is your name, sir?" the policeman asked.

"Dra . . . Madison, Madison Tanner," Dray said.

"Madison Tanner," the policeman repeated and wrote Madison's name in his ledger. "We'll need to get a statement from you. Can you come to the station?"

"Yes, of course. I'll follow you over," Dray said as he watched the young man stare back at him as the police car sped away.

After spending two hours at the police station, Dray finally made it to Crenshaw and stood in front of his house. He hoped that something would come back to him about the night he became Madison. He thought as hard as he could, and the only thing he remembered was that after he left Kuame, he went home, drank some milk, and went to bed. He remembered that he had a dream that was serene and calm, remembered wondering if he was dead and hoping he was because it was so nice and peaceful. He couldn't pull it together. The transformation was a blur in his mind. He couldn't see it happening. He remembered going to sleep and waking up as Madison. His frustration was mounting, and he wanted this to be over. He got back in the car and sped off toward Madison's house.

The next few nights were terrible. He kept having the same recurring dream of a ghost town in the desert. He knew he had to find this place, but fear that the dream may come true kept him from trying. He saw himself there, but he couldn't figure out why. The town was deserted and had been for over one hundred years. It was like being in an Old Western movie.

"Where is this?" he asked. He could not remember ever being in a place like that. He couldn't get it out of his mind and his desire to find the place grew stronger.

His frustration with dealing with Barbara was also mounting. She did very well for the first three days back, but since then, she took a turn for the worse. She slipped in and out of deep depression, and she barely talked at all. One day she was laughing and singing, and the next day she was lost. Dray was about to lose his mind. He tried very hard to cope with her, but he felt like he was losing the battle and was wondering if maybe hospitalization was the answer. Dray was also trying to get a handle on his job. He had no idea what was expected of him, and he couldn't seem to answer anyone's questions. He was losing his grip on reality; he was having a hard time figuring out what real was. Which life was real?

Dray sat at his desk at the office and wondered what to do next. The staff meeting that morning was a disaster. When William asked him about the Carter file, Dray was lost. He had no idea what to say. He hadn't even seen the file and didn't know what it was about. He stared back at William hoping for an answer, but nothing came. William realized that Madison could not answer and decided to move on. It was an uncomfortable moment. Dray knew that there would be more awkward moments if he couldn't figure out how to get out of Madison's body.

"I'm sick of this!" he yelled as he hit the desk furiously. He paced around the office in a fit of anger. He couldn't keep this charade up and he couldn't stop it either.

"I've got to get out of here. I've got to go."

He picked up his jacket and hurried to his car. He didn't speak to anyone as he passed by. He didn't even look up from the floor. He couldn't face anyone. Tears started to roll down his face and the anger and guilt overpowered him. By the time he got to his car he was beside himself. He screamed in a fit of anger and nervously turned the key. He sat in the car for a moment and tried to calm himself before he took off toward nowhere. He drove for hours, but eventually he knew he had to go home and face Barbara.

Dray pulled into the driveway knowing that he was going to have to tell Barbara that he thought she should get professional help, and that he would be going away for a while. He knew this would break her heart even more, but he also knew he couldn't stay there, not like that. He went into the library first and poured himself a drink. He looked for her and found her sitting on the back porch. He could tell this was not a good day. She was quiet and solemn. She looked up at him as he approached her and she smiled.

"Hi, sweetheart," she said.

"Hi, Barb. How are you today?"

"Oh, I'm fine. I'm fine."

"What have you been doing all day?" he asked as he knelt beside her and took her hand.

"I've been working in the garden most of the morning, but mostly I've been right here, sitting and waiting."

"Waiting for what?" he asked.

"Waiting for the sun to set," she said.

"What will happen when the sun sets?" he asked.

Her expression was peaceful and serene, unlike any he'd seen before. It was scary and calming at the same time. It was one of those feelings you get when you know something is wrong, but you don't know how to find out what it is.

"Nothing, nothing," she laughed. "Why are you here? You're early today."

"I need to talk to you." She could see the seriousness on his face. His face turned sad and uneasy. He sat beside her. He pulled her hand to his lips, kissed it, and turned to look out at the garden. "Barb, I want you to go into a hospital for a while." He looked at her to see her reaction.

"Why?" she asked.

"I don't think you are handling Danny's death very well, and I think a professional who is educated in dealing with these types of issues can help you."

"You want me to see a psychiatrist?" Her face became sad. "OK, I'll do it. I'll do what you want, Madison."

"Yes, but I want you to stay at a hospital with someone who will be able to take care of you," he said.

She couldn't believe what she was hearing.

"You want me to do what? What...I don't believe you. Why, Madison, why do you want to send me away? I know I've been a burden on you, but I can change. I'm much better now, and I can take care of myself. I don't want to be away from you. Please, Madison, please don't ask me to do this." Tears flowed down her face. She couldn't bear the thought of being separated from him so soon after losing Danny. She stood and started to pace up and down the porch, trying to sort out exactly what he meant. "I'm scared, Madison. Am I losing you too?"

"No . . . no Barbara, no, you will never lose me." He took her in his arms and held her. He tried to comfort her and told her he would always love her. He knew this was devastating for her, but he couldn't let her stay in that house alone and he had to go. He just had to.

"I don't understand. I don't understand how you can be so calm. He was your son, too, and sometimes you act like you don't miss him at all. You always seem so calm and controlled. You should be just like me, missing him. Why aren't you committing yourself? You should be just as crazy as I am, but you're not. You're not because you're glad he's gone and now you're trying to get rid of me too. Well, I'll help you, Madison. I'll help you." She ran upstairs and into the bathroom, locked the door, and opened the medicine cabinet. She found the razors and forced one of them out of the pack. Dray banged on the door and demanded that she opened it, but she ignored him. He frantically looked for something he could use to open the door.

"Open the door, Barbara. Don't do anything stupid. I love you. You know I love you. I miss Danny as much as you do. But I can't let you go on this way. I just want to do what's best for you. You should know this. Barbara . . . Barbara open the damn door!" he yelled. But nothing happened. He finally found a small screwdriver in her desk drawer and used it to force the lock open. He saw the blood on the floor and in the sink, and found Barbara crouching in the shower stall bleeding from both wrists.

"Oh God, oh God. No, no I can't let this happen." He picked her up and took her to the bed. He called 911. "My wife, she cut her wrists. I need help, I need help now."

"Your address, sir. What is your address?"

"7011 Palms Lane, San Pedro. Come now, please come now."

Dray hung up the phone and checked Barbara's pulse. It was there. It was faint, but it was there. He found scissors, cut strips from the pillowcase, and wrapped her wrists as tightly as he could. He held her arms up to stop the blood flow. The ambulance arrived within minutes and Dray ran downstairs to let them in. He turned and rushed back upstairs to show them where she was.

"Here. She's up here," he yelled.

The paramedics raced upstairs and begin working on

Barbara. They got her stable and carried her downstairs and outside. As they placed her in the ambulance, Dray wondered if he would ever see her again. He ran to his car and followed her to the hospital.

The wait seemed forever. *Damn, now I've killed two people. I shouldn't have even suggested sending her to a hospital. I should have known she wasn't ready to deal with anything like that. What was I thinking? Thinking about myself as always, about myself. God, what do you want from me?*

"Mr. Tanner," the doctor said.

"Yes, how is she?"

"She lost a lot of blood, but she is stable now. The next twenty-four hours will tell. Can you tell me what happened? I will have to report this as an attempted suicide, so there will be an inquiry."

"It was suicide. She tried to kill herself. It's my fault. I led her to it," Dray said as the doctor led him down the hall and into his office.

"What happened, Mr. Tanner?" Dr. Parrish asked.

"We lost our son, Danny, a month ago. She took his death very hard and has not been able to go back to any semblance of a normal life. She has these mood swings and terrible dreams. I tried to help her. We went on a trip just last week and I thought she was better, but she wasn't, and I ignorantly suggested she commit herself into a hospital for help—psychiatric help. Can you believe that? Who would do that? God, I can't believe I did that. I just didn't know what else to do." Dray hung his head in anguish.

"It's all right, Mr. Tanner. These kinds of things happen all the time, especially after the death of a child. Actually, you may have been right about getting her some help. Is there anyone else at home with her now?" Dr. Parrish asked.

"No, that's why I suggested it. I didn't want her there

alone all day while I was working. But I guess I waited too late to do something. I didn't realize she would go this far."

"She kept muttering that you were not her husband, that you were someone else," Dr. Parrish said.

"She says that because she thinks I am acting cold about our son's death, like I didn't care. But she is so depressed most of the time, she doesn't seem to know when I'm around. I can't lose it. One of us has to hold on. You understand, don't you?" Dray looked into the doctor eyes, almost begging for forgiveness.

A nurse knocked on the door and asked to speak to Dr. Parrish. She told him that two policemen were waiting to talk to Mr. Tanner. Dr. Parrish walked down the hallway to talk with the officers. He told them everything and explained that he was certain it was attempted suicide. The doctor suggested hospitalization for Barbara. The policemen took the doctor's statement and decided not to bother Mr. Tanner.

"We are going to keep her for a while and then I will have her moved to the ninth floor, where she can get the kind of treatment she needs. Because she attempted suicide, you can have her committed to the hospital for psychiatric treatment. You will need to sign some papers." Dr. Parrish walked out into the hallway and requested that one of the clerks assist Mr. Tanner in filling out the proper forms.

"Doctor, will I be able to have her released at any time? I don't want her to end up in a mental ward for the rest of her life," Dray said.

"Yes, Mr. Tanner. It is up to you. However, you should allow her physician to make the assessment of her ability to cope before you agree to have her released. To release her too soon could prove fatal," he said.

"Yes, I understand," Dray said. He completed the paperwork and took a moment to look in on Barbara before leaving. He drove back home to a large, empty house and tried very hard to hold onto what little sanity he had left. He walked into the library, poured a drink, sat on the sofa, and continued to drink. He picked up the phone and called Roman.

"Hello," Roman said.

"Roman, this is Madison."

"Hey man, what happened to you today?"

"Barbara is in the hospital."

"What . . . what happened!"

"She tried to kill herself. She cut her wrists. They are going to keep her for a while and then she is going to need some therapy. She's not doing well."

"I'll come over. You shouldn't be alone."

"No, please no. I need to be alone. I need to think. I am going away for a while, Roman. I need to take a leave of absence from the job."

"How long?"

"I don't know, but I will keep in touch with you to let you know what's going on."

"Where are you going? You're just going to disappear for who knows how long. This makes no sense. Madison, you should not be alone now. What can be gained by disappearing?"

"I have to do something. I have to find out about something. I can't explain it. I really don't understand it myself. I just know that I have to go."

"Go where?" Roman asked.

"To the desert."

"The desert? What the hell for?" Roman shouted.

"I don't know. Please trust me. I'll get back with you as soon as I can. Please check on Barbara for me, please."

"Yeah, sure, I'll check on her. You take care man, OK?"

"Bye," Dray said as he hung up the phone.

Dray stretched out across the sofa and went to sleep. He dreamed of the desert again. He saw an Old Western town with sand and tumbleweeds blowing everywhere. It called to him. It was hot and dry, and he saw the saloon doors swinging back and forth in the wind. The town was deserted, and he wondered why he was there. He walked toward the swinging doors and passed through them into a dark room. As he approached the center of the room, it got even darker and hundreds of eyes appeared from nowhere and stared at him. They watched his every move as he tried to find his way out. The eyes had no faces, no bodies, and no voices. He was consumed by the darkness.

Something is around Dray—a presence he can not touch or see. It lashes out at him in the darkness and he can't fight back. He turned around and around in terror, trying to see what was beating him, but he couldn't see it. He fell to the floor and fought the invisible enemy. The strikes were painful like knives cutting across his body.

He got back on his feet, stumbled through the swinging doors, and made his way back outside. He knew he was outside, because he could feel the warm, dry air and the heat of the sun, but he still couldn't see. He was still in darkness. The darkness surrounded him as he reached to touch his eyes and found empty sockets where his eyes once were.

He awakened screaming helplessly and found himself on the floor in a cold sweat. He looked around the room and remembered where he was as he reached for his glass and took another drink. He sat on the sofa in deep distress, staring at the floor and waiting for the morning sun.

CHAPTER 8

Josh

Josh knew he would need a key to enter the building, and he had no idea where his was. He waited until some unsuspecting person opened the door wide enough for him to slip inside and took the stairs up to his apartment. He didn't look like someone who would live in the building. If he was noticed, someone might call the police.

Once I'm inside, I'll be all right.

He peeked out of the stairwell door and down the hall. He didn't see anyone, so it was OK to try to make it to the apartment.

Josh kept a spare key hidden in a little notch in the doorframe behind some plaster. He reached the door and looked for the plaster, but it was not there. His heart started to pound as he ran his hand all along the doorframe. He couldn't find it.

"What the hell? I know I have a hole in the wood where I kept a key. Where is it?" He had to find it. Without it, he had nowhere to go. He checked the door to make sure it was the right apartment. "Yes, it's mine. I live here." He searched the doorframe again when the door suddenly opened.

"Who the hell are you and why are you at my door?" the tall, black man bellowed at Josh.

"This, this is my apartment. I live here," Josh stuttered as he tried to regain his composure. The man looked at the pitiful figure of a woman standing before him and wondered how she got in the building.

"I don't know you and I live here, so that means you can't live here, because I don't know you. Is this making any sense to you at all?"

Josh had no idea what to do. He backed away from the man and looked into the apartment to see if there was anything inside that may resemble his home.

"Why do you think you live here?" the man asked.

"This is where I was living before the incident."

"What incident?"

"Before I became a woman and lost my identity."

"What the hell, you crazy. Before you became a woman? What was you before?"

"A man," Josh said. "Can I look inside, just to be sure?"

"Yeah, I guess. It ain't like you could beat me up or something." The man stepped aside and let Josh enter the apartment. It was his, but all of the things he held so dear were gone. His paintings, his mahogany wine rack, leather sofa, and beautiful fur rug—it was all gone.

"How long have you lived here?" Josh asked.

"Seven years," the man said.

"What's happened to me? I was in this apartment yesterday. I know I live here."

"Yesterday," the man said as he looked intently at Josh, trying to understand. "Look, I don't know what's going on with you, but I've been here for years. My little girl grew up in this apartment. You can see where I measured her height year after year on the door frame."

He walked to the kitchen door and rubbed his hand over the markings as he remembered the joy of his daughter's youth. Josh walked over and stared at the markings and knew they were not there when he lived in the apartment. He looked out the large window and remembered how Iria was in awe of the view. Josh stared out the window for a moment and then turned and walked toward the door.

"Are you going to be all right?" the man asked.

Josh stepped out into the hallway and thanked the man for his patience. He walked back downstairs and out of the building.

Now what? I have nowhere to go. I can't stay out here on the street. What the hell am I going to do?

He wandered the street, hoping something would happen to show him which way to go. He walked past the park and decided to take refuge there for the night. He found a large tree away from the street and lrested on the ground. He had been walking all day, and he was exhausted. He laid his head down and slowly fell asleep.

The sound of the morning traffic startled him. He jumped to his feet and took a good look at himself. He had hoped that he had dreamt the whole thing, but no luck. He still had Iria's body. He walked out to the sidewalk, walked for about two hours, and found himself in a different part of town. The neighborhood was different. He noticed the black people sitting on the steps in front of old, run-down homes and young men with rags tied around their heads playing basketball in the middle of the morning.

"Hey you," a voice said from behind him. "What you doing around here? Girl, you white. You 'bout to get yourself killed, or worse," the old man sitting on the step in front of his house said. He looked at her with his old, worn, and battered face. His dark complexion was ominous against his red eyes and yellow teeth.

"I don't need anything from you, old man," Josh said.

"Oh, you need something all right. You need something. I can't give it to you, but you sure need something. You need a fix, that's what you need—a fix. Lord child, you best move on, 'cause I ain't gonna see nothing." He got up and walked inside out of sight to show that he didn't want any part of whatever happened. Josh was nervous. As a white woman, he couldn't be in a worse place. He noticed a service station across the street and a telephone booth, but he couldn't even make a call. He looked around until he saw someone who looked kind enough to help him. He hoped that his female exterior would help him.

"Can you help me?" he asked the well-dressed man coming out of the store. "I need to make a phone call. Please help me." The man pitied the young woman and gave her a dollar in change.

"Thank you, thank you very much." Josh went to the phone booth and made a call.

"Hey, Kyle."

"Who's this?" Kyle asked, not recognizing the voice.

"It's me, Josh."

"Josh, since when did you start sounding like a girl. Who is this?"

"It's me, man. I promise you, it's me."

"Do you know Josh? Is he putting you up to this?" Kyle was starting to feel that a bad joke was getting ready to be played on him.

"NO! Man, it's me. What can I do to prove it to you?" Josh thought for a moment and decided to tell Kyle something that only the two of them should know. "Kyle, do you remember the time we both got stinking drunk and went to the basketball court in the middle of the night and you got

sick and had to let go in your pants? Remember . . . we had
to ride home on the bus stinking. Remember, do you remember?" Josh pleaded with him.

"Damn that, Josh. I told him never to tell anybody about
that. I'm gonna kill his ass when I see him. You tell him his
ass is mine." Josh cringed at Kyle's reaction. He pulled the
phone from his ear when the sound of Kyle's voice
squealed in his ear.

"Wait, wait," Josh yelled as Kyle slammed the phone
down. *One call gone. I've got to make this last one count.* He dialed another number and prayed that she would listen.

"Hello," the sweet voice said on the other end.

"Angie, it's Josh." He waited for her response.

"Josh, Josh who?"

"What do you mean, Josh who? How many people
named Josh do you know? It's me, Angie."

"I don't know who you are, but you can't be Josh because
he is a man and you don't sound like one."

"Look, Angie." He started to tremble from the fear of losing his last lifeline.

"How did you get my number anyway?" she asked.

"Angie, something terrible has happened to me. I need
your help. Please Angie, please don't hang up because I
don't have any more money. Please listen to me."

"OK, so what happened?"

"I know I sound like a girl, and I look like one too, but it's
really me. Something strange happened to me last night,
and I can't explain it. I found myself moving in and out of a
different body and a different place. When I woke up, I was
in an alley and in a woman's body, and I don't know how
this happened. I swear, I swear I am not lying. Help me,
Angie, please. I need a place to sleep. Someone else is living
in my apartment and says that he's been there for years. I

don't understand, Angie. Where do I live? Where do you remember me living?" he asked desperately.

"I don't know where you live, but Josh lives in San Pedro with his parents. The sorry bastard never would work."

"San Pedro. No, Angie, I lived in Santa Monica, I'm sure of it."

"Well none of this has anything to do with me," said Angie as she prepared to hang up.

"Angie, please don't hang up, please. I need a place to stay. Just for tonight until I figure out what's happening to me and I can fix it. Please, Angie," Josh begged with all his soul. He had nowhere else to turn. Angie was curious, but not curious enough to let a strange woman in her home.

"I'm sorry, but I don't know you. I would be crazy to let a complete stranger into my home," Angie said

"But I'm not a stranger; I'm Josh."

"Look, I can't help you. I don't know you," she said

"Please, Angie. I'm coming up there. I have to talk to you. You're my only hope."

"Don't come here. I can't help you." She hung up.

Josh felt lost and abandoned by everyone he knew. He started walking toward Los Feliz. He caught a ride from anyone who would stop. When he was not riding, he was walking until he made it. He stood at Angie's door, trying to figure out how he was going to make her believe him. He knocked on the door softly and waited. Angie opened the door to find a pitiful girl who looked like she had been on the streets for months.

"Who are you?" asked Angie.

"Please, Angie, please try to be open minded. We had something special once. I need a friend right now."

"Look, I can't help you!" Angie yelled.

"Please, we were together for two years, and now you

can't give me two minutes? Please Angie, please. I'm begging you."

Angie was very concerned about this. She looked at this
frail girl hoping to see some sign of Josh, but there was
nothing.

"How did you know how long Josh and I dated? What
did he tell you?"

"I paid for the abortion, Angie. Only you and I know
about that."

"He could have told you about that."

"But why would I tell anyone, why? It's me, Angie. It's
me," Josh pleaded.

She stared at him. She wasn't frightened. The girl before
her was so frail and weak; Angie did not feel threatened.
She hesitated to say yes, but there was something, something about her. Something about this made Angie very curious.

"I know I will regret this, but come on in," she said hesitantly.

Josh stepped inside her modest one-bedroom apartment
and stood there, not knowing what to say. He couldn't sit
down because he was so dirty and soiled, so he stood in the
middle of the room looking frail and weak.

"I appreciate this, Angie," he said.

"Well, I guess a bath is in order," Angie said as she got a
towel from the closet and walked Josh to the bathroom.
"The soap is over there. Let me know if you need anything." She closed the door and left Josh inside staring at
himself in the mirror.

Josh wanted to cry, but he remembered that he was a
man regardless of the image that stared back at him. He
took off the dress and his underwear and looked down at
the breasts and the body that was suddenly his. He ran his
hand over the breasts and couldn't understand how they

became his. He looked down further and noticed the pubic hairs, and started to cry uncontrollably. He started the shower and stepped inside the tub. The warm water felt good. Inside he felt like Josh, but outside he saw Iria. He wondered where Iria was and if she was in his body.

Maybe she is me, but if she was, she would be living in my apartment.

He lay back in the tub and let the water calm him. He wanted to scream, but he knew it wouldn't fix anything, so he held back the tears and hoped that he would figure out what happened to him.

Angie found Josh a T-shirt to sleep in and a pair of jeans and a blouse he could wear tomorrow. She found some linen and made him a place to sleep on the couch. Josh walked back into the living room just in time to see her placing the pillow on the couch.

"You don't have to do all that. I'll be all right," he said.

"It's all right. Have you eaten?"

"No, not in a while," Josh said as he began to feel a little more comfortable.

"Let me see what I can find." Angie went into the kitchen and pulled together a meal for the two of them. "So, you say that you are Josh. I've been with Josh, you know, romantically and you don't look nothing like him, in a lot of ways. You know what I mean?" She laughed.

"I know this seems strange," Josh said.

"Seems strange? This is more than strange. Either you have lost your mind and you really think you are Josh, or this is one awful, stupid trick. What I can't figure out is, a trick on who? Who is the butt of this joke?"

"Angie, somehow I have been transformed into Iria. I don't know how or why, I just know who I am, and I am Josh."

"Iria, yeah, OK. Iria. And who is Iria?"

"She is someone I know. We had a thing once, and it didn't work out and we stopped seeing each other."

"So, why did you change into her? Why not Ed or George or even Mickey Mouse? Why her?"

"I don't know. That's one of the things I've got to find out."

Angie didn't believe any of it. She knew Josh and figured that this poor child got strung out and used by him like most people and she found her phone number inside his apartment and called because she had nowhere to go.

"How do you plan to change back?" she asked.

"I don't know. I don't know how I got here, so I don't know how to change back. I have to figure that out. I went to my apartment and there was someone living there. He said he's been there for years. I know I was there yesterday. I know it, Angie. I don't know what to do."

"Well, let's eat something and we'll try to figure something out."

"Does that mean you believe me?" Josh asked.

"I don't know. But I'm going to keep an open mind about the possibility of it," Angie said as she walked back into the kitchen thinking to herself how stupid this fantasy was.

Why would anybody want to pretend to be Josh? I'll play along for a while, but this girl is on her own.

Angie brought the food to the table. They sat and ate in silence.

After the dishes were clean and put away, Angie stepped into the living room to talk with this woman who called herself Josh, hoping to find out who she really was. Josh knew that Angie didn't really believe him, but he saw her as his only link to reality, so he had to keep trying.

"So, you said you know this woman whose body you now possess?" Angie asked.

"Yes, her name is Iria. We were once together and later became good friends."

"Good friends, like us?" she asked.

"Yes, but different."

"So, is she strung out?"

"What do you mean?" Josh became very defensive.

"You know how it is, Josh. There have been many of us who have crossed your doorstep and lost our lives to drugs. You seem to be a master at getting young women hooked. I'm one of the lucky ones who managed to get clean, but most of us end up on the street. Are you one of them who ended up on the street, Iria?"

"I don't know where she lives. She was using a little, but she's doing OK."

"Yeah, sure." The skeptical look on Angie's face was disheartening to Josh. He knew there was some truth to what she said, but it was not his fault. He took no responsibility for what other people decided to do with their lives.

"People do what they want to. They are going to whether it is with me or with someone else. She still would've gotten high," Josh said in his defense.

"I wouldn't have," Angie said smugly. As she stood up and headed for her bedroom, she stopped and looked back at Iria and sadly smiled. "Iria, we all get caught sometimes. It's nothing to be ashamed of. Pretending to be somebody you're not isn't going to fix it. Maybe it makes you feel better to be someone else, but why pick the man who used you and got you strung out in the first place? Josh never loved anybody but Josh. He uses people like toys. He can make you believe you mean the world to him while he gets everything he can from you, and when he's done he'll toss you out like garbage. You became a liability to his perfect life. I'm sure he couldn't present you to his fabulous friends in your condition. So you had to go, and he was able to do it without thinking twice. He has no morals and, yet, you pretend to be him. I don't understand. I really don't." She turned and walked into the bedroom and closed the door.

Josh couldn't look at her. He felt ashamed and guilty, but still couldn't accept that he alone did all this.

I'm immoral? I never really hurt anybody. People make their own choices. I never forced anybody to do anything. I never knew she felt that way about me.

He lay down on the sofa and tossed and turned until he fell asleep. He slept soundly for a few hours, but suddenly his stomach started to churn with nausea, and his body tightened with pain. He started to shake, and his mouth got so dry he couldn't swallow. He tried to endure it, but the pain in his stomach was so intense he jumped to his feet and doubled over. He made it to the bathroom, where he immediately brought up dinner.

Josh sat on the bathroom floor, hung his head over the bowl, and tried to figure out what was happening to him. He vomited over and over and fell to the floor. He curled up next to the toilet and prayed to die. Angie heard all the commotion and walked into the living room to see what was going on. She heard the moaning and groaning from the bathroom and knocked on the door.

"Iria, are you all right?" There was no answer. She asked again. "Iria, are you OK in there?" She forced the door open and noticed Josh lying on the floor. "Damn, you got the shakes. I don't have anything here to help you. Damn, I don't have the strength to deal with a drug addict."

Angie helped Josh get to his feet and into the living room. She went back into the bathroom and looked for anything that may ease his pain. She found some Tylenol with codeine that had been there for a while and decided that it may help. She rushed into the kitchen and poured a glass of water, but by the time she made it back into the living room

Josh was lying on the floor unconscious. She put every-thing down and called 911. She tried to wake him, but he didn't respond. The paramedics arrived within minutes and started the process of stabilizing Josh. They took him to the hospital, and Angie followed the ambulance to the emergency room. The admittance clerk asked what seemed like twenty questions, none of which she could answer. She couldn't begin to tell the story that Iria told her, so she told what little she knew and avoided the rest.

"Do you know her name?" the red haired woman asked from behind the counter.

"I think her first name is Iria, but that is all I know," Angie said.

"You don't know this woman?" the clerk asked.

"No, I really don't. I just met her tonight. The only thing I know is that she is probably strung out on some kind of drug."

"Well, until we get some information on her, the most we can do is stabilize her and then she's on her own."

"What you mean is until you find out if she has insur-ance she can't stay here because this place is for paying cus-tomers, not sick people," Angie said angrily, saddened by the system.

The clerk looked at her with disgust. It wasn't her fault the girl had screwed up her life. She had heard it all and was *not* in the mood.

"We'll do what we can. Whom should we send the bill to?" she asked.

"I don't know," Angie said as she walked away from the desk and took a seat in the waiting room.

The doctors worked for a few hours to revive and stabi-lize Josh. He was still sick, and the pain again became un-bearable. He started to yell and scream for something to make the pain go away. The nurse tried to calm him, but he became erratic and started throwing whatever he could get his hands on.

"I need something. I need something now. What's wrong with you people? Can't you see I'm sick? Are you going to let me die? Somebody please get me something for this pain!" he yelled at the top of his lungs. "Help me, help me."

"You're not sick, you're a junkie," the nurse yelled as she tried to keep him from throwing the water pitcher across the room.

"I'm a what?" Josh asked as he started to calm himself. His confused look waited for an answer.

"Oh, so you don't know that you are an addict? Don't look stupid. You chose this life, and now you want to act surprised that it makes you sick when you can't get it. It doesn't matter what it does to you, because as soon as you feel better, you'll forget and be back out on the street by the weekend. Now calm down, and I'll get you a pill that will help you sleep," the nurse said.

Josh was shocked. He was a drug addict because he was inside Iria. Iria was a drug addict.

Oh my God, I never thought I would have to deal with that too. Oh God, this is awful. I don't do drugs. I sell drugs. I would never use the shit. But Iria did, so I have to suffer. This bitch is starting to get on my nerves.

The nurse walked back in with a little white pill in a paper cup. She poured a glass of water and gave it to Josh. He took the pill and lay back, hoping that it would take the madness away soon. Within an hour, he was asleep.

"How is she . . . Iria?" Angie asked.

"I'll find out," the clerk said. She got up and walked away from her counter and down the hall. Angie took a seat and waited another twenty minutes before a doctor came out to see her.

"Are you Iria's friend?" the dark haired man asked. He

was tall and slender with dark, wavy hair. He spoke very softly and calmly, which made Angie feel better.

"Yes, I called the paramedics, but I really don't know her . . . not really . . . at all."

"You know she is addicted to drugs," he said. "And this facility is not equipped for the type of long term care she needs. She should be admitted into a rehabilitation clinic so she can get the counseling and support she needs. She needs to dry out. We can't keep her here past tomorrow. Does she have somewhere to stay?" "I don't know. I don't really know her."

Angie started to feel that she was taking on a responsibility that she didn't bargain for. She really wanted Iria or Josh or whomever she was to go away, but she couldn't just abandon her, so she opened her heart and said, "I'll pick her up tomorrow around noon and try to find out where she belongs."

"Thank you," the doctor said as he turned and walked back down the hall and out of sight. Angie stood in place for a minute thinking about what she just did.

"What did I do? I don't want to be bothered with this girl. Damn, this sucks." She turned and walked outside. She got inside her car and noticed that it was four o'clock in the morning and she'd have to be back by noon to pick Josh up. "What a night."

Josh had a terrible night. He woke up in the middle of the night and couldn't fall back to sleep. He tossed and turned, but he never could go back to sleep. He found himself wallowing in depression and despair all night. He felt helpless to do anything about this situation. He couldn't figure out where to start or what to do. He lay in bed watching the sunrise, knowing that he would be back on the streets today and wondering how he would survive. He thought of Angie and the cruel things she said about him and wondered if he really was as awful as she said he was. The tears started to flow, and he couldn't control his grief.

"I'm not a woman. I will not let this destroy me. I never lose, and I will not lose now." He closed his eyes and tried to get a little sleep.

By nine o'clock the nurse came in to check on him. "Hello," she said.

"Hi," Josh said.

"So you are checking out today."

"Yes, I suppose so."

"You need to stop by the desk and fill out your release forms. Will someone be picking you up?" she asked.

"I don't know," he said as he turned and stared at the window, hoping for a miracle.

"Well, I'll be back in a minute. You may want to start pulling your things together," she said as she walked out into the hallway.

Josh got out of bed and grabbed his clothes from the closet. He got dressed, and wondered if Angie would come for him.

Doctor Lansing entered the room with a cheerful "Good morning. How are you today?"

"I'm OK . . . I guess."

"Iria, what are you going to do about your problem?"

"What problem? I don't have a problem," Josh said defensively.

"Yes, you do, and if you don't figure out how to get away from the drugs, you won't live long enough to discover that you really do have a problem. If you are in denial about your drug problem, you'll never be free of it."

Josh turned away from him. He didn't want to hear it. He didn't have a drug problem. Iria did, and he wasn't Iria, so it wasn't his issue.

"OK, I won't press it. It's your choice how you want to live your life, but just in case you change your mind, here's a place that may be able to help you." Doctor Lansing laid a card on the bed with a phone number to a rehabilitation clinic. "The woman who brought you here last night said she would come back and get you around noon." He turned and walked out of the room leaving, Josh to consider his alternatives.

Josh pulled his things together and walked to the nurse's desk to check out. He sat in a chair and filled out the release paperwork and handed it back to the nurse. She reviewed the paperwork and saw that the address was missing.

"Where will we bill you?" she asked.

"I don't know. I live nowhere," Josh said.

"You must have an address. You go somewhere, don't you? Can you find anyone's address that you can use?" she asked as she began to get a little irritated by Josh's demeanor. "This service is not free. If you do not have insurance, you should seek medical assistance through the county for help. The burden to pay this falls on you."

Josh looked toward the elevators and saw Angie walking toward him. He was so glad to see her that he stopped listening to the nurse. He smiled and turned toward the nurse with a sinister grin on his face.

"Sue me," he said and walked toward Angie and into an elevator. "Thank you for coming back for me. I didn't know what I was going to do," Josh said to Angie.

"It's OK. I guess we can try to figure out something for you," she said. Josh reached into his pocket and pulled out the card the doctor gave him to the rehabilitation center. He held it in his hand and wondered if it was his only answer.

"What's that?" Angie asked.

"Nothing, just a number." Josh put the card back in his pocket and focused on what his next move was going to be.

The ride home was long and silent. Angie had no idea what to say. She wanted to help, but how? She decided to approach the question about what Iria's plans were and how she intended to take care of herself. She knew it was a risky question, because the answer may be to stay with her until she pulled herself together, but that wasn't the answer Angie wants to hear. Just as she got the courage to ask, Josh pulled the card from his pocket and stared at it.

"What is that?" Angie asked again.

"Dr. Lansing gave me the name of a rehab clinic and told me I should think about going there," he said.

"He may be right, Iria. You do need help. Where is this place?"

"It's in Inglewood." Josh showed her the card.

She glanced at it and saw the address.

"I guess it could be the right thing to do. I don't want to live off of you, and I don't seem to have anywhere else to go. God, I wish I knew what was happening to me. Why me? I don't understand why I'm trapped like this."

"We all get trapped sometimes, but you'll pull through it," Angie said.

"You don't understand. I am not Iria. I am Josh and I am trapped in this girl's body for some reason and I can't seem to figure out why or how or how to get the fuck out," Josh said with such anger and violence in his voice that Angie's heart started to race. "I wish I could get you to understand. This is a bigger problem than needing rehab. I don't know what happened to me."

"Look, I don't know if you are Josh or not, but either way, you got a serious drug problem. Maybe if you work that out, you could work out this other shit too," Angie said. She turned the corner and drove down the street. She parked the car in front of the rehabilitation center. They got out of the car and walked inside. Angie approached the lady at the desk.

"Hello," Angie said.

The older lady with a short Afro hairstyle looked up at her and smiled. "Hello, how can I help you?" she asked.

"My friend needs your assistance. Iria, come here." Angie encouraged her to approach the desk.

Josh hesitated and stood back for a moment. He reluctantly approached the woman behind the desk and said hello.

The lady looked at Josh and noticed how nervous and inattentive he was. She realized that a decision like this could be very frightening, and she wanted to make sure he understood what he was signing up to. "Are you here on your own free will?" She asked.

Josh was so depressed and hurt that he was there, he didn't hear her. He looked around the room and peered into the adjoining room to see a group of people sitting in a circle bantering back and forth at each other. He started to shiver from the thought of being there with all of those awful people. They were men and women of all races, looking hard and worn. They looked abused and beaten as if life had tortured them and left them for dead. They were ignorant, uneducated, and beneath him. He had always lived a life of luxury and comfort. He couldn't imagine sitting in a room with these failures, trying to care about their circumstances and problems.

I am not like them. I couldn't give a damn about how they got here. I've never used hard drugs in my life. I'm not supposed to be here.

"Iria, the lady asked you a question," Angie said.

"What, what did you say?" Josh asked from a state of confusion and anger.

"Are you here of your own free will?" the lady asked.

"Yes, yes I . . . I came on my own," Josh said as he peered back into the room and felt a despair he had never known before.

These are bums and drug addicts—the scum of the earth, and I am expected to sit and talk with these people. I don't think so.

"I can't do this," Josh said and started to back up toward the door.

"What?" Angie asked in an angry but firm tone.

"I can't do this. I don't belong here. I am not one of these people. I will not subject myself to this kind of life. I will not stoop this low. I'll fix this myself. I don't belong here, and I am not staying."

Josh was adamant. He opened the door and stepped outside. He took a deep breath and tried to hold back the tears that were overwhelming him. Angie looked at the lady without knowing what to say. She simply shook her head in disbelief.

"You can't make them do it. They have to want help, or it will never work," the lady said. She walked Angie to the door and found Josh standing just outside. "Young lady, I hope you live long enough to realize that you have a problem and seek help. So many young people die in denial. If you ever figure it out, we will be here."

There was an awful sadness in her voice that made Josh's heart sink. The lady stepped back inside and closed the door.

"So, what do you plan to do?" Angie asked. She was angry and she didn't care if Josh or Iria or whomever cared. "What do you expect me to do? Just let you live with me forever, hoping that someday you will jump back into the right body? This is ludicrous."

Angie walked back to the car extremely angry. Josh followed and tried to humble himself because he knew how much he needed her. Angie drove off toward home, wondering if there was anyplace on the planet she could drop this woman off and be rid of her.

"Angie, I know you're angry, and I know you don't understand, but I will figure this out. I promise you I will."

"I don't give a damn if you figure it out or not. The whole thing is stupid as hell. I'm beginning to think you're delusional. You don't have anywhere to go. What about your home? You do have parents, don't you? What about them?" she asked.

"I don't know much about Iria's family. I believe that she lived in Canoga Park, but exactly where, I really don't know. I know that she can't go back there. Something inside of me tells me that they do not want her back there. She shamed them and used them for drug money and they've disowned her."

"Iria, your parents disowned you because you need help and you refuse to get it and they got tired of trying. I know this because my family disowned me for the same reason. You see, when I knew Josh, I ended up in one of those rehab places. I know how you feel: like the bottom has been pulled out from beneath you. You feel alone, and confused, and that the people in there are there because there's something wrong with them that could not be wrong with you. You think you're different, more in control, and that you can do this by yourself. Well, dear, you're kidding yourself. If you don't get some help, you'll die on the streets."

"Just give me a little time. Just a few days and I promise I'll figure this out. I promise," Josh begged.

"A few days . . . somehow I know this is a big mistake," Angie said as she turned into a parking space at her apartment and looked into Josh's eyes. "If you *are* Josh, then this is the best thing that could happen to you. Maybe now you can get a taste of the shit you push on people."

"I never made you take anything, Angie. I never forced you."

"No, you didn't, but you didn't help me either. You were there for me when I wanted to get as high as I could, but when the bottom came, I couldn't find your ass. If I thought you really were Josh, I'd leave your ass right here on the street."

Angie stepped out of the car and slammed the door. She was so angry, she couldn't look at him. She wanted to slap him, but she knew that would solve nothing. She walked inside in a fit of anger. Josh followed, feeling as low and disturbed as possible. He didn't realize his actions had caused so much grief. He couldn't understand why he should be responsible for the choices other people made. Angie walked inside, went to her room, and stayed there all night. Josh sat on the couch and tried to keep from vomiting.

He began to pace around the room, trying to figure out what to do. He felt horrible and he knew he wouldn't be able to go very long without the drug. He was starting to panic as he thought about going back out on the streets and running into Diamond again. He lay down on the sofa and tried to calm himself. A tear streamed down his cheek. His eyes watered as fear and desperation gripped him. His insides hurt from the pain. He couldn't believe he was crying.

"I'm not a woman," he said. "I'm a man . . . I'm a man. I can't let this win. I can't let this get the best of me. I am not a woman and I am not a drug addict. I will get through this . . . somehow." He pulled the sheet over his head and cried himself to sleep.

The wind blew warm and steady. Josh found himself standing at the end of an unpaved road in the middle of the desert. He had no idea how he got there. He looked down at his body and noticed he was a man again. He smiled in relief. He looked at his hands over and over again and wondered how it had happened. He didn't care. He was just elated that he was back to his old self again. He noticed the old saloon with one door swinging back and forth. There was movement inside, so he decided to walk toward it. He passed through the swinging doors into a thick fog. He couldn't see anything. He moved through the fog slowly.

"Is anyone here?" he yelled, but there was no answer. He continued to move forward and noticed that the fog was dissipating. When the fog finally cleared, there was a cannon sitting directly in front of him. There were two Union soldiers on either side. One man lit the fuse, and the other aimed the cannon directly at Josh. Josh could see that the cannon was aimed directly at him.

This is certain death, he thought, but he couldn't move.

The cannon fired, and Josh watched as the ball of fire came directly for him. He screamed in desperation and horror as he watched the ball pass through him. He felt nothing. He looked behind him and watched as the ball passed through the saloon wall, leaving a large, gaping hole. He looked back at the two soldiers staring back at him in a surreal kind of way. They had no expression, no movement. They were like the Welsh Guards in front of Buckingham Palace who stand on post without query or regard, accepting their duty and giving their unquestioned allegiance.

Josh looked down at his chest and gasped at the round hole where his heart once was. He turned in despair and disbelief and walked outdoors. The tears started to flow when he saw his heart lying on the ground, still beating. He walked over to it and stared down at it for a moment in awe of what just happened. When he picked it up, the beating flesh was ominous and foreboding. A sense of doom grabbed him, and the hopelessness of the situation overtook him.

He walked out of town carrying his beating heart with him. His desperate cry shook him as Josh gasped for air.

He forced himself awake. He sat up and felt his chest and realized that it was all in one piece.

It was just a dream. He tried to relax.

"Damn, what was that all about?" He pulled himself together and walked to the bathroom. When he looked in the mirror and the face of Iria looked back at him, he almost wished the dream were real. "I'm moving from one nightmare to another." He washed his face and walked back into the living room. "Four o'clock, it's almost daybreak. Another day with no way out." He lay back down and stared at the ceiling until sunrise.

As morning approached, he decided to go back to his old neighborhood in San Pedro. He could hear Angie moving around in her room, trying to get ready for work. After about an hour of bumbling around, she walked out dressed in black slacks and a white blouse. He complimented her on her choice of style and wished her a good day as she readied herself to leave.

"What are you going to do today?" she asked.

"I'm going to try and find out what happened to me. That's the most important thing right now. I was thinking about going back to San Pedro. I hope that I can convince somebody to believe me. Maybe my family will be able to help me through this if I can just get somebody to recognize me."

"Well, I hope you get the answers you need, but you may want to consider going back to the clinic and getting some help for your problem. If you don't fix that, you will never see things clearly. I don't know if you are Josh or Iria, but either way, you are a drug addict and that needs to be fixed.

If I had to choose between the two, I'd stay Iria." She opened the door and walked out.

Her last statement saddened Josh.

Am I so horrible that I should give myself up? I'm not worth existing at all? That's kinda what she said. I'm not worth existing. Damn, what am I, some kind of monster?

He felt sick and wanted to run away, to anywhere. He got the phone book and looked at the bus route to San Pedro. He checked his pocket for money and came up with some loose coins left over from the dollar the man gave him. "It's not enough. How am I going to get the money? This is hard, not having money or any means to get it. Who can I call?" He thought about it for a minute and came up with no one.

No one would believe me anyway. How do people survive like this? What am I going to do?

He looked around in the apartment for any cash. A nickel or a dollar—it didn't matter. He looked into Angie's room and noticed the twenty-dollar bill in the jewelry box. As he reached for it, he told himself that it was wrong, but he had no choice.

I'll get it back to her before she knows it's missing. That's what I'll do. I'll get some money from my folks when I see them today. They will believe me, I'm sure of it.

He forced the money into his pocket, grabbed his jacket, and walked out the door.

The bus ride to San Pedro was a dreadful affair. Josh had never had to take the bus before, and the experience was demeaning. He had his first car at seventeen, and his parents took him anywhere he wanted to go prior to that. Josh's family was quite wealthy, so the hired help was always around to take care of Josh's many needs. Selling drugs was just something to do to pass time. Working was never a desire, but he knew that his father would never let him lay around doing nothing, so he pretended to be making his own money in the stock market and foreign exchanges. He pretended to work from home so his parents would never suspect that he was selling drugs to desperate, hopeless people.

Josh stepped off the bus and started walking. He turned the corner and saw the huge house he grew up in at the end of the block. He smiled in relief. Finally, a familiar place and familiar faces. He started walking toward the house when he began to notice all the movement around the house. People were everywhere.

"What's going on?" he uttered. He got closer to the red brick house and saw his family. Aunts, uncles, cousins, neighbors, and friends he went to school with were all gathering around and mingling with each other. A black limousine pulled up in front of the house. His mother, father and his sister Emily came out of the house and walked to the limousine. His two surviving grandparents joined them and they all stepped inside the limousine.

"Oh my God. Somebody died. Who? Oh no, I have to find out."

Josh walked closer and began to mingle with the crowd. He recognized Jordan, one of his many girlfriends. He walked over to her to try to find out more about what was going on.

"Hi, my name is Iria," he said as he extended his hand.

"Hi, I'm Jordan. Did you know him well?" she asked.

"No, not well. We met briefly, but I did come to like him very much."

"It's very sad that his life was cut short, so young. He was a dog, but I wouldn't wish this on anybody."

"I never did hear what happened. Do you know?" Josh asked.

"He was shot by some drug addict. We have no idea

why. It seems that they had some kind of altercation and the man had a gun. Before anyone knew what was going on, Josh was dead."

He couldn't believe what he just heard. "Josh," he whispered. He tried to contain his fear.

The girl recognized the stunned look. "Yes, I was shocked when I heard too. Poor guy."

Josh tried to retain the horror he was feeling when the image of himself lying in the coffin, lifeless and cold, dominated his thoughts and brought chills to his heart.

"It's very sad," he said.

His face turned to stone. *I'm dead? That's not possible. I'm right here. Lord, how can I get them to understand?*

"Do you have a ride to the funeral home?" Jordan asked.

"No, I wasn't planning to go, but if you have room, I'd like to say my last good-byes."

"Sure. I guess we better get going. They are organizing the line. My car is down there," she said as she pointed down the street to a blue Honda.

They walked toward the car, and Josh was cringing at the thought of his own funeral. He couldn't believe it. He looked around at all the people and couldn't believe that just a few days ago, he was part of this family and now they have no idea who he was. Jordan got in line behind a string of cars, and they started the slow journey to the church. She parked down the street from the church, and they walked through the crowd to the door. Josh hesitated.

"What's wrong?" she asked.

"I don't think I can do this," he said.

"I know how you feel. It's awful staring down at a dead body, hoping somehow that it will breathe again and this whole affair would be over. It's hard, isn't it?"

"Yes . . . yes, I've always hated funerals and I hate that the last memory of a person is that dead body. It seems unfair to the person that they should be remembered that way."

"I never thought about it like that before, but you're right; it *is* the last thing you remember. What you want to remember is the person full of life and vigor, but this event erases all of that." She reached back to try to bring Josh along with her. He almost vomited at the thought of going inside.

"I'll be all right. I'll be there in a minute," he said as he turned and walked back down the steps to catch his breath.

"All right," Jordan said as she turned and walked inside.

Josh waited at the bottom of the stairs for his stomach to calm down. He was so nervous as he watched people he had known his entire life walk by without recognizing him.

"Are you all right, young lady?" Uncle Richard asked as he tried to comfort the young lady, not knowing that the nephew he loved and nurtured stood before him.

"I'll be fine," Josh said as he held his stomach and tried to stand up straight. He struggled to get the courage to walk inside.

Slowly, he followed his Uncle Richard inside and found a seat in the rear. He listened to the minister speak about what a fine, generous person Josh was and how he would be missed. Josh looked all around and watched people cry and mourn over his demise. He couldn't believe it was real. He had to see it for himself. He took a deep breath and stood up. The choir started to sing a beautiful hymn, and Josh stepped out into the aisle and walked down to the coffin, which was surrounded by flowers and wreaths. As he got closer, his heart started to pound so loud it drowned out the voice of the choir, the crying, the sorrow, and the anguish felt by so many. As he got closer, he saw the face peering out from beneath the satin lining. He stopped and felt that he could not go any further.

I don't want to see. I don't want to know.

Something forced him to go forward, and suddenly his own face peered back at him. The body was cold and lifeless, and fear gripped him as he tried to keep his balance. The room started to spin around him, and his legs had no strength. Tears rolled down his face.

"I'm not you," he said just as his legs buckled and he fell to the floor. The minister rushed to him, along with several other people. Someone carried him into the front parlor and laid him on the sofa. In Iria's body, Josh was weak and vulnerable. One of his neighbors, Mrs. Singleton, was a registered nurse, and she came out to see if she could help.

"Is she all right?" she asked.

"I think so. Looks like she just fainted," Mr. Perry, who lived across the street from Josh's family, said, "Let me take a look at her."

Mrs. Singleton kneeled down beside Josh and began to check his pulse and breathing. "Check the first aid kit and see if there is any ammonia in there."

Mr. Perry went into an adjacent room and came back with a bottle and some cotton balls in hand. "I found it," he said as he handed it to her.

She wet a cotton ball with ammonia and waved it beneath Josh's nose. He inhaled, gasped for air, and began to cough and gag.

"Are you all right?" Mrs. Singleton asked.

"Yes, I'm fine. What happened?" Josh tried to sit up.

"You fainted. Maybe you should lay here for a while," she said as she tried to make him comfortable. "Will you be all right?" she asked.

"Yes, I'll be fine," Josh said.

"I'll be just inside the door. If you need anything just yell, OK? I'll check on you in a few minutes. Just lay here and rest a minute," she said.

"I'll be fine." He said

She walked back inside, and Josh stared into nothing-ness, in total despair. He sat up and gathered himself. He couldn't stand it. He ran for the door and down the street. He couldn't stop running. He wanted to hear the sound of his heart—the heart that lay in the dirt in his dream and was still beating for its life, his misguided heart that hurt so many people and caused so much pain. He ran until his legs ached and his chest hurt. He was in agony, and he had no idea how to stop the pain. He ran into a small church and stumbled to a pew. He sat and cried and prayed to God to help him out of this madness.

"I am not coping with this at all. I need your help now. I need to know that you really exist and that you care enough about me to help me. I don't know what else to do. I've tried everything that I know, but I don't know what to do. Please help me." His cries were desperate and agoniz-ing.

A priest standing nearby approached him and tried to help. "What seems to be troubling you? It can't be all that bad."

"I'm not me," Josh said. "I don't know who I am."

"Have you been hurt? Do you need a doctor?"

"No. What's wrong with me, a doctor can't fix."

"What is it that's so terrible? You say you don't know who you are. Who do you think you are?

"I think I am Josh Brimeyer, but as you can see, I'm not a man, so I can't be him, can I?"

"If it is a problem with your sexuality, that is not uncom-mon. Many of our children have gone astray in that area of their lives, but many have gotten back on track with God's help."

Josh knew he wouldn't understand, but he needed someone to talk to so badly. He needed to make someone understand.

"I was switched into someone else's body."

The priest looked at him in confusion and tried hard to understand what he was really trying to tell him. "How did this happen?" the priest asked.

"I don't know. I wish I knew, because I can't figure out how to get back."

"Whose body are you in?" "A girl named Iria." Josh looked at the priest and saw the disbelief on his face. "I can't make you understand. I really don't understand myself. I just need to try. I wish I could . . . I mean, if I had my life to do over, I would fix it."

"You can fix anything with faith and a strong desire to succeed. If you trust in God, whatever it is, he will pull you through it."

"Will he, will he? I'm not so sure anymore."

"You must believe and have faith that it will be all right. Is there anything I can do to help?"

"No, I'm all right. I just need to sit for a while," Josh said as he got on his knees and began to pray. The priest touched him on the head gently and walked away.

"If you need anything, we are here to help."

Josh stared at the cross and the statue of Christ and began to pray helplessly.

He dragged himself outside and began the walk back to Angie's apartment. It was nightfall, and the air had turned cool. He didn't have the energy to move very fast, so he slowly made his way through the night streets, praying that this would all be over soon. His hunger pains gripped his stomach, and his headache throbbed behind his eyes, but he kept walking. He couldn't think clearly.

Angie's place is as close to a home as I'm going to get.

All of his friends and family believed he was dead, and

even the priest didn't believe his story. He couldn't figure out what to do next, He held onto the basic understanding that if he got into Iria's body, there must be a way out of it.

People don't just jump into each other. It just doesn't happen, so there must be hope; I can't give up because there must be a way out.

Either I have lost my mind or something greater than me has control over this situation. If it is God, then maybe it will be all right. If it isn't, I am in more trouble than I can imagine. Funny, I never really believed in God or the devil before. I never thought of either of them in a real sense as if they existed right here beside me. I can't believe I have come to a point of wondering if the devil has control over me.

Josh had no idea what time it was when he arrived at Angie's apartment building. As he walked inside and approached the door, he saw the bag sitting in the hall with Iria's name on it. There was a note attached. Josh's heart started to beat faster. He became fearful of the note and what it would say. He knew she would be angry about the money, but he thought he would have an opportunity to explain and make it right. He tore the note off the brown bag and opened it.

Iria,

   I don't know you well enough to take you into my home and have you steal from me. I will not stand for it and will not allow you to take advantage of me that way. Please do not try to contact me again.

                                          Angie

I've got to explain. I can't go back out there into the street.

He knocked on the door until Angie answered. She slowly opened the door and peered through a small opening.

"What do you want?" she asked.

"Please, Angie, I know how you feel, but I can explain. I didn't really steal the money. I will get it back to you soon. I had to try and find out what happened to me and I thought that if I could go home I could find out something. I didn't really steal from you. I have to fix this mess I'm in. Please try to understand," Josh pleaded.

"I will not allow you to come into my home and disrespect me. I don't know you, and I don't *want* to know you."

The door closed, and Josh was left wondering where to go and how to survive.

Josh walked out of the building and down the street. He had no idea where he was going. He walked all night. He wandered around aimlessly until he noticed the familiar building across the street—the rehabilitation clinic. He started walking toward it. As much as he did not want to go inside, he saw it as his only hope.

What else can I do?

It was six o'clock in the morning, and the doors were locked. He crouched down on the porch, lay against the wall, and waited. Iria's frail body shivered in the cool morning air. He tried to stay awake, but he couldn't. His eyes burned from exhaustion, and his legs hurt from walking all night. As he lay against the wall, he remembered what it was like to be a man and to be strong, and wondered if he would ever know that feeling again. His eyes closed and he drifted into a deep sleep.

It seemed like only moments later when he felt himself being awakened by the lady who spoke with him the last time he was here. He opened his eyes and tried to gather himself.

"I . . . I need a place to stay," he said as he came to his feet.

"Come inside," she said as she turned the key and

opened the door. Josh walked in behind her and stood in the hallway, not knowing what to do. He looked all around and wondered if this was a good idea.

I will have to be Iria while I'm here. The'll never believe the truth. I'll have to play along until I can figure out what else to do.

"Come inside, dear," the lady said.

Josh walked toward her desk and took a seat.

"My name is Margaret Capshaw. Most everyone calls me Marge. I'm the administrator here, and I have over forty people here from all walks of life."

"Hello," Josh said timidly.

"Fill out these forms and then we will get you a hot bath and something to eat. How does that sound?" she asked as she handed him the forms and a pen.

"It sounds great," he said.

Marge got up and walked down a long corridor. She stepped into a room for a moment, and when she returned she had two other people with her, one of whom Josh recognized. It was a young lady he had dated for a while just before he met Iria. Her name was Tricia. He remembered when he gave her cocaine for the first time. She was so giddy and fun.

Josh looked at Tricia now and noticed how old and worn she looked. He thought about what Angie said to him about how he got her strung out, and he wondered if he did the same thing to Tricia. Guilt overtook him, and made him sick to his stomach. He couldn't look at her. He turned away and then he realized she wouldn't know who he really was.

"What is your name again?" Marge asked.

"Iria."

"Iria, this is Tricia and Morgan. They are going to help you get settled in. Have you completed the paperwork?"

"Yes, it's done," he said.

Marge took the forms and laid them on her desk. Josh stood and followed Tricia and Morgan down the corridor to the bathroom. Tricia began to draw the bath, and Morgan started looking for towels and soap.

"Most of us stay four to a room here, but there are three of us—Frankie, and me, and now you. Frankie's OK. I think you'll like her," Tricia said.

Josh didn't know what to say. He watched her as she moved around trying to get him everything he needed, and he tried not to start crying. Morgan laid the towels on the counter and walked out. Tricia made sure the water wasn't too hot and drew the curtain around the tub.

"OK, I think this should be fine. Let me know if you need anything else. When you're done, come down the hall to room six. I'll show you where you'll be sleeping and get you the schedule for the week," she said.

"Schedule . . . what schedule?" Josh asked.

"Your schedule of chores and classes."

"Classes?"

"They aren't really classes. It's more like counseling sessions and group therapy. You will also have a one-on-one with the psychiatrist that comes once a week. It's very good. The sessions have been great for me. I look forward to them."

"Look forward to them? Why would anyone look forward to telling some stranger about your life? The things you don't want anyone to know about, you spill your guts in front of a whole bunch of people who could care less about you and you about them. I don't look forward to that," Josh said.

"I felt the same way when I first came here, but now, I look forward to them because they helped me face my fears and realize that I'm not alone. I'm not the only person feeling the way I do and suffering through the kinds of things I have suffered. I had to confront who I am, and that was no small task," she said.

"I know who I am," Josh said. "I just can't find him."

Tricia looked at him strangely as she opened the door and started to walk out of the bathroom.

She looked back at him. "This will be hard," she said, "but it can be done. There's a reason we're dependent on drugs, and before you can conquer the dependency, you have to find out what that reason is. You can't do it by yourself. You know this, or else you wouldn't be here now."

She closed the door, and Josh undressed and stepped into the warm, soothing water. It was the first time he had a chance to really relax in what seemed like forever. He allowed himself to drift into a peaceful place for a moment. He laid his head back, closed his eyes, and tried to remember a happier time. After about twenty minutes he heard a knock at the door.

"Yes, who is it?" he asked.

"It's Tricia. I have some clothes for you. Can I come in?"

"Yes."

She opened the door and walked inside. She placed a pair of jeans, a blouse, and some underwear on the counter.

"I think these things will fit you. Let me know if you need anything else," she said as she walked out and closed the door.

Josh lay back and wondered how he was going to live in a room full of women and not let on that he was a man.

They are going to think I'm a lesbian. He laughed. *This is going to be interesting.*

He pulled himself together and walked down the hall to room six. He entered the room to find Tricia fixing the top bunk bed for him.

"This is where you'll be sleeping," she said. She walked over to a closet. "This is your side of the closet, and these are your drawers," she said as she walked over to the dresser. "We get up at seven o'clock, have breakfast, and begin our morning sessions at nine. You can rest today and start your classes tomorrow. Marge is working on your schedule, and she'll have it ready for you after breakfast."

"Does everyone attend the same classes?" Josh asked.

"No, it depends upon where you are in your growth process. For those who've been here for a while and have faced their demons, they have more duties and responsibilities than classes. But people who are just starting or those who are not progressing well spend most of their time in classes or with their sponsor. Many of us who have been here for a while will sit in on classes for newcomers to help them get comfortable with the sessions and to let them know that they can find success just as we did. As your sponsor, I will be sitting in on a few of your sessions to give you moral support if you need it." "What is a sponsor?"

"Your sponsor is the person assigned to help you through your transition from a life of drugs to a life of sobriety. It seems easy, but it is very hard, and we all need as much support as we can get, and we always will."

"What do you mean 'we always will'? Once you're done, you're done."

"No, that's not true. Once you are hooked on this stuff, you are hooked for life. You may always need help to stay clean. Some people want to return to it for a long time after leaving here, so we have help even after we leave here. I am your sponsor. I will be here for you when you feel like the bottom is falling out and you just want to run. I'll help bring you back to reality and help you cope with your withdrawals just like my sponsor helps me."

Josh was embarrassed. Tricia was his sponsor.

How bad can this get? One of the people I put in this place is going to sponsor me. If she only knew, she would probably kill me for screwing up her life and putting her in this hellhole in the first place, he thought.

"I have a ten o'clock session, so I have to go. Get some rest, and I'll check back with you later." Tricia closed the blinds and turned the lights off as she left the room. Josh lay across the bed and closed his eyes.

Josh awoke shaking. The sheets were wet from his sweat. He tried to focus as he looked around in a daze. He couldn't seem to figure out where he was. He gathered his thoughts and jumped down to the floor. Tricia entered the room carrying a cup of pills and a glass of water that smelled of nutmeg.

"What's this?" he asked.

"Take it. It will make you feel better," she said.

He didn't care what it was, he just wanted to stop shaking and sweating. His stomach felt like he swallowed a rock, and his head was killing him. He took the pills.

"Thank you. How'd you know?"

"We've all been there. It'll help calm your stomach and make the headaches stop. Your things are over there on the table. There are some clothes and a few personal things that you may need. You know where the bathroom is. Once you are done, you can join us for dinner in the kitchen downstairs. You can get there from the lobby."

Josh went into the bathroom and got cleaned up. He was terrified about going downstairs. He was not ready to confront all these people. He couldn't imagine that he would have anything in common with them. He dreaded meeting them, but he was not sure why. Part of it was his own shame. All of the people were in there because someone just like him provided them with the drug that controlled their lives.

He walked toward the lobby and stood at the top of the

stairs. He could hear all the chatter and commotion from the kitchen and wondered if they somehow knew who he was. He was so hungry, but his upset stomach made the thought of eating distasteful. He stared downstairs, wondering if he could get his food and go back to the room.

Yes, that's what I'll do.

He took the first step and headed downstairs. He tried not to look at anyone, but they all noticed him. He could feel the stares from all around the room as silence overtook the room. He tried not to make eye contact with anyone. He walked to the serving line and picked up a tray and some utensils.

"What'll you have?" the heavyset woman asked.

"I'll have the soup and a sandwich."

"What kind of sandwich?"

"It doesn't matter. Surprise me."

"Tuna it is." She handed him the sandwich. He grabbed it and a cup of soup, and then he put them on his tray. He turned to walk back upstairs. He was so nervous and wanted to escape without notice, but he feared that everyone was watching his every move.

Tricia saw him and stood up to approach him, but Marge stopped her. "She is not ready. Let her be by herself for a while. She's got some thinking to do," Marge said.

Tricia sat and watched as Josh slipped behind the wall and back upstairs. He reached the room and closed the door behind him. He sighed in relief of making it back without being bombarded by a welcoming committee and a whole lot of stupid questions. Smiling and pretending wad not doable today. He sat at the desk, ate, and enjoyed the food. He licked his fingers as he swallowed the last bite, and moved the tray to the edge of the desk.

The bed had become Josh's sanctuary, so he climbed back into it. It was the place where he felt most secure and safe.

He could close his eyes and escape the madness, and no one could enter to ask stupid questions or make judgmental statements. He was alone. As long as he didn't open his eyes, he could be alone.

Tricia shook Josh awake. "It's time to get up," she said.

Josh looked around to see the sunlight blaring through the window. He looked down to see Frankie still sleeping with the covers pulled over her head.

"Frankie, get your butt up," Tricia yelled.

"I'll get up after Iria is finished. It's better that way," she moaned. Josh climbed out of bed and grabbed his stuff from the dresser.

"Your schedule this morning is light. After breakfast you'll meet with the counselor from nine to ten. After that, get with Marge for your duty schedule. Is there anything else you need?" Tricia asked.

"No, no, I'm fine. I'll be all right," he said.

"OK, I'll see you downstairs." She turned and walked out the door.

Josh picked up the clothes and toiletries from the table and walked down the hall to the bathroom. He turned the shower on and stepped inside. The warm water felt good flowing down his body. He began to wash Iria's body and felt how small and elegant she was. He remembered when they first met and how beautiful she was. He thought about the first time they made love and the passion she had for him. He also remembered the day he introduced her to the drug, and how much she didn't want to take it.

It will be all right, he remembered telling her. *I wouldn't let anything happen to you. I love you.*

He recalled the fear in her face the first time he forced the needle into her arm, and then the look of joy as the drug entered her body. After a while, the look of want replaced the look of fear. She would do anything to get it.

Why couldn't she be stronger? Why couldn't she have forced herself to say no? If she really didn't want it, she should have been strong enough to fight it. I can't be blamed because she allowed herself to get hooked. I wish she had been stronger.

He hung his head in sadness and wished that she had made a different choice.

It's not my fault, he thought. *It's not my fault.*

He finished his shower and walked downstairs to the kitchen. Everyone was mingling, talking, and laughing. The basement was converted into a cafeteria. The galley-like kitchen was on the back wall with a serving bar. People grabbed a tray and utensils and filed down the bar waiting to be served. The young man serving behind the counter was yelling at the top of his lungs.

"Grits, eggs, toast, and ham. Eat at your own risk. Pick your poison, pick your poison."

Josh grabbed a tray and walked down the counter. After he got his food he walked toward the center of the room.

"Iria, over here." He heard the sound of Tricia's voice. He turned to find her sitting at a table with two other women on the far wall. Josh walked over and took a seat.

"Is everything all right?" Tricia asked.

"Yes, I'm fine."

"This is Darcy," Tricia said as she pointed to the rough looking girl with long dreadlocks. "And this is Janeen." Janeen was huge. She hadn't missed a meal in a long time. Her short, blond hair made her look as tough as any man.

I would not want to come up against he.

Darcy looked over at Josh's plate and saw the small amount of food and laughed. "Girl, you need some meat." Janeen laughed and her body shook the whole table.

"Yeah girl, as little as you are, I could sit on you and end it all," Janeen said. They all laughed. Tricia took some ham and eggs from her plate and put them on Josh's plate.

"They're right. You do need to eat."

"So, how long were you on the street?" Darcy asked as she looked up at Josh.

"What do you mean? I wasn't on the street," Josh replied nervously. They all looked at each other, wondering if he thought they were dumb enough to believe him.

"If you wasn't on the street, what are you doing here?" Janeen asked as she leaned forward into Josh's face. Her wide berth was a little intimidating, so not responding would be viewed by most as unwise. Josh backed away from her advance, but never took his eyes off her.

"I wanted to get help, so I came here."

"Yeah, right," Darcy said. "Let me guess, you stole somebody's money, got so high you overdosed, ended up in the hospital, and the person you stole from threw you out. So you ended up here because you had nowhere else to go."

"That's not true," Josh yelled.

"It's nothing to be ashamed of," Tricia said. "We've all been there."

"What do you mean?" Josh asked.

"I mean that all of us lived on the street at one time or another. That's where most of us end up before coming to places like this."

"You were on the streets?" he asked as he looked into Tricia's eyes.

"Yeah, for a while."

"Why didn't you stay with someone or get help?" he asked.

"I tried, but I soon learned that a junkie and straight people can't live together, so the junkie has to go since they own nothing most of the time. I burned my bridges just like most addicts and had no one who would help me, so I ended up on the street, hit bottom, and then came here at the bequest of the judge."

Josh stared at each of them and realized that their experiences were all similar, that a junkie's life was transparent to a junkie. He couldn't hide behind false impressions and prideful lies. They all knew. They'd all been there.

Accepting that he was a junkie hit him hard. It was the one thing he worked extremely hard at not becoming, but through a twist of fate, he found himself struggling with the life of a drug addict. He felt naked and like the whole world was looking at him. They mocked his weakness and pitied him. He hung his head in shame. He lost his appetite. He sat in silence until breakfast was over.

After breakfast, Josh was scheduled to meet with the psychiatrist. Everyone attended the group sessions with the onsite counselors, but periodically everyone was scheduled to talk with the psychiatrist. The visits became fewer and fewer as one progressed through the program. All new arrivals had to see her weekly, until she decided otherwise. Josh was not looking forward to this. He walked down the hall, out the back door, and across the yard to a small building. The old detached garage had been converted into an office where Dr. Pamela Seaton held her sessions. Josh knocked on the door and heard the soft voice from inside.

"Please come in." Josh entered the room with great hesitation. The last thing he wanted to do was talk to someone who was going to try and help him find himself. He walked in slowly and looked around at the small office. He noticed the window that faced the street and remembered when he was driving around in his red Porsche, free and easy.

"Iria, that is your name, isn't it?" Pamela asked.

"Yes."

"It is an unusual name . . . pretty. Please take a seat and tell me, Iria, why are you here?"

"Why I'm here." *What a strange question.* "I'm here because I don't have anywhere else to go."

"Why don't you have anywhere else to go?" Pamela asked as she tried to probe a little deeper, hoping to break the wall of denial that she believed Iria was hiding behind.

"I don't have anywhere to go because I'm having a problem right now. I've got some issues to deal with, and I don't know how I got in it or how to get out of it," Josh replied sarcastically."You got in it because you made a bad choice. Do you know what that choice was?"

"No, this wasn't my choice. If I could change it, I would, but I can't, I really can't." Josh became irritated with the line of questions. He stood up, walked to the window, and stared outside.

"Why does the window fascinate you?" she asked.

"It doesn't. It's just a window."

"What do you see, Iria? What are you looking for?"

"I'm looking for myself. The person I used to be. I can see him and I want him back," Josh said.

"Him?"

Josh realized what he had said, and turned to look at her to judge her reaction. Confusion—of course, what else could it be?

Now she thinks I'm a woman who wants to be a man, or a man posing as a woman. This is funny. He turned back toward the window and tried not to laugh.

"Iria, everyone finds themselves in good places and bad places at some point in our lives."

No shit, lady. You have no idea what a bad place is. I wish I could make you understand what has happened to me and then you would know what bad times ten is. Fucking horrible.

"I am not going to help you find the person you used to be. That person is the person who made the bad choice. You do not want to be her anymore. She is not strong. She has no self-worth, value, or self-esteem. What we are going to work on over the next few months is finding a new person, a new Iria who is strong and secure. She will know her value and will know that she is more valuable than this. She will not allow herself to be led or influenced to do something she knows is wrong. The old Iria is putting you through hell."

Josh burst out laughing. "God, you have no idea what you are talking about. I know who I am. I just can't find him. I am strong and I know that when this is over I will be back to being my old self."

"Iria, you are not the first woman to get strung out on drugs. You are not the first woman who wishes she could be somebody else in an effort to escape the pain, horror, and shame of it. You aren't even the first woman who pretends to be a man due to a lack of self-respect and worth. But, if you want to succeed at getting yourself back, you will have to be willing to do whatever it takes. You must be willing to fight to the end, and it will be an awful, dreadful fight. Many times you will think you are losing, and just when you think you are there, you will fall. It is a lifelong struggle and the question is, are you willing to fight for yourself? Are you willing to look yourself in the face and realize how much you hate what you've become and the demons that got you here? Are you willing to fight? Iria, are you willing to do whatever it takes? Because if you're not, we are wasting time."

"I guess I have no choice. I'll do whatever it takes. If I'm going to be stuck with this body, I might as well be clean,"

"Yes, you are stuck with that body, and you are right, it might as well be clean. Totally clean—the mind, body, and soul."

"OK, Doctor, let's give it our best try," he said as he prepared to leave the office.

She walked over to him and extended her hand. He shook her hand and smiled.

"We will talk again next week, and then we'll start the process of breaking down the barriers to see who Iria really is. We have to free you of the past before you can move forward."

"I agree, freeing my mind and finding my way back is all I really want."

If I don't fix this, my mind will never be free again.

After four weeks of working with Josh, Pamela felt Josh was ready to join group therapy. Marge scheduled him for a late session with Doctor Brown. When Josh entered the room, he saw that the chairs in a circle so that everyone was facing each other. He walked in, took a seat, and waited for the others to enter. One by one, they all entered the room and found a seat. Within minutes, Dr. Brown walked in with a notepad in one hand and a large soda in the other.

Dr. Brown was an older man in his early sixties with a great deal of experience in group therapy and dependency counseling. Hewrote many books on the subject and was sought after to give speeches and sessions all across the country. He came to this place because it was the place where he went through his journey back to a whole, sober life and he supported the work that was done there. He had dark black hair and a thick mustache 'that was turning gray. When people ask how he stays so young looking, he would quickly respond that it was due to clean living and lots of vitamins and minerals.

"I eat right and take care of my body. You only have one life, and I almost ruined mine once, so it won't happen again," he would say. He was very handsome and distinguished looking with a pleasant smile. He made people feel comfortable opening up and expressing their deepest fears.

"We will begin where we left off last week," he began. "But first, I see that we have two new people with us today.

Please introduce yourselves and tell us a little about your-selves." He looked over at the young man sitting to his left and nodded for him to go first.

"My name is Vernon, and I'm a drug addict. I live in Palmdale and I was a member of a gang. My mother was shot because I was messing around with some dude's stuff, and I knew then that I had to get out and get cleaned up. So I came here."

"Did your mother survive?" Dr. Brown asked.

"Yes, she survived the gun shot, but she didn't survive the cause of the wound. She's never been the same," Vernon said.

"And you, what is your name?" Dr. Brown asked as he looked at Josh.

"I'm Iria, and I have some issues I need to deal with, so I came here."

"Oh, you got some issues, all right. They're called drugs," Darcy, who sat next to Tricia and across from Josh, said. "You know, sweet gold, honey, the greatest joint in the world. You know what it is, so just say it." Darcy didn't ap-preciate Josh's disinterest and denial.

"I don't have to admit anything."

"Yes, you do. You need to face up to what you really are," she responded.

"Wait, wait a minute. Darcy, Iria will come to her own re-alization in her own time, not in yours. It"s not up to you when a person should face their enemy. You did yours in your time, and Iria will do hers in her time," Dr. Brown said.

"Jamal, why don't we start with you? Last week you were talking about your relationship with the drug dealer," Dr. Brown said.

"Yea, his name was Sky. That's a stupid name, now that I think about it." Jamal chuckled about it. "I don't know why they called him that, but that was his name. I met him through my friend Trent. I guess he really wasn't a friend since he got me into this life."

"No, Jamal, *you* got you into this life. You have to accept the decision you made that got you here, sitting across from me in this room at this time," Tricia said.

"Yeah, yeah, I guess you're right, but I thought Trent was my boy. It never dawned on me that he was into all this kind of stuff. I guess I was a little naïve about things."

Jamal leaned forward in his chair and looked down at the floor. He didn't want to face everyone. He didn't want them to think of him as a loser or an idiot. He began to squirm around in the chair, trying to get comfortable as he told his story. He took a deep breath and started talking in such a sorrowful and regretful tone that everyone felt his struggle and his message.

"I was only thirteen when I met Trent. My mama tried to tell me that Trent was no good, but I didn't listen. I was hanging out with the big boys and they treated me like I was somebody. Me, Trent, Durshuan, and Ricky used to hang out together. I was the youngest. I really had no business being with them, but I thought they were looking out for me. I thought they were my boys and that they protected me. I went to school, but I really didn't study. I didn't care. By the time I was sixteen, I was finished with school. My mama almost died when she found out I wasn't going to school anymore. She cried and cried. I remember, she kept saying, 'I've lost him, I've lost him.' At the time I didn't know what she meant, but I do now. I hurt her. I hurt her bad. I really regret what I put my mama through, and the worst part is that I let her die thinking I was a no-good nothing. I never had the chance to fix it and let her know that I could be stronger and really could make something out of myself, at least I hope so."

A tear rolled down Jamal's cheek as he turned his face away from the group. He didn't want them to see this side of him, the weak side, the side that got him in this mess in the first place.

"You are somebody, Jamal. You always were. You just let somebody else determine your value for you and you forgot. But that's all right, because we're here to help you remember who you really are and how strong you can be. You can be sure that your mama knows that you are here today trying to get it together," Tricia said.

"Yeah man, she's proud of you," Darcy interjected as she wiped a tear from her face. Her masculine demeanor made any feminine gesture seem awkward. Jamal pulled himself together and tried to continue.

"I remember the first time I tried reefer. Man, what a blast that was. I had just turned fourteen and Trent was treating me to a man's birthday. He called me little man. 'Man in training,' he would always say. That's kinda funny now. Nothing he ever did was manly. Sometimes I think he was the biggest coward of all, except for Sky. Sky was the biggest coward."

Josh listened and felt deep sorrow for Jamal, but he was stunned when Jamal named Sky as the biggest coward. He and Sky had a lot in common and Josh felt that Sky was just an innocent bystander in all of this. Just like him, it wasn't not Sky's fault.

"Why?" Josh asked.

"Why . . . why, because the murdering bastard supplied this filth and pawned it off as joy. He made me think I could handle it. 'Don't worry, man,' he would say, 'nothing's gonna happen to you. You can handle it.' The lying bastard. One time he said, 'You control the drug, never let the drug control you.' Now, how stupid is that?" Jamal said.

"If you knew it was stupid, why did you take it?" Josh asked.

"I was fourteen. He could have told me the sky was green and I would've believed him. I thought that they wouldn't let anything hurt me. I was a child, and I didn't have enough life experience to know what to expect or what could hurt me. But he knew. He was creating a life-long partnership of supply and demand. I had demands and he had the supply, until I couldn't hustle up enough money. Sky was ruthless. He preyed on young people because he knew we didn't know. He could tell us anything. First he would become our friend, and then he would become our mentor, and then our supplier. I hate him." Jamal was angry and his voice quivered with pain.

"What happened to Trent, Durshuan, and Ricky?" Tricia asked.

"Durshuan and Ricky are doing ten years for armed robbery, and Trent overdosed and died about three months ago."

"So I guess you're one of the lucky ones," Josh laughed.

Jamal looked at him with confusion and disbelief. "Lucky? Is that what you think this is, lucky?"

"You're alive, aren't you," Josh said.

"This isn't alive. I'm here on a probation program. I got caught for armed robbery and possession, but because I was just sixteen, they decided to rehabilitate me instead of incarceration. I guess they thought I could be saved." He laughed.

"What happened to Sky?" Tricia asked.

"Sky . . . he's still out there pushing his poison on innocent children, last I heard. I hope he gets what's coming to him someday."

"What's coming to him? What did he do? He didn't force you to do anything." Josh just couldn't understand why the pusher should take all the blame for the actions of these people. *They had the choice*, he kept thinking, and he couldn't understand why they didn't get it.

"It seems to me that by blaming somebody else, you take all of the responsibility for your actions away. It's his fault, not mine. It's a copout if you ask me," Josh said.

"If someone approached your twelve-year-old child and said, 'I have some great candy for you. Try it,' are you so sure that they wouldn't try it?" Dr. Brown asked.

Josh thought about it for a while and pondered the thought of a grown man approaching a child. He wondered if a child would be able to know the difference between right and wrong, and he had to admit to himself that he wasn't sure.

"I don't know."

"So you're not sure?" Janeen asked.

"I mean, at twelve-years-old they may not know what to do. I guess it depends on how he was raised."

"What if the streets raised you because you didn't know your father and your mother was a crack head?" Jamal asked.

"What if the streets was all you knew and you thought that this must be right because it's what everyone else was doing?" Darcy asked.

"A lot of these people were grown when they first tried it, what about them? Why couldn't they have made a different choice?" Josh asked.

"I'm one of them," Tricia said. Tricia's face saddened and her tone became soft and afraid as she remembered the first time she met Josh.

"Tricia, tell us your story again for the new people. I think it is important to hear how age may not always be a factor in the choices we make. We think that we make these choices because we are young and naïve, but not always.

Many times, the circumstances in our lives at any given time can dictate what choices we make. A long illness for instance can lead to a horrible substance abuse problem. Tricia's co-dependency in a love relationship led to her co-dependency on drugs. Her need to belong was strong enough that she allowed herself to become dependent on the relationship, as well as the drug, for her source of happiness.Of course, both relationships failed her. Numerous suicides have resulted from these kinds of traumatic experiences. Why she is co-dependent is what we are getting to the bottom of here." Dr. Brown as he looked at her. "Tricia."

"His name was Josh. He was the most beautiful man I had ever seen. When I met him and he acted like he liked me, I thought I had died and gone to heaven. He was tall and slim with beautiful blue eyes and golden blond hair. Every time I looked at him, my heart would melt. God, I loved him, or at least I thought I did. Really, I was in love with the idea of him. He wasn't a very nice person, so there wasn't much to love. He treated me horribly, but I couldn't see it. The few good moments made up for all the rest. He made me think I was special and that we could have a future together.

"I wanted him so much I would believe anything he said. I know it sounds stupid, and it was now that I look back on it. It was real stupid, but I wanted him, and when he gave me the drug and said 'let's have some fun,' all I could think about was being in the best place possible and making love to him at the same time. It was the best of both worlds until one of those worlds fell apart. When that special place became a nightmare, he turned into the demon from hell. He wanted nothing to do with me when I couldn't be the pretty little thing on his arm in front of his friends. I became a junkie, and he never let me forget it. I was weak. I admit that. But I was weak for *him*, not the drug, and my weakness for him got me to this point. I will never love anyone else again, not like that."

Josh was stunned. He had no idea she felt that way. He felt saddened, but it wasn't his fault that she fell in love. She should've had control over her emotions.

"What did you want him to do? What would have made it better?" Josh asked.

"He could have been honest about his feelings. He never loved me, but yet he said he did, and I believed him. He made me feel special and loved. He made me think I was important to him and I wanted to be so badly, so I fell right down the shaft, following that feeling. I wish he had not made love to me. I wish he had said, 'I'm sorry, but I cannot be with you because . . .' I wish he had told me how he really felt."

"What would you have done?" Josh asked.

"I would have been devastated. I would have left him and endured the pain, but I would not be here trying to get my life back. I fell out of love with him eventually and I would have anyway. I wish he had been honest instead of using me," Tricia said. "I admitted myself here after I pulled a gun on my mother. I was prepared to shoot her if she did not give me the money I needed to get the drug."

"Would you have shot her?" Vernon asked.

"Yes," Tricia said as she started to cry.

Without thinking, Josh stood and walked toward her. He took her hand and she stood to take his. He embraced her and tried to comfort her pain. To the group, it appeared to be one woman comforting another, but Josh was really trying to ease the pain he knew he caused. He realized the impact he had was far more damaging than he thought. After hearing what Angie said about him, he was beginning to wonder if he went too far in using his looks and charm to get women to do what he wanted, and what he had wanted were permanent customers. Josh held Tricia close and let her cry until she pulled herself together. He looked at her in the hopes that she'd see his regret, as he wiped the tears from her face.

"It'll be all right, Trish," he said.

"What . . . what did you say?" A familiar word. Trish was what Josh used to call her, and hearing it again produced a flood of emotions that overwhelmed her. She started to cry again. Josh realized his blunder and tried to recant his words.

"Tricia . . . I meant Tricia. You'll be all right." He quickly turned and walked back to his seat.

"So, Iria, you do not blame the dealer or the pusher at all. You do not see yourself as a victim of the system?" Dr. Brown asked.

"No . . . I never did, but now . . . well, maybe. I don't know anymore. I always thought that the choice was mine to make, and if you didn't like my choice then that was your problem."

"You don't think that you could be influenced or coerced into doing something that you really don't want to do?" he asked.

"No, I never did. I take full responsibility for my actions."

"Actually, that's a good thing, Iria. It means you are not displacing and you are facing up to your actions and taking full responsibility for what you do. I commend you for your ability to face up to things. Now that you are so confident of the source of the problem, it is fixable. You will not be in denial about your situation, which is a big step for most people. So, now that you know that you are the problem, what do you plan to do about it?" Dr. Brown asked.

"I'm going to get well," Josh responded.

"All by yourself?" Dr. Brown asked.

"Well . . . yes." Josh didn't understand their confusion.

"I know that you don't believe this, but you did not get in this mess by yourself, and you will not get out by yourself. If it's so easy, why are you here? There were many factors that led you here. Factors such as your parents, your peers, the school you attended, the neighborhood you grew up in, and any number of experiences, or maybe even one event that destroyed your self-esteem. The pusher influenced you, and even though you took the shot, he provided the gun. He has power over you now. Still, you do not want to see the role he played in your addiction. In your eyes, he still can't do any wrong. Iria, your whole life brought you to this point. The type of person who would allow herself to be influenced into using drugs already had a problem long before she took the drug. Taking the drug is a symptom of the problem. It"'s good that you are not displacing the blame, but it is not good that you do not accept some realities about the people in your life and how they affect you today and will tomorrow."

"I had an OK childhood. My parents were cool," Josh said.

"Really? So you think your parents would be OK with this lifestyle you have chosen? They accept pushers as just regular people?" Dr. Brown asked.

"No, of course not."

"Then, why do you?" he asked blatantly. "A child can have low self-esteem or feel unloved without being conscious of it. You may not realize the effect it has on you today. Your friends and relationships all affected you and determined who you are today and what choices you'll make today. These are the areas that must be addressed and fixed before you can be whole again. You have to find out why you are the type of person who would be associated with people who take the drugs and why you would allow yourself to fall prey to it. What is the source of your abusive behavior?"

"I'm not abusive," Josh said defensively.

"You abuse yourself. Why? What was going on in your life, Iria, during that moment of weakness when you allowed yourself to be used by someone?" Dr. Brown asked.

Josh didn't know what to say. He looked into Dr. Brown's eyes helplessly, looking for the answer. He turned toward Tricia and stared at her. He remembered Iria's love for him and how he made her feel loved and wanted. *She was special and I used her. How could I?* He looked down at the floor.

"I loved someone, too." He spoke softly as he looked back at Tricia's dark eyes. "Please forgive me," he said. Tricia looked at him in confusion, but believed that Iria was really speaking to herself.

"Iria, you need to forgive yourself," Tricia responded.

At the end of the session, Josh walked back to his room exhausted. He sat on his bed and pondered the words spoken today. His feelings were in a state of confusion, and he couldn't seem to get control of himself.

If I were myself, I would be dealing with this better. I would know what to do, what to think. I can't believe everyone thinks I was such an asshole. He couldn't face anyone, so he decided to go into the reading room and sit while everyone else had dinner.

"Where's Iria?" Marge asked as she approached Tricia in the dining room.

"She had a rough day. She's upstairs trying to deal with her first session. You know how it is. That first time is rough," she said.

"Yeah, I hope she survives this. She's so weak and frail."

"She thinks that she's up-front about it. You know, that old up-front shit. 'I take the blame for my actions. I did everything myself' crap. I think Dr. Brown gave her something to think about. It was a strange session," Tricia said.

"Oh, really? How?" Marge asked.

"I don't know. It's hard to explain. At times it seemed like she was speaking directly to me. Like we knew each other, but I know we've never met. It was strange." Tricia shrugged her shoulders, walked over to the kitchen, and picked up a tray.

Josh isolated himself in the reading room and sat with his head on the table, trying to reconcile what had happened today. *I'm not a drug addict, but I'm a pusher, and that makes me even worse. I didn't make anybody do anything; I just preyed on them. I fed them the piece of me that I hated the most. Oh God, what's wrong with me?*

When Josh walked into his room, Frankie was fast asleep. Tricia was still in the kitchen cleaning. Josh got undressed, put his pajamas on, and lay down on the bed. He was still awake when Tricia walked in and turned the light on.

"Girl, you better get some sleep. You have a busy day tomorrow," she said.

"I know," Josh said.

He watched as Tricia undressed down to her underwear. She stood in front of the mirror and brushed her dark brown curls. Her white skin was pale and worn from years of abuse, but she still had an inner beauty that could not be denied. Her small frame and long legs reminded Josh of the moments when they were intimate. He felt deep regret and wished there was a way to make it all right, to change what happened and give her back the life she had, but he knows he can't. He can't get his own life back, no less hers.

"Tricia, I'm so sorry."

"What are you sorry for? You didn't do anything," she said as she slipped out of her underwear and into her pajamas.

"I mean, for what happened to you. I wish I . . . I mean, I wish it hadn't happened to you like that," he said.

"It doesn't matter how it happens, it always ends up bad." She turned off the light and climbed into bed. "Get some sleep."

Several months passed, and Josh's rehabilitation was going well. Even though he was not a drug user, he was part of that world and now he realized the impact he had on all of the people in his life. For the first time in years, he could see himself doing something besides being a drug pusher. He saw himself with a career in counseling, maybe, or psychology. He talked to Dr. Brown about going to school and how to apply.

Josh was coming to terms with being Iria until he woke up sweating from an old nightmare. The dream that took him into the desert had begun to haunt him again. He saw his heart lying in the dirt again, and he couldn't get that image out of his mind.

Dr. Brown will try to interpret the dream, but he can't. Josh knew he would not be able to. The dream was a message to him, and he had to do what it told him to do. He knew he had to go to the desert. If he told them why he had to leave, they would not understand and would try to convince him to stay. It would not be easy to say goodbye.

After a few weeks of enduring the hellish nightmare, Josh decided to slip out during the night. He hung around waiting for Marge to leave her desk for a moment. She didn't lock the drawers until the end of the day, so Josh had easy access to her purse. He stole the key marked "back door, kitchen." Josh was hoping she wouldn't miss the key for a while. He waited in the reading room until midnight, then walked to his room to see Tricia and Frankie asleep. He picked up a bag he had prepared earlier from the floor, looked back at Tricia, and slipped out the door. He slowly made it downstairs without turning on any lights and moved himself through the kitchen to the back door. He unlocked the door, turned and put the key on the counter, opened it, and stepped outside. He turned the inside lock and shut the door behind him. Josh ran down the street and wondered if he was doing the right thing. He didn't know how he was going to get to the desert, but he knew that's where he had to go.

I need money, but there's no one I can turn to.

He walked out to the street to hitchhike a ride. Josh got his first lift to Santa Monica on the back of a truck. He stepped out on Wilshire Boulevard and tried to flag down another car. He didn't recognize the car that pulled up across the street. Josh kept walking and turning every now and then to try to flag down a driver. He couldn't tell who was behind him, but suddenly someone pulled his hair and forced their arm around his neck. Josh gasped for air and struggled to get free.

"Bitch, don't you know I will kill you?"

"Oh God . . . Diamond. Please let me go. I don't have anything, Diamond. I promise you I will get you your money as soon as I can. Please, Diamond, please," Josh begged.

"I don't care about what you can do. You were supposed to give me my money months ago. I should have killed your ass the last time I saw you, but I called myself giving you a chance, but no more. You will pay one way or the other," Diamond said.

"Diamond, I need to get to the desert for a few days, and after that I will have all your money and then some. I just need a little time. Please, I promise."

"The desert? I'll get you to the desert." Diamond dragged Josh to his car and forced him inside. Josh sat in the front seat as Diamond pulled off into traffic going toward the desert. "I can get you to the desert if that's where you want to go. Sure, I'll do that for you."

"Diamond, stop and let me out. Please, it's all right. I'll get there somehow. I don't want you to drive all the way up there. Please stop."

Diamond continued to drive the car out of the city and into the darkness of the night desert sky. Diamond drove for an hour. Josh sat in horror, not knowing what his plans were. He feared death. He knew that Diamond had killed before and would not hesitate to do it again. He felt that this could be his last night alive. As scared as he was, he wanted it to be over so badly that even death was a possible answer. His need to be free was stronger than his fear. Diamond found a deserted area and stopped the car.

"What are you going to do? Why did you stop?" Josh started to panic as fear gripped him.

Diamond walked around and opened the door. "Get out, bitch."

"Diamond, please, please don't do this."

"I told you that you were going to pay me one way or the other."

Josh stepped out of the car, and Diamond forced him off the road and back into some bushes. It was so dark, it was hard to see anything. The moon hung in the sky and provided glimpses of light as the clouds slumbered by. Diamond pushed Josh to the ground and started to remove his belt. Josh realized what was about to happen and screamed for his life. He made it to his feet and tried to run, but he didn't get far before Diamond grabbed his hair and pulled him to the ground. Josh started kicking and scratching Diamond everywhere, but it didn't seem to faze him. Diamond ripped the dress that Josh was wearing and tore the underpants off. He slapped Josh across the face over and over again.

"One way or the other," Diamond said.

Tears flooded Josh's eyes as Diamond forced his legs apart and penetrated his body. He had never felt anything so violating in his life. Diamond held Iria's small body down and forced himself into her over and over again. It seemed to last forever. Josh's stomach was sour, and his body ached from trying to fight back. He couldn't believe he was being raped. He gasped for air as Diamond thrust himself into Iria's small body harder and harder until it was over and he collapsed on top of Josh.

Josh turned his face into the dirt and cried. The humiliation was unlike anything he could imagine. He laid in the dirt as Diamond stood up, zipped up his pants, and walked away. He got into the car and drove off, leaving Josh lying on the ground, unable to move and wanting to die.

CHAPTER 9

Carlita

Carlita and David slipped out of the apartment during the nightwith no other choice. She knew she would never convince the landlord to let them stay. She decided to go home and stay with her mom until she could figure things out. She had enough money to catch the bus to east Los Angeles. She and David walked the two blocks to the bus stop and waited on the curb in the middle of the night. After a twenty-minute wait, the bus pulled up and stopped. Carlita grabbed the boy's hand, they stepped onto the bus, and took a seat in the back. She looked around and remembered that the seat she was in now was the same seat she was in when she stole the purse. An eerie feeling came over her as she remembered the moment that changed her life. She started to regret that choice, knowing now that the switch into Silvia's body must have had something to do with her stealing the money. Deep inside she understood why this happened to her, but she couldn't figure out how.

I screwed up. Somehow I've got to make it right in order for me to get back to my real self. So I have to do the right thing for the boy. I've got to look out for him to let God know that I repent and that I've changed. If I do the right thing, he'll fix it back. I know what's happening. I'm being punished for what I did. I will help the child and then it will be all right.

The bus stopped and they stepped off. She walked down the street and began to realize how difficult this was going to be. She stopped for a moment to think of how she was going to make her mother know who she was. *What can I do to convince her that I am her daughter?* She walked a little further and stopped again. *What if she doesn't believe me? What will I do?*

After walking a few blocks, Carlita saw her small house down the street. She walked toward the small cinderblock house with green shutters. The grass needed to be cut, and the few flowers had long since died from lack of water, and only the dark brown stems remained. Carlita opened the gate.

"David, wait right here. I need to speak with the lady alone. Can you do that for me?" she asked.

"Sure, Mama." He stood by the gate as she walked toward the door.

She hesitated to knock when the door swung open.

The rough voice came from the other side. "What do you want? I don't want to buy anything."

"I have nothing to sell," Carlita said.

"What do you want, then?" Juanita asked.

Carlita's mother, Juanita, was a handsome woman who was once beautiful. She had gained a few pounds, and her face was hardened with age and worry. She worries about her two sons who live on the streets to feed their drug habits, and her daughter who she hadn't heard from all day. Her black hair and dark features were striking, and she spoke with a heavy Mexican accent.

"What do you want?" she asked again. Her agitation

with the interruption was evident, and she wanted the lady to go away.

"This is going to be hard to believe, but I am Carlita," Carlita said with great trepidation. She stared into Juanita's eyes and waited for her reaction.

"I do not know you," Juanita said.

"Yes, you do. I know I do not look like me, but I am Carlita."

"Do you know where my Carlita is? Who are you? If you know where she is, please tell me."

"I am Carlita. You must believe me. Mama, I can prove it. I know things that no one else could know about you. I remember when you took me to the zoo for the first time and we went into the birdcage and I cried because all the birds flying around scared me. Do you remember, Mama? I remember the red, checkered dress you bought for me to wear the first day of school, and my graduation when I was almost late because I burned my gown and you had to mend it for me."

"How can you know these things? You have talked with Carlita? Please tell me where she is. Please, I beg you."

"I am Carlita, Mama. I am your daughter."

"What happened? How can you be Carlita and be this other person at the same time?" Juanita asked in such great confusion and frustration.

What has happened to my little girl? Who is this woman, and how does she know so much about our life?

Her feelings were all mixed up and confused. She didn't know what to think or what to do.

"Who is this?" Juanita asked as she looked at David.

"This is Silvia's son, David. I couldn't leave him after Silvia and I became one . . . or I became her . . . it's just that, she"s no longer there to care for him because now I'm her. I know this makes no sense. I can't explain it. I just know who I am." Carlita looked back at David and told him to come closer. "I couldn't leave him."

"No, I suppose not," Juanita said. "Please come inside and have a seat. Would you like something to eat or drink?" she asked as she walked into the kitchen.

Juanita was so confused and baffled. She was trying very hard to believe what this woman was telling her, but common sense told her it couldn't be true. People don't just switch like that. If this woman was Carlita, was Silvia walking around in Carlita's body thinking she was Silvia in the wrong body?

I can't believe this. This woman seems to know a lot about Carlita, but the story she tells is unbelievable.

Juanita was beginning to wonder if she should have even let the woman in.

What if she is a killer?

She walked back into the living room and found David sitting on the sofa. She handed him a glass of lemonade and looked around wondering where the woman was. David took the glass and said thank you. Juanita never looked at the boy and began to search the house for the woman. She walked down the hall and noticed the door to Carlita's room open. She stood at the door and watched this strange woman cuddle a large stuffed panda bear and a pair of ballet slippers.

"These are my things," Carlita said. "I remember . . . I remember when I wanted to be a ballerina. I never could get on my toes. I was terrible at it. My bear . . . this is my bear. Carlos won it for me at the carnival two years ago. Do you remember, Mama? Do you remember?"

Carlita wandered around the room remembering the good moments while Juanita stood in the doorway, fighting back tears as she wondered what had happened to her little girl. Carlita looked over at her and began to cry. She walked over to her and gently put her arms around her.

"Please understand, Mama. I don't know what's happening to me either. I just know that I know who I am. I'll figure it out, I promise. I promise, Mama." They held each other and cried.

"What's wrong?" David asked as he walked down the hall to see what all the commotion was about.

"It's all right, Davie, it's all right. I guess you can stay in the guest room," Carlita said as she looked at Juanita for her approval.

"Yes, yes, that will be fine," Juanita said.

Carlita walked David into the room across the hall. It was a small room with a twin bed. There was one window facing the street and a small dresser. The room was decorated in bright colors of red, yellow, and white. It looked like someone took a lot of care to completely remove any glimpse of decorating sense.

"Davie, you can stay in here." She began to pull the covers back on the bed and checked the windows to make sure they were locked.

David was looking at her strangely. He was beginning to wonder who this person was. She looked like his mother, but she was not acting much like her, and how did she know this other woman? His mother never spoke of her before. He was starting to feel very uncomfortable with staying there. He removed his clothes and found his pajamas from the suitcase he bought with him. He put them on and slipped into bed.

Carlita walked over to him and tucked him in. "Are you going to be all right?" she asked.

"Yes, I'll be OK," he said in a quivering voice.

She sensed his fear. "Don't worry, Davie. It will be fine."

"Why are you calling me that?"

"Calling you what?"

"Davie. You never called me that before. Why are you calling me that now?"

"Oh, I don't know. I kinda like it, don't you?" Carlita asked in as jovial a tone as she could.

"No," he said emphatically. "I don't like it."

David turned over and closed his eyes. He hated what happened, and he wanted to blame somebody. He knew it wasn't his mother's fault that someone stole her money, but he wished he could change it back the way it was. He was also afraid that once she walked out of that door, he would never see her again. He tried not to let his fear overtake him, but he couldn't hold back the tears as they started to flow down his face.

As Carlita walked out the room she looked back at him, knowing she was the reason for his sorrow, his fear. Sadness overtook her. She leaned against the wall and cried.

"What have I done?" Carlita walked into the living room to talk to Juanita. She sensed her nervousness and tried to put her at ease. "I know you don't understand this. I don't either, but I did something that makes me feel that God is punishing me."

Juanita looked at her and waited to hear what could be so terrible that God would do this. She was more afraid that this woman befriended Carlita, found out some things about her, and had done some terrible thing to her. Juanita wanted to disbelieve anything she said, but deep inside she couldn't help but feel that there was something genuine about this woman. She looked into her unrecognizable face.

"What did you do?" Juanita asked.

"I stole Silvia's rent money," she said.

"You did what?" Juanita asked.

"I was taking the bus to see Carlos, and this woman, this woman, Silvia, got on the bus and she was so tired she fell asleep. She didn't see me when I took her purse that was lying beside her. No one saw me. I slipped her small bag into mine and walked off the bus. I know she frantically looked all around for it, but I didn't care."

"No one saw you do this?"

"No, there were only two people on the bus by then, and they didn't see me take it, so I could have given it back, but I didn't. I just walked away. I could have dropped it and pretended that I found it on the floor, but I didn't. I just took it. I didn't know how much money was in the purse until I stepped outside, not that it would have mattered. I'd have taken it anyway. I didn't care."

"How much did you steal?"

"About eight hundred dollars."

"Oh no, oh my God, Carlita . . . why, why would you do such a thing? I taught you better than that. I know that I can't give you everything you want, but I never thought that you would steal from anyone. Why did you do this? I am ashamed of you. I do not like you. If you did this terrible thing, I see why God has turned against you. This is your punishment. You will repent, and you will pray for forgiveness and ask him to give you back your body," Juanita said.

Juanita's thick Mexican accent was punctuated with her anger. She talked very fast as her tone filled with anger and frustration. Carlita knew that she had shamed her mother and made her very unhappy. Juanita turned away from her. She was too ashamed to look at her.

"No, Mama, please. I know what I did was wrong. I don't even know why I did it, but please don't turn away from me. I need you now. I really do. If you turn away from me, I won't make it. I know I won't. Please, Mama." The tears flowed down Carlita's face as she begged her mother for forgiveness and understanding. She sat on the sofa and wept. Juanita walked over to her and stroked her hair.

"Don't worry, we will figure this out together. We'll go to church and try to make things right with God," Juanita said.

Juanita walked over to the fireplace and took the Bible from the mantel. It rested against the wall along with the crucifix and the rosary. Juanita was a religious woman, and considered herself a good Catholic. She tried to live a godly life and always hoped Carlita would too, which made her transgression even more intolerable.

"Carlita, I don't know how to fix this. I have to be honest, I'm not sure I even believe it, but I am willing to take you at your word and try to help. We'll talk to the priest and pray to God for his forgiveness. If God decides to change you back, we will be thankful, but if he decides never to change you back, and you stay this way, we will deal with that too. We will do whatever is necessary to fix it. Don't be afraid. Have faith. It will be all right."

Juanita caressed Carlita's face. Tears flowed down her cheeks as she tried to grasp the thought that her child could remain in the body of this other woman for the rest of her life. *Would she live the life of Carlita or Silvia? How can I bear losing my child to something like this? I just can't believe this is real. I just can't.*

"I'm going to bed now. Maybe I'll see things differently tomorrow. At least I hope so," Juanita said.

Juanita walked down the hall to her bedroom, went inside, and closed the door behind her. She walked over to the window, stared out at the streetlight, and watched the cars move up and down the street. She had a terrible headache and wished she could settle herself so she could sleep. She walked over to her vanity, sat in front of the mirror, and held her face in her hands and cried.

* * *

Carlita could hear David moving around in the hallway. She opened her eyes to the morning sunlight. She looked at her hands and felt her face, hoping that the new morning would have blessed her, but she found Silvia's hands and face were still with her. She got out of bed and found her robe hanging inside the closet. She looked at the clothes that belonged to her, but knew that in her present state, she could never wear them. She had Silvia's suitcase with her. She went through it and found a pair of jeans and a shirt.

Carlita walked into the hallway and saw David sitting in the living room watching television. She could smell the food from the kitchen, so she knew where Juanita was. She walked into the bathroom and stepped into the shower. The water felt good as she let it caress her body. She wondered what she was going to do today to find out what happened to her and how to fix it. She dried herself off and found her toothbrush still in the cup on the sink. After she cleaned up, she walked back to the bedroom and got dressed and made herself ready to face the day with a little optimism.

She walked into the living room and spoke to David. He was fixed on the television and barely saw her. She walked into the kitchen.

"Good morning, Mama."

"Did you sleep well?" Juanita asked.

"Yes."

"David, come get your breakfast," Juanita yelled from the kitchen. She placed a plate of food on the table and walked back to the stove.

David walked in and sat. He began to eat quickly as he listened to his mother tell this story about being trapped in another person's body. David, like Juanita, was becoming very suspicious about the situation. After Juanita heard the bus story, she was more convinced that something was wrong with Silvia and that this could not be her daughter. She didn't understand the connection between the two, but she knew that body switching was impossible. She needed to figure out where Carlita was and get this woman out of her house. Carlita didn't come home last night, so Juanita was becoming more and more worried and more and more suspicious of Silvia. She wanted to call the police, but not with Silvia in the room.

"I've run out of a few items. Do you think you and David could walk to the corner store for me?" she asked.

"Sure," Carlita said. "David, when you finish, put your shoes on and go to the store with me."

"OK," he said.

The police were notified of the body floating in the lake at eight o'clock. A man who routinely walked his dogs along the path of the lake noticed the body of a young girl floating at the lake's edge and phoned the police. A flood of people and police officers overtook the area quickly.

Two men pulled the body from the lake, placed her on a gurney, and began to examine the body. The photographers took pictures as the officers searched the area. Detective Hauser leaned over the girl and looked for some clue as to who she was and why she met such a dismal end at such a young age. This was the second case he had where a young person was killed with no apparent motive. He hoped this investigation would give him more leads than the Daniel Tanner case. Now he had two cases that would lay heavy on his mind.

"Sir, you may want to see this," Sergeant Hunter yelled from a few yards down the lake.

Detective Hauser made his way toward the grassy area covered with shrubbery and small trees. The sergeant pointed to a black purse lying in the leaves.

"Do you think this could be hers?" he asked.

"It's possible. There's only one real way to know for sure," Detective Hauser said.

"How?" Sergeant Hunter asked with great anticipation.

"Look inside," Detective Hauser said with a hint of sarcasm. He walked over to the purse and kneeled down. He put his plastic gloves on, picked the purse up, and carefully opened the flap. He found a picture identification card that matched the face of the dead girl. Detective Hauser stared at the picture and wondered how she came to this end.

Did she fall into the lake and couldn't swim? Was she killed and dumped into the lake, or was she deliberately drowned? How do you fall into the center of the lake? If she fell along the edge, she could have stood up. She had to be swimming alone and drowned or she was tossed in.

He looked around for any evidence that someone else was there with her. He searched the ground for car tire marks, shoe prints, broken tree limbs, anything that might show that she was carried to the lake. He walked around the area, looking and searching, but nothing jumped out at him.

"No one goes swimming fully dressed, so someone else must have been here."

"Nothing's obvious, but I'll find it. It's always here, the strand of hair, a broken fingernail, or a spot of blood. It's here; I just have to be patient and it will show itself. Patience, patience," he repeated to himself over and over again.

"Sir, do you see that child standing over there?" Sergeant Deberry asked.

"Yeah, where did he come from?" Detective Hauser asked as he stared directly at the child.

"I don't know. He was just there," Sergeant Deberry said.

Detective Hauser looked up at Sergeant Deberry and then he turned to look back at the child. He was gone.

"What? Where did he go?" he asked. Detective Hauser began to walk toward the location where the child was standing. "Did anyone see the child leave?"

"No, he just disappeared," Sergeant Deberry said as he looked all around, profoundly confused and unsettled.

"No one just disappears," Detective Hauser said.

"Sir, I don't know what happened. One second he was here, and then he was gone."

"Sergeant Hunter, did you see the boy that was standing here?" Detective Hauser asked.

"No, I didn't. I didn't see him," Sergeant Hunter said.

"OK then, I'm crazy, but that's all right. I knew I'd cross over the line someday," Detective Hauser joked.

"But I saw him too," Sergeant Deberry said.

Detective Hauser looked at him, smiled, and shook his head. "I don't know why, but that doesn't make me feel better."

Sergeant Deberry took a moment to think about that and suddenly realized that it wasn't a compliment. He shrugged his shoulders and walked around the area until he stumbled over a rock and inadvertently saw another purse.

"Sir, I found another lady's bag."

"Where?" Detective Hauser asked as he walked over to the area.

The detective kneeled down to pick up the bag when a shadow blocked out the sunlight. He looked up and the young boy stood in front of him. He was African American and about nine-years-old. He seemed surreal, as if he was there, but not there at the same time. The boy looked down at the purse and back into Detective Hauser's eyes.

"Who are you?" he asked.

"She's not my mother," the boy said as he looked back at the purse.

Detective Hauser looked down at the purse and back at the boy. "Who's not your mother? Where is your mother?"

"She's not my mother. She's not who she says she is," the boy repeated as he slipped behind a tree and out of sight.

"What the . . . did you see that, sir?" Sergeant Deberry exclaimed as he took a very cautious peek around the tree to find nothing. "This is getting a little too weird," he said as he looked at Detective Hauser, so confused and disturbed that he could hardly speak.

Detective Hauser stared back and forth from the purse to the tree, trying to figure out what he meant.

"I do not believe in the supernatural. You know, ghosts and demons and that sort of thing. But there's something going on here that's not in my handbook. I don't know what this all means, but somehow this purse and that death are related. The boy wanted us to find this purse. I've got to find out why." He opened the purse and found the driver's license for Silvia Watkins, age twenty-six. "Now what could a twenty-six-year-old black woman have in common with an eighteen-year-old Hispanic girl?" He stood up and put the purse inside a plastic bag, along with the other purse. "I guess the first thing to do is contact the victim's family and then pay a visit to Silvia.

Silvia and David walked around inside the store, picking up items and placing them in the cart.

"What kind of cereal do you like?" Carlita asked.

"You know what kind I like. You buy it for me all the time," he said. Carlita hesitated to respond. She couldn't let on that she was not Silvia to the boy. She thought for a moment and tried to clarify herself.

"Yes, I know. But I thought you would like to try something different."

"No, I wouldn't."

David waited to see what she would do. He suspected that something was wrong with her, but he couldn't figure out what. It was like his inner spirit was trying to tell him, but his mind wasn't able to process it. She looked the same, but she acted different. She talked different too, and she changed from the regular things they always did. He knew that because the money was stolen they had to live differently, but he still thought that she was very different and he couldn't understand why. He couldn't understand who Juanita was either. His mother never spoke of her, and now they were like best friends. David was a little scared, but he wasn't sure of what. He couldn't tell anyone because he couldn't explain it, not even to himself. He wanted to see what cereal she'd pick as she looked around at all the boxes on the shelf.

Carlita hoped for some reaction from David as she reached for the Frosted Flakes, but he did nothing. She pulled back and glanced down at him. She wondered why he was being so evasive about this.

Does he know that I'm not his mom? Why won't he tell me?

"I think we eat too much of the stuff anyway. Maybe we should try something different," she said.

David looked at her with great concern, walked toward his favorite cereal, and picked up a box. He looked squarely into Carlita's eyes and wondered who she was.

"David, I know things seem a little strange right now, but everything will be all right," she said as she realized that she just made a major blunder.

"Why are things so strange now, Mama?" he asked.

"Because I lost the money and now we have to live differently for a while, at least until I can get the money back and make things right with God."

"With God?" he asked curiously.

"Well, yeah, or . . . well, what I mean is with Mr. Bellatori, the landlord. I have to get him the money to make things right so we can go home.

"How long will that take?" he asked.

"Not long. I'm going to start working on it tomorrow. I'll take a second job if I have to. I'll do it . . . I promise, I'll do it,"

David looked at her, confused and scared. He didn't believe her. He turned away and walked down the aisle holding his box of cereal as if it were his best friend.

They walked home in complete silence. Carlita was was afraid that if she opened her mouth, whatever she said would make things worse. They turned the corner and looked down toward her house. The police cars parked in front of the house frightened her. She stopped and watched the events going on from the end of the street. She noticed Juanita standing on the porch crying. A female police officer tried to console her as she screamed in pain and despair.

"What is it, Mama?" David asked.

"I don't know, David, I don't know." She stared as she watched Juanita calm herself and began to talk to the policemen. She talked for a moment and then Carlita could see her point in the direction of the store. An uncontrollable fear came over her. She stepped behind a house and looked through the grocery bags. "David, we will take what we can carry and leave the rest."

"What, why . . . what's wrong?"

"Listen to me. We have to go and we will need some of this food, so get the stuff that we can carry and put it in this bag." David started to pull items from one bag to another until Carlita said OK. "Come on, we have to go."

"No," David said in defiance. She grabbed his arm and pulled him, and he pulled back. "I'm not going."

"You don't have a choice. You have to stay with me until I can figure out how to fix this mess I'm in. Now, come on." Carlita grabbed his arm and pulled him along with her to the nearest bus stop. A bus pulled up immediately and they stepped inside. She used some of the money she had left from grocery shopping to pay the two fares.

They sat on the bus without any idea where it was going. She was going to take it to the end of the line and worry about what to do then. David felt like his own mother had kidnapped him. He was very scared and wanted to ask for help, but couldn't.

"Where are we going?" he asked.

"I don't know," she answered as she tried to keep him from hearing the fear in her voice. She fought back tears as she wondered if she had the strength to handle this. *What am I going to do? God, I'm sorry. I'm so sorry. Please help me . . . please.*

"End of the line," the bus driver stated as he pulled to the curb and opened the door.

"Where are we?" she asked.

"San Pedro," the bus driver said.

Carlita grabbed David's hand and stepped off the bus. They stood on the curb and watched the bus drive off. She began to walk, hoping to find a place to stay for the night. As night started to overtake them, Carlita began to worry. She noticed an abandoned car in an alley and decided to sleep inside the car for the night. David saw what she was planning and began to cry.

"No Mama, please, Mama, no," he cried.

"I know, baby, I know, but it's just for tonight. I'll find someplace else, I promise. It's just for tonight."

She opened the door to the old car and they both climbed

into the backseat. She laid him down and tried to make him feel safe and comfortable. She stroked his brow until he fell asleep. She tried to make herself comfortable, but couldn't. She was afraid to close her eyes, and forced herself to stay awake for as long as she could, but eventually sleep overtook her, and she drifted into a deep sleep while praying that God kept them safe through the night.

While Carlita slept, David sat up and watched his mother sleep. He wondered how they got to this place. He didn't understand any of it, but deep inside, his gut feeling was telling him that this woman wasn't his mother, or at least not the mother she used to be. He stared at the door handle and considered getting out and running, but to where? If he went to the police what would he tell them? He couldn't' have his mother put in jail. He had already missed two days of school and he wondered if anyone from the school was looking for him.

Maybe they will find me. Someone is looking for me. I can feel it. Someone is out there trying to figure out what happened to me and they are looking for my mother, too. They will find me. I know they will.

He laid his head back, stared out the window, and waited.

As Detective Hauser drove to Silvia's apartment building, he tried to forget the look on Juanita's face when he asked her to go to the morgue to identify the body of her daughter. The look of fear and despair in her eyes was so disturbing. The shock was so great she couldn't accept it. She was too frightened to cry. If she cried she would be acknowledging the reality of it. She couldn't accept it.

"It's not my daughter," she said. "My daughter isn't there. No, I won't accept this. I don't have to go anywhere."

Detective Hauser told loved ones about losses all the

time, but this one was different, as though something from deep inside him was telling him that it wasn't true. Even though 'there was a body, somehow he knew it was not true. The feeling was so overwhelming, that he started to question what he really saw. He arrived at the apartment building and walked inside to talk to the landlord. He knocked on the door and waited for the door to open to a rough looking Italian man who appeared to be quite annoyed by the interruption.

"What do you want?" he asked.

"My name is Detective . . ."

"I don't care what your name is. What do you want?" he bellowed out.

Detective Hauser opened his badge so that the man could see who he was, what his name was, and to let the man know that his assistance would be given, whether he liked it or not. He waited for the man to make up his mind to cooperate, and he watched him squirm around, trying to cover his humiliation.

"Yeah, yeah, what can I do for you?" he asked in a more humble tone.

"Do you have a tenant living here named Silvia Watkins?"

"Yeah, yeah. Well, I did."

"You did? What do you mean?"

"She left."

"Why?"

"She couldn't pay her rent, so I told her she had to go."

"Do you know where she went?"

"No, she didn't leave me nothing. No information at all."

"Which apartment was hers?"

"The one at the top of the stairs." The landlord pointed to the landing at the top of the stairs and turned back toward Detective Hauser. "What she do?" he asked.

"Nothing. I just need to find her, that's all." Detective Hauser looked upstairs. "Are her belongings still inside?" he asked.

"Yeah, I ain't had time to move nothing out yet."

"I need to look around," Detective Hauser said. He waited for the man to acknowledge him, and then looked back at him with a quizzical smile. "Is that all right?"

"I don't know. Do you have a search warrant?"

"No, I don't, but if I have to, I'll get one."

"No . . . No, It'll be all right. Let me get the key," Mr. Bellatori said as he walked back inside and picked up his key ring from the coffee table. He searched through the handful of keys to locate the master key for the apartment doors. "This is it," he said as he started to walk upstairs. He turned the key in the lock and opened the door. He stepped inside and waited for Detective Hauser to follow. "I didn't move anything. It's just like it was when they left."

"They . . . what do you mean they?" Detective Hauser asked.

"She lived here with her son."

"Her son? How old is he?"

"Around eight or nine, I think."

"Eight or nine," he said as he began to look around the room. *It's an average home for an upper lower class income. No real surprises.*

Detective Hauser walked over to a corner cabinet and noticed a picture of a familiar face. He picked up the photograph of a young boy and immediately recognized it as the boy by the lake. He stared at the photograph and wondered how this child got there and where he was now.

"Is this her son?" the detective asked.

"Yes, that's him . . . David, that's him," the landlord said.

"This is strange. Why would this kid be trying to contact

me? She's not my mother," he whispered. "Not my mother."

"What did you say?"

"Nothing, nothing," Detective Hauser said as he slipped the photograph into his coat pocket and walked down the hall toward the bedrooms.

The detective opened the door to David's room to find a typical kid's room. There were posters of his favorite super-heroes and cartoon characters. A basketball and tennis racket lay on the floor, and an unmade bed gave the room the perfect little boy look. The room was in disarray as if they left in a hurry. Things were thrown about as if the boy had to choose between what to leave and what to take. Toys and clothes covered the bed and the closet floor. He looked all around and found nothing really suspicious. He closed the door and walked across the hall to Silvia's room. It looked the same, in disarray. He moved his way through clothes thrown about and found a piece of paper with a number to the local police department written on it. He took out his cell phone and dialed the number to the police station.

"Ninth precinct, can I help you?" the receptionist asked.

"This is Detective Hauser from the Forty-third, and I'm investigating a murder case. I need to know if a phone call was made to your station on August fifth from 213-286-5555. Can you help me?"

"Please hold." She put the phone down and locates Sergeant Wilcox to take the call.

"This is Sergeant Wilcox. Can I help you?"

"Yes, I am Detective Hauser and I am investigating the murder of the young Mexican girl found near Echo Park Lake. I found a phone number to your police station, and I want to know if a call was made to your station on the night of August fifth from this phone number."

"What is the number?" the Sergeant asked.

"213-286-5555," Detective Hauser said again, as he became more and more agitated that he had to make his request twice.

"Please hold." Sergeant Wilcox immediately located Lieutenant Dryer and informed him of the request. Lieutenant Dryer walked over and picked up the phone.

"This is Lieutenant Dryer. May I help you?"

"Yes, someone can answer my question, and I am not going to ask it again," Detective Hauser said in a disturbed tone.

"Sir, I can't help you if I don't know what the problem is."

"Ask anyone else there. They know. I've asked it twice, so someone there knows."

"Please hold," Lieutenant Dryer said. Detective Hauser waited for a moment before Lieutenant Dryer came back on line. "Sorry, sir. We needed to verify that you were with the Forty-third. We will get that information momentarily. Please hold."

"Sure, sure I'll hold."

"Detective Hauser, a call was made to this station on August fifth to report a stolen purse. The caller, a Silvia Watkins, claimed to have lost eight hundred dollars. That's all it says except for the particulars. Is that all you need?" the receptionist asked.

"Yes, thank you."

Silvia's missing purse was in the same vicinity as the dead body. *I wonder if Carlita stole the purse and Silvia found her and killed her.* He pondered the thought and walked back into the living room. He still couldn't understand the appearance of Silvia's son at the crime scene. He took a picture of Silvia from the shelf and asked the landlord if he could have it.

"Sure, I don't care. I'll be dumping all this stuff anyway," the landlord said. *She couldn't pay her rent because Carlita stole her purse and she was thrown out. That's a motive, a weak one, but a motive. People have killed for less than that.* Detective Hauser put her photograph in his pocket and turned toward Mr. Bellatori.

"Please do not remove anything from this apartment until our investigation is over."

"Investigation of what?"

"Murder," Detective Hauser said as he turned and walked out.

Detective Hauser went back to the police station and took the difficult walk upstairs. He remembered when he could run the stairs with energy to spare, and now he wondered if he'd make it to the landing without having a heart attack.

Retirement seemed so close. I don't know what happened, but I just can't seem to break free. I've got to figure out what happened here. I've got to find the kid. Something tells me that he's in trouble.

He walked through the crowd of police officers and all of the criminals and derelicts who could be found that day to his office. He threw his coat over the chair, walked around to his desk, and stared at the photographs of Daniel Tanner spread out across the desk. He added Carlita's pictures to the pile.

"I don't understand any of this. This boy gets shot down for no reason at all, and this girl is dead because she stole a purse. I may never find out who killed Daniel. It could have been a jealous girlfriend or a gang banger. I don't know. I've never seen a case without any clues like Daniel's, and now there's Carlita. I have to find Silvia to help explain what happened to this young lady."

Detective Hauser picked up Carlita's picture, stared at it,

and remembered her mother's denial. He left his office, walked across the floor to Josie's desk, and stood behind her, watching her type away at her computer. She had papers stacked everywhere and he wondered how she knew where anything was, but somehow she did.

"What do you want?" she asked without looking away from the computer monitor.

"I'll let you finish your thought," he said politely.

"No, no, I'm OK. You know, us women can do two things at once."

"What are you trying to say, men can't do more than one thing at time?" Night asked.

Night sat next to Josie and gave her hell whenever he could. His real name was Leroy, and he was a junior officer who was eager to prove himself to the team. He was so dark, they simply called him Night.

"Two things? We're lucky if we can get you to do one thing," she replied.

"What! As much as I do around here," he said.

"I've seen what you do around here and it is a whole lot of nothing," she said

"I know I'm great. "

"I don't know. We've seen you in target practice and we all wonder how many people you really see, cause you be all over the place. Shooting at imaginary people."

"That's right, and for them, I use my imaginary gun with imaginary bullets that kill imaginary people," Night said.

"You know you don't have but one bullet that the Lieutenant makes you keep in your pocket, like Barney," she said

He patted his pocket, as if he thought a bullet might be there. "Show me some action, and I'll show you some real shooting."

"If you got some real action, you'd accidentally shoot

yourself." She chuckled and shook her head. "He's a character," she said. The chatter ceased when Captain Tracell walked through the room.

"What do you want, Pat?" she asked again.

"I need to find a person," he said.

"What's the info?"

"Her name is Silvia Watkins, and I think she's connected to the death of Carlita Espinoza. She no longer lives at her last known address, and I have no leads on where she could be now." He showed Josie the photograph he took from Silvia's apartment. "She may be with this boy." He showed her David's photograph. "He's her son."

Josie looked at the photos and started to search the database for addresses, family members, jobs, police records, hospitals, and jails to see if her name came up anywhere. She found her last known job, but found she was terminated because no one had heard from her in a few days. Josie gave Detective Hauser the names of a few friends and the name of her sister, Carolyn, who lived in Nevada.

"This is all I could find for now. I'll keep searching and see if something comes up. She doesn't have much of a history, at least for someone who could be involved in a crime like this. She has no priors at all, not even a speeding ticket," Josie said as she handed him the information.

"She's connected to Carlita somehow," he said.

"She left her work and never went back. That doesn't sound like something a woman with a child would do," Josie said.

"She would if she killed someone. She and the child are running. I think I'll check with her sister first. That's where I would go—out of state and hopefully out of mind. I'll drive to Vegas in the morning," he said.

"Good luck," she said as she walked out of his office and

closed the door. Detective Hauser sat at his desk and stared out the window wondering where Silvia could be.

Carlita ran for the door in terror as she stared at her head lying on the floor. She couldn't open the door. Her hands were missing so she couldn't turn the knob. She looked back at her decapitated head and looked into those haunting eyes staring back at her, and she screamed in terror and fright. Her body began to shiver and sweat poured from her face as she kicked the door over and over again, hoping it would succumb to her force, but it didn't. It was' too strong, and she fell to the floor, drug herself to a corner, and looked back at herself.

She screamed so loudly she woke herself. She was shaking from the dream and tried to gather herself. David looked at her and watched her try to calm down.

"Are you all right?" he asked.

"Yes, yes, I'm fine. I had a dream that's all. Just a dream." She looked at him and took a deep breath. She sat still for a few minutes and composed herself.

"Did you dream that you were sleeping in an old abandoned car like homeless people?"

She looked at him in shame.

"We'll be all right, Davie. It'll be all right." Carlita opened the car door and stepped outside. She reached back inside, pulled out the bag of food, and started looking through it to see what they could eat. "Here, eat this," she said as she handed David a muffin and an apple. David hesitantly took the food and began to eat it. She found another muffin for herself and also began to eat.

Carlita walked to the corner, stared out over the street, and tried to figure out what to do now. She knew the amount of food they had was only going to last about two days. 'She was scared. David walked up behind her and acknowledged her fear.

"You don't know what to do, do you? I can see it in your eyes. We're in trouble, and it's not going to be all right. Maybe we should go to Aunt Carolyn's house."

"Carolyn . . . Aunt Carolyn, who is . . . I mean, where does she live?"

"Mama, you don't know where your own sister lives?"

"Well, yeah . . . of course I do. I just wondered if you remembered."

"What is going on?" he asked. "I don't know who you are, but you're not my mother. I want to know who you are. I'm not going anywhere with you until I know." "David, you're right. There is something going on, and I want to explain it to you, but I just don't think you'll understand, and it will only make things worse. I'm afraid. That's true. I don't know what's going to happen to us. I'm acting strange, I know, but you have to trust me. I promise you I won't do you any harm. Your mother loves you, and I promise you will be with her again, but for now you have to trust me until I can figure out what to do." "Who are you?" David yelled as he pulled back from her.

Carlita's tears blurred her vision as she tried to calm David. "Please, please, try to understand."

"Understand what?" he exclaimed.

She pulled him toward her and tried to calm him. She knew he wouldn't understand, but she had came to realize that if she lied or tried to mislead him, he would know and that would only make things worse.

"You're right, I'm not your mother, but I am her at the same time. I know this doesn't make sense, David, but I'll try to explain. My name is Carlita Espinoza, and I am the person who stole the money from your mother. I believe that God is punishing me for doing that and forced me to become Silvia."

"Why would God do that?"

"I don't know, I only know that I am Carlita, but I look like your mom. I think I'm supposed to take care of you no matter what, so I can't let you go. I have to watch over you and make sure you're safe, and then God will be pleased and give me my body back."

"So you caused this when you stole my mother's money? You put us in this mess and made me lose my mama? I hate you, I hate you, and I won't help you," David yelled and cried as he ran away from her. He ran with all his strength, but she caught him, held him, and tried to calm him.

"I won't leave you, David. I won't give up. I'll fix this, I promise. Please forgive me. I beg you to please forgive me."

She held him and they cried in deep despair and grief. Neither of them knew what lay ahead for them, but they couldn't give up on each other. They had nowhere else to go.

"Let's go find Aunt Carolyn. She'll know what to do," David said.

"OK, OK," Carlita said as she stroked David's hair and hugged him. She held his hand as they walked back to the car to get the food and started the long journey to Nevada, hoping to find Aunt Carolyn. "David, will you know how to get to her house once we get to Vegas?"

"I'm not sure, but we can try," he said

"What is her last name?" Carlita asked

"Jones," he said

"We'll check a phone book once we get there and try to find her."

"We went there a lot; I'll try to remember as much as I can," he said.

"Great . . . we'll find her somehow," she said as she took his hand and started walking.

They walked for hours. She had a little money left, but she was trying to hold onto it for food. They walked all day.

By nightfall, she started looking around for a place to stay. She noticed an abandoned building. They walked in through a side door. The inside was filthy and the room smelled of urine. There were empty beer and wine bottles thrown about and garbage piled in the corners. The floor was so dirty, she was afraid to lie on it. She found an old mattress that was just as filthy as the floor, but she decided it was her best option. She took her jacket off, laid it on the mattress, and told David to lay there. He crawled up into her jacket and she covered him as best she could. She looked around for something for herself and found an old chair. She pulled the chair close to David, sat down, and tried to relax. She couldn't really rest, not knowing what was going to happen from one moment to the next.

Carlita lingered somewhere between sleep and wakefulness, knowing the circumstances surrounding her were horrible and unthinkable. She started to drift off into a deep sleep when she felt something touching her. She kicked it away and thought that she was dreaming, but the feeling came right back. She opened her eyes slowly and screamed at the horror of mice nipping at her feet and legs and cowering all around David's body. She jumped to her feet and grabbed him from the mattress. She shook her jacket and threw the lingering mice to the floor. She picked David up and ran to the door. When she looked back, the mice were crawling over each other to get to the bag of food she left behind. After walking for a few blocks, Carlita found an alley that looked safe and somewhat clean. She found an open, clean space, laid her jacket on the ground, and told David to lie there. She sat next to him, leaned against the wall, and tried to sleep.

All the food was gone. She pulled the few dollars she had left from her pocket and counted it. *Not much.* She decided to let David sleep a little longer while she walked around to see what she could find in the alley that may be useful to them. She found a knife and yesterday's newspaper. As she began to read the paper she saw a story about a young girl who was found dead near Echo Park Lake and her name was Carlita Espinoza. Carlita angrily crumpled the paper in her hands.

"What do you want? Is this me? Oh God, is this me? What do you want from me? I'm sorry, God, I'm so sorry." She fell to the ground clutching the crumpled paper wondering what to do now that her body may be gone.

How can I get back into my body if it is gone? What am I working so hard to please you for if my body is gone and you know I will never get it back? So now what? What happens to Silvia? Does she get her body back? This is crazy. I've got to find out if this is me. Maybe there is another Carlita Espinoza somewhere. God, please don't let this be me. Where would the body be . . . the morgue? I'll go to the morgue and pray this person is somebody else. The look of fear in her eyes frightened David.

"What's wrong?" he asked

"We have to go back." "Why?"

"There's something I have to do. I need to find out something," she said.

"What?" he asked with great confusion

"Please trust me. I won't let anything happen to you."

He hesitantly took her hand and they stated walking back toward Juanita's house.

She and David hitchhiked back to her neighborhood in East Los Angeles and located the local hospital and the morgue where the body had been transferred. She walked inside and told the attendant she wanted to see the body of Carlita Espinoza.

"Are you here to identify the body?" he asked.

"Yes, yes . . . to identify the body."

"Please come this way. We have been waiting for someone to identify the body before we proceed with the autopsy." He walked into a room full of refrigerated tombs.

"David, could you please wait outside?" she asked.

David didn't have a problem with that. He didn't really want to be there at all. He immediately turned, walked out the room, and took a seat in the hallway. As the attendant pulled open the drawer, Carlita's heart sank. She knew it was her body. The first thing she saw on the exposed arm was a bracelet she bought with the money she stole from Silvia. She started to cry. He pulled the sheet back and her face stared back at her. Her knees buckled and she grabbed the table to brace herself. She thought about her dream where her decapitated head stared back at her and she lost control. She began to scream and scream as she backed out of the room and fell into the hallway. David ran to her and tried to help. The attendant helped her to a seat and got her a glass of water.

"What's wrong?" David cried.

"It's me, it's me. I can't believe it. It's really me." She couldn't control her tears. The fear of never being Carlita again meant she had to accept her fate to remain Silvia forever. "I'm dead, dead. Oh God, I'm dead."

The attendant waited for her to calm down as he tried to understand what she meant by "I'm dead."

"Do you recognize the body?" he asked.

"Yes, it's me," she said.

"I don't understand," the attendant said.

"It's Carlita Espinoza. It's me."

"You recognize the woman to be Carlita Espinoza?"

"Yes."

The attendant walked over, picked up a form, and asked Carlita to sign the form indicating that she recognized the deceased as Carlita Espinoza. When she signed the form Carlita Espinoza, the attendant took exception to it.

"Miss, I don't want you to sign the decease's name. I need for you to sign your name."

"That is my name."

"No, it is the name of the deceased. Who are you?" he asked.

"I'm Carlita Espinoza pretending to be Silvia Watkins."

The attendant remembered Detective Hauser mentioning a woman named Silvia when he was there looking at the body. He wondered if this could be the person they were looking for. There was definitely something strange about her. She didn't seem to know who she was and she had this boy with her who looked rather destitute.

"Wait here," he said as he walked to the front office and phoned Detective Hauser. He told him that a woman was here and that she may be the woman he was looking for. He described the woman and said she came there to identify Carlita's body. Detective Hauser told him to keep her there and that he was on his way. The attendant walked back into the hallway and found Carlita and David gone. He ran to the door and tried to see what direction they took, but they were out of sight. He ran back inside and called Detective Hauser to tell him that she left the building.

Detective Hauser arrived at the morgue within fifteen minutes of the phone call and talked to the attendant about Carlita's visit. He told them exactly what happened and how strangely she behaved. He showed him the form where she signed Carlita's name as her own and kept referring to herself as Carlita.

"I am dead. That's what she kept saying," the attendant said.

A team of officers stayed at the hospital to collect any evidence they could find about Silvia while Detective Hauser drove around the area hoping to see her walking. He wondered what she meant by "I am dead."

Why would she refer to herself as Carlita? OK, let's assume she thinks she is Carlita and she's just discovered that she is dead. What would she do next? If she thinks she's Carlita she would want her mother to know that she isn't dead. She would go home. She would want her mother to recognize her and reassure her that she is OK. She's at Juanita's house.

He turned the car around and headed for Juanita's house. He turned the corner just in time to see Silvia and David walk inside Juanita's house.

"Mama, it's not me. I swear to you, it's not me. I am not dead. I can't believe this is happening to me. I know this is crazy, but I am me and I can't get anybody to believe me."

"I don't know who you are. I don't know what to think. Who are you? My child is dead and you stand here with this outrageous story about bodies switching and changing and all sorts of nonsense. Get out," she said firmly.

"Mama, please, I beg you to believe me." Tears formed in Carlita's eyes as she tried her best to make Juanita understand. She fell against the wall. She could barely stand from the weight of all of this.

Juanita saw something in this woman that reminded her of Carlita. For a brief moment she could feel Carlita, her baby, her child. She could sense that Carlita was in there somewhere and that she was hurting and afraid. She couldn't give her up. She couldn't let her child be harmed. She knew it was crazy, but she had to take the chance just in case there was some truth to what this woman was saying.

"The police have been here, and they will be back. I don't know who you are. If you are Carlita, I wouldn't want you to get into trouble, so I'll help you get out of here, but once you're out of my house you are on your own. Please don't come back here until you are you again. I can't take this. It's too hard. I can't take this anymore," she cried and walked them through her bedroom to the window at the back of the house. "Please leave now," Juanita said as she opened the window and helped them climb out.

The doorbell rang just as Carlita and David climbed out the back window. Juanita closed the window behind them and walked to the door. She gathered herself and opened the door.

"Detective, may I help you?" she asked.

"Is Silvia Watkins here?" Detective Hauser asked.

"No."

"Please, Ms. Espinoza, I know they are here. I saw them walk inside your house."

"She is not here."

"Ms. Espinoza, please allow me to enter the premises." She opened the door and allowed him inside. He immediately started to search each room and found no one. "Why would you help them? This woman could have murdered your daughter."

"I didn't help anyone, and I'm not sure that she's not my daughter," she said.

What a strange statement, Detective Hauser thought. He didn't know what to say to that.

"Ms. Espinoza, your daughter is dead. You may not want to accept it, but it is true, and our prime suspect is that woman. I don't understand your hesitation to help us. How could you think that this woman is your daughter?"

"Something strange has happened to Carlita and she's in that woman's body."

"What, what kind of talk is that?"

"I know it sounds strange, but it's true. She is my daughter," Juanita said it as if she really believed it. "We will find her, and when we do, we'll get to the bottom of this. Please, if she comes back here, please contact me."

Detective Hauser walked out the door and back to his car. He knew that Silvia was in the neighborhood somewhere and it was just a matter of waiting for her to surface. He rode around and waited.

Carlita and David moved through one backyard after the other until they reached a cross street. She looked around and saw no one. She saw the bus coming a block away. She waited behind a house until it reached the bus stop across the street and she and David ran toward it just as the driver pulled the bus from the curb. The bus driver saw her and slowed the bus, giving them enough time to catch up and board. She found a seat near the rear and looked out the back window to see Detective Hauser driving by. She watched him until he was out of sight. She relaxed for a moment on the long bus ride toward San Fernando. As nightfall approached, Carlita wondered where they would sleep. As they stepped off the bus, she began looking around for an old building or an abandoned house.

"I'm hungry. Do we have enough money to get something to eat?" David asked as he held his stomach, trying to hold back the cramping hunger pains. Carlita checked her pockets and found a few dollars and some coins. She knew it would never be enough for a bus ticket to Vegas, so she decided to get him something to eat. They walked for a few blocks and she saw a McDonald's a block away.

"Come on, we'll see what we can get from McDonald's with the money we have," she said.

They walked the block and finally got a chance to use the bathroom and sit down. She walked to the counter and began to count the money she had to figure out what she could buy. She got the food and they finally ate. They finished eating and sat and watched the sun go down. They both felt better, but now she had to find a place to sleep. "Come on," she said.

David tried to be brave, but again he was afraid of what

or where they might end up tonight. They walked for a while and she noticed a department store with an out of business sign hanging across the entrance. If she could fig-ure out how to get inside, they might be safe there tonight. She walked around the building until she found a slightly open window and forced it open wide enough for her and David to climb inside.

"It's clean," she said as she smiled in relief.

David was so exhausted he didn't care. They found some old blankets used by the movers and made themselves a comfortable place to sleep. David slept soundly for a while until he felt a chill race across his body. He began to feel a presence in the room. He wondered if he was dreaming and turned over to continue his peaceful sleep. The feelings became stronger and stronger until he was forced to open his eyes. He saw her; the angel who came to him before was hovering over him in a glowing light.

She gently caressed his cheeks and smiled. She was glowing in a beautiful blue and white light. Her white and silver gown moved as if a soft breeze blew through the room. Her face was serene and pure, and she brought him comfort and peace. He was not afraid because he knew she would not harm him. He still thought this could be a dream, but it was so real. The smell of lilacs and roses and her touch on his face were so real. He smiled back at her, knowing that the moment would end soon just like before and the beautiful angel would be gone. He reached out to touch her and she pulled back.

"Not yet," the angel said. "Everything will be all right,. Don't be afraid any longer." She kissed her fingers, pressed them upon his forehead, and disappeared into the ceiling and up into the night sky.

David looked over at Carlita to see if she was awake. *Maybe she saw her too*, he thought, but Carlita was sleeping soundly. He decided not to disturb her and turned over to continue sleeping, knowing that the beautiful angel was watching over him.

The morning light came through the window and forced Carlita to wake up. She gathered herself, but let David sleep a while longer. She felt safe inside the store and decided not to rush him. She needed time to think about what would happen next.

How do we get to Nevada with one dollar and thirty-five cents? I won't try. I'll get him something to eat today and worry about that later.

David slept another hour and awoke feeling rested and unafraid for the first time in days. He looked over at Carlita.

"I believe you," he said.

"What?" She looked at him.

"I believe that you are Carlita and that somehow you have to make up for what you did. I don't know why you are in my mother's body, but I think you have to use it to get something done so God can be happy again."

"Thank you, David." She walked over to him and they hugged each other. She was so happy he wouldn't be afraid of her any longer. Now that she has his trust, they could really work together to fix this.

"Do you know what you have to do?" he asked.

"No, David, I don't. And that's why this is so difficult. If I knew, I would just do it and we could all go home, but I don't know. I just don't know," she said solemnly.

"We'll find out how. The angel told me."

"What angel?"

"The angel who came to me last night. She said that everything was going to be all right and I would not have to be afraid anymore."

"She said that?" Carlita asked as she looked at David with a little skepticism. "Are you sure it wasn't a dream?"

"No, she was real. She kissed me. It was real."

"OK, I believe you, too," she said and smiled. "Well, let's go see how we can get to Nevada. It's going to be a long day, and we don't have much money, so we will eat half way through the day, OK?" she said as she looked down at him and smiled.

"OK," he said as he took her hand. They walked back to the open window and climbed out.

Carlita and David began a long walk along the highway, hoping that someone would stop and give them a ride. After about an hour, someone did stop, but it wasn't whom she wanted to see. As the police car pulled over and stopped, Carlita began to panic. She couldn't allow them to catch her. She would never be able to explain this. They wouldn't understand. She couldn't go to jail. Who would take care of David? If she lost David, God would never forgive her and she would be in Silvia's body for the rest of her life or worse, her soul could spend eternity in hell. That was her mother's greatest fear for her, and, somehow, Carlita knew she was fighting to shield herself from that awful fate. She started to walk very fast. David could sense her fear and he became very nervous and frightened.

I don't want to go to jail. He started thinking that they would handcuff him and put him in jail for the rest of his life. He became so nervous and scared that without thinking he let go of Carlita's hand and began to run.

"Miss, please stop," one of the policemen yelled. The two men tried to catch up with her, but now she was trying to catch David.

"David . . . no, David stop!" she yelled.

David couldn't hear her. He never looked back. He ran aimlessly and was unaware that he had crossed over into oncoming traffic. He never noticed the car that was traveling at sixty miles an hourand the car that tried to avoid hitting him, but couldn't. He realized his fate when he heard the brakes squealing and squeaking. He couldn't move, and the car couldn't stop. He looked back at Carlita, knowing that this would be the last time he would ever see his mother's face. He saw the beautiful angel and reached for her, and this time she reached toward him. Their hands touched slightly just as the car plowed into his small body, throwing him five feet into the air. He landed against the median wall. Carlita's scream was heartbreaking.

"NO, no, no. Please God, no! Please don't let him die."

She ran toward his broken body and reached down to hold him. The policeman called the ambulance and finally reached the boy's body. One of the policemen ran back to get the car, drove it closer to the body, and blocked the lane to oncoming traffic. The other policeman laid David down and placed his jacket under his head. He checked to see if he was breathing and checked his pulse.

"Is he alive? Please, is he alive?" Carlita begged.

"Yes, he is breathing. Barely, but breathing," the policeman said.

The other policeman got a blanket from the car, covered David, and they all waited to hear the sound of the sirens getting closer and closer. Carlita could hardly breathe. She couldn't bare the thought of losing David.

How can I lose this woman's child? What was I thinking, walking out here on the highway anyway? How stupid was that? She beat herself up for that fatal decision. She cried and stroked David's face as she watched his breath fade away.

The driver stopped the ambulance a few feet from them, and the paramedics immediately pulled the gurney from the back of the truck. They covered David's face with the oxygen mask and lifted him inside the truck. Carlita jumped into the ambulance with David before the policemen had a chance to say anything. She held his hand as they inserted a needle into his arm and began checking his body for broken bones and other injuries. The police car escorted the ambulance to the hospital, where they quickly prepped him for surgery. Carlita waited for what seemed like forever. The three hours that it took the doctors to put the frail little body back together seemed to be an eternity. Carlita watched as they moved David from the operating room to the intensive care unit.

"Will he live?" she pleaded.

"His chances are not good. We did everything we could, but he was badly injured. We'll see how he makes it through the night," the doctor said.

Carlita sat beside him while he fought for his life. The policemen were waiting in the hallway to speak to her. They realized that what happened was tragic, but she was wanted for murder and they had to deal with that situation. One of them walked in and asked if they could speak with her for a moment. She didn't want to leave David, but she followed him into the hallway.

"Are you Silvia Watkins?" Officer Newman asked.

"Yes, no . . . I mean I am Silvia, but I'm Carlita. I don't know how to explain it. I really need to get back," she said as she started to walk away.

"Please, Miss, are you Silvia Watkins?"

"No . . . I am Carlita Espinoza, but I am in Silvia's body. I know you don't believe me, but it's true."

"OK." The officer waited to form the next question since the answer to that one proved to be more confusing than helpful. "Is that your son?" he asked.

"Yes, well he is Silvia's son, but he is not my son."

"Aren't you Silvia?"

"This is crazy and I don't have time to explain this. I must get back inside."

She turned and walked back into the room where David was fighting for his life. She looked at his helpless little body and all hope faded away. She couldn't believe she caused this much pain and anguish. She remembered the day she stole the money and mourned in regret of that one horrible day that changed her life and destroyed Silvia's, and now David's. *Oh God, he's just a child.*

Detective Hauser heard of the accident and made his way to the Valley. He located the hospital, entered into the front lobby, and inquired about David Watkins.

"He is in the Intensive Care Unit, ICU," the administrator said. "Unless you are family, you cannot see him."

"Where is ICU?" Detective Hauser asked.

"Fourth floor. Take the elevators to your right."

Detective Hauser took the elevator upstairs just as Carlita watched David take his last breath. She listened as the monitor flatlined, and the loud, piercing sound broke her heart. She stepped back as the doctors and nurses tried to resuscitate him, but Carlita knew he was gone. She slowly stepped back to the door, shaking from the inevitable loss that she would have to face. She backed into the door and peered through the glass at the two policemen standing in the hallway. She saw Detective Hauser coming down the hall. She looked around at all of the commotion and calmly walked by everyone to the exit on the other side of the room. Just before she left the room, she looked back at David.

"I'm sorry, my sweet child, I'm sorry. Goodbye." She slipped out of the room and down the hall. She saw the exit sign and darted downstairs and outside through a first floor door. She started running toward the street, where she stopped a man who fortunately, was driving to Palmdale. She got into the backseat and lay down.

"Are you all right, miss?" the man asked.

"Yes, I'll be fine. I'm just tired and need to sleep," she said. She couldn't talk. She couldn't be sociable, and she didn't try to. She had never felt so much pain. She had never had such a horrible experience, and she just wanted life to stop so she could get off. She closed her eyes and waited.

The ride took about an hour. "Any place in particular?" the man asked as he pulled over and stopped.

"No, you can let me out here. Thanks," she said as she got out of the car and watched the man drive down the street. She looked around and wondered what was next.

Meanwhile, Detective Hauser was furious. He'd missed her again. He had no idea where she could be headed. He walked outside and asked a few people if they saw the woman in the picture. One young man remembered a woman who looked like her getting in a car going north. Detective Hauser took a deep breath and decided to head north. His frustration level was increasing by the minute. He wanted to talk with David. He wanted to know why he was contacting him and why this woman who looked like his mother, supposedly wasn't.

Carlita walked until she saw a huge church directly in front of her. She walked up the steps and peered inside. She saw no one, so she stepped inside, hoping to find a place to rest. She walked around until she found a secluded spot on the floor in the back of the church behind a row of columns and a huge desk. She crawled behind the desk and cried herself to sleep.

"Miss, miss, are you all right?" the minister asked as he

tried to wake her. She slowly opened her eyes. She was so tired, her body fought her for more rest.

"Miss, you can't stay here. Please, are you all right?" he asked again. She sat up, rubbed her eyes, and began to focus on her surroundings.

"Where am I?" she asked.

"You have wandered into St. Mary's Church." He helped her to her feet. She noticed the people coming in for services and decided that she should leave.

"Oh, I'm sorry. I just needed a place to sleep. I'll be going now."

"Is there anything I can do to help? Have you had any food? Are you hungry?" he asked as he looked at her with great concern.

Who is she, and how did she get this way? How did she end up here? "I'm all right. I just needed some sleep," she said. She lost her balance when she tried to stand.

"Come with me," the minister said as he took her by the arm and walked her toward the back of the church and into another room. He told the woman sitting inside to fix Carlita something to eat and allow her to rest on the sofa for a while. He closed the door behind him and the elderly woman stood up and began to prepare a meal for Carlita.

"We don't have much," she said. "I can make you a sandwich and a cup of soup. Will that do?" she asked.

"That will do just fine," Carlita said. She was so grateful to be getting anything that her heart started to pound from the mere thought of eating.

The lady placed the dish on the table and walked over to the sink and got a glass of water. Carlita began to eat with the vigor and joy of a homeless person who hadn't eaten in weeks. Then she remembered that she *was* that person. She was homeless and she hadn't eaten. She felt her stomach sink as she humbled herself to the thought of being homeless. Acceptance of that thought gave certain finality to her plight. A single tear rolled down her cheek as she realized that God would never forgive her now that David was gone. She was left to this horrible fate forever. She finished the meal and walked out into the church. One of the ministers ushered her to a seat.

"No, I'm not dressed properly," she said.

"God doesn't care how you dress," he said as he walked her to a seat in the rear of the church.

It was a beautiful church. The sunlight poured through the stained glass windows, and the huge gold cross on the wall was breathtaking. It was a small church with a multicultural congregation. She sat in the back and tried to relax. Carlita listened to the sermon and tried to hold back the tears. It pulled at her heart and forced her to confront herself. The Reverend spoke of pride and vanity.

Pride and vanity—the two things that brought me to this point. It was as if he knew she was in the room and was speaking to her. He spoke of wanting beauty and beautiful things at the expense of others. He spoke of the deception and boasting that comes with pride and how it leads to Damnation if it becomes the God we worship.

This is for me. It was my pride that stole that money. It was my vanity that went to the mall for all those useless things. It was my pride that got David killed, and it's my pride that's got me bargaining with God for my release from the curse. I don't know what to do. I want to fix it, but I can't . . . I can't.

Carlita felt more alone than she ever had. She waited for the miracle that only God could give to change her back. She closed her eyes and waited for God to right this terrible wrong, accept her forgiveness, and answer her prayer. The Reverend spoke directly to her about the struggles of life and the joy of death. He spoke about the illumination of

Paul and the betrayal of Peter. She wondered if she stood in the lion's den would God save her as he did Daniel.

"It is through his eyes that all things are clear. Ask the Lord Jesus Christ to save you and he will. Ask the Lord Jesus Christ to heal you and he will. Ask the Lord Jesus Christ to provide for you and he will, because he is all things to all people who choose him. He is all that you will ever need."

The words shook Carlita as tears rolled down her face. She could hardly contain herself. She wanted to tell someone of her ordeal, but they would see Silvia, not her. They would see a homeless black woman whose mind was going and who couldn't remember who she was. As the offering basket was handed to her, she looked at it with great sadness. She reached for it, knowing that she could give nothing. She was embarrassed to even touch it. She handed it to the lady next to her and turned her head in shame.

"It's all right, dear, I'll put this one in for you," she said as she smiled.

Oh God, could this get any worse? Now I have little old ladies paying my tithes. One dollar, I don't even have one dollar. Carlita glanced at her and tried to smile, but couldn't. As the sermon ended and everyone started to leave, Carlita found the courage to whisper "thank you" to the lady and walked out of the building and down the steps. The man who found her under the table and got her the food was standing outside and stopped her.

"You seem to be in so much pain," he said.

Carlita didn't respond. She tried not to look at him.

"You know that God can help you."

"Yes, I know he can," she said. "That's what makes this so terrible because I know he can, but he won't. I don't understand why, but he won't."

"Maybe it's not too late," the man said.

"Or, maybe it is," she said as she walked away in despair.

Carlita walked toward the place in the dream. She had no idea where this place was, but somehow she knew she was going in the right direction. She was so tired. She walked along Highway 38 in the middle of the desert with nothing but scattered Joshua trees everywhere. She looked all around and wondered what she would do when night fell. *It will get very cold and I will not be able to stay outside.* She tried to stop someone, hoping to get a ride. She had no idea where this place was, so anywhere they were going was fine as long as the direction was north. *I must go north.* She looked so unclean and disheveled that no one would likely stop to help her. She sat on a huge rock near the side of the road and waited for something to happen.

PART FOUR

GOOD AND EVIL

According to their way I will do to them, and according to their own judgments I will judge them; and they shall know that I am the Lord.

Ezekiel 7:27

CHAPTER 10

Dray couldn't stay at Madison's home. He had to find the place in his dream. He was terrified of what he might find, but he knew he had to try. He went upstairs and put a few essential items in a black bag. He grabbed his cell phone and wallet, and checked to see how much money he had. After heading downstairs, he looked all around to ensure everything was in place. He made sure the stove was off, the air was off, and that all windows and doors were locked before he closed the door behind him. He backed out of the driveway and headed north.

He checked to make sure the gas tank was full, and he reached for his shades above the visor. The blaring sounds from the radio began to irritate him. He tried to think his way through each step that should happen, and the music was just an interruption. He turned the radio off and drove in silence, hearing only the sound of the wheels turning on the road and the sound of his heart beating as the thought of the dream kept repeating over and over in his mind. He drove past Palmdale and into the desert. Just before sunset, he turned off the road to go to a roadside diner when he saw some movement on the side of the road.

He stopped the car and looked as intently as possible to be sure that what he really saw was a woman. He looked all around to make sure no one else was around waiting to jump him. He stepped out of the car slowly and cautiously walked toward Josh.

"Oh my God. What happened?" Dray picked Josh up and laid him in the backseat of the car. "Are you all right? Do you need a doctor?" Dray asked.

"No, no, I'll be all right. I need some water. Do you have any water?" Josh asked.

"No, but I'll get some," Dray said as he got back into the car and drove toward the diner. He parked the car. "Would you like to come in and use the restroom or get something to eat?"

"Yes," Josh said.

Dray opened the back door and helped Josh into the restaurant. Josh made it to the ladies' room and went inside. He looked into the mirror and was frightened by what he saw. He looked awful. His eyes were dark, and his face was swollen from the beating and red from the desert sun. He took a paper towel and washed his face, arms, and legs. He tried to clean himself up as much as he could.

Iria's body is so frail, so fragile, and now I've gotten her raped. God, I hope she can't see what a mess I've made of it. He walked into the restaurant and found Dray. He sat and stared out the window.

"Look like you could use something to eat," Dray said.

"That's OK, I'm fine."

"Sure you are. You're starving to death. You need to eat."

"I don't need anything," Josh insisted.

Dray realized that the young lady had no money and belonged nowhere.

"What would you like?" the waitress asked.

"I'll have a burger and fries with a Coke," Dray said.

"And you, young lady?" the waitress asked as she looked at Josh.

"I'm not hungry."

"She'll have the same thing," Dray said.

"I can't," Josh said.

"I know," Dray said.

"Will that be it?" the waitress asked.

"Yes, thank you," Dray said. He watched her walk back behind the counter. "So, I know this is none of my business, but it's not everyday that you run across someone crawling around in the desert, so I would really like to know how you ended up there."

"I was left there."

"By who?"

"Nobody."

"I've never known nobody to do a thing like that before. This seems more like somebody left you there. The question is, is it somebody you know or someone who dumped you there after, you know."

"If a woman is left in the desert to die, you can pretty much figure out what happened," Josh said as he rolled his eyes toward Dray.

"Do you need to see a doctor?" Dray asked.

"No," Josh said quietly.

"Are you sure you don't want to report this?"

Josh did not want to deal with the drama that would come from an investigation. He knew an investigation would keep him from getting to the desert, and he couldn't let that happen. He was so ashamed of the incident; he did not want to talk about it at all. All he wanted to do was get to the desert and hope that whatever he finds will erase the nightmare. "For what? What good would it do?" He stared at the floor and hoped he would let it go.

"They can make sure you're all right."

"I'm all right. I just need to get to the desert," Josh said. That statement piqued Dray's curiosity.

"The desert, why?"

"I don't know. I just know I have to get there."

"Here's your food," the waitress said as she put the plates in front of them. They both ate frantically.

The waitress walked back over and asked if they wanted dessert—a slice of pie or ice cream. They declined and headed back to the car. Dray drove about one block and stopped at a convenience store before getting back on the road. Josh was lying down in the backseat, and Dray got out and went inside. He purchased some water and walked back outside. He looked across the street and noticed a woman sitting on a rock. She seemed disoriented and confused. She was talking to herself and crying. He stared at her without knowing why. *She is like him; she's lost.* He got back inside the car. He pulled out onto the road, turned the car around, pulled over, and stopped.

"What are you doing?" Josh asked.

"I think this woman should come with us," Dray said.

"What woman?" Josh asked as he sat up in the backseat. He watched Dray walk toward a black woman sitting on a rock.

Dray kneeled in front of her and smiled. "Are you all right?" he asked. "Do you need anything?"

"I'm lost. I lost him, and now I don't know what to do. I have to get to the desert to make it all right, but I don't know where to go," she said.

"You lost who?"

"Davie, I lost Davie. He is dead, and now God will never let me go back to being myself, never again," she said in a very confused manner. Dray took a napkin and cleaned her face. He helped her to her feet and walked her to the car.

"We are going to the desert. We can take you there," he said.

"You are? You are going to the desert too?"

She seemed happy to know that there may be someone else who would understand her fear. Carlita sat in the front seat and tried to relax. She felt safe for the first time since the incident occurred and she was going to enjoy the feeling for as long as she could. She looked back to see Josh staring at her. "Hi, my name is Carlita."

"Hi, I'm Josh."

"Josh, that's an interesting name for a girl."

"Yes it is," Dray said as he looked at Josh through the rearview mirror.

"Well, I'm not who I seem to be," he said.

"Yes, I know what you mean," Carlita said.

"I don't know what you mean. What do you mean?" Dray asked.

"I mean, I am not who I seem to be. That's all," Josh said again.

"OK, OK, now something is very strange here. All of us seem to be in the same mess and are trying to get to the same place. Why?" Dray asked.

"What do you mean the 'same mess?' " Josh asked.

"You know what I mean. We are all not who we seem to be. So who are you really, Josh? And whose body are you in?" Dray asked.

Josh didn't know if he should answer or not. He hesitated for a while and pushed Dray for more. He didn't want to tell first and be the only one in this particular mess, as Dray called it.

"No, man, I don't know what you mean. What do you mean?" Josh demanded.

"Yes, you do, Josh. I know it. There's something strange about all of us, and for some reason we have been brought together. There was a reason for this. I can feel it. You are not Josh, but you are trapped in Josh's body, or you are Josh and you are in somebody else's body. Which way is it?" Dray asked.

"Who are you, Josh?" Carlita asked as she stared into his eyes. Josh hesitated, but it would be nice to be able to talk to somebody about this who may understand. He took a chance and spoke.

"My name is Josh Brimeyer and I am in Iria Tinsdale's body."

"What about you, Carlita?" Dray asked.

"I am Carlita Espinoza, and I am in Silvia Watkins's body."

"Yeah, well, I am Darrel Hunter, people call me Dray and I am in Madison Tanner's body," Dray said slowly and methodically. "Now the next question is, how did we all end up this way? Josh, what did you do to Iria?"

"I didn't do anything to her. We were lovers and we stopped being lovers. That's all," Josh said.

"Hold out your arms."

"Why, what for?"

"Hold them out, Josh," Dray demanded,

Josh slowly extended his arms and exposed the awful blackened needle marks that followed the veins up and down Iria's arm.

"You're a drug addict. Just as I thought. I don't know much about drugs, but from the looks of you, my guess would be heroin. Am I right?" Dray asked.

"I'm not a drug addict. Iria is, but I'm not."

"So, you got her hooked," Carlita said.

"She got herself hooked. What about you, Carlita, what did you do to Silvia?" Josh asked.

"Everything. I stole her rent money, and she and her son were thrown out of their apartment. I was living on the street with her son, David."

"Where is David now?" Dray asked.

"Dead."

"Dead? What happened?" Josh asked.

"It doesn't matter. All that matters now is that he's dead. God will never forgive me, and I will be in this body forever."

"Did you kill him?" Josh asked

"No," said Carlita, "he was hit by a car, but I put him in harm's way. It was my fault."

"So, it was an accident," said Dray.

"No, it was my responsibility to take care of him, and I didn't. God will never forgive me for that . . . never." The sadness in her voice was painful to hear.

"What did you do, Dray?" asked Josh

"I killed Madison Tanner's son, Daniel," Dray said.

They were silent. They didn't know what to say.

"Why?" Carlita finally asked.

"I wanted to get into a gang. That's sick, isn't it? I can't believe I did it."

"You are a murderer? Oh, hell no, I can't believe that," Josh said as he stared at Dray in disbelief that he was sitting in the same car with a murderer.

"Don't play shocked, Josh, as if what you did wasn't the same thing," Dray said.

"I don't kill people," Josh said with defiance.

"What do you think drugs do—make people wealthy and prosperous? It's a slow death. It may take longer, but the outcome is the same. They're still dead. What you do is create the walking dead. Most of those people might as well be dead for what good their lives are after they get hooked on that stuff."

"Oh no, I ain't even in your league. I would never kill anyone."

"Have you looked at what you did to Iria's body? She was raped and left for dead in the desert. Don't you get all high and mighty! She"s as much dead as Daniel is. In fact, I think Daniel is better off," Dray exclaimed.

"Stop! It doesn't matter. All of us are wrong! Sin is sin regardless of what we did. We are equally bad. There are no degrees to sin. Sin is sin, and that's all. We are all going to hell," Carlita yelled. They stopped talking and sat in silence, remembering how they came to be at this place, at this time, and wished they had made different choices.

Her scream was deafening as he watched the car plow down the road. She tried to control the car, but the brakes were malfunctioning.

"No brakes," she screamed as the downward spiraling road forced the car to go faster and faster. He tried to help her control the steering wheel from the passenger side, but fear of the inevitable lunged toward them as the car shifted too far to the right and flew over the cliff.

"Jump!" he yelled as he flung the door open. "Jump!" Bones cracked as he hit the rock, forcing excruciating pain to radiate throughout his body. He gathered himself and turned just in time to see the car hit the bottom and burst into flames. "Mary!" he cried. He forced himself to move in a feeble attempt to reach her, but he couldn't. She was gone. "Mary," he cried as he leaped forward, clutching his chest. His body was sweating profusely and the sound of his heartbeat frightened him. Detective Hauser tried to calm himself and lay back down in the bed.

"Mary," he whispered.

The detective had found a motel in the middle of

nowhere, surrounded by the desert. He reached over and picked up his watch from the nightstand. He was still shaken by the dream. It was the same nightmare he often had. He remembered the night like it was yesterday, the night his life changed forever.

Patrick Hauser was a late bloomer. He was not an attractive man, so when Mary Simmons fell in love with him and said yes to the big question, he became a whole new man. He was able to put all of the pain and humiliation of years of teasing and rejection behind him and begin a new life. She loved him and he loved her. He knew that God had found her for him and he cherished her with every breath he took.

Detective Hauser knew that his line of work was dangerous and that he could get hurt or killed at any time. He had testified against many criminals, which resulted in jail time, life sentences, and even death for some. But he never thought Mary could get caught up in the madness of someone's vindictive revenge. A convict who had served ten years in prison blamed the testimony of then Officer Hauser for his misfortune. He wanted revenge, and Mary wanted to visit her mother that day. She wanted to drive, and Pat couldn't say no to her.

She was a capable driver, but someone had cut the brake line, and four years after God gave her to him, he took Mary away. Detective Hauser has been waiting for the past five years for God to reunite them and end his pain.

"Four o'clock," he whispered as he held his watch in his hand. He got up and walked to the window of his ground floor room. The shadow of the figure standing beneath the street light was familiar. He stared at the person and realized that the person was staring back at him. He reached for his pants that were thrown across a chair and put them on as he ran out the door in his bare feet. He raced across the parking lot and gasped when he recognized the figure to be David Watkins.

"How can this be? I saw you dead yesterday. I saw you, so you can't be David. Who are you?" he asked.

"They are close," David said.

"Who is close? Who are they?" Detective Hauser asked. "How can you be here?" he asked again as he stared at the boy.

"She's not my mother. They are in trouble," David said as he looked north down the long road toward the horizon.

"Is she north of here? Is Silvia with them?" he asked as he turned and looked toward the horizon, hoping to see something, anything. He turned to face David again, but he was gone. Detective Hauser looked around, but there was no trace of him, no sign that he was ever there.

Dray noticed the truck approaching him. It was very dark and the roads were empty, so it was easy to see on-coming headlights in the night sky. The stars in the desert sky twinkled like diamonds dancing in the moonlight. He looked up at the sky for a moment to marvel at the beauty of it and then back down to the road.

Something's wrong. Where is the truck? It was there. I saw it. Maybe it turned off, but where? I should see headlights or tail-lights somewhere.

Dray scanned the flat land that was spread out before him and saw nothing but desert brush and Joshua trees. His heart started to pound. He was frightened, but he didn't know why. He checked Josh in the rearview mirror and then he looked at Carlita as she uncomfortably tried to rest. Suddenly headlights came from nowhere and he found himself looking directly into the front grill of the huge truck. He watched the truck speed toward him and he screamed in desperation.

"Oh shit!"

Carlita was startled awake. "Oh my God! What is it?" she yelled.

The front grill of the truck transformed into the horrific face of the entity that visited Dray in Madison's house. The truck lunged toward them as the mouth of the ghostly aberration opened wide, seemingly to swallow them whole. Dray hit the brakes and swerved to the left, forcing the car over the road and down an embankment. Josh was oblivious to the incident. He was thrown to the floor. Carlita's wrist hit the dashboard and she screamed. Dray struck his head against the steering wheel and suffered a severe concussion. Carlita held her arm in agony and cried from the pain. Dray laid his head back and tried to gather himself as he slipped into unconsciousness. Josh pulled himself from the floor and looked around to see what happened.

"What the hell happened?" Josh asked as he forced the back door open. He pulled himself out of the car and leaned against the car for a moment. He began to focus when he heard Carlita crying. He looked back at her, trying to wake Dray. "What's wrong?" he asked frantically. "What happened?" He opened Carlita's door and helped her out of the car.

She looked back at him, crying desperately. "He's hurt. I can't wake him."

Josh walked around the car and opened Dray's door. "Dray," he yelled. "Dray, man, wake up, wake up." Josh softly slapped him across the face and Dray opened his eyes. He looked at Iria's small, pretty face and smiled. He could barely keep his eyes open. Josh wondered how he was going to move Madison's heavy body from the car and up the embankment. Josh reached behind him and pulled him to the ground. "You have to help me," he yelled at Carlita.

"I can't. My arm is broken," she cried.

"Damn," Josh said. He leaned Dray against the car and forced him to sit up. "Wake up, man. You can't fall asleep," he said. He began to look around for a flat piece of wood and found an old piece of ply board a few feet away. He tore a band of material from Iria's dress and used the board as a splint to brace Carlita's wrist.

"This will keep your arm stable. It may not hurt as much," he said. She stopped crying and thanked him for his help. "Try to make it to the street and flag down anybody you see," he said.

"I'll try," she said as she began climbing up the hill to the street. Josh turned his attention back to Dray and tried to drag him up the hill. He moved Madison's heavy body a little at a time. Iria's frail body struggled with every step. Josh was so frustrated because he knew he should have the strength to do this, but he couldn't. He slipped and fell and cut his leg on a sharp branch. He screamed from the pain. His level of frustration overwhelmed him and he cried out to God, "Why!" He began to cry. Iria's emotions took over and he cried. "What the hell do you want from us? What do you want us to do? I can't take this anymore. I can't be her anymore. Please help me, God. Please!" Tears streamed down his face as he sat on the ground holding Dray, who had Madison's life in his hands.

Detective Hauser got in his car in the early morning before sunrise and headed north. He had no idea where he was going, but he had decided to listen to David. He couldn't figure out how David was appearing and disappearing, or even why, but there was a reason. He knew it now. There was something happening to him. This case was different than any other he had worked on before. He'd had an eerie feeling ever since Daniel Tanner was killed. Then there was

Carlita Espinoza's mysterious drowning. He began to rely on David's guidance and heeded his warnings.

"He wants me to go north. There're in trouble . . . in trouble. I wonder who they are," he whispered as he drove into the darkness.

Josh gathered his strength and pulled Dray little by little until he reached the road. He laid Dray on the ground and fell in the grass from exhaustion. Carlita was standing at the edge of the road looking both ways and seeing nothing. It was pitch black.

"This is hopeless," she said. "No one is going to come down this road in the middle of the night. No one except a crazed madman who will probably kill all of us."

"Right now that doesn't sound too bad," Josh said as he sat on the ground. He tore another piece of cloth from the dress and wrapped his injured leg. Carlita looked around at Dray as he started to moan and regain consciousness.

"What's going on? What happened?" Dray asked. He touched his head and cringed from the pain.

"You ran the damn car off the road. That's what happened," Josh said.

"You didn't see it," Carlita said with anguish and fear in her voice. "The truck . . . you were asleep, so you didn't see it."

"See what?" Josh asked.

"The front of the truck. It changed. It changed into something horrible. I thought it was going to kill us. I knew we were dead," she said.

"What are you talking about?" He looked at Dray and asked the same question, hoping to get a more sensible answer.

Dray forced himself to sit up. His head was throbbing, and his sight was slightly blurred. He knew he was hurt, but he couldn't tell how bad it was, and he was a little afraid that if he didn't get help soon, he wouldn't make it.

"The front of the truck that was coming toward us turned into the face of evil," Dray said.

"What? Both of you are hallucinating," Josh said. "This is crazy. I'm the one fucked up on drugs. If anybody has a hallucination, it's going to be me."

"I've seen that face before," Dray said.

"What do you mean?" Carlita asked.

"That evil face, I've seen it before. It came to me at Madison's house. It asked me how did I want to spend eternity. It was evil and foul."

"You are describing the devil," Carlita said.

"Yes, I suppose I am," Dray said.

"What? But why? Why would the devil be chasing you? You see? I told you that being a murderer ain't no joke. You go straight to hell for that shit," Josh said.

"You know, Josh, I'd pay all of Madison's money just to shut you up," Dray said.

"What? Man, I just saved your life, and that was no easy task," Josh said.

"I know, I'm sorry," Dray said as he struggled to stand. He walked over to Carlita and looked down the road. "I think we should start walking."

"Walking to where?" Carlita asked.

"You are in no condition to walk anywhere," Josh said.

"I don't think we should stay here. We need to be moving," Dray said.

"Which way should we go?" Carlita asked.

"North, we were going north," Dray said.

"Which way is north?" Josh asked.

Dray looked at the sky.

"Well, the sun is coming up over there, so that's east, so this way must be north," he said as he started walking.

They all had fear in the pit of their stomachs. Carlita started praying. She asked God and Silvia to forgive her and asked God to take David's soul into his hands. She feared that her journey through the desert would lead to hell and damnation.

Dray knew the devil was after him, but he intended to fight. He would not surrender his soul without a fight. He reflected on his life and wondered about the choices he made. The fights he had with his mother seemed so trivial now, and he realized he wasted energy on foolish things. He thought of Daniel and Barbara and wondered what life would be like if he hadn't met Kuame. "What if," he whispered to himself? "What if?"

"What is that?" Carlita asked. "Is that a car?"

"Yeah, I believe it is," Dray said.

They stopped walking and waited as the car got closer and closer. Josh began to feel very nervous. He stared at the car as it came into view. It was a red Porsche. Josh recognized the car. He remembered that he had a red Porsche that had an unusual black stripe on the hood and a crystal unicorn hanging from the mirror that reflected the sun through a prism of colors. He could see the unicorn swinging from the mirror. He stopped breathing as he watched the car ride by with an image of himself behind the wheel. Josh saw himself the way he once was and shuddered with fear.

"That's me," Josh yelled. "That's me. That's my car and that's me driving it." His eyes followed the car as it slowly drove by. The figure inside looked at Josh and smiled as he glided by as if on air.

"What are you yelling about?" Dray asked.

"That's my car. That was me, I mean the me that I really am. I can't be here. This can't be real. I saw myself dead. I saw my body."

"None of this is real," Dray said as he looked at Josh. "You saw your body, your dead body?"

"Yeah, I saw it," Josh said.

"I found out that I was killed too and my body was cremated," Dray said. He looked at Carlita. "What about you? Is your body gone too?"

"Yeah, I drowned and the police think I did it . . . I mean Silvia. They are looking for me," she said.

They looked back and forth at each other in silence.

"With our bodies gone, we have no way back, do we?" Carlita asked.

"I don't know. I'm hoping that whatever we find at our final destination will give us the answer to that question," Dray said as he walked toward Josh, who was still staring down the road at the Porsche that slowly moved into the horizon. Dray grabbed his shoulder. "Come on, man . . . come on."

The hours passed slowly as they made their way north. Dray's headache was getting worse and his vision was fading. He forced himself to keep moving and tried not to think about it. Carlita said a different prayer every few miles and Josh was starting to complain about being hungry. Carlita started a new verse. "The Lord is my shepherd, I shall not want. He . . ."

"Oh please, will you shut up! If God gave a damn he wouldn't have put us in this mess in the first place," Josh yelled angrily.

"You can't blame God for this situation. We did this to ourselves," Carlita said.

"We are not the first people to commit crimes and do bad things, and not everyone goes through this kinda hell," Josh said.

"How do you know?" Carlita asked.

"I just know it, that's all. God is playing with us. Yeah,

he's playing a game at our expense. He's having fun watching us suffer," Josh said.

"Shut up, Josh. Just shut up!" Dray yelled as he stopped for a moment and looked back at Josh. "Do you have any idea how stupid you sound? God doesn't have time to play games. He's too busy trying to keep us from killing each other."

"Well, I guess you failed that test," Josh said viciously.

Dray could barely see Josh, but he focused his sight long enough to see Iria. He remembered that he couldn't beat the hell out of him because he was a woman, so he refrained from killing him and tried to calm himself.

"What's that?" Carlita asked.

"What?" Dray asked as he squinted to see what she was asking about.

"At the intersection. It looks like a truck stop," she said.

"Where?" Dray asked as he tried to focus.

"Yeah, I see it. Great, maybe we can get some food," Josh said.

"Yeah, maybe, but I don't have any money," Carlita said.

"Me neither," Josh said as he pats his pockets, hoping to find some coins.

"I have Madison's credit cards and a few dollars on me. We should be all right," Dray said.

"Great, let's go," Josh said as he walked another half mile to the Cal City Truck Stop. The small store sat on the corner of an intersection that had no name. It was deserted looking. The old rundown store had two gas pumps and an outhouse for the truckers.

"I can't imagine anyone working out here," Carlita said. "Oh my God . . . look." Carlita pointed to the red Porsche parked in front of the store.

"That can't be right. We saw that car going south and it didn't come back to pass us," Dray said.

Josh walked to the car and looked inside. He noticed his black leather jacket and his compact disc case. He recognized the initials on the case, JB. *It's mine.* He looked at the unicorn hanging from the mirror and remembered when this was his life. Without saying a word, he walked inside the store. He looked around until he saw a man standing in the back of the store. Josh recognized him and wondered if he should approach the man. He watched the man who looked just like him pick up a few items and walk toward him. Josh was stunned. He couldn't move. It was like watching a ghost, a ghost of himself. The tall, blond man stopped at the counter and the gruff looking man behind the counter tallied up his total.

"Four twenty-five," he said.

The tall, blond man paid the storekeeper and walked toward the door. He walked past Josh without a word. Josh was frozen and could not take his eyes off of the man. As the man walked past him, he stopped.

"Do you believe in the law that you reap what you sow?" he asked.

Josh turned to look back at him, but couldn't speak.

"Do you, Josh?" he asked.

He knows who I am. His heart began to beat rapidly as fear gripped him.

"Do you know what karma is? It"s the belief that what you do in this life, you will pay for it in the next. What do you have to pay for, Josh?" The man's face turned demonic and foul.

He looked into Josh's eyes and asked the most disheartening question. "How do you plan to spend eternity, Josh?"

He grinned as his face transformed into this hideous image. Josh was scared to death. He began to shake. Dray and Carlita stood at the door and watched the man transform back to the image of Josh and walked by without a word. The storekeeper showed no reaction, as if he didn't see the image of evil before him. He continued to work behind the counter as if nothing was happening. He noticed the young girl standing just inside the door looking scared and disoriented.

"Are you all right, miss?" he asked

"She's fine," Dray said and he walked in and took Josh's arm as they watched the likeness of Josh walk out the door.

"He's evil," Carlita said.

"Josh . . . Josh, man, you all right?" Dray asked as he walked Josh to the counter and tried to calm him. "Don't worry. We will fight this. If we stay together, we will fight this and we will go home."

Dray tried to calm Josh. Looking into Iria's face and seeing her so frightened made him feel helpless. He had to remind himself that she was a man and that he had to refrain from any emotional contact. "Let's get something to eat," Dray said. They began to walk around the store, making their personal selections, and piled the counter up with cookies, chips, sodas, and candy.

"Well, these aren't the healthiest things to eat, but it's the best we can do," Carlita said. Each of them took their bag of junk food and walked outside. Josh hesitated when he reached the door. He was afraid that the man was still there and that he wouldn't be able to escape his wrath. Dray noticed Josh's hesitation and walked out ahead of him.

"It's OK. He's gone," Dray said. Josh stepped outside and calmed himself. He looked back as they continued to walk north, wondering if he was his own worst enemy. It was starting to get dark, and Carlita was becoming very nervous that they would have to spend the night outside. She knew that the desert could be an unforgiving place at night.

"We need to start looking for a place to sleep tonight. We have to rest," she said.

"Yeah, you're right," Dray said as he held his head in his hand and tried to deal with the excruciating pain. Josh looked around for someplace to sleep. Finally, he noticed a mound with large rocks at the foot of it.

"Maybe we could stay there," he said as he pointed to the mound. "We could sleep on the side away from the wind and use the rocks as shelter."

Carlita looked around. "It may be the best we can do," she said. "Besides, Dray needs to lie down. If we don't get him to a hospital soon, we may lose him. How far is it?" she asked.

"It will take about twenty minutes to walk over there," Josh said. In silence, they began to walk in the direction of the rocky mound, which took them away from the main road. Dray stumbled to the ground in pain and yelled out in agony.

"Oh God, we've got to get him some help," Carlita cried.

"How? What? Where can we go? We are out here in the middle of nowhere looking for a place that probably doesn't even exist. How are we going to get to a hospital!" Josh yelled.

"I don't know," she cried. "I don't know."

They felt the pressure to try and save Dray's life, but neither of them knew what to do or how. The whole journey was becoming hopeless, and they all wondered if going back would be a better choice. Carlita knew she couldn't return without facing prison, and Josh knew he couldn't survive without the drugs, so the streets would eventually kill him. Dray was in so much pain, he couldn't think of anything but relief. It didn't matter how hopeless it was; they all knew they had no choice but to somehow go forward and hold onto the small slice of hope they all had.

Josh and Carlita picked Dray up and carried him forward as the wind forced them back. *It's as if the elements are working against us*, Josh thought. They fought the wind and pushed forward.

Detective Hauser saw David standing on the side of the road. He pulled over from his long drive and stopped the car. He looked out the window at David and watched him walk to the edge of the embankment and look down. He looked back at Detective Hauser as if urging him to come and see. The detective got out of the car and walked to the edge. He looked down to see the wreckage of Madison's car at the bottom of the embankment. His heart started to pound as he ran down to the car and searched inside. *Nobody's here.* He began to look around, but he couldn't find anyone. He noticed blood on the side of the car where Dray laid his head.

"She's hurt," he whispered. He climbed up the embankment to the street and looked all around, hoping to see some sign of where she was. "They are in trouble. You must find them."

"They? She must be traveling with someone. Where are they? Why me . . . why must I help them?"

"She told me that you would help," David said.

"She . . . who is she?" he asked

"You must help them. If they die, he will have their souls," David said.

"What, what, who will have their souls . . . What?" he asked. *This gets more confusing by the minute.*

David turned and pointed north. He stared into Detective Hauser's eyes as he stepped off the embankment into nothingness.

"He can not harm you." The voice that came from the thick air vanished as quickly as David did into the night.

Detective Hauser ran over to the edge to see what happened, but there was nothing; no sign of David. This whole experience had been so unreal that David's disappearance did not alarm him. He walked back to his car and started the drive north. He drove for a while until he reached the intersection where the corner store was. He got out and walked inside. He asked the man behind the counter if anyone had stopped by, specifically a young black woman. "Yes, I remember her," he said. "She came in here with a man and another woman."

"Do you know which way they went?" he asked.

"That way," the storekeeper said as he pointed north.

"Thank you," Detective Hauser said as he walked out of the store and back to his car. "As long as I've been driving, I should be in another state by now. This is crazy. I feel like I'm going around in circles. It's getting dark, and I'm getting nowhere. I'll go another thirty miles, and then I'm heading back."

He drank the cup of coffee he purchased from the store and looked all around, hoping to see anything. He noticed smoke several yards off the road. He saw puffs of smoke coming from a mound in the distance that faded into the evening sky and he felt that David was helping him to see it. It was as if a line of light carried his eyes straight to the source of the smoke. He got back into his car and headed toward the smoke. He drove over the desert floor and stopped the car just at the foot of the mound and walked around to the other side. He looked into Silvia's frightened face and felt a sense of relief that the search was finally over.

"Silvia Watkins," he yelled. "I need to speak with you about the death of Carlita Espinoza. Please come with me"

"My friend is hurt. Please take care of him, and I'll do whatever you want," she said.

Detective Hauser climbed up the mound a little and saw

Dray lying unconscious on the ground. Josh had made a small fire from some brush and sticks nearby, hoping to help keep them warm through the night, but never thinking that it would be seen from the highway. Detective Hauser looked into Iria's face and back at Silvia.

"This is Madison Tanner, Daniel Tanner's father. What is he doing out here with the two of you? What's going on?" Detective Hauser looked at each of them suspiciously. "Did the two of you bring him out here to extort money? Are you trying to do the same thing to him that you did to Daniel? I guess Daniel didn't cooperate, so you had to kill him and now you're working on Madison, is that it?" he asked.

"A car accident, we were in a car accident," Josh said. "We are all together. He was not kidnapped or anything like that. If that's what you're thinking, you're wrong. We are together."

"The car that went off the road a few miles back". Detective Hauser said.

"Yeah," Josh answered.

"Why would Mr. Tanner be with you, an obvious addict?" He asked as he grabbed Josh's arm and looked at the tracks, "And you, a murder suspect. I'm not buying this. I think we all should go to the station and answer a lot of questions." "We have to get him to a hospital first, then we'll go with you," said Carlita as she looked at Dray with fear that he wouldn't make it.

"OK, help me get him to the car," Detective Hauser said as he reached down to pick up Dray. He was wondering how Madison Tanner found himself in the middle of the Mojave Desert with these two people. The obvious reason was that the two of them were trying to steal money from him, but couldn't because he got hurt in the car accident. If they could get the money, they would have left him for dead.

CHAPTER 11

They took Dray to the hospital emergency room in Palmdale, where he was admitted and rushed into surgery. A doctor looked at Carlita and determined that she only sprained her wrist. He wrapped it and gave her some pain pills. She was released into Detective Hauser's custody. They began the two-hour drive south to the Forty-third Precinct, and he walked Josh and Carlita inside, past the front desk, and into a back room.

"Sit," he said as he pointed to the table surrounded by four chairs. The detective left them in the room alone.

Josh and Carlita sat close to each other. Carlita felt trapped and helpless. She looked around, hoping to find an escape route, but hung her head and began to cry when she found nothing. Blank walls surrounded her with small barred windows at the ceiling. Josh took her hand and held it.

Detective Hauser and Captain James Tracell entered the room, both looking very disturbed. Detective Hauser was yelling as he entered.

"I think we have enough evidence to hold her! That's what I'm saying."

"What evidence . . . What?" Captain Tracell asked as he looked at Josh and Carlita. The look of fear in their eyes moved him. He hoped this was a big mistake and that they'd done nothing wrong, but a crime had been committed and someone was responsible. But he hoped it was not them.

"Silvia," Captain Tracell said as he read through Detective Hauser's brief. He took a deep breath and looked at Detective Hauser and then Carlita and Josh. "Silvia, please follow Detective Hauser," he said as he opened the door and waited for her to walk out.

Captain Tracell was a stern man with seventeen years on the force. He'd seen it all from beggars, thieves, murderers, dealers, and lunatics and now he was about to hear Silvia's and Iria's story. He was waiting for the same "I'm innocent" plea that he often heard and the onslaught of tears that usually accompany frightened and alone women. Carlita looked at Josh as he held onto her hand until it started to slip away and fear gripped her. She looked beyond Iria's eyes and into Josh's soul.

"Josh, be strong," she said. He faked a smile and nodded his head. Carlita walked down the hall and into another room. The room looked the same as the one she just left. She was frightened and wondered if she would ever see outside again.

"Have a seat," Detective Hauser said.

Carlita walked to the end of the table and sat down. She held her hands together and stared down at the table. She could hear sounds from outside—the cars moving by and the chatter of people walking along the sidewalk. The sun was bright as the light filtered through the small window behind her. There was a faint smell of cigarette smoke in the room, reminiscent of a distant time when brutal interrogations took place in smoke-filled rooms such as this one.

"Do you need anything?" he asked. "A glass of water, maybe."

"No, no, I'm fine," she said as her voice quivered.

"Silvia, let's talk about Carlita Espinoza. How do you know her? What was your relationship with her?"

"I did not have a relationship with Silvia. I didn't know her. I stole her purse and ran. I've never really met her."

"So, you are not Silvia Watkins?"

"No, not really, well maybe on the outside, but really Silvia and I never met. She was asleep when I stole her purse, so she didn't see me."

"You're not Silvia."

"No, I'm not."

"You look just like Silvia."

"I'm not her."

"Then, who are you?"

"I am Carlita Espinoza." She looked him squarely in the eyes and waited for his response of disbelief.

"We found Carlita's body a week ago—dead."

"Yes, I know, but it was my body, not me. Look, I know this doesn't make any sense to you."

"You got that right. Now look, maybe you didn't mean to kill her. Maybe you struggled over the purse and you accidentally pushed her into the lake. Is that what happened?"

"No, I don't know how I ended up in the lake. That seems strange to me, because I've never been there."

"Who has never been there, you or Carlita?"

"Carlita, me, I've never been there. I don't know if Silvia has been there or not. I've never met her."

"But you are her."

"No I'm, not! No, no, no!"

"Enough of this," Detective Hauser shouted as he started

to pace around the room. He looked at her and shook his head in confusion.

"Is David your son?" he asked.

"David," she sadly whispered

"Is he your son?" he asked again, even more abruptly.

"He was Silvia's son, but he was in my care when the accident happened." Tears swelled in her eyes and rolled down her cheeks. She couldn't bear the thought of him and his tragic death. She hung her head and cried. "I let him down," she cried. "He was my responsibility, and I failed."

"Who gave you this responsibility?"

"God," she said without flinching.

"God," he repeated softly as he looked directly at her, wondering if she really had lost her mind. "Why would God give you David to care for?"

"He didn't give me David. He gave me Silvia's body, and I had to take care of David because he thought I was his mother."

The look on her face was frightening to Detective Hauser. *Could she really believe this?*

"Well, I think you took David on the run with you after you killed Carlita, and in the confusion of things, David lost his life."

"I wasn't on the run. I was trying to get to Redemption. I was trying to save Silvia's life and save my soul." She chuckled. "I guess this does sound a little bizarre." She smiled as she looked down at the table while holding her hands together. She patiently waited for whatever would happen next.

Detective Hauser sat in the chair staring at her as she stared at the table. In all of his years on the force, he had never heard a story quite like this one. He stood up and walked to the door. Just as he reached for the knob, he turned and looked into her face.

"What if I told you that I've seen David?" "Yes, I know. You saw him at the hospital."

"No, I mean since then. I've seen him."

"That's not possible. He's dead," she said angrily.

"He came to me and told me that you were in trouble. He told me where to find you. How else could I have found the three of you in the middle of the desert? He helped me."

"I don't believe you."

"Yes, it sounds a little farfetched, doesn't it? If this sounds too hard to believe, imagine someone believing the story you just told me."

Detective Hauser looked into her dark eyes, turned, and walked out the door. He walked down the hall to a door that read "Private, Authorized Personnel Only." He opened the door and walked inside. He looked at Josh and saw Iria's blue eyes. He walked around the table trying to start a conversation, but he stumbled on the words until something reasonable emerged.

"So, you are . . . I mean you say you are . . . or rather, who are you?" he finally asked.

Josh had just as much trouble answering. He was wondering what Carlita might have told him, and he was afraid to say anything that may contradict her statements. He couldn't look at Detective Hauser and tell the lie he was getting ready to tell. He couldn't tell him the truth because it would only confirm him as a lunatic.

I have to play the game. Say what they want to hear, and maybe you will be allowed to leave.

"My name is Iria Tinsdale," Josh said.

"Iria, how do you know Silvia Watkins?"

"Silvia, I don't know anyone named Silvia."

"The woman who you were in the desert with is Silvia Watkins. You don't know her?"

"Oh yeah, Silvia. Yeah, I know her, sure I know her," he

laughed. "I thought you were talking about another Silvia that I don't know, yeah...yeah, I know Silvia." He looked away from the detective, knowing that he just made a fool of himself.

"Do you know the woman or not?" Detective Hauser asked with a hint of agitation in his voice.

"Yeah, I know her. I said I know her."

"How do you know her? What is your relationship with her?"

"I just met her. I really don't know her that well. Me and Dray, we was driving and saw this woman on the side of the road who looked like she needed some help, so we picked her up. I really don't know anything about her."

"You and Dray? By Dray, are you referring to Mr. Tanner?"

"Mr. Tanner . . . Dray. I don't know. Look, all I know is she was sitting on the roadside and needed some help. That's all."

Josh had been fighting the cravings for the drug ever since he left the rehab clinic and his support group. He didn't want to re-enter that world, but he feared he was losing the fight. Josh had come to realize that once you become dependent on drugs, that the cravings and pains may never end. Even after all this time, he still wanted it. His body ached for it. He met people at the rehab clinic who stayed off of it for years and still couldn't let it go. At the time, he couldn't understand, but he did now. All he could think about was getting the drug. "I'm weak. Sometimes I am so weak. I can't help it."

"Can't help what? What do you want?"

"What? You know what I need. Why are you asking me something stupid?"

"No, Iria, I don't know what you need. I don't even know who you really are. Who is Josh?"

"Josh?"

"That's what Silvia called you earlier. Who is he?"

Josh could barely look at him. He turned away and hung his head.

"I used to know someone named Josh. He was a selfish bastard. He's dead," Josh said.

"How did he die?"

"I don't know, and I don't care."

"What is your relationship with Mr. Tanner?" Detective Hauser asked.

Josh was starting to get very frustrated with all the questions. "Mr. Tanner? Who the hell is Mr. Tanner?"

"Maybe I should say Dray."

"Oh yeah, I know Dray. That's my boy. Poor Dray, he is stuck in that white man's body." Josh was craving the drug, so he was not thinking clearly. He was wondering how much longer this was going to go on. His focus changed and now he needed to make some decisions. He needed to get to Dray and he needed the drug. His internal struggle was just beginning.

"Mr. Tanner's body?" Detective Hauser said.

"Yeah, yeah, how'd you know?"

"Lucky guess."

Detective Hauser was beginning to become very frustrated with the madness. *Everybody is somebody else. People don't just jump around from one body to another, and it seems that Daniel Tanner's death may be tied to this somehow.*

The detective remembered reading about the death of a gang member, Darrell Hunter, better known as Dray. He wondered if Dray was linked to Daniel, but Dray was dead too. But that didn't mean that he couldn't have killed Daniel before he died. This was getting more and more interesting. How can Dray "be his boy," as Iria put it, and be dead?

"Look, I need to get out of here. How much longer are you going to keep us?" yelled Josh.

"What is it? What's the hurry?" he asked.

"I want to check on Mr. Tanner and see how he's doing, that's all," said Josh

"I guess I can't hold you, but letting you out on the street, knowing what you may do may not be the best thing to do," said Detective Hauser. "Please stay in town, I will want to talk to you again."

"What about Silvia?" Josh asked

"Not yet, I have a few more questions for her. Carlita Espinoza is dead, and there seems to be some connection to Silvia, so she may have to stay a little longer."

Detective Hauser stood and walked to the door and told Josh he could leave.

"Can I see Silvia?" he asked.

"No, I think it's best if you don't see her." He found an officer to escort Josh out of the building. He walked back down the hall and into the room where Carlita was waiting. He entered the room, telling her about Josh.

"Your friend had to leave."

"I need to see him," she said as she stood and started toward the door.

"No, no, I don't think I can let you go so easily. He's not completely off the hook either. He could be in trouble for harboring a fugitive if we can prove that he knew who you were and was helping you get away."

"What was his story?"

"Why don't you tell me how the two of you met?"

"He and Dray picked me up on the side of the road."

"Where were you?"

"I don't know. In the desert somewhere. I was lost, tired, and alone. Dray and Josh drove by and stopped to give me a lift. As it turns out, we were all trying to get to the same place."

"And this place is . . . ?"

"Redemption."

"Redemption? Where is Redemption?"

"I don't know. We were looking for it when you found us."

"Why are all of you looking for it?"

"We have to find it or we will never get our bodies back. Don't you see, it's our only way to save us from our sins," she cried. "I have to go. I have to see Josh."

"You mean Iria."

"Yes, I mean Iria," she said as she walked back to the chair and sat hopelessly. "God, what are we going to do?" she whispered.

Captain Tracell entered the room. He looked at Carlita and back at Detective Hauser.

"Detective, I need to speak to you," he said.

Detective Hauser walked into the hallway following Captain Tracell. "I read all of the statements from everyone on the scene. There is a link. I don't understand how David fits into it, but there seems to be something going on between Carlita and Silvia. I don't think we should let her go. She was on the run before and most likely, she'll run again. Read her her rights and get her an attorney."

Detective Hauser walked back into the room and saw the frightened look on Silvia's face. He was angry about what he had to do, but he didn't have much choice.

"Please stand," he said. He walked over to Carlita and pulled her arms behind her. He cuffed her wrists and began to read her rights.

"You have the right to remain silent. You have the right to an attorney. If you do not have an attorney, one will be appointed to you. You have . . ."

Carlita phased out. She couldn't hear a word he was saying. She couldn't focus on anything but walking to the jail cell. She never imagined she would be walking to a jail cell for a crime she didn't commit. She couldn't cry anymore. She couldn't think. Her mind was moving from point to point remembering her life as it once was. This moment would define the rest of her life.

It's over; I will spend the rest of my life in jail. There's no way to win.

Detective Hauser asked her if she understood everything he just said.

"What . . . what?" She looked at him with a confused and dazed expression.

"Did you understand what was just said to you?" he asked again.

"Yes, I understand," she said rather than to have him repeat the whole thing again.

Detective Hauser grabbed her arm and walked her down the hall into a small room where she was fingerprinted and photographed. She tried to calm herself. She felt like she would explode at any moment, but she was too numb to do it. She couldn't think about what to do or what to say. She was taken to a small room where a female guard was waiting to search her.

"Don't worry, everything will be all right. This doesn't mean you're guilty. This simply means that you are a suspect, and until the jury finds you guilty, you're innocent. So don't lose hope. This may not be permanent. Do you have a lawyer?" the guard asked.

"No, no I don't," Carlita said solemnly.

"Don't worry, they'll get you one. Come with me. Do you need to contact anybody?"

"Yes, but he's in the hospital, somewhere in Palmdale, I

think. I forgot the name." Her voice quivered as she desperately tried to hold back the tears.

"I'll find out." The guard walked her through a set of locked doors and into an area of holding cells. Carlita's heart sank as she finally saw the reality of her nightmare.

"Oh my God, it's like being in a cage," she cried.

"Try to relax. Hopefully, this will all be over soon," the guard said as she opened the door to the cell and ushered Carlita inside. She closed the door behind her, walked back down the hall, and through the doors.

Carlita could hear the doors opening and closing behind her. She looked around at the horrible place, sat on the cot, and cried.

CHAPTER 12

Dray walked out of the saloon and felt the warmth of the sun on his face. He couldn't see, but he knew he was outside. He felt his face and where his eyes once were are empty sockets. He yelled for mercy and fell to the ground.

"You must come to me, Dray," a soft, loving voice spoke from the wind.

Dray could not see her, but he knew she was there, standing next to him.

"You must come to me if you want to be saved." Soft hands touched his face and caressed his brow.

He reached up, took her hands, and stood up. "Where do I have to go?" he asked.

"You must come to me. You must bring them to the place in your dreams or he will take your souls. Bring them. God doesn't want to lose you. He has you now. He has all of you. Come to me. Come to Redemption," she said.

"I'm afraid. I can't see," he said as he touched her face to see who she was. His heart calmed from the sweet smell of roses and lilacs. He smiled and felt a peace that he hadn't had in months. She placed her hand on his eyes.

"God loves you. Don't leave him," she said as she removed her hand and he opened his eyes.

He looked into her dark brown eyes and smiled. She was beautiful, just as he expected. Her brown, curly hair blew in the wind and her soft, white skin glowed in the sunlight. He reached out to touch her and she disappeared into the wind, leaving only the whispering of the words, "Come to me."

Dray felt the warmth of the sun on his face. He thought he was in the desert, but when he opened his eyes, he saw sunlight shining through a window.

I'm in bed. How did I get here? I feel a little better.

He turned over to see Josh sitting in a chair next to the bed sound asleep. He stared at Iria's pretty face and small body. He wondered what it could have been like if they had met as their real selves. The door opened and the nurse walked in.

"Hello, Mr. Tanner. How are you this morning?" she asked.

"I'm fine."

She walked over to him and checked the machines. She checked the intravenous tube and read his chart.

"Things look better now. For a moment we thought we were going to lose you. If you had been a day later getting in here, we may not be having this conversation," she said.

"How long have I been here?" "Three days. The young lady arrived two days ago. It seems that she caught a ride up here from LA She said that she had nowhere to go, so she's been staying here. She seems to really care about you. Is she your daughter?"

Dray stumbled with the answer, uncertain about what to say. He realized that yes was the safest answer that would provoke the least amount of questions. "Yes . . . yes, my daughter."

"She's very pretty. What is her name?"

"Iria."

"She's pretty. She's very quiet, barely says a word. She seems to be on some sort of medication that makes her sleep. I hope she'll be all right."

"She's been under a lot of stress lately. I'm sure she'll be fine," Dray said.

"She may want to go home and get some food and sleep in a bed now that you're going to be OK," the nurse said as she walked toward the door. "I'll get the doctor to look in on you. He'll be glad to hear that you finally woke up."

"Josh . . . Josh, wake up," Dray said after the nurse had left. Josh began to stir around. He opened his eyes and smiled to see Dray awake and talking. "Josh, what's going on? Where's Carlita?"

"Man, they got her locked up. It looks bad. They think she killed Carlita," Josh said. "And they think we're helping her. They told me not to leave town, and I guess someone will be here to talk to you now that you're awake. I've been interrogated by the best of them. They want me to say I know something about Carlita's death and that I was helping Silvia, but they couldn't pin anything on me, so I have to stay in town for further questioning. I don't know how we're going to explain ourselves out of this."

"How are you holding up?" Dray asked.

"I'll admit, it's hard," said Josh

"We'll never get out of this if you lose it. We have to do this together. We need for you to be stronger than you ever have."

"No matter how bad I want it, I promise I'll stay clean. I was in a rehab clinic before you found me in the desert. I've been doing really well, but you know how it is; once you have this monkey on your back, it's hard to shake. I don't want to need it, I just do. I guess I needed more treatment, or Iria did."

"Maybe you should have stayed," Dray said.

"I wanted to, but I couldn't. I had to get to the desert just like you, so I left. I thought I was over it, but I guess I still get the shakes every now and then. It's going to take time, man. Time, that's all."

"Time is a luxury we don't have, and somehow, we have to put your issues on the back burner and focus on Carlita. She should be the most important thing right now. She has to be what we focus on now," Dray said.

He looked at Josh sadly. He realized that Josh was in over his head and would have a hard time controlling this. He wanted to be sympathetic, but he knew he had to be firm with Josh or he'd lose him.

"Look, I'll admit I don't know much about drug addiction. I've got other issues, but please, man, try as hard as you can to stay clean. It's the only way we're going to make it."

"I know man, I know. It'll be all right. Maybe having something else to focus on beside myself will help. All I needed was a reason to try, and now I have one."

"You really got to mean it, Josh. Our friend is in trouble, and you need to be here one hundred percent."

"Yeah, that's what I mean. I know Iria didn't have control, but I will. I promise." Josh took a deep breath and prayed to God for strength.

"We've got to figure out a way to get her out of there. We have to make it to the desert. I know now that's the place where we can be safe. I don't know how I know, but I feel that we have to get there or this will never change," Dray said. "Something evil is trying to take control of us, and we have to fight it. We have to get to the desert or else nothing will change. We'll lose our souls."

"What? Our souls? What are you talking about, man?"

"I don't know for sure, but I had a dream and a woman came to me."

"Man, this ain't the time to be dreaming about a woman."

"No . . . no, the woman was like an angel. I mean, she was different. She told me that we had to get to the desert, to Redemption. It was a message. We have to go, and we have to go together, I believe it's our only chance," said Dray

"I don't know if I want to change back," Josh said. Dray looked at him with uncertainty.

"What do you mean?"

"I'm not sure I like the old me anymore."

"Yeah, I kinda know what you mean. Either way, we've got to save Carlita."

Carlita sat in a small room waiting for the court appointed lawyer to come in. She was staying at the courthouse until the arraignment. She was so broken from the interrogation that she could hardly think. She tried to tell them who she really was, but they wouldn't listen. Now they thought she was trying to play crazy to get off with an insanity plea. She couldn't stop crying. She felt hopeless, and she really didn't want to talk about it anymore.

"Hello, Silvia," the attorney said. "My name is James Logan. I will be your attorney. May I?" He pointed to the chair across the table. He walked over and sat across from her.

She barely acknowledged him.

"Silvia, I have read your testimony several times, and I don't know how to feel about it. I mean, it is a wild story. People don't just jump into other people's bodies. But you seem to know a lot about Carlita, which seems very suspicious. What was your relationship with the deceased?"

"She is not deceased."

"The police pulled her body from the lake. Her fingerprints match those of Carlita Espinoza. They found her purse with her identification card in it with a picture that looks just like the deceased. It's hard to believe that Carlita is not the young lady that was found dead. Where do you think she is?"

"I am not going to keep telling this story. I am Carlita. My mother is Juanita, and I live in East LA. I know who I am."

"Have you looked at yourself? You are not Hispanic."

"I don't look like me because I am in Silvia's body. I don't know why; I just am."

"When the detective found you in the desert you were with Madison Tanner, who is one of the best corporate lawyers in the state, and Iria Tinsdale, a well-to-do young lady who ended up on the streets with a bad drug problem. How do you know these people? Were you and Iria working together and you kidnapped Mr. Tanner for money? You have to admit, the three of you are an unlikely combination for good friends. What's going on here?"

"They are my friends. They are in trouble too."

"In trouble how?"

"Dray is Madison Tanner, and Josh is Iria Tinsdale."

"Who is Dray and who is Josh?"

"Dray killed Madison Tanner's son, and Josh was the one who got Iria hooked on drugs, so they ended up in their bodies. I took Silvia's money, so I ended up in her body. We all did bad things and now we are paying for it."

"Madison Tanner's son, you mean Daniel Tanner? This guy named Dray killed Daniel Tanner?"

"Yes."

"So, let me get this straight. Dray is Madison because he killed Daniel, Josh is Iria because he strung her out, and you are Silvia because you took her money? Do you hear how impossible this sounds? Do you think a jury will believe this story? Would you believe it?"

"I don't care. It's true," she said as she wiped the tears from her face and hung her head in despair.

"We are going into the arraignment next Wednesday. I hope you can come up with something better than that before then. I will be back tomorrow to see what we can do to keep you out of jail."

The attorney got up and walked out. He walked down the hall and out the front door. He saw Detective Hauser standing at the bottom of the steps talking to someone. He walked up to him.

"Detective," the lawyer greeted.

Detective Hauser turned to acknowledge him. "Do I know you?"

"No . . . I'm the court appointed attorney for Silvia Watkins. I just left her. I know I should not be speaking to you about this, but did you ever find Daniel Tanner's killer?"

"No. We figure it was a drive by. Why?" Detective Hauser asked cautiously. He didn't want to reveal any information to a stranger.

"Just wondered. Thank you," he said as he walked away, leaving Detective Hauser confused and wondering if Silvia could have been involved with the death of Daniel Tanner too.

Detective Hauser was more confused than ever. He went back to his office and took another look at the pictures of Daniel Tanner and Carlita Espinoza. He tried to make some kind of connection between the two of them and Silvia.

"Carlita steals Silvia's purse. Silvia has money in it. She

finds Carlita and kills her for it. She kidnaps Madison Tanner for money and kills Daniel in the process. I'm thinking about her as if she was six feet tall, weighing 210 pounds. She's not Conan the Barbarian. She's five feet, three inches tall and weighs all of 110 pounds. There's no way she overpowered both Madison and Daniel. What is the connection? I have to figure this out. And David, why is David coming to me? Why was it so important that I find them? God, I'm so tired. I know David was coming to me for a reason, but what is it? Finding them changed nothing. Does he want justice? Does he want to see Silvia pay for the crime? But she's his mother. Why would he want his mother to go to jail? But he said that she isn't his mother. 'She's not my mother' . . . he said. God, please."

Detective Hauser rubbed his hands over his face in great frustration and sat in the chair, staring out the window until dark, wondering what to do next. As night fell, he decided to go home. He walked to his car and took the thirty-minute drive to his apartment. He went inside, turned on the television, fixed a drink, and tried to relax. He looked in the refrigerator for something to eat and found some leftover Chinese food and warmed it in the microwave. He couldn't get Silvia off his mind as he tried to focus on the news. He heard what was being said, but he was not really listening. When the food was all gone, he walked into the bathroom to shower. Steam filled the room. *The heat feels good.*

He undressed, put his robe on, and began to brush his teeth when the image of David appeared in the mirror. He turned quickly and saw nothing behind him. He was not frightened. He knew David had been trying to help. He was startled, but he wanted him to come back to find out what to do next. He finished brushing, stepped into the shower, and let the warm water run down his body. He closed his eyes and began to meditate for a moment and the image of Mary came to mind. He remembered her touch and her laughter, the smell of the roses she always had in the house, and the lilac perfume she wore. He fought back the tears, finished his shower, walked back into the living room, and made another drink. He carried the glass into the bedroom and placed it on the nightstand, got a book from the dresser, and got in bed. He took a drink from the glass when he heard the voice from the other side of the room.

"You have to let her go."

"David, please David, tell me what to do."

"You have to let her go."

"Who, let who go?" he asked.

David walked closer to the bed. "You have to let her go. If you keep her she will never reach Redemption. He will have her soul. She will die. You have to let her go."

"Are you talking about Silvia?"

"Yes, Carlita," David said.

"Carlita is dead."

"Carlita lives within. You have to let her go. She told me you would help them."

"My God, what do you want me to do? Who is she? Who said that I would help them? Please, David, stop talking in riddles and tell me what to do! What is going on?"

"Carlita, Josh, and Dray must make it to Redemption. You must help them."

"I'm not sure who Josh and Dray are. I hear their names, but I can't figure out who they really are. Who the hell are they? I can't do this anymore. I'll be as crazy as Silvia, thinking I'm somebody else. I've got to take myself off this case. This is too hard." He rubbed his eyes for a moment and when he looked up, David was gone. He was not surprised. David came and went suddenly. *You look up and he's gone.* He lay down, hoping to sleep, but knowing that the night would be long and troublesome.

When morning came, Detective Hauser decided to have a talk with Silvia. He entered the courthouse early and asked to see her. The guard called her down to the meeting room. She walked into the small room where Detective Hauser sat, looking exhausted and hopeless. It was obvious she was crying all night and that she was very frightened by what was happening to her. She sat in the chair across from him and said nothing.

"Silvia, how are you? Are they treating you all right?" he asked.

"Yes," she said solemnly.

He squirmed around in his chair for a moment, feeling pretty uncomfortable about what he was about to say. "Do you remember that I told you that David has been coming to me?"

"Yes, but you never said why. David is dead. I killed him. I got him mixed up in my mess and I killed him. Why would he be coming to you?" she asked as her eyes swelled with tears.

He reached into his pocket and handed her a handkerchief. "I don't know. He seems to think that I can help you and your friends. Do you know why?"

"What did he say?"

"He said that Carlita lives within. He often says 'she is not my mother,' and that I had to get you to Redemption. Do you know what he is talking about?"

"Yes . . . he's right. I am Carlita; I just can't get anybody to believe me. I can't tell it anymore. We all did bad things, and to pay for it, we were put in the bodies of the people we hurt. I know that makes no sense."

"Right now I'll believe anything," he said. "Explain to me again who Josh and Dray are."

"Josh got Iria strung out. He's a drug dealer. And Dray killed Daniel Tanner," she said.

"Daniel Tanner, so David was right. Josh and Dray are connected to you through this need to reach Redemption. David also mentioned Josh and Dray. He knows who they are. Who is the woman who told him that I would help you?"

"I don't know of any woman. I don't know who that could be."

"David keeps speaking her, but he never says who she is."

"I don't know about any woman," she said. "Do you believe me?" she asked as she looked into his eyes.

"I have to. It's too close to what David said. There are some supernatural things going on here, and I'm in it somehow. I have to get all of you to Redemption. Where is that?"

"I don't know. All we know is that it is in the desert somewhere."

"How do you know that?"

"We all have theses dreams about the same place in the desert, and somehow we all know that we have to get there. But now I'm locked up. I don't have a chance of getting there. I don't know what to do."

"I have to go. There's someone else I need to talk to. I'll be back tomorrow hopefully with a plan." He got up and called for the guard.

The door opened and Carlita's first ray of hope walked out the door.

Detective Hauser left the courthouse and traveled to the hospital where Dray was recovering. He walked inside and asked the clerk for Madison Tanner's room number.

"He's in room 412," the clerk said. "The elevators are down the hall."

Detective Hauser walked down the hall and hit the elevator button. He stepped inside as the door opened and took the short ride to the fourth floor. As he reached the nurses station, the head nurse stopped him.

"Sir, visiting hours begin at two o'clock."

He pulled his badge from his pocket and flashed it.

She stepped back with concern that she may have an unsavory character on her floor. "What room are you looking for?" she asked.

"Room 412," he said. She pointed down the hall and stepped back out of his path.

"Thank you," he said. He walked down the hall to room 412. The door was ajar and he stood outside listening for a moment. He could hear voices talking.

He walked inside to find Madison Tanner and Iria Tinsdale planning Silvia's escape.

"It won't work," Detective Hauser said as he walked in.

"What do you want?" Dray asked sternly.

"I want to talk to you. I spoke with Silvia a few minutes ago, and she told me the story of a lifetime. She said that you are Darrell Hunter, the man who killed Daniel Tanner, and that this woman is really Josh Brimeyer, who sells drugs to innocent people, one of whom was Iria Tinsdale. She said that you were switched up because of the bad things you all did, and now you need to get to a place in the desert to fix this. Is this crazy talk or what?"

"It's crazy talk," Josh said as he walked to the window and looked outside, ignoring any further conversation on the matter.

"David has been coming to me and telling me that I have to help you," Detective Hauser said.

"David who?" Dray asked.

"Silvia's child. You know, the boy who was killed."

"Don't believe him, Dray," Josh said.

"Dray? Why did you call him Dray? This is Madison Tanner, isn't it?" Detective Hauser asked.

"I was confused because of what you said. I . . ."

"It's OK, Josh, I think he knows what's happening. So Detective, let's talk. What do you want to know?" Dray asked.

"I want to know everything," Detective Hauser said as he took a chair from against the wall and pulled it next to the bed. He sat and patiently listened to the most spellbinding story he had ever heard.

As Dray began to talk, he told the detective everything that happened to him, from the time he fired the gun until now. Josh jumped in with his story, about the beating he took from Diamond and the Porsche he saw that haunted his memory. Dray talked about Carlita, and how she became Silvia, and that all of their bodies were dead. Josh told how he saw his body in the coffin during the funeral, and Dray told how he found out that a member of a rival gang killed him. He said that Carlita's body was found in the lake after she became Silvia. He said that Silvia did not kill Carlita. She never met her. Carlita stole Silvia's purse with her rent money in it and was switched into her body to endure her grief.

"Tell me about Redemption. What is that, or rather where is it?" Detective Hauser asked.

"Redemption is where we have to get to, to save ourselves," Dray said. "We don't know where it is. We only know that it is in the desert somewhere. That's where we were going when you found us."

"What happened? How did you hurt your head?"

"Something happened out in the desert that is hard to explain. I lost control of the car and had an accident."

"How . . . what happened?" asked Detective Hauser

"I was driving. It was so dark I couldn't see but a few yards ahead of me. I saw the headlights of a truck in the distance and then suddenly, it was gone. The next thing I knew, the truck was coming straight toward us. The grill of the truck turned into some kind of demonic creature that scared me to death. I thought sure we would be killed. I swerved off the road and over the embankment."

"What do you think you saw?" Detective Hauser asked.

"I don't know, it sounds crazy, but we thought it was the devil," said Dray.

"The devil." Detective Hauser looked at Josh and waited for his response.

"I didn't see it, but Carlita did," said Josh.

Detective Hauser thought about it for a moment and tried to stay focused.

"Why the devil?" Detective Hauser asked.

"We think it is trying to stop us. Trying to keep us from getting to Redemption," said Josh.

"He will have their souls," said Detective Hauser. "That's what David said, 'he will have their souls.' Oh God, I hope we are not up against anything like that."

"We . . . are you going to help?" asked Josh.

Detective Hauser decided not to respond to that right now. He didn't know the answer himself yet. "If you don't get to Redemption, you will lose your souls. What does that mean?" Detective Hauser asked.

Dray and Josh look at each other, uncertain about what to say to that.

"I think we have a limited amount of time in these bodies before they go back to the people who own them. If we don't make it to Redemption soon and we lose these bodies, the devil will take our souls, I guess. I know that sounds ridiculous, but it's the only way I can explain it because our bodies are gone. So maybe God is giving us a chance to redeem ourselves, but we have to get to the place in the desert to do it, and there's something evil out there that's been trying to stop us," Josh said.

"The devil?" Detective Hauser asked.

"Well . . . something evil," said Josh.

"It's just twelve o'clock and I already need a drink," Detective Hauser said. "I've never heard such fiction before, but even worse, I'm starting to believe it. There is nothing real about any of this that I can grab hold of as fact or truth, but it's obvious that something strange is going on with the three of you. I've worked many cases, but I have never seen anything as bizarre as this. I'm fighting myself every minute not to fall into the insanity of it, but I can't seem to step out of it. For some reason, David is pulling on me to do something, but for the life of me I don't know what."

"He wants you to free Carlita," Josh said.

"How can I do that? I can't just ask for her release. On what grounds? She needs to save her soul? I don't think so."

"That's why we have to come up with a plan," Dray said. "We have to save her."

"Can't the two of you go to Redemption and Carlita go later?"

"No, I know that we have to go together. For some reason we have been brought together to make sure that each of us gets there. It won't work if one of us is missing."

"What if one of you gets hurt or retained, like Carlita, and just can't make it. What happens?" asked Detective Hauser.

"We have to make sure that doesn't happen. The lady in my dream will protect us from any harm. That's why I feel that we can get Carlita out and make it to Redemption," said Dray.

"What lady?" asked Detective Hauser.

"The angel who told me I had to come to her and I had to bring them with me. She said that we had to go to Redemption to save our souls."

"An angel. I have lost my mind," Detective Hauser shook his head in disbelief and knew that his next words were going to change the direction of his life forever. His retirement, his pension, his sanity would all be lost. "OK, let's get started," he reluctantly agreed.

CHAPTER 13

Detective Hauser walked into the jailhouse early the next morning. He asked to speak to Silvia Watkins and was ushered into the waiting room. He spent most of the previous day with Josh and Dray, and now he wanted to look into Silvia's eyes, hoping that he would get a glimpse of Carlita.

Silvia walked into the room, looking tired and disheartened. Her brown complexion looked pale and lifeless.

"Did you sleep well?" he asked.

"No, I stayed up all night fighting hope. After talking to you yesterday, I felt a ray of hope, and I'm afraid to latch onto it."

"Don't be afraid," he said. "Never give up. That's what he wants you to do."

"He . . . you said he. You believe me," she said as she began to feel the burden lift a little. "God, I didn't think anyone would. But what can we do? How can I get out of here?"

"Don't worry, Redemption is possible," he said with an interesting grin on his face.

She looked at him with a little concern and tried to figure out what he was talking about. She thought about it for a moment and looked back at him. She smiled as she realized what was meant by redemption. *It's the place,* she thought. *The place we have to get to.*

"I am ready to go to Redemption. I am ready to repent," she said.

The detective provided her with a clue, and he smiled a little when he realized she understood. He stood up, touched her shoulder, and walked to the door. He called for the guard and looked back at her just before stepping out of the door. He walked down the long corridor, through the lobby to the front door, and looked outside. For the first time since Mary's death, he felt alive. He had purpose and a sense of urgency that invigorated him. He was on a mission. Somehow he felt that his own soul was in jeopardy, and whatever was going on may just lift him up from the bowels of depression that he'd been in for five long years. He scurried down the steps with a determination he hadn't known for a long time.

"We've got to make this work," he whispered. "We've got to. I just wish I knew why."

Dray wrote Madison Tanner's name on the release papers as he signed himself out of the hospital. He grabbed his things, walked down the hall to the elevators, and down to the lobby where Josh was waiting for him.

"Are we ready?" Dray asked.

"Yes, Detective Hauser left me a car," Josh said.

"I think we should stay at Madison's house and work on this. We can hole up there until Carlita is moved," Dray said as they walked to the parking lot.

The ride to San Pedro was long and the traffic was horrific.

"I hate Los Angeles traffic," Dray said.

"Yeah, I would say it's gotten worse, but I've never
known it to be good," Josh said.

Eventually, Josh pulled into the Tanners' driveway in one
of the city's elite neighborhoods. "So, Madison wasn't doing
too bad for himself, this is nice," Josh commented.

"Yeah, I guess," Dray said. He really didn't care. All he
wanted was to go home to his small, humble room and his
mother.

They walked inside, and Dray looked around to see if
Barbara might have been there. He walked into the kitchen,
but she was not there and it didn't look like anyone had
been there for a while.

She must still be in the hospital.

He walked back into the foyer.

"Why don't you settle down in the library for a moment?
I'll be right back," Dray said as he pointed Josh in the right
direction.

He walked upstairs and entered the empty bedroom, and
it felt strange. He looked around and could feel Barbara's
presence in the room. He remembered the horrible days of
watching her grieve over Danny, and he could barely contain himself. He wanted to run, but he knew he couldn't.

He found some clothes and changed and walked back
downstairs. He walked into the library and over to the
liquor cabinet. "Would you like a drink?" he asked Josh.

"Definitely," Josh said. "But first, are there clothes in this
place I can wear? I'd like to shower and clean up a little."

"Sure." Dray put the drink down and walked back upstairs. Josh followed him. "This will be your room. There's
a bathroom inside."

Josh walked into the massive room and was in awe of the

splendor of the room. "I had a room like this once. It seems long ago. Now I live like a pauper on the streets. What I wouldn't give to have my life back. Man, why would you want to leave this? I think I'd say goodbye to Dray forever if I could have this life. Hell, I ended up as a drug addict. You got a rich, man, and you want to leave and go back to being a gang-banger? What the hell's wrong with you?" "I can't stay. Every time I think of it, I become deathly ill. For some reason I can't stay as Madison, but I can't leave him either. So this must not be forever. One way or the other, I will be back to myself. The question is, will I be alive when it happens?" "Well, at least I know you thought about it. I sure would have. I guess that hasn't happened to me, because I'm not trying to stay in this body, no way," Josh said as he walked into the bathroom and turned the water on, undressed, and stepped into the shower.

Dray searched Barbara's clothes to find something that was small enough for Josh to wear. Iria's little body was almost half the size of Barbara's. Dray found some old clothes in the back of the closet that Barbara probably hadn't worn in ten years. He walked out of the closet just as Josh walked out of the bathroom completely naked. Dray stared at Iria's beautiful body and felt himself lusting for her. He tried to control himself. He looked down at the floor as he placed the slacks and blouse on the bed. He turned and walked out of the room just as Josh realized what happened. He looked down at Iria's body and felt the embarrassment of a woman who was unintentionally caught naked.

"Oh my God, I keep forgetting I'm a woman." He remembered the look on Dray's face and burst into laughter. He fell on the bed laughing, knowing that he got Dray aroused and he would get nothing.

Dray heard him laughing from downstairs.

"It's not funny, man. Get dressed and bring your ass down here," he yelled.

Josh got dressed and walked downstairs. He found Dray in the library finishing the drink he started earlier. "Hey, man, I'm sorry about that. I'll have to be more careful."

"No problem. I'll just take lots of showers, exercise a lot of control, and get drunk and drunker," Dray said as he took a big swallow and prepared to pour himself another drink. He searched the caller ID directory for Roman Cantell's number, hoping he would know where Barbara was. He found it and hit the memory dial.

"Hello," the voice from the other end said.

"Roman, it's me, Madison."

"Man, where the hell have you been? Are you crazy to just drop out of sight like that? Man, this is crazy. I thought I saw you on the news hooked up with some black woman who killed somebody. What is going on, Madison? Your position at the firm is gone. We waited for as long as we could, but we needed someone to step in and take on your workload. Man, this is crazy. Where are you?"

"I can't go into all of that now. Where is Barbara?"

"Barbara, you don't know? You mean you lost touch with your own wife too? Are you insane?"

"Yes, I suppose I am. Now, where is Barbara?"

"She was committed to the mental hospital. She tried to commit suicide again, and they decided to keep her. When they couldn't find you, they contacted her mother and she came to sign the papers. Something had to be done. When she went home and you were gone, she lost it. She thought she had lost you and Daniel, and she couldn't take it. She slit her wrists again and your neighbors found her lying in the backyard, almost dead."

"Have you seen her?"

"Yes, which is more than I can say for you. I don't believe you abandoned her this way."

"How is she?"

"How do you think? She is walking around barely aware of what's going on around her. That's how she's doing. She's not really *doing* at all."

"You have every right to be angry. But please try to understand that I didn't ask for this to happen to me, and I have to fix some things before I can get my life back."

"Fix some things? What things? Get your life back? Man, what kind of trouble are you in?"

"I can't explain it, Roman, just trust me. I mean Barbara no harm. Please look in on her for me, and I'll call you as soon as I can."

"What do you mean as soon as you can? You can't just drop out of sight again. We need to talk. We . . ."

"Goodbye, Roman," Dray said, and then he hung up the phone.

Dray couldn't bear the thought of the mess he made of this man's life. He fought back the tears and poured himself another drink.

"I've lost his job, his wife, his son, and soon this house will be gone. I can't let this happen. I need to fix this, and I'm going to."

Dray's determination and resolve to make things right was evident. He felt the guilt and shame that he should have felt for even thinking about killing another person, the shame he should have felt for putting his mother through so much drama and turmoil. He knew now what she was trying to tell him about being a man and being respected. He couldn't see it then, but now it was all very clear.

"It's being responsible for myself and for those who matter to me. I am responsible for the good and the bad things that I cause. I am responsible for making my life work, and there is no one to blame but me if it falls apart. I didn't try hard enough, didn't want it bad enough. I am a man . . . I am a man . . . a man," Dray whispered.

"Come on, man. It'll be all right. We're about to fix all of this," Josh said as he walked over to him and put his hand on Dray's shoulder.

Dray saw Iria and wanted to hold her. He wanted to feel the body of a woman in his arms and smell her scent. He looked at Josh and stared into Iria's eyes.

"Josh, man, you better get the fuck away from me before you become the second Mrs. Tanner and be loving it, you know what I mean?"

"Yo, man, it ain't even like that." Josh threw up both hands and backed away. "OK, man, no more touching." He laughed as he stepped back to the sofa. He sat down and took a drink.

"It ain't funny, man. It's been a long time; you know what I mean? So don't fuck with me, man. I mean it," Dray said.

"Don't worry, man, I had one experience, and I don't want to have another," Josh said.

"You mean what happened in the desert, the day I found you?"

Josh did not want to talk about the night Diamond raped him and left him for dead in the desert. He held back from saying any more, but deep down inside he wanted to talk about it. He wanted to express how it made him feel. *Yes, I was raped. I was raped and I never had a chance to deal with it.* He swallowed and turned away. He walked to the window and looked outside.

"You never did say who did that to you."

"Iria's pimp, a man called Diamond, dragged me into the desert, raped me, and left me there. I crawled to the street where you found me. He beat me unmercifully and the pain and humiliation of it was more horrible than anything I could imagine. I always thought those women who yelled rape over-exaggerated the impact it had on their lives. I mean, they have sex all the time, so what's the difference? It would be like having sex with a stranger, which is something most of us do. But I was wrong. It is a horrible thing to experience. I don't think you ever fully recover, because you feel so violated and shameful. I'm sure every woman who has been through it asks herself what she did to deserve it."

"This guy, Diamond, sounds like an animal. You have no guilt to bear."

"I have guilt about what I did to Iria. He was really raping *her*. As much as I try to distance myself from her problems, I can't. Maybe I did cause them, or helped to cause them. I don't know. I just have a hard time bearing all the responsibility for it. But the folks at the rehab center said it was a joint effort to screw up someone's life, and that a lot of people are involved. I realize I had an impact on her life that could have led to her addiction, and not just for her, but for many others. Iria became my girl, and I blew her off when she became an embarrassment to me. I didn't help her. I threw her out. I'm the reason she was on the street. Just like you, I hope I can fix this." Josh stared out the window and wondered if he would ever get a chance to say I'm sorry.

"Let's get some sleep. We have a busy day tomorrow. We both got lots of business to take care of."

They walked upstairs and closed their doors, both hoping to get a good night's sleep.

Detective Hauser entered the courtroom and looked to his left to see Dray and Josh sitting in the back. He walked toward the front and sat near the defense's table. There were only six or seven people in the courtroom.

Juanita Espinoza was sitting in the front row, hoping to see the woman who was accused of killing her child again, the same woman who stayed in her home, the woman who opened up her heart to Juanita, and the woman who Juanita trusted. She didn't know how to feel about it. A part of her believed that Carlita could be one with this woman through some miraculous means, but it seemed so mythical that she dismissed the possibility. She watched as a guard entered the room from a side door, escorting Carlita in. Carlita took a seat beside her lawyer and looked back to see her mother sitting behind her.

"Mama," she whispered as she stared into Juanita's eyes. Juanita looked back at her, hoping to see some sign of her daughter in the woman who sat before her.

The room filled up with friends, family, and the curious to see what the judge's ruling would be.

"All rise," the bailiff said as Judge Robert Walton entered the courtroom.

The judge was a handsome man with graying hair. His tall frame towered over everyone, even when he was sitting. His manner was calm and assured. He read through some papers on his desk and asked to hear from the prosecution first.

Ms. Katlynne Simmone stood and established herself as the lead prosecutor on the case. She looked back at her associates, Dennis Matlin and Corey Flintock. She walked toward the judge and began to speak. She talked for about twenty minutes about the facts of the case. She pointed out that it was Silvia Watkins's purse that was found near the victim, and how Silvia fled from the police for weeks in an attempt to escape prosecution. She explained that Silvia had a motive when she was thrown out of her apartment because she couldn't pay the rent, and she went after Carlita because she knew Carlita had stolen the money.

"She didn't go looking for her to say hello, or to introduce herself as the woman from whom Carlita stole. Instead, she went there to make her pay for what she had done. Now she is pretending to be the very woman she murdered. Classic case for any first year psych student. This woman knows who she is. She knows what she did, and she should pay for it. It isn't rocket science," Katlynne said. "Your Honor, Carlita had no enemies. She created no long list of people who wanted to kill her. However, someone decided to take her life. The only person with a motive to kill Carlita is sitting across from you," she said as she pointed to Silvia and walked back to her seat. "I hope we do not let this game she is playing affect your decision to proceed."

Katlynne sat down and looked over at James Logan, Carlita's attorney. He slowly stood up while tapping a pencil on the table. He walked toward the judge.

"Your Honor, we have no idea what happened, and we won't know until we are able to break through the gridlock that has Ms. Watkins in such mental confusion. Ms. Watkins has no recollection of ever meeting Carlita Espinoza, nor does she know who stole her money. She was on the bus and she fell asleep, and when she awoke, her purse was gone. There were many people transiting on and off the bus, and because she was asleep, she couldn't have seen this young lady. How would she have known to search for Carlita if she had no idea what she looked like? She didn't know where Carlita lived or what happened after she stepped off the bus, because Silvia didn't see her."

"What do you mean by her mental confusion?" the judge asked.

"For some reason, Ms. Watkins believes she is Carlita Espinoza. She believes that Carlita's body has been switched into hers so she can pay penance for her actions."

"What actions?" the judge asked.

"The action of stealing Ms. Watkins's purse," James Logan said.

"Are you saying that the woman before me admits to stealing her own purse?" Judge Walton asked. "Approach the bench, please." Katlynne and James walked forward.

"What are you saying, James? What do you believe is the problem with her state of mind? Can she stand trial?" the judge asked.

"I don't know. I think we should have her observed for a few weeks to see what the professionals think of this. It's too weird for me," he said.

"Your Honor, please, I beg you not to fall for this hoax. This woman is running a scam, and she is going to play this role so she can get an insanity verdict out of this," Katlynne said.

"Maybe you're right, but what harm can it do to find out?" James asked.

"Lots of harm. With this charade, she will have any number of psychologists believing her story and coming in here with some split personality disorder, or some other foolishness that will confuse a jury and add a whole lot of additional weight to a case that is pretty cut and dry."

"I don't think this is so cut and dry," Judge Walton said. "We really don't know if she saw the young lady or not. If she really was asleep, then she can't know who took the purse or where to begin to search. So why the charade? If we can believe the sleep story, why pretend to be someone else, especially the victim? I don't know, Katlynne, I tend to lean toward giving her the benefit of the doubt. She does not have a history of any wrongdoing, so why start now?

Her history does not lean toward a woman who would get angry enough to kill someone over money. It makes no sense. Besides, who would steal a purse from someone while they are looking at you? It is very likely that she did not see the young lady when the purse was stolen," Judge Walton said as he sat back in his chair. Katlynne and James returned to their seats and awaited the judge's recommendation.

"I will not rule on this today. I recommend that Ms. Watkins be remanded to the state hospital for observation to ensure that she is capable to stand trial. I'll set a date to reconvene . . ." He thumbed through his calendar and found an open date. "Let's reconvene on October first. That's three weeks from today. I expect to see a report on my desk in two weeks." He hit the gavel and stood to walk out.

"All rise," the bailiff bellowed as the judge walked out of the courtroom.

James Logan turned to Carlita and smiled. "Well, this is the first step to saving your life," he said.

"You can't save my life. No one can." She stood up and walked toward the door.

A voice came from the crowd. "Silvia."

Carlita looked behind her and tried to recognize the person who called out Silvia's name. "Do I know you?" she asked.

"Sil, you don't know me?"

"No, I'm sorry I don't." She turned and walked toward the door as a guard held onto her arm. Carlita disappeared behind closed doors.

The woman stood in the middle of the courtroom, dumbfounded at the response she got. She didn't know what to do. As she turned to walk out, she noticed the older, grumpy man staring at her.

"Do you know Silvia?" Detective Hauser asked.

"Yes, who are you?" the lady asked in a soft, lonesome tone.

"I am Detective Patrick Hauser."

The woman looked a lot like Silvia. She was tall and slender and quite pretty. Her dark eyes were sad and a bit red from crying. She wore a short haircut and appeared to be quite conservative and soft-spoken. Her voice quivered when she spoke as she tried to hold back tears. "You're the one who arrested her, so maybe you can tell me what the hell is going on with my sister," the woman said.

"Your sister? Silvia is your sister?" Dray asked as he moved closer to hear the conversation.

"Yes, and who are you?" she asked as she turned toward Dray and Josh. "I know my sister. She would never do anything like this. All of this is crazy. She would never kill anyone, and she wouldn't be crazy enough to think that she could be somebody else either. I don't know what's happening to her, but something is definitely wrong. She didn't even recognize me. I don't understand that. How could she not know me?" She hung her head and clutched her purse close to her chest as she wandered off in thought for a moment. Dray broke the silence.

"I'm Darrell Hunter, and this is Josh Brimeyer. We have a very strange story to tell you that involves your sister and Carlita Espinoza. It's going to be unbelievable, but it's true. Let's get a bite to eat and talk," Dray said.

They all walked out and down the street to a local diner, where they told Carolyn Watkins-Jones the heart-stopping story.

Dray found a hotel near Madison's home where Carolyn decided to stay. They knew that they would need to talk with her, so they wanted her nearby. After dropping Carolyn off, they stopped and picked up some Chinese food and arrived at Madison's house at six o'clock in the evening.

Carolyn was left alone wondering about the fantastic story she just heard. She walked into the bathroom and stared into the mirror and tried to control her fear. She started to cry at the thought of her sister being a part of this fantastic hoax that cost David his life. She couldn't believe it. She splashed some water on her face, hoping it would help to calm her, but all she thought about was how awful this whole thing was and how David lost his life to this fantasy. She couldn't believe that Silvia would be involved with people talking about body-switching and to involve David was just crazy to her.

She doesn't use drugs, or at least she didn't used to. "There's got to be more to it. There's gotta be."

She hung her head and cried. She walked back into the room and sat on the bed in a daze. She wasn't sure if she ever wanted to see those people again, but she *did* want to hear that strange story again. She thought that maybe she'd misunderstood or didn't hear it right. She stared out the window and began to wonder if they weren't all crazy. Tears rolled down her cheek as she thought about Carlita and what her poor mother must be going through.

Could she have done it? I have to ask. As crazy as it seems, it's obvious that something has happened to her. The Silvia I know would never be on a busy highway with David and let him get away from her. Oh God, David is gone. I can't believe it. My baby boy is gone. I can't allow myself to believe this nonsense. This is incredible, but what other explanation is there? What else can it be? She lay across the bed and cried herself to sleep.

"Do you think Carolyn will be all right?" Josh asked.

"I don't know. I don't think she believed us," Dray said.

"I know I wouldn't."

Dray took a deep breath. "I guess not." He picked at the Chinese food and tried to eat it, but couldn't.

Josh helped himself. His appetite was fine. Just as Dray prepared his third drink, the doorbell rang and his heart sank. "Lord, who can that be?" He slowly walked to the door and peered through the peephole. He saw Roman and stepped back from the door. He didn't want to talk to him. He couldn't tell him the truth, but to ignore him wasn't good either. He didn't want to completely ruin Madison's friendship with this man.

"I know you're in there, Madison," Roman yelled. Dray slowly opened the door. He looked into Roman's eyes, turned, and walked away. Roman followed him into the house. Dray walked toward the living room, but Roman could hear sounds from the library and decided to investigate. He took one look at Iria and formed his own conclusion. "So, this is what you've been up to Madison? Playing with little girls?"

"It's not like that, Roman," Dray said as he entered the library behind him. "Everything is not as it seems. You just have to trust me. I will fix everything, and it'll be just like before. I just need a little time."

"What the hell are you talking about, Madison? Fix what? Now look, you have a very sick wife and a job that's on the verge of being gone forever if you don't get your act together. I know you've been through a lot, but you are not the only person on the planet who has lost a child. You have to figure out how to recover from it and move on, and you've got to get Barbara back to being Barbara. You do remember Barbara, don't you?" he asked sarcastically as he glanced at the pretty young woman sitting on the sofa, not knowing that she was really as much of a man as either of them.

"Look, I know I've been acting strange, but I can't help it right now, and you just have to understand. That's all, Roman. You just have to understand. I can't explain it. Please."

Dray's pleas fell on deaf ears. Roman wanted to know what was going on, and if he couldn't get an explanation, then the conclusion was that Madison was having an affair, and that's all there was to it.

"Go away, Roman. I will call you as soon as I can. Please, just go." Dray turned away from him and stood over the fireplace.

Roman looked at him, hoping to get more, but realized the futility of it and angrily walked out. The door slammed behind him, and Dray's level of frustration turned into a loud scream as he threw the glass into the fireplace and walked out.

Josh sat on the sofa and stared at the floor, not knowing what to say or do.

Dray turned over and pulled the covers over his head to block out the light, and Josh, who slept on the sofa in the library, started the day with another drink. He didn't know how much longer he could handle the cravings. The liquor was helping a little, but it was only temporary. He told himself that he could overcome the urge to find the heroin, but deep inside he knew he would have to find the stuff soon or he wouldn't be able to make it.

I'll fight it, he thought. *I'll be strong. It'll be all right.* He took another drink and walked upstairs to clean up.

By nine o'clock, Carolyn was knocking on Madison's door. Dray was in the kitchen, attempting to make breakfast, when he heard the knock. He dreaded answering it.

It's either Roman or bad news about Barbara.. He slowly

walked to the door and opened it. He was pleased to see Carolyn on the other side.

She stepped in.

"Good morning," she said

"Good morning," said Dray. "I'm in the kitchen trying to cook breakfast.

She could see that Dray's feeble attempt was failing.

"Would you like some help?" she asked.

Dray looked around at the mess he'd made and quickly said yes.

She washed her hands and started cracking eggs into a bowl. She prepared the eggs and coffee, and Dray made the toast. Just as they were preparing to sit and eat, the doorbell rang.

"I hope it's not Roman," Dray said. He walked to the door and was glad to see that it was Detective Hauser. He opened the door and invited him in.

"We are just starting breakfast, would you like to join us?" Dray asked.

"No, thank you," he said as he entered the kitchen and said hello to everyone. "Well, maybe a cup of coffee."

Detective Hauser sat at the table with them and gave them the latest news about Carlita. "She is going to be moved tomorrow. They're taking her to Hillside Hospital, and she will stay there for ten days. She'll be under strict observation, and guards will be around her at all times. Getting her out of that place will be impossible."

"Maybe we can keep her from getting there," Josh said.

"What do you mean?" Dray asked.

"Wait, wait one minute. What are all of you talking about? You are not going to try to get her out. That will only make things worse. We have to let this play out in court and see what happens," Carolyn said.

"Let me tell you what will happen. She has two choices. One: ten years to life, or two: life in a mental institution. Neither of those are good options," Detective Hauser said.

"Besides, if we don't get her to Redemption, she will die soon," Josh said.

"The hell with all that nonsense. If you try to get her out, they will kill her and you," Carolyn said.

"We have to take that chance," Dray said.

"Not with my sister's life, you don't."

"She's not your sister. She's Carlita Espinoza, and she is on board with this. If we don't do it, your sister is gone for good anyway. This is the only way we know of that has a chance of getting both people back," Dray said.

"We have to try. I know you don't completely understand this, but for whatever reason, we have to get to this place in the desert. I am putting my career on the line and maybe even my life, but I know I have to do this. If you are not going to help us, please don't do anything to stop us. Promise me that you won't, because if you do, you will never see Silvia again," Detective Hauser said.

Carolyn looked at him with disbelief. "I really can't figure out why you are caught up in this. You arrested her and now you believe *this*?" she said.

"I know it's crazy. I didn't believe any of it at first, but I am sure of it now. There's something greater than all of us involved in this. David has been coming to me. He is urging me to help. Even more than that, he won't let me *not* help. I am compelled to get involved and I don't know why. Somehow I feel that it is the right thing to do. I know I have to try at all costs."

"Even if it means your life?" she asked.

"Yes."

"What if you're wrong and there's nothing going on, and these people are using you?" she asked.

"To what end?"

"Using you to keep themselves out of jail."

"I thought of that, but I can't account for David. Why is he coming to me? He convinced me that this was real and wants me to make sure it happens, at any cost. I don't know why, I just know that if I don't do it, I won't be able to live with myself," he said.

She looked at him and saw the determination in his eyes and his willingness to give his life for this.

"David is dead. You don't think that something could be wrong with you also? I mean, how many people do you know who see dead people on a regular basis? You may be just as crazy as they are. He isn't speaking to anyone anymore."

"I don't expect you to understand, but you have to admit that something is different about your sister. Something has changed," he said.

"Yes, it's called stress. She's under more stress than most of us can bear. She lost her child, and now she's suspected of killing someone she never met. I would lose it too, but it doesn't mean something supernatural is happening," Carolyn said.

"How do you explain Josh and Dray?" Detective Hauser asked.

"What do you mean?" she asked.

"They are also caught in someone else's bodies, but they aren't under that kind of stress. How do you explain them?"

"I don't know. I don't know that I believe they're caught in anyone's body other than their own," she replied.

"Why would we make this up?" Josh asked.

"I don't know, but I do know people don't just jump around between bodies, and I also know that dead children don't come back and talk to strangers."

"You're right, I doubt that this happens every day. Somehow I believe that this is happening to us for a reason that we cannot know right now, but we will know once we reach Redemption," Dray said.

"You don't even know where that is. How will you ever find it?" Carolyn asked.

"God will show us," Dray said.

"Now that really is crazy," she said.

"You have to trust us if you ever want to see your sister again," Detective Hauser said.

"I don't seem to have a choice. If I don't, my sister will go to jail for life."

"It will be all right. I know it," Dray said.

"I hope you're right," she said as she turned back to her food and moved it around on her plate in deep thought.

"What can we do to keep her from getting there? What did you have in mind, Josh?" Detective Hauser asked as he turned the conversation back to Josh's thought.

"Well . . . let's think of what we can do to get her out of that van before it gets to the hospital. Having you as an inside man may be very helpful," Josh said as he looked at Detective Hauser and smiled.

They sat around the table for most of the day, talking and brainstorming ideas until they came up with the perfect plan. After a few hours of working out the finer points, they felt comfortable that everyone knew their job.

"When will she be moved?" Dray asked.

"Tomorrow at two o'clock, which is good. It will give me some time to confirm the route and make any changes if we have to," Detective Hauser said.

With everything in place, Josh decided to take a walk. "I need some air," he said as he walked toward the door.

"Josh, why don't you take the car and pick up something for dinner tonight?" Dray said as he reached in his pocket and pulled out his wallet. He pulled out fifty dollars and handed it to Josh. Dray located the keys at the end of the table and tossed them to Josh as Josh walked out the door. "Are you sure that's a good idea?" Detective Hauser asked.

"What do you mean?" Dray asked.

"He's a junkie, and he is going to find the stuff if he can."

"No . . . no, I don't think so. Josh knows how important this is. He won't let us down."

Dray's faith in Josh was skewed. When he looked at Josh, he really couldn't see Josh, only the outward image of Iria, so sweet and soft. He forgot who he was dealing with sometimes. Dray didn't have much experience with drugs. He never got involved in drugs, and he wasn't in the gang long enough to find out much about the effect that drugs can have on the body and the mind. He had no idea what Josh's motivation was or his determination when it came to the pursuit of the next high. Dray looked through the window as he watched Josh drive down the street, and got a sick feeling in his stomach.

What did I just do?

Josh drove toward the store to pick up dinner. He had the money in his hand, and he planned to do the right thing. He drove past the first store.

This store has very high prices. I'll find somewhere cheaper.

He drove for twenty minutes and saw another store. He pulled into the parking lot when he realized that this store might not have what he wanted.

This store is not one of the big chains, so I may not find what I need.

He continued to drive. He began to notice a change in the neighborhood and realized that he had gone too far. He saw another store and pulled into the parking lot.

I guess I better stop here before I get lost. He had his hand on the money in his pocket when he looked across the street at the transaction taking place. He pulled the money from his pocket, looked at it, and wondered how much he would need to buy the food.

I may not need all of this. This is a lot of money. I only need a little bit to get me through the night. How much money can that take? It can't do any harm as long as I get the food.

"I'll put this away," he said as he pulled off twenty dollars and put the rest back into his pocket. He walked across the street and approached the scruffy looking man with tattoos canvassing his arms and chest. His pale, white skin was dry and weathered, and his face was sunken from the loss of many teeth.

"What you want little lady?" the man asked.

"I need a little help," Josh said.

"I can't help you. I can't even help myself," he said as he turned away from her.

"Yes, I believe you can. My need is very small."

"Yes I suppose it is," he said as he turned to face her and smiled. "The smallest I have is a twenty."

"That's just what I have," Josh said.

"Good, good. Let's see what we can do to help you." The man reached into his pocket and pulled out a bag of white powder. "You look like a lady with a strong need. I believe this will suit you fine."

"I can't use no cane."

"I know, I can tell. You want the big dawg. I got you covered." He handed Josh a bag of heroin and took the twenty. Josh slipped the bag into his bra and began to walk away.

"Hey, little lady, do you have someplace to kick it?" the man asked.

"No . . . but I only need a place for a minute, you know."

"Yeah, yeah, I know. I got you covered," he said as he walked toward a row of houses down the street. He walked up the steps and into a building that looked like it was condemned. The door was hanging off the hinges and the paint was crumbling off the walls. The types of characters transiting in and out were the lowest of the low. Josh thought about Madison's beautiful home and wondered why he was in this place. The sharp pain in his stomach reminded him of his mission. *A few minutes*, he thought, *just a few minutes*.

Josh walked past room after room and looked inside to see men and women with needles in their arms and straws up their noses as they took that deep breath to pull in as much of the drug as they could. He passed rooms of woman seducing and fondling other women, and men performing intercourse with women and men. Every possible horrible act imaginable was happening inside the condemned building the authorities probably thought was empty.

The dealer led Josh to the end of the hall and through a door where five people were sitting around, either getting high or passed out. The room was filled with dirty mattresses on the floor for those who needed to sleep it off. The cigarette smoke was suffocating. Liquor bottles and beer cans were thrown about everywhere. The stench was sickening, and the bewildered looks on people's faces were horrifying.

Josh looked into the eyes of the people around him and saw hopelessness and despair. He saw the kind of life Iria was living and the many people he supplied drugs to when he was selling. He was living large, not knowing how the people who kept him in luxury were living. Now he had a habit to feed, and regardless of how humiliating it was, he needed it and would do anything to get it.

He walked to the back of the room with the man and sat at a table. The man took a hypodermic syringe and doused it in alcohol. He gave Josh a piece of tubing and the syringe and helped him tie the tubing around his arm. Josh forced the needle into his arm and waited to feel the affects of the drug. His body immediately relaxed as he began to feel light and euphoric. He couldn't remember what he was supposed to do, and he really didn't care. He looked around the room and watched everyone move around in slow motion. He could hear everything everyone was saying, and the sound of his heart filled his ears. He watched everyone moving back and forth, and he laughed at the man at the sink who tried desperately to pour a glass of wine, but kept missing the glass. Eventually, the man gave up and drank from the bottle.

Josh felt the joy of the high like never before. He told himself that his mind was open to a more spiritual plane, and his conscious mind was no longer in control. He believed that he was one with God and balanced for an eternity. He wanted this feeling to last forever. He had forgotten where he was. He tried to stand, but stumbled. He caught himself and laughed at his clumsiness.

The man watched Iria stand against the wall and studied her body. He walked over to her and began to caress her body. Josh tried to stop him, but he was so high he couldn't seem to move his arms and hands right. The man touched Iria's breasts and Josh moved away from him. Josh stumbled to the front room and tried to make it to the door, but it seemed too far away. He looked at the door and started to panic. He knew he was in trouble, and he also knew he was in no position to do anything about it. There was no one to help him, and none of these people would care.

The man grabbed him from behind and forced him to the floor. Josh tried to fight, but his arms had no power. His legs were pinned down. The horrible man forced Josh's panties off, and before Josh could scream, the man was inside Iria's body. He forced himself on Josh with all the people in the room looking on. Those that could speak cheered him on and wanted to join in on the fun. Josh couldn't believe this was happening to him. He lay on the floor while one man after the other mounted him and force their unwashed, filthy bodies into him. One man held his arms, while another penetrated his body. His breasts were exposed and became anyone's toys to play with.

"Yeah, little girl, that's right, give it to me. I know you love it. It's all yours," one man screamed as he climaxed with demanding force and vigor. He rolled over onto the floor, and another took his place with the same vengeance and lust.

They took Josh over and over again. He cried and fought with what little strength he had, but he couldn't make them stop. Eventually they were done with him and left him to his humiliation. He couldn't move. He lay on the floor all night in pain.

Dray paced the floor for most of the night waiting for Josh to return. Detective Hauser left to check on Carlita's move. By ten o'clock, Dray knew that Josh was not going to make it. He couldn't believe Josh would let them down this way. He couldn't control his anger. He picked up the wine bottle from the table and threw it against the wall. He started thinking that maybe he should try to find Redemption alone.

Maybe I will have a better chance if I go alone. I can't let them destroy my chances of getting back to myself. It's not my fault about what happened to Carlita. I feel sorry for her, but I can't fix it, and Josh, well, he deserves his mess. If the drug is more important to him than we are, then let him stay in Iria's body and damn him. He thought of Iria and realized that she deserved to have her life back, and so did Silvia.

"I can't just abandon them even though I wish I could."
He lay on the sofa and fell asleep in the library.

The ringing of the phone woke him at about eight o'clock
in the morning. He stumbled to his feet and walked to the
phone.

"Hello."

"Did he come back?" asked Detective Hauser

"No, there's no sign of him."

"Damn, what are we going to do? We can't leave him."

"I don't know. I guess we'll just have to wait and hope he
shows up," Dray said.

"If he's not there by noon, we'll have to scratch the plan
for today and regroup after we find him."

"Find him? How can we find him? I wouldn't know
where to look," Dray said.

"Let me worry about that. I'll get back with you later,"
Detective Hauser said.

The detective hung up and walked to his car, frustrated
by Josh's actions. This may be their only chance at saving
Carlita. He knew that letting Josh out of sight was not a
good idea, but he couldn't really say much. He really didn't
know them well enough to make judgment calls, but he
knew how a junkie acted when he needed a high. He
should have pressed Josh to stay last night, knowing what
the possible outcome could be, but he allowed his need to
trust to dominate his judgment.

"It won't happen again," Detective Hauser said as he
drove off in search of Josh.

Josh's aching body wouldn't let him move from the floor.
He opened his eyes and looked around at his horrible,
filthy surroundings and remembered what happened to

him the night before. He screamed and cried. He screamed the way he wanted to last night but couldn't. He sat up and looked around for the horrible men who raped him. He couldn't recognize anyone. The man from the street corner was gone. *Now may be the best time to try and get out of here.*

Josh tried to stand, but he became so dizzy and disoriented that he lost his footing and fell. He cringed on the floor and fought with himself for letting this happen to him. He tried again and pulled himself up. Just as he made it to the door, a large figure forced him back inside.

"Where you going, bitch?"

The black man was furious, and Josh knew he couldn't agitate him without serious consequences. Josh stepped back against the wall and stood still. The large man stared at him as he walked by into an adjacent room. Josh listened as the men in the back room discussed the size of the next pickup and where it would be coming in.

"Ten kilos," the man said with the thick, Italian accent as he lit a cigarette and took a long drag.

"What's the price?" the tall, black man asked.

"You know what the price is, I won't go over that with you again."

"No, no, man. You got to come down off that."

"I can't help you, man. That is the price. I can do business elsewhere," he said as he stood up and walked toward the door.

"What's the location?" the black man asked. The Italian man stopped and listened.

"At the Pier. It's called the Ocean Front. Tonight at ten," the Italian man said.

"I'll be there with the cash," the black man said.

The Italian man walked out the door and never looked back. Moments later, the black man glanced at Josh as he walked past and out the door. Josh's heart began to calm.

He was certain that this would become another horrible night.

Josh sat on the floor to calm himself when his body started to shake for the drug. He noticed a man in the kitchen and decided that if he could get just a little, he could make it out of there. He walked into the kitchen with a twenty in his hand. He had ten dollars left and he planned to hold onto it. He bought twenty dollars worth of heroin and walked back into the room and out the door. He walked down the street and found an empty alley that he could hang out in while he filled his body with the wonderful drug. He crouched behind a trash can and waited for the wonderful feeling to come so he could go. He sat next to the wall and sank into oblivion.

Carlita walked out of the courthouse with her hands cuffed behind her and tears in her eyes. She looked around, hoping to see some sign of Detective Hauser, Dray, or Josh. She studied the back streets and every parked car. As she walked to the van parked in the rear of the building, her heart sank. She was hoping to get some sign, some hope that they would rescue her. She stepped inside and wondered what it would be like to be in a mental asylum, to be studied like a mentally ill person who wasn't really ill.

If I pretend to be Silvia, I'll go to jail for murder. If I say who I really am, I'll spend the rest of my life in an asylum. Oh God, how awful.

Two guards sat with her in the back of the van as the driver pulled into the street and headed toward her final destination. She kept hoping that something would happen. She waited and listened for every sound that came from outside. There were no windows in the back of the van, so she couldn't see anything. They sat in silence. The ride seemed to take forever, but all too soon, it was over.

She could tell when the driver pulled into the driveway. Her heart pounded with fear. Her hopes for a rescue vanished as the van stopped and the guards opened the rear doors. She stood and stepped outside.

Four men wearing the traditional white uniforms guided her inside. The guards followed them to the front office where one of them signed the forms to release her into the custody of the nurses and doctors in ward six of the hospital, where mentally ill convicts served their sentences and waited to die. She watched the guard fold the papers and stuff them into his pocket. Carlita's eyes followed them as they exited the building.

She turned toward the large woman behind the desk. Her face was soft and calming. Her brown hair hung in her face as she read Carlita's file. She tucked her hair behind her ear, looked up at Carlita, and smiled.

"So, you seem to be in a bit of trouble, don't you?" she said softly.

Carlita's face saddened as she struggled to speak. She couldn't find the words. *I can't tell this story again.* She stared into Mrs. Downings' brown eyes, hoping that she would understand and that somehow she would see her, the *real* her inside.

"Well, let's get you settled in," she said as she walked Carlita to the door and out into the hallway. "Come on," she said. Carlita walked slowly behind her and tried her best not to scream.

How did I get here? she kept asking herself as she looked around at the white walls and locked doors.

Mrs. Downings stopped at a nurse's station.

"Please sit here," she said to Carlita as she pointed to the bench against the wall. She walked behind the counter and spoke to the head nurse on duty. She handed her Carlita's file and discussed the particulars and the significant points.

"This is Mrs. Dressel. She will help you get settled in and provide you with whatever you may need. Try to relax and get some sleep, looks like you could use some." She caressed Carlita's shoulder. "Don't worry, Silvia. We'll get to the bottom of this," Mrs. Downings said.

The nurse walked Carlita to the room. The room was a very sterile and impersonal white room. The twin bed divided the room into a functional area on one side with a dresser, mirror, chair, bathroom, and closet. The other side was the personal area with a writing table and chair, a small bookcase, and a reading lamp. The window faced the front of the building so she could see all the activities and goings-on from the street in front of the complex.

"If you need anything to help you sleep, just press zero on your phone and someone will come in." Mrs. Dressel said. "If you hit zero on the phone, it rings at the front desk, so if you have any problems, just hit the button. You cannot make any calls outside of this complex from this phone. If you want to make a personal call, you have to get permission from your doctor, and there is a room down the hall for making outside calls. Understood?"

"Yes," Carlita said timidly.

"Your daily activities and diet will be determined by your doctor."

"When will I see him?" Carlita asked.

"Doctor Mitchell will be by tomorrow to speak with you, so just try to relax and get some sleep. Oh, by the way, the break room is down the hall and to your left. It's where the television is, and where other social events are held. You are welcome to participate if you like. However, I doubt that you will be here very long." Mrs. Dressel walked out and closed the door.

Detective Hauser drove around the city, hoping to find Josh stumbling around somewhere. They missed their opportunity to rescue Carlita, and now the detective was focused on keeping Josh alive. He stopped in the local bars and liquor stores and tried to describe Iria as best he could. He stopped the local junkies and prostitutes standing on the street corners, hoping for a trick, and asked if anyone saw a petite woman with long, blond hair and bright blue eyes. After four hours, he stopped a crackhead and offered him a few dollars for some information. The small, frail man listened for a moment, but waited to see the cash before he told the detective anything. He looked at Detective Hauser and smiled.

"Yeah, I seen her," he said.

"Where?"

"I don't know. I can't remember."

Detective Hauser pulled twenty dollars from his pocket and laid it in the man's hand.

"She was at the crack house last time."

"There are hundreds of crack houses around here. What are you talking about? Detective Hauser said as he grabbed the man's collar.

"Wait, wait, I got your answer. Just hold on." The man pulled back and gathered himself. "She was down on Swan Street. Down at Kat's house. You know the one I mean."

"Yeah, I know." Detective Hauser turned and walked back to his car.

He drove to Swan Street and found the house. He parked nearby and walked inside. He couldn't believe that people lived this way for the love of a drug. He went upstairs and looked all around. He knows his white skin, clean face, and washed hair made it obvious he was an outsider. He nervously walked into the large room at the top of the stairs. A large, black man noticed this strange character and walked toward him.

"What do you want?" he asked as he got directly in Detective Hauser's face, making it known that he was the leader.

Looks like he is the leader of a pack of filthy wolves.

"I just want to know if you've seen a young woman about five feet, three inches tall, blond hair with blue eyes. Have you seen anyone like that?"

"Hey, anybody see a blond chick with blue eyes up in here?" the black man asked as he walked around the room, laughing and joking. "You seen her, man?" He laughed as he approached a man standing in the far corner, one of the men who raped her. They all laughed as they all denied seeing her. He walked back toward Detective Hauser. "Well, don't look like we seen her," the man said as he moved closer to the detective in an effort to intimidate him. "Besides, what she do? She ain't no whore or nothing, is she?" he asked, laughing as he moved even closer to Detective Hauser, which forced him to step back. The detective never took his eyes off of him.

"Well, thank you for your time," Detective Hauser said as he backed out of the room. He walked down the hall sideways so as to keep one eye on the room. He headed downstairs and out the door. He walked briskly to the car and stepped inside.

"Josh was there, all right, which means that he can't be far away. He's in this area somewhere," Detective Hauser mumbled to himself as he pulled from the curve and headed down the street.

The detective continued to ride around in the general area for several more hours. Just as it started to get dark, he decided to park the car and walk. He moved around between buildings and alleys until he spotted the small, unkempt, sick body lying against the wall. He walked toward Josh, and as angry as he was, he could only pick him up and carry Iria's body home.

He put him in the backseat of the car and drove back to Madison's house, where Dray was waiting to kill Josh. Dray watched Detective Hauser carry Josh inside and take him upstairs to the bedroom. He laid Josh on the bed, and Dray stood in the doorway looking at the detective pamper Josh.

Dray was so angry. He couldn't believe that Detective Hauser was being so calm.

"Maybe you should have left him. It seemed that that's where he really wants to be," Dray said.

"Of all people, you should understand what it's like to be strung out," Detective Hauser said.

"Why . . . why of all people should I know? Because I'm black you automatically assume that I know all about drugs?"

"No, that's not what I meant. You were trying to get in a gang. What do you think gangs do?"

"We didn't do that."

"Oh please, you had no idea what you were getting into when you killed Daniel Tanner. That was just the beginning of the kinda shit you would've had to do to stay in that gang. The selling of drugs is a big part of what keeps a gang rich. What do you think they buy those expensive cars with—their allowances? You need to grow up, Dray."

"No, we weren't like that."

"Gang members don't work for a living. How do you think they make money? A little fairy gives it to them? No! They sell drugs, run prostitution rings, and kill people. Gangs just like yours paid Josh for selling the shit. If it weren't for people like you and Josh, this young girl would be having a real life right now, instead of cowering in a gutter. No matter what, I have to take care of her. It's her life I'm trying to save," Detective Hauser said angrily. He turned back toward Josh, removed his shoes, and pulled the cover over him. "He will be sick in the morning. We'll have to get him something. I'll see what I can do. The next eight or nine days are going to be horrible. He's so weak, he may not survive."

"He has to. Without all of us, we can't make the journey," Dray said.

Carolyn walked in, stood behind Dray, and looked inside. "I see you found her . . . or him . . . or whatever. Now what do you plan to do?" she asked.

"We'll have to wait until Josh is clean, and then we'll try again," Detective Hauser said.

"Try again? How?" Carolyn asked.

"They have to bring her back in two weeks. That gives us enough time to get Josh clean and work on another plan. Out of all the drugs to be hooked on, heroin is the worst."

Detective Hauser tucked Josh in the bed and walked back downstairs. Dray and Carolyn followed him into the library. The detective poured himself a drink. Dray was stunned. For the first time, he saw a vulnerable side of the great Detective Hauser. This whole ordeal was frustrating the detective to the point of exhaustion. He finished his drink and walked toward the door.

"I'll see if I can get something that will help him get through the next few days. I don't know how yet, but I'll figure something out."

The knock on the door startled Carlita to her feet. "Come in," she whispered as she stared at the door with great anticipation of who was on the other side.

"Hello, Silvia," the handsome young man wearing a white shirt, jeans, and a white medical coat said. He looked nothing like the traditional, old, white-haired psychiatrists. The young, black man approached Carlita and extended his hand. His pleasant smile put her immediately at ease. "May we sit for a moment and talk?"

"Yes . . . please," she said as she pointed to the chair opposite hers at the small table. He sat and began to read through her file.

She waited and watched him as he pondered the particulars about the case. *He's very handsome. It was worth getting sick just to see him. Down, girl, down. I've got to get out of here. That's all that matters.*

"Do you mind if I call you Silvia?" he asked.

"No, I guess it's my name." He looked at her and smiled at the uncertainty of her answer.

"You guess? What do you think your name is?"

"Carlita. I'm sure that's what it says in the file; that I'm wacko and think I'm the person I'm supposed to have killed."

He looked at the file and back at her.

"In so many words, yes, that's what it says. Is it true?"

"To the best of my knowledge, it's not true."

"Well, I guess we'll have to figure out what the truth is while you're here. Unfortunately, you are here for only two weeks, which really doesn't give us much time."

"You're not supposed to cure me, just determine if I'm crazy or not."

"You're not crazy. You may be sick, but not crazy."

"Sick in the head, same thing." She smiled

"Do you think you are sick in the head, as you say?"

"No," she said sternly.

"Then why do so many other people think that something is wrong?"

"Because they can't understand what happened to us. I don't blame them. I really don't understand it myself."

"Can you tell me what happened?"

"I wish I didn't have to, but I knew I would, so here it

goes again. My name is Carlita Espinoza and I am in Silvia Watkins's body. It all started when . . ."

Josh was in so much pain he could barely breathe. Iria's little body was shaking all over, and he wanted to throw up, but he hadn't eaten, so there was nothing to come up. He sat on the side of the bed, holding his stomach and his head at different times. Carolyn and Dray were downstairs in the library when they heard Josh's moaning and crying. They rushed into the room to see if he was all right. Dray was still angry with Josh for blowing Carlita's chance for a rescue, so he had a hard time being sympathetic.

"You all right, man?" Dray asked as Carolyn walked toward Josh and sat beside him.

"My God, you're soaking wet. You've got to get out of these clothes."

Carolyn helped Josh into the bathroom and ran a cool bath. Josh sat in the tub. The water felt good. He relaxed for a moment.

Dray walked toward the bathroom door. He stopped before walking in.

"What happened to you?"

Josh hesitated before speaking. He didn't know what to say. He stared at the water and wished Dray would go away and relieve him of the humiliation of apologizing.

"What happened, Josh?" Dray asked again. "Where is my car?"

"Dray, I got caught, man, that's all, I got caught."

"Caught? Caught by who, by what?"

"You know, man. I ended up in a bad place and I got caught."

"You mean you *went* to a bad place and got caught. You didn't just end up there. You left here with the intentions of ending up there. I don't believe you, man," Dray said angrily.

"No, no, I didn't intend for this to happen. I was clean, man, I was. It wouldn't hit me so hard if I hadn't been so clean. I shouldn't have left here. That was the problem. It was that store and all those people hanging around."

"Man, next you gonna blame the bird that flew by and dropped shit on you so you had to get high. Any excuse will do. There's a store two blocks away where no one is hanging around selling drugs. Why didn't you stop there? I know why, damn you, man. I just don't believe you would do this to Carlita."

"Carlita, what about Carlita?"

"Damn, man, don't you remember? We were supposed to get Carlita out of jail yesterday, but now she's locked up in an insane asylum. Thanks to you." Dray was so frustrated that he hit the wall so hard it cracked.

"Oh no . . . I forgot. Oh man, I'm so sorry." Josh realized the consequences of his choice and regretted it immensely. He laid his head back on the tub and cried. "Damn, I didn't mean for this to happen."

"You didn't mean? You are a drug addict. An addict doesn't mean for anything to happen except getting high. You were supposed to help Carlita and all of us fix this mess we're in more than you wanted to get high. But I guess I was wrong. I'll never forgive you for this," Dray said. "And now Madison's car is gone too."

Dray backed away from the bathroom door and walked downstairs. The doorbell rang just as he entered the library. He walked into the foyer and opened the door. Detective Hauser entered carrying a brown bag. He walked into the kitchen and poured the contents onto the table.

"I snatched this from the lab. One of the technicians told me to give him these first for two days, and then these." He picked up two vials of pills. "He said to wean him off of these by giving him less every day until the eighth day, and then stop. He said for me to hold onto these so that when he has a relapse he can take these instead of going back to the streets. Where is he now?"

"Upstairs in the tub. Carolyn is with him."

Detective Hauser and Dray walked upstairs to find Josh lying on the bed in agony. Carolyn covered his shivering body and tried to comfort him. Detective Hauser walked into the bathroom and got a glass of water. He gave Josh one pill and the water.

"What is it?" Josh asked.

"It'll make you feel better," Detective Hauser said as he put the glass on the nightstand. "Try to stay strong, Josh. I will be out of pocket for a while, so you follow Dray's instructions, and he'll pull you through this, OK? You'll be all right," he said.

"Where are you going?" asked Josh.

"Just out of sight for a while. Just until you get better."

He patted Josh on the shoulder and walked downstairs.

"Dray, I'm not going to be here, so make sure he gets these daily. Just like I said, a little less every day. He'll worry you about giving him more, but don't. We want him to kick it, but we don't want him to die trying. That's all these pills are for, to keep him from dying. I'm going to disconnect myself from you for a few days. I don't want the department to think I'm involved in any way. Maybe I can get in to see Carlita. Get Josh through this, and I'll be back when it's time for Carlita to return to the jail. We'll try again."

"It might be easier to get Carolyn in to see her. She is her sister," Dray said.

"Yeah, that would be easier. I'll get back with you," Detective Hauser said. He shook Dray's hand and walked out.

Dray listened to Josh's moaning sounds from upstairs and wondered how he was going to deal with this for the next eight days. He walked into the library and poured himself a drink. He noticed that the liquor cabinet was looking pretty grim. "I guess I need to restock soon." He smiled as he drank the last of the vodka and cranberry juice. He walked back upstairs to find Carolyn trying to comfort Josh. He was tossing and turning in the bed and shaking desperately.

"There's nothing you can do for him. The pill should help him sleep. Let's go get something to eat," Dray said.

"Are you sure it's OK to leave her? Anything could happen. I don't think we should go."

"Maybe you're right. I'll go get something."

Dray walked back downstairs and found the keys to Barbara's car on the foyer table. He backed the car out of the garage and headed down the street. He had no idea where he was going. All he knew was that he had to get out of the house. He couldn't be in the same place with Josh right now. Dray was still very angry and felt a little betrayed. Their one opportunity vanished because of Josh's desire for drugs.

Dray drove for an hour until he found himself at the ocean. He couldn't seem to remember how he got there, but he parked. He walked toward the water and watched the waves curl in from the vast, open distance while the wind blew over him. He remembered for a moment what it was like to be free of worry and enjoying life. He remembered joking with his mother and laughing. Playing ball in the park and making the homerun, being young and free. The look on Daniel Tanner's face as he clutched his heart and wondered why came to his mind as he fell to his knees and cried. The water washed over him as he prayed for forgiveness.

"I'm sorry. God, I'm so sorry."

Dray drove Carolyn to the hospital to see Carlita. Detective Hauser was able to get permission for the visit. Dr. Mitchell thought it was a good idea for Silvia to see someone from her past. Maybe Carolyn would jolt her memory enough to start dismantling the illusion of Silvia being Carlita, and force Silvia to see who she really was. If it was a fraud, he thought Silvia may break down when she saw her sister. This was what Dr. Mitchell hoped for. Carolyn walked inside and waited in the lobby. Dr. Mitchell approached her with his hand extended.

"Hello Ms . . ."

"Mrs. Jones . . . Carolyn Watkins-Jones," she said as she reached out to shake his hand.

"Please follow me." He walked Carolyn down the hall and through two sets of double doors. He passed his badge over the badge reader, and the doors automatically opened. When they reached the nurse's station, he asked her to complete the visitors form. She completed the form and walked down the hall.

"Carolyn, tell me about Silvia. Can you think of anything that would push her into complete separation from herself?" Dr. Mitchell asked.

"I don't know. At first I thought it was because of David. Losing him had to destroy her, but . . ." She hesitated.

"But what?"

"After I spoke with Madison Tanner or Dray or whoever he is, it seems that she had this illusion before David's death, so I don't know what could have caused this."

"Really? Who is Madison Tanner or . . ."

"Dray, they call him Dray."

"Are Madison and Dray the same person?"

"Yes, just like Silvia and Carlita, and there's another one they call Josh, who is Iria. Josh and Iria are also the same person. It's the strangest thing I've ever seen. They all walk around pretending to be somebody else."

"But why, did they say?"

"They all did terrible things and now they have to pay for it. I can't explain it. I want to believe it, but it's too impossible."

"It would be for anyone. Why would you want to believe it?"

"It's either this, or that my sister is a murderer, and I can't believe that either," she said as she stared into his eyes.

"Yes, I see your point." He opened the door to Carlita's room. Carolyn walked in. She stared at Dr. Mitchell as she walked by the bed and stood in the center of the room.

"Hello, Sil," she said softly.

Carlita was staring out the window watching all the people walk around. "Do I know you?" she asked.

"Sil, you know who I am."

"I'm sorry, but I don't. Silvia Watkins may know you, but I don't know you. Who are you?" Carlita asked as she turned and looked into Carolyn's face.

"Silvy, enough of this. I won't play with you. This is too serious for you to be playing with me. You know me and Judith, Roger, Casey, and Soda," Carolyn shouted.

"Soda? Who is Soda? Why would anybody name a person Soda?" Carlita asked with a puzzled look on her face.

"Soda was our dog. Remember, you said he looked like root beer soda, so we started calling him Soda. You don't remember?"

"I can't remember because those are Silvia's memories, not mine," Carlita said.

Carolyn walked to the chair and sat down. She couldn't believe it. Either she was really Carlita or she was very good at disguising herself, and if she was disguising herself, she must have killed Carlita and was using this mental trip thing to escape going to jail. Or she really was Carlita, just like everyone had been telling her.

"I never really believed it, but now I'm not sure." She stared at the face of Silvia and wondered who she was. "You know they found Carlita's body? If you are her, are you planning to stay in Silvia's body forever?"

"I hope not. We were trying to get to this place in the desert where we thought we could change back to our old selves, but the police stopped us. Now that it doesn't look like I'm going to make it, I don't know what's going to happen."

"Redemption," Carolyn said.

"What?"

"Redemption . . . the place you were looking for, it's called Redemption."

"Yes . . . yes, that's right."

"What happens if you don't get there?" Carolyn asked.

"We lose our souls." Carlita turned to face the window and looked out over the street at all of the people moving around in their day-to-day routines. "We all live right on the edge of Redemption."

"I have a message for you from Madison."

"You mean Dray."

"Yes, I guess so." Carolyn said with some confusion and frustration.

"What is it?" Carlita asked.

"Redemption will be found on the way back," Carolyn said.

Carlita smiled. She never turned away from the window. Now she knew that they didn't abandon her. Something went wrong.

"How is Josh?" Carlita asked.

"He had a setback, but he's doing better."

"I understand."

Carolyn stood and walked over to Carlita. She caressed her shoulder.

"I don't know if you're my sister or not. I know that Sil would never kill anyone or lose David so carelessly. This is a maddening story, and I hope you are telling the truth, but it's hard to believe. I am going to give you the benefit of doubt and believe you, so please do whatever you have to, to get my sister back," she said, knowing that hope was out of reach and only by the grace of God would the madness end with any joy. She kissed whom she believed to be her sister on the forehead and used all of her strength not to cry. She turned and walked out.

Dr. Mitchell was standing just outside the door. Carlita knew that he was listening through the door, hoping to see a glimpse of Silvia, something to help him prove that this whole thing was a fraud. But he heard nothing that would convince him that she was lying. Carolyn walked out the door and saw Dr. Mitchell standing in the hallway. He walked her back to the lobby.

"What do you think?" he asked.

"She's sick. I didn't tell her that I think she's sick. If she really thinks she's Carlita, then I guess I'll have to play along until she understands what's happening to her. The story is far-fetched. It is unbelievable. But, it seemed that she would have flinched when I mentioned Soda. She loved him madly. His death devastated her, but she didn't react at all. She really doesn't know me. I can tell. She's not playing. She really doesn't know who I am. She's really sick."

"You really thinks she's sick? There's no chance that she could be faking this?" he asked.

"No, I don't think she faking. I really believe she believes it, and that scares me."

"Why?"

"Because something pretty bad must have happened to cause this. I can't imagine what."

"I don't know either, and I'm not convinced that it's not a fraud to keep from going to jail for murder. I've seen some pretty elaborate performances, so don't be surprised if she really is faking. I will do everything I can to find out. I promise. Thank you for coming."

"You're welcome. I wish I could have been more helpful."

"On the contrary, you gave me a starting place."

Carolyn extended her hand and wished him luck.

"Please save my sister's life," she begged as she turned and walked outside.

Dray waited in the parking lot. He saw Carolyn walking back to the car. He opened the door, stepped outside, and walked toward her.

"How'd it go?" he asked.

"She didn't know me," Carolyn said as she walked past him and proceeded to open the car door.

"I didn't expect for her to know you. What I want to know is how is she doing? How is she holding up? Did you give her the message?"

"Yes, she got the message and I think she understood. She seemed to be doing well. The doctor thinks she is trying to deceive him, so he is waiting for her to break at any time, but I don't think she will." Carolyn got inside and hung her head in despair.

Is my sister gone forever. Is she dead? She rode back to Madison's house in silence.

Days went b,y and Dray watched Josh fight for his life. Josh spent the last three days in a panicked, paranoid state that "they" were after him. He could never truly identify who "they" were, but nevertheless, he was scared to death. Dray gave him the pills every night to help him sleep just like Detective Hauser said. Josh awoke every morning with the urge to escape and find some of the life-giving drug. He believed he would die without it. He was locked in the room most of the time. Dray and Carolyn made sure one of them always had Josh in their sight, save the visit to Carlita. He woke up promising that he would never do it again, trying to get them to stop watching over him.

"I am better now. I'm through it. I know it this time. I really mean it," Josh repeated over and over again. He'd plead his case in the morning, and by nightfall he was begging for more.

"All I need is one more pill and I'll be all right. That's all I need, and then you can be finished with me. I can't make it off of the little bit you're giving me. Can't you see I'm dying?"

"If it wasn't for Iria, I'd let you die," Dray said.

"Oh, yeah, you would say that. You never liked me anyway. You don't understand what it's been like, living my life. It ain't been easy."

"It was easier than Iria's life, thanks to you," Dray said.

"How dare you, you sorry ass motherfucker! How dare you judge me? You murderer. You don't have the right. I would never do what you did and you have the nerve to judge me? I'll kill your sorry ass, I'll kill you," Josh exclaimed as he lunged toward Dray in a fit of rage.

Dray grabbed Iria's small body and threw her back on the bed.

"You're right. I don't have the right to judge. Maybe we should all die." Dray picked up the bottle of pills, walked out the door, and locked it. He could hear Josh screaming and crying. He looked at the pills and wondered if he was doing the right thing.

"Don't even think about it," the voice came from behind him.

"Carolyn, what do you mean?"

"I know what you're thinking, and don't. You can't coddle him. If you give in, he wins and loses at the same time. He's an addict. He will try every ploy necessary to wear you down. I've lived through this before. The only thing that will change him is admission, acceptance and time. He needs time to fight, fail and fight some more, but without acceptance, he'll never start fighting and then he is defeated. There's no hope of recovery. He has to suffer through it. That's his only hope."

"You were strung out before?"

"No, but my husband was, and it didn't end well. I became an enabler for him. I thought I could help him. I thought we could get through it together, but I was wrong."

"What happened?"

"He died."

"I'm sorry."

"Don't be. It was his choice to try the stuff, and his weakness that made him stay out there. One would think that with all we know about drugs today, no one would ever try it, knowing it can only lead to one thing—addiction. I don't get it."

"You know how people are. We all think we are invincible and that we can control anything. It's the 'it won't happen to me' attitude, until it does."

"Yes, and then it's too late." Carolyn took the pills from Dray's hands and stuffed them into his pocket. "He'll survive. He'll keep you up all night, but he'll survive," she said as she turned to walk downstairs.

"Can you stay tonight?" Dray asked.

She stopped at the top of the stairs and looked back at him.

"I don't know. It's not that I'm frightened, I just wonder if I should associate myself with all of this."

"Carolyn, it's your sister. You are already associated, and I really need your help with dealing with Josh. Please. I really can't do this by my self." Dray stared at the door as he listened to the moaning sounds coming from the other side. "Please."

"All right. I'll stay until he is back on his feet."

"Thank you." Dray walked down the hall and into a guest room. Carolyn followed.

"You can stay here. We can get your things from the hotel in the morning. "Is it all right?"

"Yes, it's fine. Do you have a robe I can use tonight?"

"Sure." Dray walked down the hall into his room and found one of Barbara's robes and gave it to Carolyn. "There are toiletries in the bathroom you can use. Let me know if you need anything. Thanks Carolyn."

The pitiful look on Dray's face saddened her. She knew he was suffering from all of this and needed as much help as he could get, and now that Detective Hauser wasn't around, Dray was left alone to deal with Josh's issues as well as his own.

"Yell if you need me," she said as she closed the door behind him.

Dray went back to his room and got undressed. He slipped in under the covers and closed his eyes for the night.

The deafening scream from down the hall jolted Dray to his feet. He ran out of the room in his underwear and entered Josh's room. Carolyn quickly put the robe on and dashed into the hallway. They entered the room to see Josh screaming in a horrific dream that he couldn't seem to wake up from.

"Josh . . . Josh, man, wake up . . . wake up, man," Dray yelled as he shook Josh until he opened his eyes and calmed himself. Dray held Josh in his arms while he cried, shook, and shivered like a frightened child. "It's all right. It'll be all right. It was just a dream, OK, a dream," Dray said.

Carolyn went into the bathroom and came out with a glass of water.

"Here, drink this," she said as she handed Josh the glass. Dray took the glass and helped Josh drink the water. "It's all right now," Carolyn assured Josh as she sat at the foot of the bed.

"Oh God, Dray, it happened to me again. I . . . I was at that awful place and it happened again," Josh cried.

"What happened?" Dray asked.

"They raped me. They raped me over and over again. I couldn't move. I couldn't do anything. There were so many of them. I couldn't move."

"Oh no, it's all right now. I promise you it will be different now," Dray said.

"How, how can it be different? I'm a junkie and I will always be a junkie. I can't do anything about it. I can't get out of this body, so I'll always be this way. They raped me over and over again. What was I doing in that horrible place? I can't go back there. I won't go back there. Please don't make me, please, please!" Josh exclaimed as he pulled on Dray's arms to hold him tighter, hoping that he would always be in this secure place. The memory of the rape was excruciatingly frustrating to accept. Josh cried as Dray laid him down and pulled the covers over him.

"I can't let him suffer like this. Go look in my shirt pocket and get one of the pills," Dray said.

"No," Carolyn said.

"Look, we can't just let him shake like this all night. Get the pills."

"No, you shouldn't give him anything. He will not die, and if you start doing that, he will learn exactly what he needs to do to get more pills, and you will be having this kind of behavior over and over again."

"Are you saying that he's lying?"

"No, that's not what I'm saying. What I'm saying is that if he realizes that by doing this, it will get him a pill, he will start to fake, lie, and dramatize everything and you won't know the difference. We will stay with him tonight and do whatever we can. He had a bad dream. He remembered something awful, but he will survive, and we shouldn't try to help him by keeping him high. He will survive. Trust me, he'll fall asleep in a while."

"I hope you know what you're talking about."

Dray walked out of the room in a fit of frustration. Carolyn stepped into the bathroom to wet two washcloths. She walked back to the bed and sat beside Josh. She laid a cool cloth on his forehead and the other on the back of his neck. The cool feeling was pleasing to Josh as he began to calm himself and relax. Carolyn sat with him, refreshing the cloth over and over again until Josh fell asleep. She stretched out across the lounge chair by the window and covered herself with the throw that was draped across the chair. She stared at Josh for any changes until she too fell asleep.

Detective Hauser entered the courthouse, hoping to find out all that he could about Carlita's return to the jail. He stopped in at the guard's station and asked what was on the agenda for the next few days. Sergeant Hatch was kind enough to show Detective Hauser the roster. He reviewed the list and found the scheduled time for Carlita's pickup from the hospital—two o'clock on Thursday. Now he needed to find out what the planned route is.

"Do you know who the driver is for the two o'clock pick-up on Thursday?" he asked.

"No, not yet. Why do you care?" Sergeant Hatch asked.

"Just wondering. You know this is my case and I just want to keep abreast of what's going on with it. That's all."

"Yeah, well, you know they won't make the assignments until Thursday morning for that day's schedule."

"Yeah, you're right, I forgot." He put the roster down and walked out.

Detective Hauser drove to Madison's house to let Dray know that whatever they were planning to do, they must be ready by two o'clock on Thursday. He pulled into the driveway to see Dray standing outside talking with the local police. Detective Hauser walked toward them.

"What's going on?" he asked Dray.

"They found my car."

"Great," Detective Hauser said as he turned and walked toward the house. "I would like to speak with you, Mr. Tanner, when you're done." The detective knew that he must appear to be there on official business. He could not give any appearance that he was in collusion with Dray and Josh. His name could not be connected with theirs at all, except as the detective handling the case.

"I'll be right with you, Detective," Dray said as he signed some paperwork for the police officers so they would release Madison's car. He thanked the officer and went inside.

"What's up?" Dray asked Detective Hauser.

"We must be ready by two o'clock, Thursday. How's Josh?"

"He's much better. He's probably in the kitchen, since that's where he's been living for the past two days. He's still up quite a bit at night, but he is over the shakes and the sickness."

Twelve days into Josh's recovery, he was up on his feet and eating everything in sight.

"Yes, his nervous system is all whacked out, so he can't rest at night. That will get better with time. After a while, we can give him some sleeping pills until he begins to fall asleep on his own." They walked into the kitchen to find Josh and Carolyn drinking tea and laughing.

"That's good, that's good to see you smiling," Detective Hauser said as he walked over to Josh to shake his hand. "How are you, Carolyn?"

"Fine, I'm doing OK, I guess."

"I heard you went to see Carlita."

"Yes."

"How'd it go?"

"It depends upon how you want to look at it. It's good in that she didn't remember anything about our life together, and if she's Carlita, she wouldn't. It's bad in that my sister is gone," she said sadly.

"I'm hoping we can get your sister back. If we make this move on Thursday, we may make it to Redemption and save both people. I have a good feeling about this. Somehow, I feel that someone or something is working with us to make sure this happens."

"Do you mean David?" Josh asked.

"No . . . maybe, I'm not sure who it is. I just know that there are outside forces working to ensure this happens. We are getting help from somewhere."

"I hope so," Carolyn said. "I truly hope so."

"OK, we need to plan this out. This is our last chance. We can't afford to blow it," Dray said as he looked into Josh's eyes.

"I know, I know. It won't happen again, I promise. I'm on board. What can I do?" Josh asked.

"There can only be a few routes that they can take, so let's look at each of them and plan for each of them. We won't know which route they are going to take until Thursday morning, and by then it will be too late to plan this out. So we will be prepared regardless of which route they choose. We will name each plan something different so we'll know which one is in play on Thursday morning," Detective Hauser said.

"Let's get started," Dray said as he took a seat at the table and Detective Hauser unfolded a street map.

They talked into the night, reviewing every possible outcome and every "what if" scenario. By ten o'clock Wednesday morning, they were ready. Just as they were lying down for a few hours of sleep after working all night, Carlita was walking into Dr. Mitchell's office for the last time.

"Good morning, Silvia," Dr. Mitchell greeted her.

"Good morning, Doctor."

"It seems that we didn't make much progress while you were here."

"No I suppose not," she said

"I'm sorry about that. I wish I had more time to discover just how real this is to you.

"It is the truth; that makes it real," said Carlita

"It may be very real to you, but you have to admit that what you're asking me to accept is physically impossible. So it's not hard to think that something devious could be going on. I realize that there are seemingly unexplainable things that happen in our world, but usually there are concrete explanations for most things. This situation provides no evidence of the supernatural or some weird science or even a miraculous event occurring. It's just your word that you switched bodies with a body that was found dead. So Carlita, where is Silvia now?"

"What do you mean?"

"I mean, if you are she, then where is she? Is she in your body and thereby dead instead of you?"

"I don't know. Maybe she is dormant inside of this body waiting for me to get out. Once I'm released she will go back to being herself."

"But where will you go? Your body is dead."

"Look, I don't know. If I had all the answers I would fix this and be done with it, but I don't know," she lashed out at him.

"I would love to believe you, Silvia, because a young lady is dead and you're the only suspect, and I hate to think that you could do such a thing, but what you're asking is physically impossible. You have to admit, it sounds a little crazy."

"Hell yes, it's crazy. If it wasn't happening to me, I wouldn't believe it. I know I'm asking you to accept the impossible, but I don't know what else to ask. It is what it is. I am Carlita and I am inside Silvia."

"I want to believe it, but it doesn't matter if I do or not. What matters is do you really believe it?"

"Do you think I do?"

"I'm still not convinced that you do."

"I guess it doesn't matter as long as I'm trapped in jail for murder, or in a hospital for being insane. I'll be trapped in Silvia's body forever or we will both die. It's over." She hung her head as Dr. Mitchell walked toward her and touched her shoulder.

"My God, what happened to you?" he asked.

"I stole her money."

"Silvia, people do bad things all the time. The world is made up of hate, lust, and greed, all of which someone is committing daily. Why should this happen to you and not one of them?"

"Maybe it does happen, just differently. Maybe every one of those people eventually get what's coming to them. The difference with Josh, Dray, and me is that we got a chance to connect the dots. I'm paying for my deeds immediately after doing them, so I get to connect the punishment to the crime. I guess most people never know. By the time they pay for it, the crime is forgotten. They don't understand why bad things are happening to them. But it is payment for an earlier crime or act of indiscretion. It's the same thing."

"Why do you think you are paying for yours this way, so immediate, unlike most people?" he asked.

"I don't know. I really don't know. That's the answer I'm searching for."

"I wish I had time to work with you. Two weeks just wasn't enough."

"When do you have to have your report to the judge?"

"I plan to have it to him by Friday, why?" he asked

"I just wanted to know how much time I had before he reads the verdict that I am completely mad, or that I am the biggest con artist on the planet, and decides the rest of my life. Will you tell him that I can stand trial?"

"Is that what you want me to say?"

"Yes, because there's nothing wrong with me, and I deserve to go to prison for killing David," she said.

"Did you kill David?"

"Yes."

"How?"

"I let him get away from me and he was struck by a car."

"It was an accident."

"No, I had no business trying to run away with him. I should have been thinking of him first, but I tried to save my own ass, and he died. I will always regret losing Silvia's child."

"You mean your child."

Carlita looked at him and smiled.

"You just don't get it, do you?" She stood up to walk out and stopped. "I guess the judge will decide if I'm insane or a murderer." She looked back at him. "Doctor, was there ever a time in our conversations that you started to believe me?"

"No, I could never accept something as impossible as this as fact."

"Well then, we really are wasting time. If you are closed to it, then there can only be one answer: I've lost my mind. So to continue talking is a waste of time."

"No, we are not wasting time. If you have lost your mind, as you say, then my job is to help you find it."

"I know this is the craziest thing you've ever heard. It is for me too. If someone told me this a year ago, I would have told them to see a doctor. It is unbelievable, but it"s happening to me, and I know I'll never get you to understand or believe me. There's nothing for you to cure. I am who I am," she said as she walked out.

A guard was waiting to walk Carlita back to her room. She walked inside wondering if they would rescue her this time, or if she would be back in a jail cell awaiting her fate. She got down on her knees, prayed for forgiveness, and asked God to give Dray, Detective Hauser, and Josh the strength to carry out their plan to free her.

The following morning Carlita prepared herself to leave. She pulled together her few personal items and put them into a bag. Even though she could have been going to a worse fate, she was ready to leave. She sat on the bed wondering what the outcome of the day's events would be and praying for success. Dr. Mitchell stopped by to say good-bye. He knocked on the door.

"Come in," she said. He stepped into the room and grabbed a chair from the far wall.

"How are you today?" he asked.

"As well as I can be under the circumstances."

"I'm going to recommend further treatment in my report. I wanted you to know that."

"I know you think that's helping me, and I thank you for that."

"Be strong, Silvia. We will get you free of this, someday."

"Yes I think you're right, I will be free someday," she said as she hung her head and stared at the floor, patiently waiting for whatever might happen next.

"Goodbye Silvia," said Dr. Mitchell as he stood and walked out.

Thursday morning was wet and dreary. Detective Hauser was up at five o'clock. He went over the plan one more time and got dressed to get to the courthouse early. He needed to find out about the route as early as possible. He went into the bathroom and started the shower. He pulled his clothes together and laid them across the bed. He walked back into the bathroom, which was filled with steam, brushed his teeth, and stepped into the shower to begin his morning.

Dray was also up early. He couldn't sleep knowing that whatever happened today would decide the rest of his life. He sat on the side of the bed for a moment and began to doubt the plan. He went over the plan in his mind and there were so many holes he couldn't see any way it could work.

"We have to try," he whispered.

He went into the bathroom and brushed his teeth. He

started the shower, stepped inside, and let the water run down his back. He noticed how much weight Madison's body had lost because of the stress he'd been under. "Well, if nothing else, Madison, you'll be slim and trim."

Carolyn lay in bed. She didn't want to face the day at all. She wanted no part of the scheme, and had decided not to become involved.

I can't afford to go to jail if this fails. I have children to take care of. I can't get caught, but God, I pray that this works.

She'd decided to go home to Vegas and check on her children. A tear rolled down her cheek as she remembered the way Silvia once was. She couldn't imagine her life without her, but she feared that she might never see her again, at least not the woman she once knew.

Josh was adamant about not screwing up this time. He was up and ready to go. He stood in the bathroom mirror, staring at Iria's pretty face. Sadness came over him when he thought of her enduring the life that he endured over the past few months. He couldn't imagine her surviving, but he knew she would have.

She's a fighter, he thought. "I promise you, if I get us out of this mess, I will find you and I will do everything in my power to help you. I promise." He walked to the tub and started the shower. He stepped inside and smiled at the hope that it could all be over today. "Today is the day, no matter what."

Dray and Carolyn were finishing their first cup of coffee when Josh walked downstairs.

"Would you like something to eat?" Dray asked.

"No, I can't eat, but I'll have a cup of coffee, if you don't mind."

Dray poured Josh a cup of coffee and carried it to the table.

Josh sat down and stared into the coffee cup. His mind

began to wonder and hope. "What if this works today and we make it to Redemption? This could all be over."

"Yep. I can't imagine how it would happen. We all got here in very different ways. I hope I can remember."

"Oh no . . . I don't want to remember any of this. I wish I could forget it now, no, not for me. I want it to be over and gone," Josh said.

"If you don't remember, you will do the same thing again. Nothing will change," Dray said.

"Hopefully, the experience has changed your heart, and maybe you will make different choices even if you don't remember," Carolyn said.

"I hope so," Dray said as he took a swallow of the coffee and headed back upstairs. The doorbell rang, so he turned to walk back downstairs. He opened the door to find Detective Hauser waiting with the morning newspaper in hand.

"Morning," he said as he stepped inside.

"Good morning. Would you like a cup of coffee?" Dray asked.

"Yes, that sounds good."

Detective Hauser followed Dray back into the kitchen. "Good morning, everyone."

"Hey," Josh said. "So I guess this is it."

"Are you up to it, Josh?" Detective Hauser asked as he slanted his eyes toward Josh and waited for a response.

"Ready as I'll ever be."

"Did you find out about the route?" Dray asked.

"Yes, it's going to be plan C."

"Great, OK, so we know what to do," Dray said. "We don't have much time left. We need to be in place by one o'clock. Everyone get your things together, because we won't be coming back here. Pack light. We have no idea how long we will be running."

Dray, Josh, and Carolyn walked upstairs to pull themselves together. Detective Hauser sat at the table and drank a second cup of coffee. He made sure the appliances were turned off and he met everyone in the foyer.

"Let's do it," Josh said as they walked out the door, dreading the day and hoping for the best. They knew if they failed, they would never get another chance.

"I'm going to the precinct, and then I'll meet you at Venice Boulevard," Detective Hauser said as he walked to his old car.

Dray and Josh took Barbara's car and drove Carolyn to the airport. "I hope for all your sakes that what you're about to do is right. You are putting your lives on the line," Carolyn said.

"We realize the risk, but we have few options. Without this, someone will die, either me or Madison, so I have to try to save both of us if I can, and this is the only way I know how," Dray said.

Carolyn looked into their eyes, hoping to see some sign of either sincerity or deception so she could judge the situation. She saw neither.

Dray pulled the car to the curb in front of the Southwest terminal, looked at Carolyn, and smiled. He knew she would never understand, and he was hoping their plan would work so she would never have to.

"Good luck," she said. "I will call you tomorrow to see how things went."

"If it goes well, you can call Silvia and talk about old times," Dray said as Carolyn stepped out onto the curb and said goodbye. She walked into the airport and out of sight.

"She's right. This is very dangerous," Josh said.

"I know, but we still have to try, no matter what happens. If this doesn't work, we may all find ourselves in jail."

"If we survive at all," Josh said. He looked into Dray's eyes and said, "Let's do it."

Dray put the car in gear and drove out onto the street. It was one o'clock and they were preparing for the most important day of their lives. Their souls were at stake. They could not fail. Dray drove for thirty minutes and pulled over. He looked at the instructions given to him by Detective Hauser, and then looked around to find the location.

"There. That's where we're supposed to wait," Dray said as he pointed across the street. He drove one block and stopped.

"Hi Jerry," Detective Hauser said as he greeted the driver of the van.

"Hi, Pat. How the hell are you, man?"

"It's been good . . . good."

"What can I do for you?" Jerry asked.

"Since this is my case, I want to ride with you to the hospital."

"Sure man, I don't care."

"Thanks," he said as he jumped in the front seat. Two guards jump into the back of the van.

Jerry drove for forty-five minutes and entered the hospital driveway exactly at two o'clock. The two guards jumped out and went inside to get Carlita. She was waiting in the lobby with a guard. One of the men signed the papers to release her back into the custody of the police department, and they escorted her to the van.

Detective Hauser watched through the side mirror as two guards carrying guns walk Carlita to the van. Her hands were cuffed, and she was wearing blue jeans and a gray smock. He watched as they walked her to the rear of the van, and he was hoping that her facial expression wouldn't give him away when she saw him sitting in the front seat.

Carlita was scared to death. She knew where they were

taking her, and she was afraid that once she was there, she would be there for the rest of her life. They would think she was insane if she kept telling everyone that really she was Carlita. But if she couldn't get anyone to believe her, they would think she killed Carlita.

It's hopeless.

She remembered that Detective Hauser said she would make it to Redemption as she looked up and saw him sitting in the front seat. She was surprised, but she showed no reaction. She reached the door and stepped inside the back of the van.

Jerry opened the small glass window that separated the front cab from the rear of the van. "Is everything ready back there?" he yelled.

The bulletproof glass and the metal gate that separated the driver from the passengers seemed a little over the top for such a docile person as Carlita, but as far as they knew she was a criminal, a murderer who could murder again.

The sergeant yelled back, "Yeah, everything is good back here."

"OK," Jerry said as he pulled the van out onto the street and headed toward Los Angeles..

Detective Hauser turned to look directly at Carlita. He kept a straight face and hoped that she would too. She took a deep breath and tried to refrain from smiling. She sat back in her seat and wondered where Josh and Dray were and what the plan was. They rode in silence for about ten minutes.

"How have you been getting along since Mary passed?" Jerry suddenly asked.

The question caught him off guard. He hesitated to answer. "At first it was hard, but I managed to stay sane, I guess."

"Are you dating?"

Detective Hauser chuckled and started to nervously rub his hands together. "No . . . no, I . . . well I can't seem to . . ." he stumbled all over the answer as he tried to figure out how not to be embarrassed. "I haven't had much time for that, you know, with things being so busy and everything."

"Man . . . you need to get back out there. It's been five years, hasn't it?"

"Yeah, I guess it has." Detective Hauser noticed a toolkit on the floor. He slowly reached down and opened it while Jerry continued to give advice about his love life.

"You need to meet people and enjoy yourself before you forget how," Jerry said as Detective Hauser pulled a screwdriver from the toolkit and placed it on the side of the seat.

"I suppose you're right."

Detective Hauser felt very uncomfortable with the conversation, but found it to be the perfect distraction for when he put his hand into his pocket. He looked around and realized that they were coming to the rendezvous point. He looked back at Carlita as if to signal her to get ready. She stared back at him to acknowledge his signal.

The guards bantered on about whom the next Muhammad Ali would be and last night's football game. Just as the driver turned the corner, Detective Hauser saw Josh and Dray waiting on the side of the road. He pulled a hypodermic syringe from his pocket with enough drugs in it to keep the driver asleep for two days. Detective Hauser jabbed Jerry's arm. Detective Hauser held him as he pumped the entire contents of the syringe into his arm.

"What the hell you doing man!" Jerry yelled. "We got a problem up here," as the van started swerving across the road.

The guards reached for the sliding window in the middle of the metal gate, but before they could open it, Detective

Hauser forced the screwdriver between the window latches, which stopped it from opening. The detective handled the steering wheel as he moved into the driver's seat and forced Jerry's body to the other side. The guards knew the glass was bulletproof, so it was hopeless for them to shoot at Detective Hauser. They sat and waited in a state of confusion and desperation.

The van was moving erratically across the road. Detective Hauser saw Dray and Josh waiting. He hit the brakes and Jerry slumped over the seat in a deep sleep. Detective Hauser pulled off the road into an alley. Josh and Dray followed the van into the alley and flung the back doors open as soon as the van came to a complete stop. They demanded that the guards get out of the van. They stood with guns cocked and ready to do the unthinkable, if necessary. Dray had been in this position before, but Josh was nervous. He could hardly keep his hands from shaking. The guards drew their weapons and one of them fired. Dray heard the sound of a bullet stream by his head.

That was close. He knew he was in it deep now, and there was no turning back. He fired back and got the guard in the hand. The guard dropped the gun, and before he could reach for it, Dray ordered him not to move. The other guard aimed at Josh. Josh froze with the gun shaking in his hand.

"Step back!" the guard yelled as he stepped off the van while pointing his gun at Josh. Josh continued to point his gun at the guard. Just as the guard stepped out of the van he was struck from behind and fell to the ground.

"Get out," Dray yelled to the guard who was inside the van nursing his injured hand.

The guard stepped out. He looked at Detective Hauser and yelled.

"Are you crazy? What are you doing? You won't get away with this. Man, you're crazy. All of you are crazy."

Dray took their cellular phones, handheld radios, keys, and weapons.

"All you have to do is get down on the ground with your hands behind your head," Josh said.

Josh was scared to death, but he loved the adrenaline rush he got. He loved playing the role of a gangster, something he had always wanted to do, but never had the courage for. He always thought he would be wearing an Italian suit, nine hundred-dollar shoes, and carrying a machine gun, but this would have to do. Dray found the key to unlock Carlita's handcuffs. Detective Hauser pulled Jerry out of the van and laid him on a dirty mattress nearby.

"He's just sleeping. Tell him I'm sorry, but I had to do it," Detective Hauser said to the guards as he looked back at Josh and Dray to see that everything was in place.

Dray waved his hand, indicating that they needed to go now. They all jumped back into the van, Detective Hauser pulled the van back onto the road, and they headed north. Detective Hauser knew that someone was going to radio in, and when the guards didn't answer, there would be the manhunt of the century.

He drove relentlessly, without truly understanding why. He thought about what just happened and realized he just lost his pension and possibly his freedom. If they got caught, the jail time could be the rest of his life. He knew he was in trouble, but he couldn't seem to stop himself. He felt strongly that something or someone was pulling him to do this and he couldn't stop it. He thought of Mary, and knew that she would be very proud of him for helping them. She would want him to be a better person before he was a better policeman. He smiled at the thought of her and felt her warm touch on his heart. He drove for more than an hour and looked around at the terrain. Before he knew it, he was in the desert.

"Jerry, what's up, man? Where are you? You was supposed to check in thirty minutes ago." The voice came across the radio.

Dray's heart started to pound. Josh stared at the radio and Carlita covered her face in anguish.

"Well, here it comes. In a minute we are going to be joined by the entire Los Angeles Police Department," Detective Hauser said. "God, we could use a lot of help right now."

They rode in silence for another hour. Detective Hauser had no idea where he was going, but he knew he had to get there. He kept thinking of how crazy this was, and now he was beginning to wonder if he made the right choice. Just as he was wondering about Jerry and the other officers, he heard the sound of helicopters overhead and checked the rearview mirror. He could see the dust being stirred up by the line of police cars plowing down on them. His heart began to race as he tried to think of an escape plan. He looked around the desolate desert and saw nothing. It was flat and open.

Dray heard the helicopters and opened the back door to look out. He saw the cars coming and felt his heart sink. He sat back down and the look on his face told the whole story.

"We are caught, aren't we?" Carlita asked.

"We can't be. I'm not going to jail as no woman. We gotta do something," Josh said.

"It'll be all right," Dray said as he hung his head and tried not to look at them.

"Oh my God! Look!" Detective Hauser yelled.

"What . . . what is it?" Josh asked as he moved to the front of the van. "I see it. Do you think that's it?" Dray and Carlita looked out the front window to see a small desert town. It appeared abandoned and it fit the image in their dreams.

"It's real, it's really out here," Carlita said as she smiled. "We are going to make it. We'll be all right." She was elated as she moved back to her seat and cried.

Dray looked at the town, but he couldn't seem to feel the joy about finding it that they felt. He wasn't sure how he felt.

"Let's get there fast. Step on it, man," Josh said as he laughed with a sigh of relief.

Detective Hauser picked up speed as he headed toward the town. He checked the mirror and saw the swell of dust getting closer. He drove as fast as he could, and suddenly he found himself in front of an old saloon. He jumped out of the van and ran to the door. Dray, Josh, and Carlita jumped out of the back door and ran to the swinging double doors. They stopped just before stepping inside. They stared at each other, each hoping that the other one would take the first step. Carlita was anxious to get this over, one way or the other, so she pushed the door open and stepped inside.

The bar resembled the old saloons of the early West. There were old wooden tables and chairs scattered about and a huge bar with a large mirror behind it. Bottles of whiskey and beer canvassed the wall behind the bar, and glasses sat on top as if waiting for the next customer. The wooden floor was covered with dirt and sand that crept in over the years, and the windows were opaque so little sunlight seeped in. The kind lady who stood behind the bar welcomed her with open arms. Carlita was excited to see her and ran to embrace her. Josh walked in behind Carlita and smiled.

"It's just like the dream. We made it." He looked around and smiled. He was sure he would become his old self again and be free to live his own life. His excitement overwhelmed him and he began to cry. He felt ashamed and weak because he was a man, but he carried Iria's emotions and he couldn't contain himself.

Detective Hauser noticed Dray's hesitation.

"What's wrong?" the detective asked.

"I don't know. It just seems strange to me." Dray looked behind him out over the desert. He looked up at the sky and inside the saloon. He saw how happy Carlita and Josh were, and he did not want to take their joy away from them, but he felt odd and out of place. He looked behind him again. "Do you notice how quiet it is?"

"Yeah, now that you mention it. There isn't a sound."

"The cars that were behind us, where are they?"

"And the helicopter, it's gone too."

"Something is wrong. I don't know what, but something is wrong," Dray said. They looked inside the saloon and watched the lady prepare them something to eat.

"Please, come on in," she sweetly said as she waved her arms for them to enter. Detective Hauser walked inside and took a seat. Dray followed him and watched the lady's every move.

"You've had a long journey. You must be tired and hungry. Well, you're home now. Just relax and don't worry anymore about anything," she said as she went behind the bar and filled a pitcher full of beer.

"Where are we?" Dray asked.

"Why, honey, this is Sanctuary," she said as she smiled at him.

"Sanctuary," Dray repeated with concern. "Who are you?"

"I'm your salvation." She walked to the table with a pitcher of beer and went back for the glasses.

"Why are we here?"

"You are here to have anything you need and everything you want."

Dray sat and drank the beer. He was very thirsty and

would like a good meal for a change. He tried to relax, and he began to accept that they had found Redemption.

"Redemption," he whispered. "What did you say the name of this place was?"

"Sanctuary, sweetie, Sanctuary." the lady said.

His heart sank. He knew something was wrong, but he couldn't figure out what. He stared at her, hoping that something would happen to relieve him of the hole in the pit of his stomach.

The day turned to night as they sat around the table eating, drinking, and talking. The beer quickly turned into glasses of whiskey and before long they are laughing and crying about their ordeal. Josh was wondering when the transformation would take place to put them back into their old bodies.

"When do I become me again?" he asked

"There's time, child," the lady said. "Plenty of time."

"How much time will it take? It seems that it should've happened when we walked in," said Dray.

"We are going to change back, aren't we?" asked Carlita.

"Yes, but first I have something for all of you. I know you will love it," she said.

Detective Hauser silently watched the lady as she walked into a back room and came out with a bag. She reached inside and pulled out a beautiful bracelet. It had diamonds and sapphires in a beautiful gold setting. She walked over to Carlita and laid it in front of her.

"Isn't it beautiful?" she asked Carlita.

"Oh my, it's magnificent," Carlita said as she reached for it. She laid the bracelet over her wrist and admired it. "It's the most beautiful thing I've ever seen."

"Would you like to have it?" The lady offered.

"Oh no, I couldn't take it. It's yours. Why would you want to part with it? It's so beautiful. No, I couldn't."

"Oh no, I insist. It's for you. Look how beautiful it looks on your arm. It really would make me happy if you would take it."

Carlita didn't know what to say.

"Why would you give away such an expensive piece of jewelry?" she asked.

"Yes, why?" Dray whispered.

The lady walked over to Josh and handed him a small vial full of white powder.

"What is this?" he asked.

"It's what you want," she said.

Josh looked at Dray and Carlita with desperation in his eyes. He knew what it was and he also knew he did not have the strength to turn his back on it. He held it in his hand and imagined the glorious high he could get from just a little bit.

"I can't take this," he said.

"But it's what you want, and I'll always give you what you want. You are here to be taken care of. You will never have to worry about what's going on in the world again. It's your sanctuary."

She walked over to Dray and placed one hundred thousand dollars in front of him.

"Oh my God," Carlita yelled.

Detective Hauser and Josh stood up simultaneously and took note of the awesome gift. Dray looked at the money and tried to believe that there wasn't a price to pay. He couldn't accept it. He looked at the lady and started backing out of the room.

"Everyone, put everything down and let's go," he said

"Let's go? Let's go where?" Josh asked.

"I'm not going anywhere. This is the first time I haven't been afraid in months. I'm not leaving," Carlita said. Dray continued to back up toward the door.

"Josh, please don't take it. It's a trick. Please," Dray said.

"You don't understand. I need it, and besides, it's only this one time. I'll do this and I will never need it again because she's going to put me back and I'll be back to my old self. And I'm not hooked on this stuff, so it will only be this once."

Josh opened the vial and poured the white powder onto the table. He placed a little on his tongue and enjoyed the tingling feeling it gave him. He took the straw that the lady readily provided to him and he began to inhale the heroin with every piece of his body. He relished in the feeling and the ecstasy of his body getting what it had been craving. He couldn't stop. He couldn't save any. He devoured it and sat back in the chair, oblivious to the price he would have to pay for that one moment of joy.

"Noooooo!" Dray yelled. "Oh no, man, please don't do it. Don't give yourself away."

Dray stepped out the door and found himself standing in nothing, as if he was inside a blank page of a white piece of paper. He looked all around, but no one was there. He began to yell and scream, but to no avail. No one heard him.

"Where am I? Where is everybody?"

He felt lost. He had no idea where to go to get free of this. "Is this in my mind? I don't know what's going on here, but somebody needs to let me the hell out of here," he yelled. He was scared. He turned around and around, but there was nothing, but white emptiness. More and more white. He fell to his knees and yelled.

"Oh God, please . . . please help me." He saw a figure in the distance and tried to focus. He got up and started to walk toward the person. "Hey," he yelled. "Hey, over here." He began to run toward him. His heart started to pound louder and he ran faster. He started to slow his pace when he began to recognize the figure.

Dray quickly stopped and stared into Daniel Tanner's eyes. He looked down to see him holding his chest. Blood was running from his chest where the bullet entered his body. He removed his hand and looked down at the hole in his chest. He walked toward Dray, raised his cold, bloody hands, and began to wipe Dray's face with the blood. He stared into Drays eyes and smiled.

"How do you plan to spend eternity?" Daniel asked.

Dray started to back away in terror.

Flashes of the life Daniel Tanner would have lived moved around him. Dray saw Daniel's wedding and the birth of his children, his house and the celebration of birthdays and graduations, grandchildren, and aging.

"You see, I would have had a long life, but you stole it, and now I'm going to take yours," Daniel said. Daniel looked into Dray's eyes and saw his greatest fear. "Your eyes, you are afraid of losing your eyes. That's funny for someone who can not see even with eyes. You would be the same with or without them. He waved his hand over Dray's face and stole his eyes. Dray screamed and fell to the ground. He covered his face in agony and prayed to God for forgiveness.

"I can't see, please God, please give me back my eyes. I will be better I promise, I promise," he cried.

A young man in a wheelchair came toward him. He was solemn and forbidding. He slowly inched his way closer and closer.

"Why are you crying?" the man asked.

"My eyes, I lost my eyes," cried Dray.

"Stand up, there's nothing wrong with you."

Dray stopped crying and stood up in a state of panic. He felt his eyes and realized that it was all an illusion. His eyes were still there and he could see. He looked down at the man in the wheelchair and stepped back as the young man moved closer.

"Do you know who I am?" the man in the wheelchair asked.

"No, I've never seen you before," Dray said.

"Sure you have. The evil in me is the same evil that's in you."

"I'm not evil," Dray yelled.

"Please . . . you are the worst. There are three or four productive lives that you're going to snuff out in a blink of an eye. The only thing stopping you is this moment of guilt. If this madness ended tomorrow, you would be right back out there killing for fun."

"No, I won't, I know better now," Dray cried.

"You are trying to find Redemption, aren't you?"

His evil face looked up at Dray. His tiny body melted into the wheelchair that confined him. His dark, stringy hair hung in his pale face as he maneuvered the wheelchair around. His eyes were dark and sunken and his crippled body stiffened with every movement. He was in great pain that seemed eternal and agonizing.

"What do you know about Redemption?" Dray asked.

"Because I am like you. I tried to get there, but I couldn't because I'm stuck in this chair . . . this damn chair."

"How did you end up like this?"

"Oh, I was as stupid as you. I was an athlete." He chuckled. "I know that's hard to believe now, but I was a runner. I could do a mile in under six minutes. I was great. But there was someone better. His name was Langston, and I hated him. He was tall and brown and charming. He was black just like you, and he was talented just like you could have been. I couldn't let some black boy get the better of me all the time, you know. He got all the attention, all the trophies, and all the women. You know what I mean. We were on the same team, but I could never beat him. I was always second, always the runner up. I got sick of it."

"Why didn't you stop running or move to another town?"

"Oh no, that would have been the right thing to do, but you know how that is, Dray, we don't always do what's right, now do we?" He smiled. "I let my pride and hate consume me. One night I dressed up in dark clothing, covered by face with a ski mask, tiptoed behind Langston, and plunged the knife into his spine, deeper and deeper. He fell to the ground, never to walk again."

"So, he survived."

"Yeah, I didn't want to kill him. I just wanted him out of my way so I could win." The man smiled horribly.

"So did you?"

"No, the next day I tried to get out of bed, but I couldn't. I screamed and the people who ran into the room were Langston's people not mine. His mother and father were trying to calm me. I was in a hospital bed in more pain than I had ever known. They kept calling me Langston and telling me that's who I was. I kept telling them that I was Allen Banks, but they wouldn't listen. I lay in that bed for weeks and went through surgery after surgery until one day I was allowed to leave the room to begin therapy. When I saw myself in a mirror and there was Langston's face looking back at me, I screamed. I tried to run, but of course I couldn't. They picked me up from the floor and put me back in the wheelchair. I found out later that week that my body was deceased. Someone had stabbed me in the back. They showed a picture of me on the television. They like for you to know that you're dead before they tell you the bad news, you know . . . that you're going to hell. Funny, don't you think?"

"No, I don't think it's funny at all," Dray said angrily. "How did you get your body back? You're not black now."

"Once you die, they give it back to you, but you get to keep the misery and pain that you caused."

"Who gives it back to you?"

"You know, the evil one."

"Did you make it to Redemption? Do you know where it is?"

"That's funny," he laughed. "Do I look like I made it? No, I never could get anyone to believe me, so no one would help me look for it, and so my eternity was sealed."

"What happened to Langston?"

"He's fine, running every day. You see, I took his pain and crippled disfigured body with me to have through eternity. So I sit here alone, waiting for nothing."

"If I make it, my body will come back to me and I will be fine."

"You will spend eternity alone, carrying Daniel's pain as his body slipped into death. You'll know the guilt and anguish of empty aloneness and cold pain. There's nothing worse than the guilt that eats away at you forever. It's like a bloodstain that you can't get off your hands. You can feel it, but you can't see it. It's all around and inside of you. It's the great destroyer. You will lose your mind a thousand times over, again and again."

"But we are here now. This is Redemption. We are saved."

"Yes, Dray, you are here. This is where you are supposed to be, here with me forever and ever," Allen said. As he began to grin an ominous look overshadowed him. "I know where Redemption is."

"Where is it?" Dray begged. "Is this it?"

"No, this is your sanctuary. This is where you'll spend eternity," he laughed.

Dray began to back up. He ran as fast as he could into nothing, until he stumbled and fell to the floor.

Dray yelled to God for mercy. He was so intensely distraught he didn't realize that he was back in the saloon lying on the floor in agony.

"Dray, Dray, what is it, man? What's going on?" Detective Hauser asked as he got down on the floor and shook Dray until he recognized him.

Dray looked around and realized where he was and stood up. He felt his face and checked his hands for blood. He looked frightened and disoriented. He was sweating and his heart was pounding.

"Are you all right?" Detective Hauser asked.

"No. We have to get out of here. Remember we are looking for Redemption, not Sanctuary. Think about it. Who would give you anything and everything for free? We have to go. There are horrible strings attached to everything we get. We can't stay."

Dray looked at the lady with fear and anger. He took the bracelet from Carlita and threw it back at her. She laughed as she caressed Josh's forehead.

Josh lay back in the chair and drifted into the same blank space Dray was in. He was suffering from withdrawal pains. He had the shakes bad. He tried to stand up and walk toward nothing, hoping that wherever he ended up, it would be better than where he was now. He saw Iria standing in front of him. She walked toward him and kissed him on the cheek.

"I love you," she whispered.

She began to walk toward a door and he followed her. He was heaving and shaking in agony. His face was sunken and his teeth were rotting. She opened the door to a room that was empty except for the table that sat in the center of the room with a small vial and mirror on it. He cringed at the sight of himself looking so worn and tattered.

It's me, the old me, but what happened to me?

He couldn't bear to look at himself. He could only think about the pain. He looked at the vial and then at Iria.

"Will this help me?" he asked.

"Yes," she said. He began to walk toward it, but when he reached for it, it disappeared. He pulled back and it was there again. He reached again, and again it was gone.

"What is this? I thought you said it would help me."

"It can."

"Why can't I have it?"

"You can," she smiled.

He reached again and the vial faded into nothing and reappeared when he pulled back.

"This is crazy. It can't help me if I can't have it!"

"But you can. Just keep reaching for it, keep needing it, wanting it, and you will have it someday."

"God, I'm so tired. I'm in so much pain." He fell to his knees. "How long will this pain last?"

"For an eternity."

He looked at her. "What do you mean?"

"This is your eternity. You will always want and reach for what you can't have, and you will endure the agony and pain of wanting. It's the same pain you helped me and so many others come to know and love."

"I'll die before I live through this."

"You can't die."

"What do you mean?"

"You can't die. This is your eternity. You will reach for the elusive vial forever. You will always believe that you can have it."

Pain gripped Josh's stomach as he screamed in horror.

Carlita pushed the lady away from Josh as she heard his piercing scream. Josh stumbled outside.

The woman grabbed Carlita's arm, and Carlita drifted into darkness. She couldn't see anything.

"Help me! Will somebody help me? Where am I?" Carlita screamed as loud as she could.

The horror of the dark space was frightening to an extreme. She forced her hands upward, but something stopped her from pushing too far. She moved from side to side and realized that she was confined to a small, dark box. She began to yell and scream in horror. A faint light began to fill the space. She began to see her surroundings and realized that she was in a coffin. She cried in horror.

"Carlita," a voice spoke from out of nowhere.

She looked to her left and saw David lying beside her. His ashy, pale skin and dark, sunken eyes were cold and somber.

"Davie, oh God, Davie, what are you doing here? Where are we? What's happening to me?"

"You let me die, and now you will live a neverending death. Here you will be, and here you will stay throughout eternity."

"I will die in this box?"

"You cannot die. You will spend eternity wishing you could," he said as he began to disintegrate into sand.

Carlita screamed for mercy until she felt her body jolted backward as Detective Hauser pushed the woman back. The woman screamed in agony when Detective Hauser's hand touched her. She stepped back. It was obvious that she was in pain, but why?

The detective looked at his hands and wondered what happened. The lady lunged toward him again and he grabbed her face and forced her back. His hands burned her face as she screamed in agony. He stepped back.

"She protects you," the lady screamed.

"Who . . . who protects me? Who?"

"She has you, but I'll have them. They are mine," she said as she rushed toward Carlita. Dray reached for Carlita and grabbed her before the evil woman could reach her. Dray pulled her through the swinging doors, back into the desert sun where Josh was waiting.

"Who are you?" Detective Hauser asked as he stared at the woman standing by the bar.

"I will have their souls," she said as she began to laugh, an awful deadly laugh.

Detective Hauser walked out of the saloon toward the van. Suddenly they were all thrown off their feet when the van burst into flames and burned to the ground. They couldn't believe this. Now they would have to walk, and Josh was in no condition to carry himself. They had walked about two miles when Detective Hauser saw an image standing on a mound. He knew it was David. He couldn't make him out completely, but he knew.

"There's David. Do you see him?"

"Oh no . . . David." Carlita shuddered. She couldn't bear to look at him. She turned her face away from him. "I can't let him see me. I'm too ashamed. I can't see him. Please don't make me," she cried.

"He is our only hope. We have to follow him," Detective Hauser said. He turned around and noticed the police cars a few miles back. "We have to hurry." He picked up the pace and began to walk faster.

Josh was still feeling the effects of the drug and he couldn't get his bearings. He began to walk very fast, but in the wrong direction.

"Hey man . . . where're you going?" Dray yelled as he caught up with him and pulled him in the right direction.

Dray looked into Josh's eyes and feared the worst. "Man, when you come down, this is going to be bad," he said. He held onto Josh's arm and tried to help him keep up. They walked for a while when Josh fell to the ground. He lay across the dirt, exhausted and battered. Iria's frail body was lusting for more of her wonderful drug. The cravings were so strong that Josh was already trying to figure out how he would get the next hit.

"Dray . . . Dray, look man, all I need is just a little bit more, and I promise you that I will be all right. I won't need a lot, nope, not a lot. Just a little bit. You see, man. Can you help me? I'll pay you back, I promise. I feel that I can be stronger and get through this. I really do. I just need to get over this hump and then everything will be good, man, good. You gonna help me man . . . well, are you?" Josh asked as he sprawled out in the dirt.

Detective Hauser, Carlita, and Dray stopped walking and looked at him with total disgust on their faces.

"We are about to get caught by the police, and he's play-ing in the dirt. We don't have time for this," Carlita yelled. Detective Hauser walked over to him and helped Dray lift him to his feet. They wrapped his arms around their shoul-ders and began to carry him.

"Each of us were tempted. You wanted the bracelet as much as he needs the drug. Remember that," Dray said.

"You wanted your money too," she said.

"Yes, yes I did. So neither of us are in a position to judge the other," Dray said. "It seems that it's our job to protect each other and make sure we all make it."

"You're right . . . sorry. I know I wouldn't be here if he hadn't helped free me, you're right." She turned and began to walk. She looked back and noticed the police cars were getting closer. "We need to move faster," she said as she began to run.

They made it to the mound where David was standing, but he was nowhere to be found. They began to run. They ran as fast as they could. Dray and Detective Hauser were carrying Iria's body such that her feet were not touching the ground. They couldn't get any real speed with her body pulling on them. Carlita's fear was mounting as she saw the inevitable happening. She knew that if they were caught, they would be sentenced and sent to jail for years. She could end up in a mental institution or on death row for murder. She began to cry as she ran toward nowhere. She couldn't see an ending to this. She couldn't understand how all of this came to be and why she was fighting for her young life for one act of indiscretion.

It's not the act, she thought, *it's the heart. The heart has always lusted for things, and I was willing to do anything to get them. I have always been greedy and unconcerned about the needs of others. I don't know why. I just wanted so much. I'm sorry, God. Please don't let us die.* Tears rolled down Carlita's face as she looked back at Dray and Detective Hauser carrying Josh, and she saw the police cars upon them.

"Run!" she yelled as she turned around and ran with all the strength she had. Detective Hauser and Dray stepped up the pace. They wanted to leave Josh, but they knew that they couldn't. They had to go together. Sweat rolled from their faces as the sun beat down on them. The heat was unbearable and Dray struggled to stay on his feet.

"STOP, STOP RIGHT THERE!" a policeman yelled.

A half dozen police cars pulled up and stopped side by side, blocking their return path. They looked back, but never stopped running. They couldn't help it. Detective Hauser knew that if they didn't stop, the police would shoot, but he couldn't stop either. His heart was beating so fast he struggled to breathe. He thought of Mary and remembered her beautiful face. He thought that once this was over, he might be with her. He ran, knowing that the next breath he took might be his last.

"STOP OR WE WILL SHOOT! STOP, PUT YOUR HANDS ON YOUR HEAD, AND GET DOWN ON THE GROUND!" the policeman yelled.

"Detective Hauser, Pat, please, Pat. Please don't make me kill you. Please talk to me and tell me what's going on. I know you must have a good reason for this, but if you don't talk to me, I can't help you. Please, Pat, please," a policeman begged.

Detective Hauser recognized the voice as Captain Tracell. The sound of a friend calling his name stunned him. He began to slow his pace, which caused Dray to stumble. Dray fell to the ground and hit his knee on a rock. He screamed from the pain. Detective Hauser looked back at Captain Tracell with sad eyes, wanting so much to tell him why. He wanted him to understand, but he knew that if he went back, the outcome would be dreadful. It seemed that either choice was a bad choice at this point. The sound of Dray's scream startled him and he focused back on Dray and Josh. As he helped Dray up, Josh began to walk toward the policemen. He was oblivious and had no idea of the danger he was in.

"Grab him!" Carlita yelled. Detective Hauser looked up and ran toward Josh.

"Damn." He grabbed Josh's arm and pulled him back.

They began to run. They ran knowing the outcome and decided to end the nightmare right then.

"THIS IS YOUR LAST WARNING," Captain Tracell yelled.

The captain's plea fell on deaf ears. They didn't look back. They kept running, and suddenly they felt a cool breeze that seemed to calm them and remove all fear. They could hear the gunshots blaring and could feel their bodies being ripped apart by the bullets. Blood flowed everywhere as they fell. Dray grabbed his heart and looked down to see the blood pouring out of Madison's body. He felt deep regret and remorse for what he did as he fell to his knees. Josh felt the bullet rip through his back and shatter his spinal cord. He fell to his knees with his hands held open and laughed as he fell into the dirt. Carlita turned around to see her killers.

"Free me," she yelled at the top of her lungs as Silvia's body was riddled with bullets and she fell to the ground, facing Dray. She reached out to him as she passed into death. Detective Hauser reached out to the image of Mary. He could see her and knew that they would be together now. He smelled the roses and lilacs and smiled as he fell forward into the dirt. Captain Tracell was so angry. He wanted to bring them back. He hated that this had to happen.

"Why this way? What was going on, Pat? What where you doing with these people?" The captain looked around at his officers and asked them to close off the area and call the coroner and an ambulance. He walked toward the bodies, hoping that Pat was still alive. Captain Tracell kneeled down beside him and checked his pulse. He was gone. He stroked his hair.

"Goodbye, old friend," he sighed. "OK, folks, let's get this area cleaned up before dark. We need to be out of here before the night crawlers come out." He walked back to his car, leaving the cleanup in the hands of Sergeant Deberry.

"Who is that, Sarge?" Officer Stillwell asked.

"What . . . who?" Sergeant Deberry asked as he turned around to see a young boy standing by the bodies. "I've seen him before."

"Where?" Officer Stillwell asked.

"At the lake where they found Carlita Espinoza's body," he said. Sergeant Deberry walked toward David. He got within five feet of the bodies and couldn't go any further.

He couldn't lift his leg to go forward. He took a few steps back and decided to try again. He got within five feet and he couldn't even fall forward. "What the hell is going on?"

"What's up, Sarge?" Officer Stillwell asked as he walked toward him.

"I can't go past this point," he said.

"What?" Officer Stillwell said as he tried to take a step, but couldn't. "I don't understand this. The captain was just over there," he said as he pointed to Detective Hauser's body.

The captain was standing by his car. He could see what was happening, but he couldn't understand why they wouldn't walk beyond that point.

"What's stopping us?" Officer Stillwell asked.

"I don't know, but I think that boy has something to do with it," Sergeant Deberry said.

The policemen gathered at the edge of the crime scene and watched David move from one body to the next, touching them. David walked to Dray and place his hand across his forehead. The light of life streamed through his hand and into Madison's body and his eyes opened. His wounds disappeared as if they were never there.

David moved to each of them as if gliding. He seemed surreal and warm. He had a soft, blue-white aura around him. His angelic motion was calming and free. David touched Carlita, Josh, and Detective Hauser and they all stood without injury. They looked at themselves and wondered how this happened. They felt themselves die. They remembered their last breath and now they were standing and breathing as if nothing happened.

Dray looked back and saw Sergeant Deberry staring at him, in shock. Dray smiled. He knew they made it.

"Hey Sarge, where'd that town come from?" Officer Stillwell asked as he stared into the desert at an old Western town that seemed to have appeared out of nowhere.

Sergeant Deberry was stunned. He couldn't speak. He couldn't explain any of this and was wondering what he was going to tell the coroner when he showed up and there were no bodies. *I can't tell him that the dead bodies got up and walked away. But that's really what happened.*

"OK, does everyone see this, because I don't want to be the only person trying to explain this," Sergeant Deberry said.

"I don't think we should explain this. They will think we are all crazy or something," Officer Waterson said.

"We have to say something," Sergeant Deberry said. "They will think we got heatstroke or something. Either way, how can I explain the disappearance of the bodies while I'm looking at them?"

"I guess we'll have to tell the truth," Officer Stillwell said as he watched the four dead bodies walk toward the desert town. The other officers turned and looked at him in amazement of such a profound statement.

Captain Tracell walked toward the area where the bodies were and tried to step across. He couldn't step beyond the outer rim of the scene. "What the hell is this? Pat, Pat, wait; please let me talk to you. What's going on here? You can't just be dead and then be alive. It's not possible. Pat, talk to me," he yelled.

Pat looked back at him and smiled. "We had to get to Redemption. We had to save our souls."

Dray looked at Detective Hauser, surprised at the statement.

"What do you mean? There was never a threat against your soul," Dray said.

"Yes, there was. It's been lost for years. I never knew it until now," Detective Hauser said. They continued to walk toward the town, knowing that they now had a chance to redeem themselves.

PART FIVE

REDEMPTION

Therefore all things whatsoever ye would that men should do to you, do ye even so to them; for this is the law of the prophets.

Matthew 7:12

CHAPTER 14

Josh began to shake. He couldn't figure out what had just happened. He kept feeling his body and his face, and he wondered if he was dead or alive.

"Are we dead?" he asked.

"No," Dray said, but just as he said it, he realized that he wasn't sure either. He looked at Detective Hauser, hoping to get an answer.

"We should be dead, and I think that we were. I saw Mary when I was lying in the dirt back there. I saw her, I know I did. This is so strange. What happened to us?" Detective Hauser asked.

"I know what happened. We got shot and we should be dead. That's what happened," Josh said.

"We can't die," Carlita said. "Once we crossed over into Redemption, we can't die. We made it. Back there, we made it." She giggled and smiled with joy and excitement.

"I'm still not sure why I'm here," Detective Hauser said. "I guess I'll find out soon."

Dray, Josh, and Carlita walked toward the ghost town

that so vividly appeared in their dreams. Everything was just as they saw it with the swinging saloon doors and the tumbleweeds blowing from behind the old buildings. The few buildings that were left were falling down. The sand had overtaken much of the town. They could imagine the Old West playing out here with shootouts, bank robberies, and saloons full of people who started out looking for a different way of life, and ended up here, out in the middle of nowhere. Dray was afraid to move.

If I enter will I lose my eyes? Dray started to step backward when Detective Hauser stopped him.

"I have to know. What happens to all of you? In your dream, what happens?" Detective Hauser asked.

Dray hesitantly spoke. "In my dream, I enter the saloon and in the darkness, I lose my eyes."

"No, it's not my eyes. I lose my heart. A cannonball was fired through my chest and blew my heart out onto the dirt road," Josh said as he felt his chest to make sure the hole wasn't there. "What about you, Carlita?" he asked.

"I lose my hands, and I can't open the door, and my head has been decapitated. Since I can't open the door to get out, I'm looking at my head that's looking at me."

They all lived with the fear that the dreams were real and the lessons were yet to be learned. They stopped at the door as fear gripped them. They held onto each other.

"I can't go in there," Carlita said as she stared into the darkness.

"Yes, you can. We have to. We came this far and if we don't, what will happen may be worse than losing your hands," Dray said.

Detective Hauser stepped inside and turned back. He urged them to come in. He looked around the room as it filled with light, and he wondered why he had to be there. He didn't have any dreams of this place, nor did he commit any crime. He saw a bartender to his right and people moving about, talking and drinking like in any other bar. He stood at the door and tried to put purpose to his journey.

"OK, we have to go. We have to face it, whatever it is. We can't stay like we are, so our only option is to take our chances."

Dray abruptly stepped inside. They followed him. To their surprise, the place was bustling with people as if they had stepped one hundred years back in time. They stood at the entrance and watched the movement of people when a voice from the bar startled them.

"What'll you have?" he yelled over the crowd. Dray tried to be calm and walked toward the bar. "What's your poison?" the bartender asked.

"I'll have a beer," Dray said.

"One beer coming up." Dray took a seat at the bar and Josh found a bench near the back wall that he stretched out on. Carlita began to walk around, staring in amazement of the events unfolding in front of her, and Detective Hauser sat at a table near the door.

"What is all this? This isn't in the dream," she said.

"Maybe the dream has changed," Dray said.

"But why?" she asked as she found a chair at a table and sat. She was very shaken. She felt that something was yet to come that would terrify her. She was trying to be brave, but her heart was pounding from fear.

Dray sat at the bar drinking his beer and looked forward to the next one. "This is a strange place, sitting out here in the middle of the desert," he said.

"Strange . . . why strange?" the bartender asked.

"I mean, where do all these people live? There are no homes or apartments anywhere nearby. I don't see any cars. How did they get here? It just seems strange," Dray said.

"Cars have not been invented yet."

"Yet . . . what do you mean, yet?" The bartender laughed. "How do you know what they are if they haven't been invented yet?"

"I know a lot of things. There are things about you that are even stranger."

"About me? You can't know anything about me. What's strange about me?" Dray asked. "I just think it's strange that all of these people are here without any way of getting here. I mean, we're out in the middle of nowhere."

"You got here," the bartender said. Dray looked around.

"So, you mean all of these people are just like me? Did they get here the same way I did?"

"Some of them."

"Is this the end? Is this where we'll be forever?"

"That depends."

"On what?"

"On you. It's your choice."

"It wasn't my choice to end up here."

"Sure it was. The moment you put the gun in your hand, you made the choice."

Dray was shaken by the bartender's statement. He wondered how he knew about that, and he was frightened that yet again they had fled to the wrong place. He remembered that they died, and now he was here. But he wasn't sure if the place was Redemption or another trick.

"This whole thing is strange. I don't understand any of it. Did we die only to end up here forever?" Dray asked.

"Yes, what you did was strange, all right," the bartender said as he continually wiped the dust off of each glass and placed them in the rack.

"What do you mean, what I did?" Dray asked with a look of concern on his face. *How can this man know anything about what I did or will do?* "You know, killing that young man. I think that was strange."

Dray jumped up from the stool and stepped back. He stared at the bartender, wondering if he was the police or a bounty hunter of sorts.

"What . . . you thought no one knew?"

"How can you know? You don't know anything."

Dray's heart started pounding. He was puzzled by the man's reaction. *He knows I killed someone, but yet he seems to be a good sport about it. He doesn't seem to care.* Dray was very apprehensive about the bartender's motives. *Why, what does he want?* He laughed at the thought. *I don't have anything, so it doesn't matter what he wants, because I don't have it.* Dray sat back at the bar and calmed down.

"I didn't kill anyone," Dray said.

"You're lying," the bartender said in a steady tone that never showed any expression or emotion about anything.

The bartender was a medium-sized man with short, black hair. His olive skin was like the people of the Mediterranean. He had a very melodic sound when he spoke. He continued wiping the bar and cleaning the glasses. Dray didn't respond. He didn't know what to say. Somehow this man knew what he did. Any response would just add to the lie. He knew he couldn't hide it from the strange man.

"How do you know about that?" Dray asked.

"I know everything about you."

"What, how could you? We've never met."

"I am always with you."

"I don't know you. How can you always be with me if I've never seen you before? That makes no sense."

"Dray." The bartender looked at him and smiled. "That is what they call you, isn't it, Dray?"

"Yeah," Dray said hesitantly.

"Dray, do you think things happen for a reason?"

"I don't know. I'd like to think they do, but sometimes it

seems that we are just lumps of flesh bouncing off the wall into each other, going nowhere."

"Do you believe in heaven?"

"No. If there really is a God he should fix this mess."

"He can't fix it. That's your job, not his."

Dray laughed sorrowfully. "What can I do? I'm nobody."

"You can save one life, the life of Daniel Tanner."

"Oh God, how can you know about Daniel? How do you even know who I am? I look like Madison Tanner. I don't even look like myself. Are you a ghost or something?"

The bartender smiled, but never looked at Dray.

"Like you said, I've never seen you, so I don't know what you look like," the bartender said. "What form your body takes is irrelevant."

"I don't understand."

"No, you don't. You don't seem to understand anything, and you don't want to. That's the sad part. You don't want to."

"Yes, I do."

"Do you understand that if everyone made the choice not to kill someone, murder and war would cease to exist? So your choice adds to the ills of the world. Just one person can make that big of a difference. You made a difference in Madison and Barbara's life, didn't you?"

"Yeah, Barbara . . . I, I don't know what will happen to her."

"You don't care. You killed her life just as you killed Daniel. Her spirit is dead. Life as she knew it will never be the same. Hopefully her faith is strong enough that she will know the greater good and survive, but she will never recover totally."

"I didn't have any choice. I was born poor, and I will die poor."

"Poverty does not equate to ignorance and selfishness.

You had the chance to remove yourself from any environment, but you didn't try. It was too hard, and you didn't want it badly enough to work hard enough. You feared failure, so you didn't try at all. You didn't try to work at it, and fail, and work some more. You didn't have the courage to try. When your fourth grade teacher was trying desperately to teach you, what were you doing?"

"Acting a fool," Dray said with a sheepish grin on his face.

"That was a choice."

"I didn't understand then. I was a child."

"The others seemed to understand. It was easier for you to act up and not have to prove yourself than it was to try and fail and be laughed at for failing. You decided at nine years old that failure hurt, and you thought you weren't smart enough, so you stopped trying even then. That was a choice. At any time you could have changed that direction, but you didn't. At fourteen, instead of going to school, you hung out with your friends. That was a choice."

"We were having fun. How do you know all of this?"

"Really? That was having fun? Getting drunk and puking all over yourself? That was fun?"

"It seems kinda stupid now."

"It was stupid then, too. It is your choice to remain poor and ignorant. It is your choice to try to succeed, or languish and fail. It is your choice to care for all things or to go through life like a vulture feeding on the death and despair of others."

"I'm not ignorant. I don't feed off of the death of others."

"Yes, you do. Only an ignorant man would allow himself to be influenced by anyone to take another person's life simply for the glory of it. That's ignorant. That kind of man feeds his deadly spirit by the physical death of others."

"I took the only way I knew," Dray said in defiance. He

was getting angry and wanted this lesson to be over. The bartender gave him another beer. Dray looked at it and wondered if he should.

"Dray, you could have studied hard, went to college, and become a businessman and a family man. You could have joined the military and had a proud profession protecting your home and country. You could have graduated from high school and become a laborer and earned a decent living. You may not have been rich, but you would have lived with high moral values and dignity. You could have been there for support to anyone who needed you, even your mother. A man living paycheck to paycheck is a better man than the one who causes despair in the lives of others for selfish gains. You were not willing to fight for yourself. Are you worth fighting for?" He looked directly at Dray for the first time in the conversation and waited for an answer.

Dray took a moment to respond. His confusion was obvious. He wasn't sure of his own value, his own self worth.

"Am I worth fighting for?" he asked himself as he pondered the answer. He thought about all the choices he could have made and thought that if he had gone in another direction then he would be worth fighting for, *but now? Who am I now? I offer nothing.* But then he thought that maybe he could. "Yes . . . yes I am worth fighting for. I am going to choose differently if I ever get out of this mess." He remembered the shooting of Daniel and the look on Kuame's face when he accepted Dray as a member. "I don't know if I'll ever get back to myself, but things will be different if I do."

"How?" the bartender asked.

Dray thought of the possibilities, and he thought of his mother, who he had hurt so many times over the years. "I would not pull the trigger. I would not be in the gang or living on the street as I was. It would be different."

"I suspect that you are saying this because of the predicament that you're in now. It is hard to know if you are sincere. Would you be saying this if you were in Dray's body, and not Madison's, and the past few months did not happen?"

"If I were in my body, I would not be here. It is Madison's life and Daniel's death that led me here. Maybe things do happen for a reason. Maybe by going through this, I'll have a chance to change my life."

"But if you go back to being Dray, either Kuame will kill you, or you will go to jail for killing Daniel. Either choice is a bad choice."

"Yes, I know, but I will deal with it somehow. I shouldn't have taken a life to save my own. I just wish there was a way to make this up to my mom."

"So, you would be willing to give your life for Daniel's?"

"Well, as you pointed out, it's not worth much anyway," Dray said as he shrugged his shoulders.

The bartender smiled, slid a wineglass into the rack, and began cleaning the countertop.

Dray looked over at Josh. "He needs some help. He's in pretty bad shape," Dray said.

"Here . . . give him this. It will make him feel better." The bartender poured something into a glass and handed it to Dray. Dray walked over to the table and gave the glass to Josh.

"Take this. It will make you feel better," Dray said.

Josh looked at the glass and wondered what was in it, but he really didn't care if it killed him as long as it took the awful pain away. He drank the liquid and laid his head on the table.

Dray looked back at the bartender and wondered how he knew so much about him. *How can he reach inside of me unlike anyone ever has, and see so much?* The bartender glanced up at Dray briefly as if he could feel Dray's stare, and then he went back to cleaning the counter and arranging the glasses. Dray watched as Josh fought the pain and tried to rest.

Carlita moved around the room. She noticed a man standing in a dark corner.

"Who are you and why are you standing over there in the dark?" she asked.

"I am blind, so I'm always in the dark."

"Oh, I'm sorry," she said sadly.

"There is no need to be," he said.

"You may be blind, but you do not have to be alone." She stared into the corner, trying to get a better look at the man.

"It is because of my heart that I am alone, not my blindness."

"Your heart, what does your heart have to do with your eyes?"

"It is because of my vengeful heart that I lost my sight."

"How?"

"I stole something from someone. Something very precious."

"You stole something? What . . . how could stealing something make you blind?"

She slowly walked closer to get a better look at the man. Where the light struck his face she could see that he was a small, thin Hispanic man with beautiful black hair that hung in his face. He was very handsome with soft, sculptured features.

"People who steal cannot see."

"That's not true. I can see," she said fervently.

"Oh, so you are a thief?"

"No . . . maybe, once or twice I may have borrowed things and forgot to return them, but I intended to. I just forgot."

"Only once or twice. I guess that makes it OK. You should be proud of yourself."

"I wouldn't say all that. I mean, I know I got my faults, but all in all, I'm not a bad person."

"Oh, I see, because there's no physical harm, your deed is justifiable. I wonder if Silvia Watkins feels the same as you do."

Carlita stepped back. The blind man frightened her. "How do you know about Silvia? What are you, some kind of psychic?" She stepped back again slowly. She began to look around to see how she would escape if she had to.

"No, I'm not psychic, but now that I'm blind, I see many things that I could not see before."

"You can't see," she said nervously. "You are blind." She was afraid. *How does he know these things about me? Who told him and why?* She started to walk away. She stopped and looked back at him. "What did you steal?"

"I stole someone's sight."

She became very curious and wanted to know more. She moved a little closer.

"How?"

"I threw acid into a woman's face and blinded her. It is just as well. That's what I tell myself."

"Why?"

"Because now she can't see her disfigured face."

"That's horrible. Why would you do such a thing?"

"Because I could. The opportunity presented itself and I took it."

"You're sick," Carlita said in disgust. "She must have hurt you pretty badly for you to do something like that."

"There is nothing she could have done to warrant that . . . nothing," he said in a tone so sad and sorrowful that Carlita found herself fighting back tears. "But I guess there is a justifiable reason to steal someone's livelihood, their home, their child, their means of survival. I guess it's better to know that someone is eating from trash cans because you wanted to go shopping. It makes you all warm and fuzzy inside, doesn't it?" He chuckled.

"It's not funny." Her face was red with anger.

"Why?"

"I don't know what's happened to me, but ever since I stole that money, I have been different. My life changed. I became her, and I've been living on the street and begging for food and money. We stayed in alleys and abandoned cars. It's been awful. I didn't intend for this to happen. I didn't know." She began to cry. She hid her face in her hands and cried.

"What do you think people do with the money they earn?" he asked very firmly to let her know that crying would not get sympathy or erase what happened.

"I don't know. I guess they pay bills and buy food and stuff like that."

"So, when you steal the money, how do they do those things and what happens when they don't?"

"I don't know."

"You mean, you don't care."

"Yes, I do," she said as she tried to clean her face with her hand. "I do care."

"Oh, really? Why . . . because you are having this experience? You find yourself trapped and you can't fix it, so now you want to repent and pretend to care. Is that why?"

"No, I mean yes, I mean . . . I don't know. I guess I was pretty bad. I don't know why. I guess it was easier than working for it. I never thought about how it would affect anybody, until now. It's horrible. I'm horrible. Silvia will never see him again. I can't imagine what that must be like. I'm so sorry, so sorry."

He stepped out of the shadows and walked over to her. He stroked her hair.

"You see, it is the heart that is blind, not the eyes. Whatever you can see with your heart, you can fix." He gently kissed her forehead and used his cane to walk to the bar.

She turned and watched him order a drink and converse with the bartender. Dray walked over to her and hugged her.

"Are you all right?" he asked.

"Yeah, I guess so."

"These people in here are a little strange, aren't they?"

Dray looked around at the various characters in the room—the bartender, the blind man, a woman in a wheelchair, a man with one arm, a burn victim, and a child with a metal plate in her head. It was a smorgasbord of accidents and injuries throughout the room. Dray was starting to wonder if this place was a holding station for people who were sick or injured and were waiting to move on to another place, heaven or hell. Everyone appeared to have an injury except the bartender. There was nothing physically wrong with him. He couldn't figure out the bartender. What was wrong with him? There was nothing wrong that Dray could see. He watched the woman in the wheelchair stop at Josh's table. She sat there for a while watching him try to sleep.

Detective Hauser was mesmerized by all he saw. He searched the room looking for some clue as to why he had to be there. He looked at the bartender and nodded his head in recognition. The bartender nodded back. He watched Dray try to comfort Carlita and noticed the woman in the wheelchair staring at Josh. He felt a cool breeze from behind him and he turned abruptly to see who was there.

"Hello" the small voice said.

"Hello" he responded hesitantly. He stared at the little

girl and noticed the metal plate in her head. "Are you here for me?" he asked.

"Here for you? No, David said that you were a nice man."

"You've seen David?" he asked.

"Yes, he is my friend. He said that you were very lonely. Why?"

"I lost my wife some years back."

"That made you sad," she said as she began to twirl around and around. "Did you know you still had God?"

"Yes, no, I don't know. Maybe I didn't. I couldn't think of it at the time and now, I'm not sure."

"You think he left you, don't you?" she said.

"I suppose so; some part of me does," he said as he turned back around and stared at the table and wondered if he really felt that way.

"That's all right; a lot of us feel that way. That's why we act so crazy some times; we think he forgot about us," she said.

"Hasn't he?"

"Of course not, you silly man." She laughed and started twirling around the table. She stopped and walked up to him. "Do you like my dress?" she asked as she pulled on it so he could see how pretty it was.

"Yes it is a beautiful dress."

"I got buried in it. My mama bought it new."

Detective Hauser stared at her. He was amazed that the statement she just made didn't shock him. Her relationship with David told him that she had some connection with the other side and after everything that had happened to him lately, nothing much surprised him anymore.

"How did you die?" he asked.

"I fell. It was wonderful. I cracked my skull, see," she said as she pointed to her metal plate.

Detective Hauser was amazed at her statement.

"It was wonderful? Why? You died?"

"Yeah, I know, but the moment before the end I was flying in the heavens. I wasn't scared because I knew God had me. I could see the beautiful angel beside me as I fell. She was there to take care of me on the way. I think because I'm so young, we are still connected to things that grown-ups can't see. David knew too, an angel came to him. The angel told David that you would help them, and you did, just like she said."

The girl was cute with long, blond hair on one side and a metal plate on the other side of her skull. She seemed to have been full of life before the accident. She was about ten years old. She had a lot of energy, which annoyed Detective Hauser a bit. His eyes followed her around as she moved around the table and from one end of the room to the other. Ever so often she would stop and say something.

"If you did nothing wrong, why are you here with these people?" he asked.

"Yep, just like you, I didn't do anything wrong. I'm here to tell you about your angel."

"My angel? I don't have one."

"Sure you do. That's why I had to tell you, because grown-ups don't know they have one, but you do and she is always with you. You have been so sad and unhappy that even your angel is sad, and we want you to make her happy again.

"How?" He looked at her strangely. *How can I make an angel happy? I should have known that whatever awaited me would be so farfetched that I would never achieve it.* "You will see," she said as she started running back and forth across the room.

Detective Hauser looked at the bartender, hoping for something more. The bartender acknowledged his stare, but continued cleaning the bar. Detective Hauser sat and waited for a sign. He looked around the room and noticed the woman in the wheelchair talking to Josh. He wondered if Josh had the strength to fight the pain that came with coming down from a high.

He's a survivor; somehow he'll make it, thought Detective Hauser as he watched and waited for the next move.

"It's hard, isn't it?" the woman in the wheelchair asked. Josh looked up at her.

"What . . . what . . . are you talking to me?" he asked.

"It's hard, isn't it?" she asked again.

"What's hard?" Josh lashed out at her.

"Being crippled."

"I'm not crippled," he replied as rudely as possible. He was obviously disturbed by her interference with him trying to get some rest.

"Yeah, I see, you can get up right now, walk out of here, and do anything in life you want to do. So, go ahead, do it." She turned and pointed to the door as if daring Josh to take that first step.

"I can if I want to. I'm able to do anything I want to do. I can walk right out of here."

The woman in the wheelchair looked at Josh, looked at the door, and then looked back at him and waited for him to take the walk. He knew he couldn't do it, no matter how much he might have wanted to. His body wasn't going anywhere. He had the shakes so badly he couldn't breathe without agony and pain, so there was no chance of him walking. He was in so much pain. He looked at her, knowing that somehow she knew he couldn't move.

"OK, I can't do it now, but I will. Just give me a minute."

"Famous last words: 'I will someday.'" She smiled at him and shook her head. "It takes great courage to overcome a disability."

"I am not disabled!"

"Oh, so you can function just like everyone else? Oh, oh, I forgot. You can't do it now, but you will someday. I got it."

"Yes."

"Really?" She gave him a quizzical look as she waited for him to recognize his condition and face his greatest enemy—himself.

"Yes, well, no, I mean yes, I did once." Josh remembered his nice apartment, sleek, fast car, and his great wardrobe. His loss saddened him as if he lost a dear, old friend.

"Yeah, I know what you mean. I did once too."

"What happened?"

"I liked my scotch and soda. I was the life of the party, so they say. I was always there and always drunk. One night I decided to sneak out the party through the back door without saying goodbye, and that way no one would know I was gone. You see, that way I didn't have to hear about drinking and driving and 'somebody take her car keys' or 'will somebody drive Paige home?'"

Josh sat up to listen. "What happened?"

"Amazingly, I got out of the yard without killing anyone, but just a few blocks down the road, I wasn't so lucky. Just as I approached the intersection, the light turned red, or so they say. I couldn't tell. I didn't know there was a light. I didn't see the car coming across the street on my left. I kept going and plowed right into them. The mother died on impact, and her daughter will be in a wheelchair for the rest of her life. She was sixteen with a boyfriend, a prom, and graduation to experience, but now she can hardly feed herself. I never took the blame for it. Of course, it was a faulty light system or they were driving too fast or something. While I was in jail for manslaughter, I woke up one morning and couldn't walk. They say it's psychological because I never accepted what I did. Maybe, I don't know. I know I can't walk. I crippled someone, and now I'm crippled. Did you cripple someone?"

"No, I never crippled anyone. I don't hurt people."

"You are lying. You are hurting someone now."

He looked at her with anger and resentment of her prying and needling him about something she knew nothing about. "What if I am, so what?" he lashed back at her.

"Why?"

"I don't know."

"What's happening to you?"

"I don't know. It's strange," Josh said. He was exhausted from the inner struggle, and the fatigue was starting to wear him down. "I woke up one morning in somebody else's body. I know it sounds weird, but this is not who I am."

"Who are you?"

"I am a man, and I live very well."

"Wow, that is hard to believe. So, you're really a man and you're not really an addict?"

"No, no, my name is Josh Brimeyer and I'm a salesman."

"What do you sell?"

"Things," Josh said as he stumbled and tried to come up with something credible. "I sell hardware."

"What kind of hardware?"

"All kinds. Damn, why do you ask so many questions?" He really felt stupid. He knew she knew he was lying, but he was too far in to stop now. "It really doesn't matter, does it?" He withdrew into a silence, hoping she would go away.

"I was a saleswoman too, in a way," she said. "Yep, I sold pain and lots of it. I sold pain and hurt and disappointment to a lot of people. Being an addict hurts everyone around you. It is a horrible way to live. I regret the day I met the man who introduced me to drinking. I lost my husband

and my job. But even worse, I started drinking with my children, so they are alcoholics too. I share no blame for their demise. They should have known better, should have had more control. I share no fault at all." She was saddened at the loss of their beautiful lives. "I didn't try to stop them or help them, but still it's not my fault."

"You're right, it's not your fault. They could have said no or they could have been strong enough to stop. Just because someone gives it to you, does not mean you have to keep taking it."

"You are so right. So, I guess this bag of heroin I have in my pocket will be of no use to you."

The woman reached into her pocket, pulled out a small bag of the drug, and laid it on the table. Josh stared at it. He started to salivate. He wanted it more than life itself. He reached for it, but pulled back. He couldn't take it. He had to play along, because he just boasted about his strength and control.

"Why would you have this stuff?" he asked.

"I have an addictive personality. It is a sickness, and people who prey on that sickness for their personal gain are thieves. They rob people of their lives, of their well-being and joy. They kill the spirit and let the body live in a state of chaos and despair. We are just empty shells moving around with no purpose except staying high. It's what I live for. I guess you wouldn't know anything about that since you are in control." She moved the drug closer to him. "Who got you hooked, was it a friend?" she asked.

"Yes, a friend," he said as he stared at the bag and began to rub his hands together, holding them tightly. He hoped one hand would keep the other one from reaching for the bag.

"Someone who you thought cared about you? It is amazing how we trust people who make us feel good about ourselves. Love is a strange beast, isn't it? It's so joyous and so painful."

Josh stared at the heroin.

"It calls to you to enjoy the love and the pain. It will love you, embrace you. It wants you as much as you want it. But you are in control, and the person who sold these drugs to you knew that you would always be in control, and would be able to stop anytime. Didn't you, Josh?"

He couldn't stand it. He pushed the drugs aside and rushed into the restroom to throw up. He gagged over the toilet for a few minutes, but afterward he felt better. Whatever he drank made him bring up the poison that had his stomach all twisted in knots. He stared in the mirror and watched the image of Iria stare back at him. He could see her eyes. *She is in here. She is calling for me to help her, but I can't. I can't even help myself.* Josh walked back into the room and over to Carlita and Dray.

"Why is this happening to us? Who are these people and what do they want with us?" Josh asked.

"I don't know, but it seems that each of them did something terrible and they are paying the price for it just like we are," Dray said.

"Do you think we will have to stay here forever like them?" Carlita asked.

"I don't know," Dray said as he looked around at all of the strange people. "I don't know."

"That blind man over there threw acid in a woman's face and blinded her. Isn't that terrible? Now he's blind," Carlita said, as she became very sad and scared that this was some kind of purgatory.

"That woman crippled a child and killed the mother because she was driving drunk. She said that for no reason one day she just couldn't walk," Josh said.

"I can't figure out the bartender. There seems to be nothing wrong with him. Why is he different? He seems to have some kind of control over the others. It's like he is the center of this place," Dray said as he looked at him, hoping that something would appear to show why he was there.

"It doesn't matter. We are just as guilty as they are. We ruined lives or we helped to bring about their demise. One thing's for sure; none of us can profess to have helped anyone. I don't care about these people. I just want to find a way out of here and back to myself," Carlita said.

"She's right," Josh said. "I want to get back to who I was." He walked over to the bartender. "What is happening to us?"

"What do you want to happen to you?" the blind man asked.

"What should happen to you?" the woman in the wheelchair asked as she moved around the room joyously whirling her chair around as if it were a toy. Her childlike manner was refreshing and annoying at the same time.

She's like a child. She makes me happy, but I wish she would stop, Detective Hauser thought.

The bartender continued to wipe the glasses and clean the counter. He looked into Josh's eyes, but said nothing.

"I want to go back to being who I was, I think," Josh said.

"I don't," Dray said.

"Me neither," Carlita said.

The bartender looked at Dray and smiled. "Who do you want to be?"

"I want to be like you," Dray said. "I want to have purpose and meaning in my life. I want to make something out of myself and make my mama proud."

"And you, Carlita?" the blind man asked.

"I want to undo what I did and never do it again, or anything like it. I'm so sorry I lost Davie. I was responsible for him, and I failed. I would give anything to undo that."

"Yes, it would be different," Josh said as he walked back toward a table and sat down.

Detective Hauser watched and listened to what was going on. He listened to everyone's story and noticed the movement of the people at the bar. He looked at the bartender again, thinking that if anyone could tell him why he was there, he could.

"Why am I here?" Detective Hauser asked.

"Why, you are the main reason we are all here," the bartender said.

"Me?" He pointed to himself. "What do I have to do with any of this? I haven't done anything wrong. I didn't commit a crime. What purpose do I have in all of this?"

"You committed the greatest crime, and you committed it against yourself."

"What do you mean?" he demanded in a frustrating and confused tone.

"You are living with guilt. You can't let it go, and even though it is not an earthly crime, the Creator knows your heart is bitter and broken. Your heart carries so much pain, so why continue? It was decided that you should bridge the gap and move on. But then, we thought that a journey might give you back your life force. A journey that would force you to search your inner self for strength and hope that would give you peace until your end comes and the plight of these young people could be the focus of your journey."

"So, they went through this because of me?"

"No, you found your passion because of them."

"Why, why would you care about me? Why would my 'inner self' matter to any of you? Where would I be moving on to? I don't understand any of this," Detective Hauser said.

"You know, life is a strange thread. We think that we start

at one point and continue walking the line until we get to the end. We think it is a forward path. I've always wondered why," the bartender said. "This thread can be shaped in many different ways at different times in our existence. It's the same thread, whether you are in the body or not. It's the same thread that moves you from one existence to another. For many, life is a circle. At the end of life, you go back to where you began. For others, it is a zigzag. In sync today and out tomorrow, and then this existence ends abruptly and another begins. You breathe every day, but your life ended five years ago."

"With Mary," he whispered as he hung his head.

"Yes. Letting go is more difficult for you than most. I suppose it has something to do with your ego, or the lack thereof."

"I still don't understand what my lesson is. It seems that each one of these young people learned a valuable lesson, but what can I learn? How not to be guilty? Please give me more than that.

"You had to find your angel. You had to find your reason for living, your connection with God. Your sadness bridged the gap between life and death, and the sorrow was an overwhelming burden to bear. You had to find your angel," said the bartender.

"I just lost my life back there. There's got to be more than that. What angel? Who could that be?"

"There's more than that," the bartender said. He looked to his left and David stood at the end of the bar. Carlita ran to him and hugged him.

"Davie, you're all right. Please forgive me. I'm so sorry," she said.

"Don't cry. Things happened, as they should. I had to get them together," he said.

"Who?" she asked. David looked at Detective Hauser.

"Your angel told me that you would help," David said as he looked at the figure standing in a dark corner behind him.

Detective Hauser stood and walked toward the figure. He stopped when he recognized her face.

"Mary, my angel" he whispered. She stepped forward and stared at him. He embraced her and began to cry. "Oh God, Mary. How can you be here? I've missed you. Did God bring you back to me?"

"My love," she said, "I knew that if you felt that they were in trouble, you would help them. I knew that you would do whatever you had to do to get them here, and you did. You even sacrificed your own life. Your heart is still passionate and strong, and you needed to know that. You needed to know that you have life within you that is fading and losing to sorrow. I carry your sorrow, I carry your sadness with me, and I can not cross into eternity with it. You have to let me go. I can not go and leave you in this sorrow, it is because of me that you carry this pain. You had to come so that we could free your heart and remove your pain, free my soul and remove my guilt. I was the one driving; I was the one who had to go out that day. If you had been driving, it may have been different, but I insisted and now you're hurting and I will carry your pain always. I am always with you, and God loves you so much and does not want you to cry any longer. If your heart remembers that, you will find the peace you so desperately need. We will be together again, know that to be true. I love you and miss you, but I don't want you to stay here. We will be together again, but not now, please go back and enjoy your life. They think you should cross over, but I knew that you still had a passion for life, it just needed to be awakened and this journey did that for you. I want you to live."

"I'm not leaving you, Mary. I will not be without you

again." He kissed her hands and stroked her face. "Please don't make me go back to nothing. I have nothing," he said.

"My dear, you have life, and this is not a place for the living. You can't stay," she said.

"Then I'll die." He looked at the bartender and acknowledged his statement. "He just said that I needed to move on. I'm no good in this life without you, and I won't stay." He took his gun from his belt and pointed it to his head. She screamed as she reached for the gun and stopped him.

"No," she yelled. "You have a life. You cannot take it. God will never forgive you if you take it. Please, my dear, don't give up your life. Please try for me. We will be together in time. I love you and want to be with you, but not at the expense of your life force, and now I know you still have a passion for life. You just needed a reason. It's still there; your joy is still there. Don't give up on yourself." She took the gun from him and placed it on the bar. She held him in her arms and stroked his hair.

He held her and cried.

"Mary, I don't want to live without you anymore." He laid his head on her shoulder and cried. "If they are ready to take me, let me come with you."

"Life is God's gift. Never give up on it," she said as she held him tightly.

"I don't understand any of this," Dray said. "How does this help us? How does this get us back to who we were? Is this Redemption? Is this the place that's supposed to help us?"

"No, this is not Redemption. Redemption is not a place. It is a state of grace. All of you have gone through a horrible experience and through it came a revelation of the inner self. The evil one fought for you and almost won, but I could see that the journey forced you to see yourself differently and each of you would make a different choice knowing what you know now. But I wonder what choice you would make if you had no knowledge of the events that took place over the past few months. Has your inner spirit changed from the experience? It's hard to say without reliving the past," the bartender said.

"Re-living the past, how can we do that?" asked Josh.

"Anything is possible in God's world," said the blind man.

"What about Detective Hauser? Why can't he stay with his wife? Both of them seem so lost without each other. It seems like there should be a way," Carlita said.

Josh walked over to Carlita, placed his hand on her shoulder, and looked into Dray's eyes.

The bartender smiled at Carlita. He could see the look of concern in their eyes.

"Yes, maybe there is a way, maybe there is," he said. He was pleased that they were willing to give of themselves for someone else. "If there is anything we can do to help him, we'll do it. He has helped us more than most people ever have. If it wasn't for him, I would be dead in an alley," Josh said. "God, I wish we had a second chance. We would make this all different. If we only had . . ."

Josh stopped in the middle of his sentence. He was overwhelmed when all the people in the room started to glow. A beautiful white and blue light began to radiate from each of them. Josh, Dray, Carlita, and Detective Hauser were in awe of the sight. They should have been scared, but it was so calming and serene that they wanted to take it all in. The light eventually filled the room, and each person became a silhouette of glowing light. Then the light became more intense and blinding. The forms of bodies illuminated into pure light. It was so bright they covered their eyes as the warmth from the light bathed their bodies. The light became too bright to endure for a second, and then it was gone.

When Dray opened his eyes, he found himself standing in the alley across the street from Macy's grocery store. He had a gun in his hand. He nervously looked down at it as he saw Daniel Tanner walk out of the store to his car. He knew what to do. He prepared himself and pointed the gun directly at Daniel. He was panicking, hesitating, and his stomach turned sour. He couldn't understand why.

I can't do it. This isn't right.

He dropped his arm and watched Daniel drive away, knowing that he had just lost his own life.

What am I going to do now? I can lie, but they will find out. I can't say I didn't do it. They'll see me as a coward and kill me for sure. Just as he dropped his arm and realized he just gave his life for Daniel's, he felt a bulge in his right pocket.

He leaned against the wall and put his hand in his pocket. He felt something unusual and when he pulled his hand out he was holding five hundred dollars. He had no idea how it got there, or who it belonged to. He started to run. He wiped the gun down with his shirt and tossed it into a trash can. He finally made it home, ran inside, and hugged his mother.

"Boy, what is wrong with you?" she yelled at him. "Why are you acting so crazy?" She caressed his face and looked into his eyes lovingly.

"I'm fine, Mama. I'm better than I've ever been. It's so good to see you. God, I've missed you." He lifted her from the floor in a big hug and kiss. "I don't know why, but it seems like a long time since I've seen you?" he laughed.

"Missed me? Boy, you haven't been anywhere. What are you talking about?"

He put her down and smiled at her joy to see him so happy.

"Mama, if you had somewhere to go, away from here, where would you go?" he asked.

"Boy, what are you talking about?" She moved through the apartment picking up things and putting them back in their proper places.

"Where would you go?" He had a serious look on his face. His manner seemed mature and masculine.

"I'd go home, where I grew up in North Carolina where our family is Irene and Janice, and my cousins Edna Ruth and big mama Pearl. We would hang out all night just like we use to." She laughed. "Yes, I'd like to go there." She smiled wistfully at the thought of going home to loved ones.

"OK, let's get packed." Dray went into her room and pulled out the suitcase from under the bed.

"Dray, have you lost your mind? We don't have the money to go anywhere."

"Yes, I do, and I didn't steal it. I worked for it, and I'm going to get you out of this ghetto tonight," he said.

"But Dray you just can't show up in North Carolina on someone's doorsteps and say, 'I'm here.' We can't leave tonight," she said.

"Yeah, you're right." Dray walked into the living room and made a phone call. "Hi, Aunt Janice, this is Dray in California."

"Dray, how are you, baby? Is everything all right?"

"Yeah, everything is fine. Aunt Janice, can I speak to Uncle Willie?"

"Sure honey, hold on." Janice put the receiver down and found her husband, Willie. D

Dray threw a kiss to his mother as she stood in the hallway watching her son take charge. It was like watching a movie unfold in front of her.

"Uncle Willie, this is Dray."

"Hey man, what's up, what can I do for you?"

"Uncle Willie, I want to bring my mama home, and I was hoping you could help us find some honest work. Something for me too, so I can help support her. We can find our own apartment and we won't have to live off of anybody. Can you help me?" Dray asked.

"You sure this is Dray? Dray from California. The Dray who never thought about work, no less actually doing any?"

"Yeah, it's me. I plan to do right, Uncle Willie. I'm going to finish school and work nights. I won't let you down," he said.

"Dray, if you really want to work, I got a job for both of you. I can find something for your mama, and you can work in my shop in the evenings until you find something that you want to do. I think this is great. You wouldn't be all the way out there anyway if it weren't for that crazy ass father of yours, God rest his soul. Janice will be happy, that's for sure. You and your mama just come on."

"Thanks, we will be there in a few days. Thanks, Uncle Willie." Dray hung up and called the bus station. "When is your next bus to North Carolina . . . Charlotte, North Carolina?"

"We have a bus leaving at twelve o'clock midnight headed for Charlotte, North Carolina. You'll have to switch in Mississippi. The trip will take about four days. The drivers will change every twelve hours and take breaks every four hours, but we will get you there," the young lady on the phone said.

"Thank you," Dray said. "Reserve two seats for that bus under the name of Darrell Hunter."

"Thank you, sir." The young lady began typing all the information into the computer. "Thank you, Mr. Hunter. You have two seats reserved on bus number 29 for Charlotte, North Carolina. Please check in two hours before departure and have your picture identification available. Thank you."

"Thank you," Dray said and hung up the phone.

"Dray, we can't leave tonight. What about our things? And I have to contact my job. I can't just up and leave like this."

"Look around, Mama. What's in here that's worth keeping? Everything we need will fit in a box. Most of this stuff is in the past. It's from a life we are going to escape from, and we only need to take our clothes and ourselves. So grab a few precious things, like pictures and books, and let's go. We are leaving tonight. We are looking forward now, Mama, into the light."

Dray hugged her and looked into her eyes. She realized the seriousness of his conviction and started to cry. They were tears of joy and excitement for going home. She was not sure why Dray had changed so suddenly, but she was not scared or upset with the idea. She wanted to do this for a long time, but life kept getting harder and harder, and the time never came. The money was never there.

Dray's mother walked into her room and started to pack all of the things she thought she'd need to start a new life. She pulled her Bible from the shelf and held it close to her breast as she looked around the room. She was not looking back with fond memories, but rather she was realizing that the wait was finally over and maybe this was the way it should have been done all along.

Faith, she thought. *We'll walk out on faith and let God give us the strength we'll need to begin again.* She put everything of any value into that old suitcase and walked into the living room, ready to go.

Dray pulled together a few things and threw them in a duffel bag and was standing by the window waiting for his mother to finish. He looked outside into the night hoping that they made it to the bus station before Kuame started looking for him. The gang members were going to realize that he should have been there by now, and they would begin to wonder if he took the coward's way out and ran. He knew he didn't have much time, but he allowed his mother to take her time and soak this all in. This was a sudden change, but he knew it was the right thing to do. He knew somehow that he wouldn't falter, for if he did, it would cost him his life. He had a strange feeling of peace. He was always torn inside and broken, never feeling balanced and free, belonging nowhere. He thought about what he almost did, and he cringed at the thought of taking someone's life.

How could I? Who am I to make the decision that a person should die today? I can't believe I could be that cruel. He watched his mother take one last look around as she walked to the door and opened it.

"I'm ready," she said and she turned and walked out. Dray walked behind her, reached up, and turned off the lights. He didn't look back.

Josh found himself standing outside one of the local bars. He looked all around, feeling a little out of place. He knew the place, but for some reason it seemed different tonight. He walked into the club and wandered around the room for a few minutes. He stopped at the bar and got his usual gin and tonic. He looked over to his left and saw the most beautiful woman he'd ever seen. She was small, with wide blue eyes and long golden hair. Her smile was welcoming and her laugh was joyous.

How lovely, he thought.

She caught his eye and began to stare. He decided to walk over and meet the woman of his dreams.

"Hello. Would you like to dance?" he asked.

"Yes," she said as she smiled and stood to take his hand. He guided her to the dance floor and held her in his arms.

"Hi, my name is Josh Brimeyer."

"Iria Tinsdale," she said with this shy look on her face. She smiled and nestled herself into his shoulder.

"Iria, that's a very pretty name. It fits you," he said lovingly.

Josh and Iria spent the evening together getting to know each other over peanuts, pretzels, and wine. They laughed and shared their inner feelings as if they'd known each other for years. She looked at her watch and realized it was two o'clock in the morning. She stood to say goodnight.

"Do you have to leave?" Josh asked. "We're having such a good time."

"Yes, it's late and I have things to do tomorrow, but I hope there will be another time."

"There will be if it's up to me."

"It's up to you," she said as she turned to walk out the door. He walked her to her car and they continued talking.

"So, what did you say you do for a living?" she asked.

Josh had been avoiding the answer to that question all night. He couldn't tell her that he was a drug dealer, and he didn't want to lie. He felt very strange about even talking about it, as if it wasn't really who he was. He stumbled around for the answer for a minute and realized that he really wasn't a drug dealer, at least not anymore. For some reason, he couldn't see himself doing that ever again. He couldn't give another person that poison and pass it off as a wonderful thing. His conscience was pushing back and he didn't know why. Any other time he would have pursued her as another customer, but he couldn't even imagine doing that to her or anyone else. He opened his mouth and what came out surprised even him.

"I've saved some money over the years and I'm going back to school in the fall," he said.

"That's great. What will you study?"

"Counseling . . . I want to study counseling for substance abuse. Hopefully I'll get my degree in some form of counseling and therapy. It's a field I can relate to, I think. I don't know why, though."

She smiled and hugged him.

"That's wonderful, Josh. My father is a psychologist, and I'm sure he would be willing to help you in any way that he can."

Josh kissed her tenderly and she held him close, wishing the moment would never end. He took out a pen and paper and wrote his phone number down. He tore the paper in half and handed her his number.

"What's your number?" he asked.

She took the pen and paper, wrote her number down, and handed it back to him.

"If I don't call you, it's because I lost this, so you call me if you don't hear from me tomorrow. I really don't want to lose touch with you," Josh said. He kissed her again and said goodnight.

Josh watched as she pulled away and drove down the street. He looked around for his car, reached into his pocket for his keys, and pulled out the bag of drugs that he usually carried with him. He stared at the bag and closed it in his hand. He walked over to a trash can in the back of a building and tossed the bag in.

I don't know why, but I can't . . . I just can't. Tomorrow will be a beautiful day and I will be a different person. He walked away with Iria on his mind, leaving his former life in that trash can.

* * *

Carlita watched Silvia board the bus and prepare for her long ride home. She stared at Silvia as if she knew her. Silvia was so tired. She worked two jobs to maintain a home for her son, David. As hard as she tried, she could not keep her eyes open. Carlita watched the woman as she fell asleep, leaving her purse exposed.

It's Friday. She probably got paid today. I sure could use the money. Carlita moved to a seat that was closer to Silvia. People were getting off the bus at every stop. As the bus got closer to the end of the line, fewer people were on board. *It's almost empty now. No one would know.*

Carlita reached over to take the purse as Silvia slept. She reached, but she couldn't seem to reach far enough. She hesitated. *What's the problem?* She reached for it again and stopped. *I can't do it. This is crazy. No one will ever know, but I can't. It's different this time. I don't know why. Somehow I know she needs it more than I do. It feels funny, like I'm stealing from myself . . . weird.*

"Miss, miss," Carlita said as she woke Silvia.

"What . . . what is it? Did I miss my stop?"

"No . . . no. I just wanted to tell you to put your purse away before it gets stolen."

"Thank you, thank you so much," Silvia said as she looked down and noticed the purse lying on the seat. She was very grateful. "I have my rent money in here and without it my son and I would be out on the street tonight. Thank you very much."

Carlita smiled and exited the bus at the next stop. She looked back and thought about the possibility of living on the streets. Somehow she felt the kind of pain and anguish that came with that kind of hopelessness, and wondered how a person endured it. She could relate to it somehow, and she was relieved that the lady on the bus would have a home to go to tonight.

Silvia pulled her purse close to her and thanked God for the kindness of a dark haired girl.

Dray read the newspaper as he waited to board the bus to North Carolina. He was focused on a story about a detective who was accidentally shot to death by the LA County Police in the desert last night. He read further to find that Detective Patrick Hauser was pursuing a murder suspect when the police, who were looking for the same suspect, saw a person from a distance and reacted without clearly identifying the man. Detective Hauser was mistakenly shot and killed. He lost his wife, Mary, five years prior and had no surviving relatives. The shooting appeared to be an accident, but the Police Department would conduct a thorough investigation. The officers in question were suspended until the investigation was complete. The search continued for the murder suspect.

"I hope his soul is with God," Dray said.

His mother looked at him in disbelief.

"What did you say?" she asked.

"Somehow, I know this man. I'm not sure how. I know he was a good man, and I hope his death was not in vain, and that God will take him."

"Dray, I didn't think you believed in God."

"I know, it's strange for me too, but somehow I know that all of us are just a step away from Redemption."

LOOK FOR MORE HOT TITLES FROM

Q-BORO
BOOKS

DARK KARMA - JUNE 2007
$14.95
ISBN 1-933967-12-9
What if the criminal was forced to live the horror that they caused? The drug dealer finds himself in the body of the drug addict and he suffers through the withdrawals, living on the street, the beatings, the rapes and the hunger. The thief steals the rent money and becomes the victim that finds herself living on the street and running for her life and the murderer becomes the victim's father and he deals with the death of a son and a grieving mother.

GET MONEY CHICKS - SEPTEMBER 2007
$14.95
ISBN 1-933967-17-X
For Mina, Shanna, and Karen, using what they had to get what they wanted was always an option. Best friends since day one, they always had a thing for the hottest gear, luxurious lifestyles, and the ballers who made it all possible. All of this changes for Mina when a tragedy makes her open her eyes to the way she's living. Peer pressure and loyalty to her girls collide with her own morality, sending Mina into a no-win situation.

AFTER-HOURS GIRLS - AUGUST 2007
$14.95
ISBN 1-933967-16-1

Take part in this tale of two best friends, Lisa and Tosha, as they stalk the nightclubs and after-hours joints of Detroit searching for excitement, money, and temporary companionship. These two divas stand tall until the unforgivable Motown streets catch up to them. One must fall. You, the reader, decide which.

THE LAST CHANCE - OCTOBER 2007
$14.95
ISBN 1-933967-22-6
Running their L.A. casino has been rewarding for Luke Chance and his three brothers. But recently it seems like everyone is trying to get a piece of the pie. An impending hostile takeover of their casino could leave them penniless and possibly dead. That is, until their sister Keilah Chance comes home for a short visit. Keilah is not only beautiful, but she also can be ruthless. Will the Chance family be able to protect their family dynasty?

Traci must find a way to complete her journey out of her first and only failed

LOOK FOR MORE HOT TITLES FROM

Q-BORO
BOOKS

NYMPHO - MAY 2007
$14.95
ISBN 1933967102

How will signing up to live a promiscuous double-life destroy everything that's at stake in the lives of two close couples? Take a journey into Leslie's secret world and prepare for a twisted, erotic experience.

FREAK IN THE SHEETS - SEPTEMBER 2007
$14.95
ISBN 1933967196

Librarian Raquelle decides to put her knowledge of sexuality to use and open up a "freak" school, teaching men and women how to please their lovers beyond belief while enjoying themselves in the process. But trouble brews when a surprise pupil shows up and everything Raquelle has worked for comes under fire.

LIAR, LIAR - JUNE 2007
$14.95
ISBN 1933967110

Stormy calls off her wedding to Camden when she learns he's cheating with a male church member. However, after being convinced that Camden has been delivered from his demons, she proceeds with the wedding.

Will Stormy and Camden survive scandal, lies and deceit?

HEAVEN SENT - AUGUST 2007
$14.95
ISBN 1933967188

Eve is a recovering drug addict who has no intentions of staying clean until she meets Reverend Washington, a newly widowed man with three children. Secrets are uncovered that threaten Eve's new life with her new family and has everyone asking if Eve was *Heaven Sent*.

LOOK FOR MORE HOT TITLES FROM

Q-BORO
BOOKS

OBSESSION 101
$6.99
ISBN 0977733548

After a horrendous trauma. Rashawn Ams is left pregnant and flees town to give birth to her son and repair her life after confiding in her psychiatrist. After her return to her life, her town, and her classroom, she finds herself the target of an intrusive secret admirer who has plans for her.

SHAMELESS- OCTOBER 2006
$6.99
ISBN 0977733513

Kyle is sexy, single, and smart; Jasmyn is a hot and sassy drama queen. These two complete opposites find love - or something real close to it - while away at college. Jasmyn is busy wreaking havoc on every man she meets. Kyle, on the other hand, is trying to walk the line between his faith and all the guilty pleasures being thrown his way. When the partying college days end and Jasmyn tests HIV positive, reality sets in.

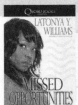

MISSED OPPORTUNITIES - MARCH 2007
$14.95
ISBN 1933967013

Missed Opportunities illustrates how true-to-life characters must face the consequences of their poor choices. Was each decision worth the opportune cost? LaTonya Y. Williams delivers yet another account of love. lies, and deceit all wrapped up into one powerful novel.

ONE DEAD PREACHER - MARCH 2007
$14.95
ISBN 1933967021

Smooth operator and security CEO David Price sets out to protect the sexy. smart, and saucy Sugar Owens from her husband, who happens to be a powerful religious leader. Sugar isn't as sweet as she appears. however. and in a twisted turn of events, the preacher man turns up dead and Price becomes the prime suspect.

LOOK FOR MORE HOT TITLES FROM

Q-BORO
BOOKS

DOGISM
$6.99
ISBN 0977733505

Lance Thomas is a sexy, young black male who has it all: a high paying blue collar career, a home in Queens, New York, two cars, a son, and a beautiful wife. However, after getting married at a very young age he realizes that he is afflicted with DOGISM, a distorted sexuality that causes men to stray and be unfaithful in their relationships with women.

POISON IVY - NOVEMBER 2006
$14.95
ISBN 0977733521

Ivy Davidson's life has been filled with sorrow. Her father was brutally murdered and she was forced to watch, she faced years of abuse at the hands of those she trusted, and she was forced to live apart from the only source of love that she'd ever known. Now Ivy stands alone at the crossroads of life, staring into the eyes of the man who holds her final choice of life or death in his hands.

HOLY HUSTLER - FEBRUARY 2007
$14.95
ISBN 0977733556

Reverend Ethan Ezekiel Goodlove the Third and his three sons are known for spreading more than just the gospel. The sanctified drama of the Goodloves promises to make us all scream "Hallelujah!"

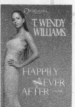

HAPPILY NEVER AFTER - JANUARY 2007
$14.95
ISBN 1933967005

To Family and friends, Dorothy and David Leonard's marriage appears to be one made in heaven. While David is one of Houston's most prominent physicians, Dorothy is a loving and carefree housewife. It seems as if life couldn't be more fabulous for this couple who appear to have it all: wealth, social status, and a loving union. However, looks can be deceiving. What really happens behind closed doors and when the flawless veneer begins to crack?